TRAIL ANGEL

TRAIL ANGEL

DEREK CATRON

FIVE STAR
A part of Gale, Cengage Learning

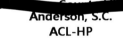
GALE
CENGAGE Learning·

Farmington Hills, Mich • San Francisco • New York • Waterville, Maine
Meriden, Conn • Mason, Ohio • Chicago

LIBRARY OF CONGRESS CATALOGING-IN-PUBLICATION DATA

Names: Catron, Derek, author.
Title: Trail angel / Derek Catron.
Description: Waterville, Maine : Five Star, a part of Cengage Learning, 2016.
Identifiers: LCCN 2016003814 (print) | LCCN 2016015636 (ebook) | ISBN 9781432832803 (hardcover) | ISBN 1432832808 (hardcover) | ISBN 9781432832735 (ebook) | ISBN 1432832735 (ebook) 9781432833794 (ebook) | ISBN 1432833790 (ebook)
Subjects: LCSH: Widows—Fiction. | Soldiers—Fiction. | Wagon Trains—Fiction. | Bozeman Trail—Fiction. | Brigands and Robbers—Fiction. | Nebraska—Fiction. | Montana—Fiction. | GSAFD: Western stories. | Love stories.
Classification: LCC PS3603.A89776 T73 2016 (print) | LCC PS3603.A89776 (ebook) | DDC 813/.6—dc23
LC record available at https://lccn.loc.gov/2016003814

First Edition. First Printing: August 2016
Find us on Facebook– https://www.facebook.com/FiveStarCengage
Visit our website– http://www.gale.cengage.com/fivestar/
Contact Five Star™ Publishing at FiveStar@cengage.com

To Lori, whose unflagging encouragement—
and patience—gave me the strength to pursue a dream.

CHAPTER ONE

From the banks of the flat, broad river, Annabelle Rutledge Holcombe looked east toward everything she had known. The Missouri flowed slow and brown here. She credited the humility of the locals who called it the "Big Muddy." Closing her eyes, she pictured the harbor and the limitless expanse of ocean that stretched beyond the barrier islands. With water lapping against the dock, she could almost imagine herself home in Charleston. Only the smell wasn't right. She missed the tangy freshness of salt water. It was cleaner than the reek of offal, butchered beef and whatever else washed downstream from Omaha's stockyards.

She opened her eyes. Compared with the harbor, the river was hardly any barrier. It would be nothing to swim across. Disappear someplace where no one depended on her, where no one could be disappointed in what she had become. She was a good swimmer. A stream had cut past the fields near her home, isolated enough from both neighbor and slave that no one saw where she went on the rides she took to flee, if only briefly, the dreary days and stifling heat of planting season. After her swim, her dark hair would be wet beneath her riding bonnet, but no one ever noticed, not even her husband.

Perhaps no one cared enough to remark on it.

Annabelle shut her mind to such thoughts. It had only been a few years, yet those days before the war might have been another lifetime. She had dreamed of escape even then, so it made little sense that she should feel wistful now. She should embrace the coming journey, the chance for a fresh start. An opportunity to put memories of the war and her life before at a distance, not only of time but the width of a continent.

Turning at the sound of her father discussing terms with the wholesaler, Annabelle listened with mounting concern. She hesitated to apply the word "negotiate" to such a one-sided exchange. John McCormick was the grocer Annabelle's father had contacted before they left Charleston to ensure they could get the provisions they needed. Something had changed in the time it took the family to travel by rail to Omaha, and Mr. McCormick sought a better deal.

"I'm afraid that's the best price I can offer," McCormick said.

"But that's not what you stated in your letter." Annabelle cringed to hear the plaintive note in her father's voice.

"Prices change, Mr. Rutledge. As a businessman, I'm sure you understand."

Langdon Rutledge was not yet an old man, but the war had aged him. His once-dark beard turned salt-and-pepper with the war's start and then, seemingly overnight with the ruin of his import business, went completely white. They had all lost weight during the war, but her father's new shape suited him poorly. No one trusted a hungry-looking businessman.

Unlike most of the men they knew, her father had not expected a quick and easy end to the war. He had been to Boston and New York. He had seen the Yankees' factories and warehouses. He had witnessed immigrants pouring off boats, restless with ambition, like ants stirred to a frenzy. Yet he kept his reservations to himself. Such doubts were practically treason when every true son of South Carolina burned with such patriotic zeal they would sizzle if you threw water on them.

Her father had stood by when the boys announced their

intention to fight. Annabelle knew he couldn't stop her headstrong brothers, but she wondered if her mother blamed him for not trying. News of their deaths abandoned her mother to an all-consuming grief. Her father fell numb to it, a reaction even more disturbing to Annabelle. He was the same when the generals seized what they would from his storehouses, compensating him with worthless Confederate graybacks. Whatever spirit had driven him to build a thriving business had flickered out like an oil lamp run dry.

By war's end, her father was a broken man. Even a year later prospects weren't good for rebuilding in a South that Annabelle knew would soon be dominated by carpetbaggers and scalawags. She had read in newspapers how miners in Montana pulled out ten million dollars in gold in one year. Men were getting rich with little more than a pan and a pick—tools they had to buy from somebody. Why not her father?

War left Annabelle a wealthy widow, at least until the federal tax collectors figured out how to steal South Carolina's plantations from their owners. Selling when she did provided the stake for a new start. More than gold, they needed hope, and there was none of that in Charleston.

Planning the journey west rejuvenated her father, at least to a point. Her mother's spirits were lifted when Annabelle's aunt, uncle and three young cousins joined them. Since no man would conduct business with a woman, her father and her uncle Luke organized most of the details, recruited a company of fellow travelers, and negotiated specifics over how much each would carry without risking a breakdown of wagons or ox teams. Her father still knew how to cut a deal.

Closing one was another matter.

McCormick was a fat man with a grizzled beard and a bald head that reflected the morning sun when he turned his back to her father, their business concluded. Other customers were gathered outside the dockside warehouse waiting for the wholesaler's attention. He appeared startled when Annabelle blocked his path, smoothing the folds of her black calico dress as she cleared her throat.

"Mr. McCormick, your new prices are unacceptable. You will fulfill the terms outlined in your letter." Though still a young woman with little more than a score of years, time as a plantation mistress lent an authority to Annabelle's voice. The other customers, all men, turned to watch.

Despite his girth, McCormick had to look up to see Annabelle's face. He appeared puzzled, his features pinched tight as if squinting against the May sun. He turned to her father, the question apparent on his face.

"My daughter," her father said.

Before he spoke, Annabelle reached out, pinching and twisting the lobe of an ear so that the portly fellow looked at her. "I will not be ignored, sir. I do not know what passes for manners on the frontier, but where I am from a gentleman never turns his back when addressed by a lady."

McCormick reached for her hand but reconsidered when she tightened her grip. He doubled over at the waist instead, his ear turned toward her to relieve the pressure, mouth agape in a silent scream. He began to nod in agreement but halted at realizing the wisdom of remaining still.

Running a plantation had taught Annabelle that some men responded only to a show of strength, particularly when a woman delivered the orders, yet she recognized this as a rash act. Something about the way McCormick turned from her, leaving her looking at the side of his head, the lobe dangling like some baited hook, set her off. She was tired of seeing her father beaten down by events and men who just a few years earlier would have been groveling to serve him. Aware of the crowd's attention, she flushed. Swallowing back the doubt that tickled

10

the back of her throat, she pressed forward.

She could not recall ever having held a man's earlobe, and its softness surprised her, like an overly ripe berry. She wondered if it would burst should she squeeze hard enough. McCormick seemed to have read her mind for his open mouth began to emit a sound.

"No-no-no-no-no!"

Annabelle held firm. "In your letter, you stated that you would fulfill our needs at a discounted rate if we purchased the bulk of our provisions from your establishment."

As she pivoted to face her father, McCormick groaned, his boots making a sharp clacking sound against the wooden dock as he maneuvered to relieve the pressure on his ear. "Father, do you have the list?"

He read: "Flour, two thousand pounds. Bacon, fifteen hundred. One hundred pounds of coffee, two hundred pounds of sugar, one hundred pounds of salt."

Relaxing her fingers enough so the man could stand upright, Annabelle faced McCormick. She didn't need to consult the list.

"At three dollars per one hundred pounds of flour, ten cents per pound of bacon, nine cents a pound for sugar, two dollars for a hundred pounds of salt and fifteen dollars for a hundred pounds of coffee, we owe two hundred and forty-five dollars. We will pay you an additional five dollars for sixty pounds of dried fruit, making it an even two hundred and fifty."

Her fingers tightened, forcing McCormick to bend at the waist again. "And you will throw in forty pounds of jarred pickles, Mr. McCormick, because you value your reputation as an honest tradesman—and because we are paying in gold, not your dubious greenbacks."

With a final twist of the wrist, she released him. McCormick fell to his knees.

Annabelle looked to her father.

"Do we have an agreement?" he asked McCormick.

The customers' laughter drowned out the response. Annabelle relented on seeing McCormick nod, his hands cupping his ear. He shrank back as she stepped forward, a hand extended to seal the deal.

"Just pay the boy," he said with a nod toward a colored man standing wide-eyed at the warehouse door. "He will get what you want."

Her hand still extended, Annabelle waited a beat longer before turning away.

The colored man loaded their provisions into the buckboard her father had rented for the day. He remained silent while they watched the loading. *Perhaps I should have left things to him. He might have rallied if I'd given him a chance.*

Looking at the man her father had become, Annabelle knew better. The skin beneath his eyes had sagged and darkened, creating half-rings that appeared like perpetual frowns beneath dull eyes. He'd lost most of his hair, too, and had taken to wearing a hat as if he were a rancher or cowboy. She worried if she had been mistaken to uproot her parents, even if the life they knew was disintegrating around them.

Annabelle smiled at her father, hoping a cheerful face might mask her thoughts. They were committed now. Better they look to the future. They had a meeting that night with the other members of their company. She hoped Caleb, their hired man, had the wagons in order. Her father planned to introduce the guides he believed could lead them on a shortcut to Montana, saving weeks and hundreds of miles. Annabelle struggled to conceal her uneasiness, wondering if she'd been right to leave those affairs to him. The guides he had chosen had been Union officers, one an old colonel, the other a notorious killer with an almost mythic reputation. As if following a pair of Yankees weren't bad enough, a freed slave rode with them.

"It won't be so bad," her father said.

Annabelle didn't know if he spoke of the journey or the meeting with the guides. She couldn't see that it made a difference.

"I know, Father."

He seemed to welcome the lie, and Annabelle permitted him to take her hand and lead her to the wagon.

CHAPTER TWO

Caleb Williams pulled at the harnesses leading the oxen. Stupid brutes. They had eaten the grass where he left them the previous day but were reluctant to move on. Beating the larger one with a switch, Caleb directed it and the rest followed.

"Now which one am I?" he muttered. "The dumb bastard getting beat on or the dumber bastard who follows him?"

The ox offered no response as Caleb followed at a walking pace. He couldn't hurry it. *They are strong, but there's no haste in them. They don't rush to eat and, with no balls, nature don't motivate them, either. They just work and chew.* If Rutledge and his high-and-mighty daughter thought of Caleb as no different from an ox, well, that was their mistake, Caleb thought.

It had been Caleb who told them to get oxen. Some drivers preferred mules because they were faster. But a mule wants to eat grain—which would be in short supply once they left town. Plus, mules aren't as strong as oxen, so you need more of them. Rutledge had listened, then showed his shrewdness. Caleb had told him it would take two yoke to pull the wagon, but Rutledge got three pairs so that if any died along the way they would still have enough for the journey. Caleb hadn't thought of that.

Looking around for the extra hands, Caleb flinched as a gunshot echoed across the flat meadow.

"Missed him. Damn."

"Told you."

A second shot and Caleb cringed again, a reflex he hadn't

14

shaken nearly two years since the last time anyone had shot at him.

"Hah. You missed him, too."

Caleb had sent the Daggett boys to get rope, figuring he needed to send both because they had but a single brain between them. Now he regretted the decision, realizing one brother's capacity for finding trouble was multiplied by the other.

"What are you idiots doing?"

Willis, older by a year and fatter by half, gestured with his revolver, first at Caleb, then toward the grass just off the path, as if that explained everything. "I saw him first."

"You missed him first," said Clifton, the smaller and fairer of the two. He believed himself the smarter one, no great distinction as far as Caleb could tell.

"Watch where you point that thing," Caleb told Willis, swatting his gun hand. Little more than wastrels from Georgia, the brothers were eager to make their fortune in the gold fields but lacked the funds to get there. Rutledge hired them to drive a pair of his supply wagons, but he left it up to Caleb to make sure they knew how.

Standing beside the brothers, Caleb wondered how long it had been since they bathed. He was probably just as ripe; he just no longer noticed. Then he saw the snake. "It's a rattler," Willis said.

"I can see that." Thing was mad now and coiled for a fight, making it no smarter than its would-be assassins.

"He's a big one, ain't he?" Clifton said.

"It's nothing compared with the moccasins I used to shoot back home," Caleb said. He drew his Navy Colt and carefully aimed along the beaded sight.

"You missed him, too," Clifton hooted after the shot sailed high.

A look from Caleb silenced the runt. Damn revolvers. He had taken the gun off a dead officer in Mississippi. Practically only good for hand-to-hand fighting. Adjusting his aim, he fired before either Daggett wagged his tongue again. The snake exploded with the impact.

"Ew!" Willis started toward the carcass, pulling out a knife. "You want the rattle?"

Caleb returned to the job. There would be plenty more snakes to kill on the trail. "I want you boys to help me finish moving the oxen."

"What's the hurry?" Clifton asked.

The fool had already forgotten. "The meeting's tonight. All the wagon drivers are going to be there. I mean to be there, too."

"Oh, yeah."

Like the Daggett boys, Caleb merely worked for Rutledge and hadn't actually been invited to the meeting. The boot-licker had gone and found himself guides he said knew a shortcut to Montana, but Caleb would be damned if he was going to follow some Yankees and their Sambo. Not without taking their measure.

Rutledge was smart but soft. He had been just a quartermaster, living at home in Charleston, reading his books, balancing his ledgers, climbing into bed with his wife every night and complaining that the "boys" hadn't won the war already so he could get back to making money. He never crawled through mud while people shot at him. He didn't march until the shoes disintegrated under his feet. Rutledge lost two sons, Caleb gave him that, but that only made it worse that he would hire bluebellies.

The war had been over barely a year. Maybe that was enough time for a man like Rutledge to forget it had been Union soldiers who killed his sons. *Maybe that's what makes rich men the way they are*. It wouldn't occur to Rutledge that Caleb might have an opinion on what the bastards had to say. Or that maybe Caleb, having served honorably in the war himself so far as Rutledge knew, might have something more to offer than his sweat and muscle.

Once reaching fresh grass, the oxen ambled ahead without more encouragement. As long as nothing disturbed them, they wouldn't wander, but Caleb wanted them watched. Plenty of cattle thieves in the territories. Besides, that's what Rutledge paid these fools for. Rich men like Rutledge needed others to do their work, and with the Sambos free, Caleb knew who would be toting the wood, fetching the water and driving the wagons.

"Get used to it, boys. You are the new slaves."

Willis looked bothered. "We ain't slaves."

Clifton nodded. "We're free to go where we want."

"Then why ain't you in Montana, already making your fortune?"

Accustomed to dealing with his brother, Clifton had the habit of stating the obvious. "You know as well as us, we got to get there first. We ain't got no money for that."

"So you'll be a slave until we get to Montana. And if you don't strike it rich, you will be somebody's slaves so you can eat and sleep under a roof."

Willis looked confused, but Clifton smiled as if he had it all figured out. "We ain't slaves because they *pay* us."

Caleb laughed. "For the pittance a rich man pays, you are worse off than a slave." Willis would never understand, so Caleb turned to Clifton. "If you took a woman and had some brats, is a rich man going to pay you any more for the same work just so's you can feed 'em?"

Caleb knew that answer only too well, though he didn't like to think on it, much less talk about it. He had watched men die in terrible ways, but no death troubled him like the one he had not been present to see, the one that happened because he had been too poor to give his sweet Laurie everything she deserved.

"At least a slave could have a wife and children, if they weren't sold somewheres else. Maybe even see a doctor when they get sick. Best you can hope for is to save a dollar or two to buy a poke in a saloon and hope your *master* will have you buried when you die."

Clifton's knitted brows told Caleb the boys still didn't understand. He was about to let the subject go when the youth smiled slyly and pointed a finger at him. "You ain't getting paid much better than us. If we's slaves, you a slave, too."

Who was dumber—the bastard getting beat on or the bastard who follows him? Throwing his hands in the air, Caleb stormed off. Let the boys think they got the better of him. Let Rutledge think he had the better of him. Caleb didn't care. He had his own reasons for seeking salvation in the gold fields that no one else need know. He just had to bide his time and be as clever as Rutledge.

When Caleb dreamed of Montana, it wasn't a pile of gold nuggets he saw. No. Caleb dreamed of the look on the faces of men like Rutledge when they learned just how clever he had been all along.

CHAPTER THREE

The wagons in the company Annabelle's father and her uncle Luke had organized were gathered on the outskirts of Omaha. The sprawling camp had grown since the family's arrival two weeks earlier.

Annabelle now counted fifteen wagons. She'd lost count of the oxen and cattle gathered around the camp, though her nose always knew they were there. The notion of safety in numbers was especially important to her mother and aunt, who had read too many Beadle books about women taken by marauding Indians. That meant her father and Luke couldn't afford to be choosy about who joined the wagon train. Southern lawyers and store clerks. Yankee farmers. Would-be miners of undetermined allegiance.

Every man among them believed it was his fate to be rich, either by panning for gold or by selling something to those who did. The gold made them determined, but it didn't make them confident of driving teams of ox-pulled wagons across unsettled country filled with hostile Indians and who knew what else.

Her father had been delighted to meet men in town who not only had made the trip to Montana but knew how to handle themselves in a tough spot.

It shouldn't matter that they were Yankee officers who had marched with that devil Sherman, torching cities and homesteads along the way. As her father kept telling everyone, they owed allegiance now only to each other and the shared hope of arriving in Montana quickly and safely. Resentments about the war were best put behind them, he told Yankees and Southerners alike. It was a generous philosophy, but convincing men to buy into it would be another matter.

As they waited for the guides, the men clustered in tight groups split nearly on geographic lines. Luke stood with the rest of the Southerners, mostly bookkeepers, bankers and businessmen who failed to find work after the war. They were only too aware of the limits of their frontier skills, but that didn't mean they had given up their pride.

Like quarantined patients, the women and children had been left on the other side of camp. Though it chafed her to have to act so, Annabelle took a pot of coffee that had been warming on a stone next to the fire and sidled among the men, smiling prettily so none would be offended at having her privy to their discussions.

"You're not bothered by all these Yankees?" one of the men asked as she poured coffee into her uncle's tin cup.

"It's only for the journey," he said. "Where we're going, it's practically a southern colony. Why do you think they call it *Virginia* City?"

"That ain't half of it," one of the others said. "They wanted to name it Varina, after Jeff Davis's bride, but some Yankee judge went and changed the paperwork."

Annabelle noticed her father watching as she circulated. With a nod, she alerted him to a man grousing about the former slave who traveled with the guides.

"I heard they got a Sambo with 'em."

"A freed slave," her father corrected.

"His name really Lord Byron?"

Her father shrugged. "They encouraged him to take a free man's name. As the Colonel tells it, this was the freest-sounding name the man knew. It's a tale I believe he enjoys telling."

"I didn't know Yankees had a sense of humor," another said.

Annabelle moved to where the northerners were clustered. Most were farmers, drawn by the prospect of homestead land. They hoped to make a good living feeding the burgeoning population around the gold fields. Miners had to eat, and most of their food had to be hauled in from Salt Lake City and other distant parts.

"If it's a guide we need, why not hire a single man?" one of the Yankees said. He was red-faced with drink and his voice carried above the rest. "Do we need to hire three?"

Annabelle motioned to her father, who hurried to the man's side. Her father's voice was barely louder than a whisper, a vain effort to have the red-faced man match his tone. "We'll be thankful for the extra labor when we must watch the stock at night."

"I'll be thankful for the extra guns if we run into trouble," another man said.

Annabelle drifted toward the third group in their company, the one her father called the bachelor miners because none traveled with families. They were the poorest of the lot, mostly southerners, though none seemed to hold loyalty to any cause but getting rich. That made them the most eager to reach Montana, feeling every day they were in camp was another day somebody else might find the gold they already deemed theirs.

Her ears perked at mention of the gunman who served alongside the Colonel. He had such an outsized reputation even Annabelle heard stories in town.

"What kind of name is Josey Angel?" asked the youngest of the miners, a boy from Indiana.

"It's not his real name, Nancy-boy."

The youth ignored the insult. "Well, what is it?"

The older miner looked peeved to be pinned down on something he didn't know. "It's Josef something. Something

Polish, even harder to speak than Indian."

Seeing the youngster's uneasiness, another miner started in. "I heard he killed his own troops 'cause they couldn't say his name proper."

"They would have hung him for that," the boy said. He didn't look certain.

"I heard he killed the witnesses."

The man laughed and others joined in, a game to see who could stretch the tale to the most ridiculous lengths. They might have talked all night, swapping opinions like poker chips because that was all they had.

Everyone fell silent when the two riders arrived. Annabelle watched, wondering if everything she had heard was really nothing more than tall tales.

CHAPTER FOUR

Josey Angel was nothing like Annabelle expected.

The afternoon light was fading as he rode up with the Colonel, and the newcomers were silhouetted as they dismounted. Stepping from the shadows of one of her family's wagons, Annabelle followed the younger man with her eyes as he picketed the horses in the grass. He was smooth-faced and slender, like a childhood beau she had known from church. Yet there could be no mistaking him.

He wore twin gun belts, one at his waist like a cowboy, the other one higher, near his ribs, so that the gun handles pointed forward. The butt of a rifle extended behind one shoulder. He looked ridiculous to Annabelle, like a boy playing bandit, but the men stood back when Josey Angel passed.

People had their reasons for calling him what they did. Angel of Mercy. Angel of Death. The choice depended on which side a man fought. Some said Josey Angel had killed more than a hundred men. Others, that he slaughtered that many in a single day in Kansas. Or maybe it was Georgia. In one telling, after he ran out of Confederates he turned on his own bluebellies and killed them, too. Any Southerner could appreciate that story.

While Josey Angel saw to the horses, Annabelle turned her attention to the Colonel. He approached with an old cavalryman's walk, bowlegged, his booted feet tender against the ground like he trod on hot coals. She stepped up on the tongue of the nearest wagon for a better look.

The settlers had built a fire to ward off mosquitoes, and in its orange glow she saw the Colonel had a lean, weathered face and a gray mustache that drooped over his mouth like a perpetual frown. He wore a buckskin coat like the trail guides in dime novels, and Annabelle wondered if he dressed that way to reassure prospective clients.

As her father introduced him one of the miners called out, "What do we need with Union cavalry?"

That set off a flurry of exchanges that required all of her father's diplomacy to quell. "The war's over," he said. "These men have been to Montana. They can help us."

"Why do we need anybody?" one of the Yankees said. "The trail's been traveled so many times, it's practically a road." A few others found sense in that. Before her father responded, the Colonel stepped forward.

"That's true enough," he said in a voice so mild some of the men asked others to repeat what they heard. Those in back crowded near while the Colonel filled a pipe, his movements deliberate, like he had all night to complete the task. His long nose and sharp gaze reminded Annabelle of a hawk, but his eyes, alight with the fire's flicker, twinkled with good humor.

His pipe filled, the Colonel continued. "Following the Platte will get you through Nebraska, into what some people are calling Wyoming. What will you do then?" He leaned in, drawing a piece of kindling from the fire to light his pipe.

"Take the South Pass?" Annabelle wasn't sure who had spoken. It sounded more a question than statement, but others took up the idea. One said he had read about the South Pass in a guidebook.

The Colonel turned his head. "Have you ever been through the South Pass?" No one said he had, and the Colonel continued as if that were the answer he expected.

"The pass cuts through the biggest mountains you'll ever see.

The trail's so steep at points, you'll need ropes to pull your wagons up, one at a time. Other times, you'll have to put both big rear wheels on one side of your rigs to keep 'em from tipping down the mountainside. It's hard going."

"But that's how every wagon gets west," the oldest miner said. He turned to his fellows. "Why should we be afraid? Other men, no better than us, have gotten through."

"I don't doubt your qualities," the Colonel said, his voice just as mild as earlier. "The South Pass is the lowest point you will find in the mountains, and it's the way I would take you if you were Mormons headed to the Salt Lake or homesteaders going to Oregon. If you weren't in a hurry, I'd tell you to wait for the railroad. Some say it will be done in a year or two." He grinned at the miner. "But I reckon all the gold will be gone by then."

A hush fell over the men. They stopped moving and shushed anyone who interrupted. The Colonel drew on his pipe as if daring to be contradicted. He took another draw.

"The problem in reaching Montana is that the South Pass takes you *south* and west," he said, looking to the miner as he emphasized the word. "You want to go *north*. That means you'll have to double back to reach Montana's gold fields."

He raised his voice as he addressed the full crowd. "You'll be crossing those mountains, not just once, but twice if you take the South Pass." This stirred the men. The Colonel looked to the one who had spoken earlier. "What does your guidebook say about that?" The man looked away.

While the others talked among themselves, Josey Angel appeared at the Colonel's side, his hands fidgeting like it was an effort to stand still in a crowd of strangers. He listened as the old man whispered something. Nodding, Josey Angel looked to be taking a head count—or choosing targets. The others fell silent.

Her father cleared his throat, drawing attention away from

the heavily armed newcomer. "Colonel, you've spoken to me of the Bozeman Trail, your shortcut, but the men here have heard it's closed."

"It was closed, to settlers, at least." The Colonel studied the pipe's bowl as if he'd tasted a bad leaf. "It's going to reopen this year. The government's treating with the Indians, and the army plans to build three forts along the trail this summer. They might be open by the time we get there."

"Indians? It sounds dangerous," said a banker from Atlanta who traveled with his family.

"Every trail west is dangerous," the Colonel said. "But more men die from accidents, disease or stupidity than Indians."

Caleb Williams spoke out. A thick-limbed handyman who had worked for Annabelle's husband before going off to war, his wife died in childbirth while he was gone. He returned home as Annabelle's family prepared to leave. After her father hired him to drive one of the supply wagons, he seemed eager to display his worth.

"We don't need these Yankees to protect us from Indians," he said. "Don't we all have guns? Aren't we all men?"

"Some of us have families," a lawyer from Savannah said.

The men renewed their argument. The Colonel didn't seem concerned, puffing at his pipe and whispering to Josey Angel again. After the men talked themselves out, the banker with two children spoke up.

"How do you know the Indians will make peace?"

The Colonel emptied his pipe with a few raps against the heel of his boot. "I don't, not for a fact. Any man who tells you otherwise is not to be trusted. That's why a sensible man takes precautions."

He looked at Josey Angel as he said the last part, then stood to his full height and crossed his arms, like posing for a photograph, his message clear to Annabelle. *Whatever we're pay-*

ing them, he means to show it's a bargain.

"Even with peace, the trail's not easy," the Colonel continued. "It's not marked like the Oregon trail. There are deep ravines that run into cliff faces so steep they can't be crossed. There are badlands where, if you don't know where the springs are, the alkaline water will poison your stock."

He paused and looked at the faces of those gathered nearest. No one spoke.

"If you know where you're going, you will pass through the richest hunting ground in the world. Great herds of buffalo, elk, mule deer and antelope. Fat prairie chickens, grouse and quail." He let those words sink in, seeming to enjoy the look on the men's faces as they imagined themselves stalking such game.

Then he finished with a flourish that left every man's eyes alight with a different kind of hunger. "Follow me and you will come to the gold fields of Montana having saved four hundred and fifty miles and at least six weeks through the mountains."

He looked at his empty pipe, seeming to deliberate whether he had time for a second smoke and deciding against it. He looked to have no doubt of the company's verdict, even as the men moved off to discuss what they had heard.

Annabelle came to him and offered coffee, hoping to hear what he discussed with Josey Angel. The Colonel declined with a wave of his pipe, as if he could indulge in only one proclivity at a time. Josey Angel, still silent, looked past her as if she weren't there.

Standing so close, she saw that his cheeks were thin and his shirt loose, like a son who takes his father's clothes before he can completely fill them out. He was older than he appeared at first, probably close to her age. Weariness hung over him, like he had seen more years than he lived. His eyes were just as restless as his fidgeting hands, sweeping across the people before him.

Men with guns didn't frighten Annabelle. She had known

many soldiers, but a gunman seemed different. A soldier was told when to fight, and after the battle he put down his rifle. A gunman always had to be alert, the fight never done. *Not until he was dead.*

Annabelle shivered at the thought as Josey Angel's eyes found her. She felt herself turning red through the chest and face and cursed her foolishness for reacting so.

The whole time she had been watching Josey Angel, his face had been blank, as if all emotion had bled away from an unseen wound. When she looked back to see his eyes still on her, she realized this wasn't true. The tiniest twitch at the side of his mouth betrayed him, a movement so slight it would have gone unnoticed on anyone else. Yet on Josey Angel's blank face it registered as—*what?*—a smile? An involuntary shudder chased the heat from her face.

Annabelle was a strong woman. Her mother would say too strong, repelling men when she should be alluring. Her mother didn't understand, and Annabelle had never been able to tell why she had vowed no man would hurt her again. No man could, so long as she stayed strong.

That was why men with guns didn't frighten her. A woman posed no threat to such men. A man who looked at her the way Josey Angel did, that was different. A man like Josey Angel made her feel weak.

CHAPTER FIVE

Josey woke to find the Colonel watching him. The old man had added wood to the fire at their campsite. Wet with dew, it sizzled and popped like echoes of gunfire. The smell of wood smoke brought back memories he preferred to forget.

"Bad dreams?"

"Can they be dreams if you lived them?" Josey couldn't have been asleep long, but his back was sore. He reached beneath his blanket and found a small stone and cast it aside. "Doesn't that make them memories?"

"Not when you sleep." The Colonel smiled. The gesture raised the droopy gray mustache like a cocked eyebrow. "Then they're called dreams."

"Or nightmares."

"Nah. You can't have a nightmare about something you lived through."

Josey frowned. *Those are the worst kind.*

They listened as the last of what was alive in the wood burned away. After the Colonel's speech, it had taken the emigrants only a few minutes to decide to hire the guides. They'd requested another day for final preparations, which suited the Colonel and Josey, particularly after they got half their fee in advance. Returning to camp, they found Lord Byron had a meager supper of beans and cornbread already going, and the men enjoyed the prospect of better meals ahead with the well-stocked travelers.

Now Byron snored softly in the bedroll nearest the fire. The freed slave had begun following the Colonel and Josey as they marched through Georgia and he had never left. Byron could sleep through most anything so long as Josey and the Colonel were near.

"Wish I slept half as well," Josey said as he sought a comfortable position.

"I thought you'd sleep easy, now that we've got a paying job. Aren't you happy?"

The Colonel generally carried the conversation for both, but in the dark he couldn't see Josey's nod. "I am happy," Josey said.

"I thought so." The Colonel expected to be right in most things, but being right wasn't always enough—he had to explain how he came to his conclusion, a small pleasure Josey wouldn't deny him. "I couldn't be sure because your face when you're happy is so much like your face when you're sad. Or your face when you're angry, come to think of it."

The Colonel got up. He didn't go far, and Josey heard the old man's dribbles against a stone.

"Don't worry about the people," he said when he returned. "You and Byron will range ahead, keep us out of trouble, find us a good campsite with water and grass."

"I can do that."

"I'll deal with the people."

The Colonel didn't need a response to confirm he was right, and Josey was relieved he didn't have to explain himself. A coughing fit overcame the old man, his dry heaves tearing through the night. He spit into the fire. "Guess I talked too much."

"Didn't know that could happen," Josey said, drawing another cough mixed with laughter. The Colonel had been trying to shake the cough for weeks.

"I knew a job would put you in a better mood. Now you can quit worrying about money."

"Now I can worry about the Sioux."

The Colonel waved a gnarled hand. "You always find something."

"I suppose you're not concerned."

"The army's negotiating a peace treaty," the Colonel said. He didn't sound convinced, tried a different tack. "The Sioux didn't bother us."

"We didn't have wagons. Or women and children."

Byron's snoring cut off as he snuffled in his sleep. They waited for the big man to quiet before speaking again. The Colonel nodded toward Byron. "The two of you should go to town tomorrow and use part of the advance to get supplies. Get as many rounds as you can."

Josey had never needed to be told to load up. He looked closely at the Colonel, but the old man returned his gaze to the fire. "Peace treaty, huh?" Josey rolled away from his friend and drifted off so quickly the Colonel's next words sounded like they were part of a dream.

"Go to sleep, Josey. We've got a long ride ahead, and there will be no rest where we're going."

CHAPTER SIX

With more than one hundred rooms, the Herndon House occupied a full block, rising four sturdy stone stories above Omaha. Annabelle didn't mind that the place had no running water and stoves in only a few rooms—a feature for which management charged extra. In a town that still housed many of its people in log houses with sod roofs, the Herndon qualified as palatial. A four-poster bed, four walls, a ceiling—these were amenities Annabelle and her mother would be denied for the next few months. If for this alone, Herndon House proved worth the splurge of three dollars a night, a savings of fifty cents since they did without a stove.

The plank sidewalk that fronted the Herndon House gave out at the end of the hotel, and Annabelle lifted her heavy, black skirts while picking her way on the unpaved street, rutted by wagon wheels and littered with manure. At her urging, the women had dispensed with their crinolines. The wide skirts would be the death of one of them cooking over an open fire. Annabelle intended to rid herself of corsets as well. If anyone asked, she would blame the sacrifice of fashion on the need to reduce weight in the wagons.

With her mother, aunt and young cousins in tow, Annabelle led the way five blocks along Farnham Street to M. Hellman & Co., a dealer in ready-made clothing and other goods. She and her father had completed most of the purchases they needed for the trip, along with the goods they hoped to sell in Virginia

City, yet there remained some final things they needed.

It distressed Annabelle to see how much more expensive things were here than in Charleston. They would be even costlier in the mining towns, where many stores accepted payment in gold dust but not greenbacks. She had read that during one winter the price for flour rose to twenty-five dollars a sack. Every hundred pounds they bought here for three dollars would not only feed them along the way but help them afford to eat when they reached Montana.

Hellman's bustled with activity, and the family split up on entering the store. Wandering to a table covered with women's clothing, Annabelle spied on the others with a feigned casualness. Her mother looked at candles. Her aunt Blanche took the children—fourteen-year-old Caroline and her brothers, twelve-year-old Mark and ten-year-old Jimmy—to study the selection of hard candy behind a glass counter on the other side of the store.

Certain their attention was diverted, Annabelle reached for the garment before her. Made of basic gray wool, it resembled an undergarment or gymnasium costume. Annabelle knew better, only because she had seen young northern women dressed in a similar fashion. Her mother described the outfit as scandalous, but where her mother saw immorality, Annabelle saw a bold practicality. She had associated bloomers with abolitionists and members of the temperance movement—until venturing to a new world where bloomers would be more practical than crinoline and corsets.

Holding the fabric to her waist, Annabelle imagined the fit on her body. Hoping to keep out of view of her mother and aunt, she turned her back to the others—and bumped into Josey Angel.

"Ma'am," he said, with a respectful touch of his broad cavalry hat. He looked at her, at the bloomers, then back at her.

Flustered, she could think of nothing to say. She waited for him to speak, but he stood dumb, holding an armful of ammunition boxes. His face betrayed only an arched eyebrow and that twitch at the corner of his mouth she recalled from the previous night.

Quickly replacing the bloomers, Annabelle turned to move, but he remained in her way. "Are you going to greet me like a proper gentleman or stand there like an ox all day?"

He stepped back and offered a curt bow, which only kept her penned in. "Are we acquainted?"

Annabelle scoffed. She wasn't vain, but Josey Angel had looked directly at her the night before. Men did not forget her so readily.

"Not formally, no, but you met last night with my father, Langdon Rutledge." His damnably impassive face offered not even a flicker of recognition. "I was there," she added. His eyes were dark and soft, but they revealed nothing. He was either a skillful actor or he honestly had no recollection of her. Annabelle couldn't decide which irritated her more.

"I am Annabelle Rutledge Holcombe," she said with more shrug than curtsy. Still seeing no reaction, she sighed and extended her hand. Balancing his boxes, he took her hand but still said nothing. *A country bumpkin.* "And you, I presume are Mr. Angel—"

"Anglewicz. But, please, call me Josef."

"Mr. Angel-witch," she said, wincing at the pronunciation.

He released her hand quickly. "My apologies, ma'am. My memory isn't what it used to be."

He became aware he blocked her path and apologized again. "I intended no disrespect." He might have looked sincere if his face showed anything, and Annabelle wondered if she'd misjudged him. *It had been dark around the fire. Maybe he hadn't seen well enough to recognize me.*

He slipped away before she thought of something to say in

amends, so she moved off to find her mother.

Still deliberating over the boxes of candles, her mother raised her head and smiled. "Find anything you like?"

Annabelle looked back toward the bloomers and Josey Angel. "I have everything I need."

"Are you feeling all right, Annabelle? You look flushed."

"I'm fine."

Her mother ignored her abrupt tone. "I think we might want more candles," she said. With her wide mouth and dark eyes, she had been a great beauty, the kind of woman men describe as handsome now that gray spotted her dark hair and lines creased her expressive face. She had retreated into herself on losing Annabelle's brothers, emerging again only once they started the journey. "I would hate to run out. I hear the prices we'll find on the trail are criminal."

"War profiteering is criminal, Mother," Annabelle said. Thinking of their plans for Montana, she added, "These prices are merely opportunistic."

Her mother laughed. "Do you think we'll have the opportunity to sell these candles for twice this price in Montana?"

"I should think at least three times," Annabelle said.

"We should buy more," her mother said with a sly grin.

They spent another hour in the store, even though they needed little. Annabelle studied jars of fruit, boxes of dry goods and stacks of clothes for no reason other than the uncertainty of when she would find such bounty again.

The shopkeeper was bundling their purchases and the children sucking on peppermint sticks when several men rushed out of the store. Her mother must have asked about the fuss because one shouted over his shoulder as he left. "There's fixing to be a gunfight."

Annabelle looked for Josey Angel. *Surely, he is far away by now.* She grabbed her packages. "Mother, can you see to the rest?" She charged out the door before hearing her mother's reply.

CHAPTER SEVEN

Annabelle pushed through the crowd gathered on the wooden boardwalk outside Hellman's, her slender frame riding the tide of townspeople until she saw Josey Angel. He stood near the hitching post outside the store with a pair of Indian ponies and a black man who looked too large to ride such a small horse.

Three men faced them. From their look and demeanor, Annabelle assumed they came from the saloon across the street. One wore a tattered, gray Confederate coat. All were big enough to make Josey Angel look small in his baggy shirt as he stepped toward them, his hands held wide from his gun belt.

The man in the middle wore a bolo tie and a crisp white shirt beneath a vest. A neatly trimmed mustache accentuated the grin on his face as he spoke, a finger pointed in Josey Angel's face. Annabelle wondered what prompted the trouble, whether the men were acquainted or had fought in the war. She knew Josey Angel had the kind of reputation men might want to measure themselves against. *Two cocks in the yard. Could it be something so foolish?* Unable to hear what they said, she eased closer.

The man in the bolo stepped forward and knocked Josey Angel's hat from his head, then rested his hand on his belt, just above the white-handled pistol on his hip. Josey Angel didn't move.

"I heard you killed more men than any soldier in the Union army," the grinning man said. "I always wondered. Are you fast?

Or did you just rely on that Henry rifle of yours and shoot 'em down like hogs at the slaughter?"

If Josey Angel responded, Annabelle didn't hear. She'd heard stories of western gunfighters, heroic figures who might gun down three men before they fired a single shot. She assumed these to be the fevered imaginings of dime novelists. Watching Josey Angel, the way his eyes narrowed and never wavered from the men standing before him, she wondered if there might be some truth to the tales.

"I don't think he heard you, Harrison," the man in the gray coat said.

The man called Harrison stood face to face with Josey Angel. "See, I figure it's easy to stand behind an army, shooting away at *boys*—" he spit the last word for emphasis "—while they reload and you can just keep firing away. Empty your rifle, pull out a revolver. Empty that one, pull out another."

The man was half a head taller, and he stood on his toes to hover over Josey Angel. The men beside him had their hands on their weapons, waiting for a response. "Is that how you killed so many?"

"Sometimes."

Josey Angel never flinched. He no longer looked boyish to Annabelle. The night before, he had worn two gun belts with a rifle strapped to his back. The rifle was now with his horse, and he wore only one gun belt. His hands hung loose at his waist, betraying none of the fidgeting she noticed earlier. They were near enough to his holstered pistols that the men facing him focused on his hands, too.

Harrison seemed to expect Josey Angel to say more. When he didn't, Harrison's grin returned wider than ever. "Sometimes?" He tried to laugh, but the sound held no humor. "I suppose the rest of the times, you just stood back and shot down men who never saw it coming, like hunting deer in the woods."

"Sometimes it was like that, too."

Harrison shook his head, still grinning like playing a game. "It doesn't take any courage to gun down unarmed boys or stand behind a tree and murder men who don't see the fight coming. It's different when a man is right before you, gun loaded and ready. I wonder if you've ever killed a man who saw you coming."

"Sometimes."

With that last word, the crowd fell away, everyone scrambling to a safe distance. Annabelle felt rooted to the spot, unable to tear her eyes away. She perspired just standing there. The air felt heavy, like before a summer storm when the wind dies and the clouds are primed to explode. She looked from one man to the other, wondering who would move first, surprised she cared so much about who should be left standing.

CHAPTER EIGHT

Caleb reached for the grease bucket slung under the wagon bed and saw Rutledge riding toward camp. Grease had to be applied to the wagon's wheel bearings, and Caleb didn't trust anyone else to do it right. He remained on the ground at his task as Rutledge arrived, looking awkward on his rented draft horse.

"Hello, Caleb," he called as he carefully dismounted. "I'm sorry I'm late. You didn't have to wait. I'm surprised to see you here."

The Daggett boys had already run off, eager to blow their advance wages in the last saloon they would see before Doby-town and Fort Kearny. Caleb had no intention of following their lead.

"I met some friends of yours on the road and told them I thought you had gone to town," Rutledge said. He walked the horse to the wagon. "If you wish to borrow the horse you might catch them."

Friends? There weren't many people living Caleb even liked, much less anyone who fit that description. He stood and took the reins from Rutledge, trying to sound indifferent as he asked about them.

"They looked like soldiers," Rutledge replied. "Least they had been. One wore an old Confederate coat." Leaving Caleb to tether the horse, Rutledge moved his bony ass to the back of the wagon.

"Did you get their names?"

Examining the contents of the wagon, Rutledge almost missed the question. Every day he repacked the damn thing, moving boxes and sacks and reorganizing with a logic that altered with each dawn. At first he packed all of his family's belongings into a single wagon, leaving three wagons for the goods they planned to sell in Montana. Then he struck on the idea of spreading the goods among all the wagons and packing the things the family would need most in the rear of all four wagons. "No. I don't think so," he said, his distraction obvious. "I figured they served with you. Said they knew you."

Caleb tried to keep his voice even. "What were they like? None of them were familiar to you?"

"Hmm?" Rutledge climbed into the wagon, a new logic no doubt upon him when he turned to face Caleb. "Oh, yes. Big fellows. You know, soldiers." He clambered farther into the wagon, then stopped as if a new thought occurred to him. "One of them was different."

"Different in what way?"

Rutledge thought a moment, stroking his white beard. "He looked a bit of a dandy, really. One of those fellows who spends a lot of time in saloons. Not like the others at all."

Harrison. Caleb had avoided town. Too many people there. Too many chances to be recognized. Damned talkative Rutledge. Caleb wanted to take a whip to him, an idea that never would have occurred to him before the war. Things had changed between them. Or maybe the world was changing. A rich man was out of his element here. Caleb still worked for Rutledge, but the differences between them weren't as great as they'd been. The differences would be even less once they reached Montana. Caleb would be the rich man, and the likes of Rutledge would fall over themselves to win *his* favor. Caleb needed to get there quickly. He saw that now.

"I wish we were gone already." He drew a drink from the

water bucket tied to the side of the wagon. "We've been talking about this for days, and nothing seems to get done."

The placating tone in the rich man's voice proved just how much things had changed. Instead of issuing commands, Rutledge pleaded. "You were the one who told me we had to wait until spring to make sure the grass would be high enough to sustain the stock."

"But May's almost gone and we're still waiting. Other companies are headed out. If we don't hurry, all the sweet grass will be gone when we get out there."

"We had to organize. You know a larger party will be safer."

"I just don't like waiting."

"I don't either, Caleb." Rutledge jumped down from the wagon, landing awkwardly but keeping his footing. He sprang up with a smile. "They say 'discretion is the better part of valor,' my boy."

Caleb looked at him, his forehead crinkled in thought. *This man has no business heading to Montana.* "I don't know what that means, Mr. Rutledge."

Rutledge chuckled. "It means don't let the gold fever get to you," he said, patting Caleb on the shoulder.

Caleb bit back a response. *If I can just get to Montana, men like Rutledge will no longer talk down to me.* He imagined again what that would be like. Rutledge speaking to him as a gentleman. Even his pretty daughter would have to look at him differently. Annabelle never let Caleb forget his place when he worked for her husband. It pleased him to picture her reaction when he was the richest man in Virginia City. He had to live long enough to see it, and Rutledge was right. There was safety in numbers.

"I guess that's what I've got," Caleb said, forcing a smile. "Gold fever."

CHAPTER NINE

Of the three men lined up before him, Josey focused on the one called Harrison. The other two would follow his lead. Harrison spoke like they were familiar, but Josey had no memory of him. This wasn't the first time he had come across men eager to prove themselves against a myth and war stories. He had gone west hoping to put it behind him.

As soon as Harrison took the swipe at his hat, Josey knew this wouldn't be a shooting fight. If Harrison meant to kill him, he would have pulled already. Must have figured he could goad Josey into something stupid, but Josey's concern was for Lord Byron. *If these three take to beating on me, how long before Old Hoss starts on them?* Harrison would hang for shooting Josey in cold blood, but he might not feel inhibited about shooting a black man.

A fluttering of black fabric, like the flapping of raven's wings, swooped from the crowd and obscured his view of the gunman. Next thing Josey knew, a dark-haired woman stood before him. She turned to face him.

Oh, hell.

"I've changed my mind." The woman—Mrs. Rutledge or Holcombe or something—spoke in a tone accustomed to giving orders. "I'll need your help getting these back to the hotel."

She extended her slender arms holding the parcels with her purchases. *Annabelle.* He had just enough time to recall her name before catching the parcels, saving them from the mud. A moment of stunned silence fell over the crowded street as every-one took in the young widow, her stern face making it clear she would tolerate no objections. Annabelle wheeled and faced the three men. Even Harrison's grin fell. The spectators, who'd fallen back moments earlier when gunplay seemed imminent, eased in again.

"What's this now?" she said. Her accent dragged out the question and left no doubt of her provenance. "Is this what passes for Southern courage?" The men looked at each other for an answer. "My brothers made the ultimate sacrifice at Sharpsburg. If they had waited until the odds favored them three to one, they might be alive today, haunted by the memory of their cowardice."

The men looked down, finding something in the muddy street to arrest their attention. If they had hoped this would shield them from the lady's wrath, they were mistaken.

"I don't suppose you were at Sharpsburg?" One of the men shook his head, but Annabelle didn't pause long enough for a response. "Of course not. If you had been there, you would not be here. You wear the uniform," she said to the big fellow in the tattered, gray coat, "but I can't believe you saw many battles. At least not from the front."

A few in the crowd snickered. Josey didn't know what to think. This woman had treated him with hostility in the store. Now she fronted him like a shield, so close he smelled flowered soap in her hair. She startled him when she turned, addressing him like a truant child. "Come along. No more dallying."

Harrison and the others stood mute as Josey stooped to retrieve his hat, balancing the parcels in a single arm. The boxes obstructed his view and left him groping in the mud. The sight of the shamefaced bullies and the cowed gunslinger proved too much for the crowd. The tension hanging over the street exploded into a release of laughter.

Finding his hat, Josey followed Annabelle, ignoring the jeers and one wiseacre who accused him of hiding behind a woman's skirts. The three men stared at Annabelle. She sighed, playing to the crowd. "I weep for what's become of Southern gallantry nearly as much as I do for my poor, dear brothers."

The men stepped back, one staggering into another so that they almost tumbled into the mud as Annabelle strolled past, expertly sweeping up her skirts high enough to step onto the wooden sidewalk without stumbling.

"Thank you, *gentlemen*," she said. She paused long enough for the men to take her hint. The one with the gray coat removed his hat, nudging the man next to him to do the same. The grin returned to Harrison's face as he removed his hat and gave Annabelle a deep bow.

Josey followed the woman onto the wooden walkway. Harrison called after him, "Some other time, Josey Angel."

CHAPTER TEN

While the others were in town, Caleb stole away to a fishing hole near camp. A bend in the river looked deep enough for cat-fish to lurk through the heat of the day. He would be happy there even if he didn't catch anything.

Fishing always brought him closer to Laurie. He thought of his late wife as he baited his line.

Her family had lived in a dirty little shack not far from Caleb's favorite fishing spot outside Charleston. They were about the poorest white people Caleb knew, even poorer than his family. Walking on the cart path that passed alongside their property, he often saw her seated on a crate in the afternoon shade.

Most of the paint had peeled away from the old house, and the front porch leaned to one side despite stones piled up to bolster it. Laurie was the oldest of five children and spent most of her time looking after the rest. She shelled beans or mended clothes while the little ones wrestled or raced in the yard, screaming like savages. Caleb always waved a howdy-doo, and she rewarded him with a shy smile that seemed bright even in the shadow of the porch.

Caleb felt sorry for the girl. Her father worked too hard and too long in the fields to be anything but mean. Her mother, whom Caleb never saw, had been made frail by birthing so many children.

One day Caleb caught more redfish than he could eat on his own. He had tired of carrying them by the time he passed

Laurie's house, surprised to see her on the porch, deep in the evening shadow, when the children weren't about.

"You're just going to walk by without so much as a hello?"

They were the most words she had spoken to him. She stood from her crate, her simple shift glowing in the gloom, revealing just enough curve to her hips and bust to put a gulp in Caleb's throat. He mumbled something about his hands being full, going toward her as he spoke, unaware of moving his feet. Like being reeled in.

Laurie took half his catch that day, and Caleb felt richer for it. After that, whenever Caleb got away to fish he stayed until he caught enough to give some to Laurie. Some days he waited, hidden among the trees near her house until he saw her. More than once when he caught little, he gave her what he had with an excuse that he was dining at the house of a friend or family member. These were inventions, for Caleb had no family left and no friends as close as that. In thanking him, Laurie made him feel more man than he was.

One day Laurie said, "It sure is nice, you bringing me all these fish. But when are you going to teach me to catch them myself?"

"Teach you?"

"Why, you think I can't learn just because I'm a girl?" A hand moved to her hip, and her lip curled into as much of a pout as her little face could muster. He stammered an apology as she laughed, the sound so sweet he didn't feel foolish for inspiring it.

He never learned what she told the children when she came away with him. That first day he told her everything he knew about fishing, probably twice, and he worried that the next time they were alone he would have nothing to say. But it was easy talking to Laurie. He told her about his mama and pappy. He even told her about the brother who died from fever when Ca-

47

leb was a boy. He couldn't remember the last time he'd talked about that.

They first kissed on a fishing outing. Other things happened, too, memories burned into Caleb's mind like a brand that marked him as Laurie's forever.

"You can have me if you want," she told him that day, a breathy whisper that made her sound like a stranger.

He pulled away. Confusion and hurt clouded her eyes, a question coming to her lips. He shook his head. "I want you, Laurie, more than I've wanted anything. But not like this."

Her face rose to meet his, another kiss coming to her lips, the last kiss, he knew, before he lost himself inside her. He waited for her eyes to meet his.

"I will have you as a husband takes a wife, Laurie. I don't have much. We may have even less together. But I will marry you as proper before God as any plantation owner's daughter."

They married by Christmas. By the new year, as they figured it later, Laurie was with child. Caleb had never been happier.

While they readied for the wedding, the country elected Abraham Lincoln. Caleb wondered why people thought it should matter to him who was president in Washington. Some told him to wait and wed after the war. *What war?* He told himself it was just talk. Caleb didn't like to think of what happened after that.

A yellow-breasted meadowlark flittered in the brush nearby, drawing Caleb's mind back to the moment. An afternoon spent away from the wagons left him with just a couple of catfish and a sadness so deep it felt like a millstone on his shoulders. The others would be back from town soon, but Caleb lingered a few minutes more. Laying his pole beside him, he leaned back against the narrow stump of a cottonwood someone had cut down for firewood. Closing his eyes, Caleb recalled the day he proposed to Laurie. He unfastened the buttons on his pants, imagining the feel of another hand against him.

He pictured her in one of the fine dresses the ladies of Charleston wore before the war, colors bright as wildflowers, silk soft as butterfly wings. Laurie's hair hanging long and loose over bare shoulders, tiny waist cinched up so tight her bosom nearly spilled out of the low-cut bodice.

"I'm a rich man now, Laurie. I could buy you all the things you deserved."

Caleb fell slack at the thought.

Laurie would ask how he came by so much money.

They had been poor, but they had everything they needed. He had never felt shamed before her. Now he covered his face, wishing to forget the blood that had stained his hands, wipe the memories from his head of the men who died to satisfy his greed.

The sound of approaching horses startled Caleb, and he hurried to refasten his pants. He reached for the line of fish beside him and turned to rise when he saw the Colonel, Josey Angel and the black man they called Lord Byron.

"Get your hands on anything worth keeping?"

Caleb flushed as he considered the Colonel's meaning. The old man's weathered face revealed nothing behind the drooping mustache. "Not much." Caleb held up the line of catfish. "They're not biting."

The men laughed. "Best be glad of that," the Colonel said.

As they rode off Caleb heard him say to the others, "You can't expect to catch much if all you're doing is playing with worms."

CHAPTER ELEVEN

Annabelle's father imagined himself a cowboy already, so he left with the Daggett boys to check the oxen as soon as he and Annabelle arrived at the camp outside Omaha.

She went to the wagons to find a place for the candles and other supplies purchased in town. The task should have been simple, but every time she returned to the wagons her father had repacked things. It always took a few moments to discern his newest strategy.

As she studied the wagon's contents, Josey Angel rode up on his gray Indian pony. She had sent him off soon after the confrontation in the street outside Hellman's store. "Perhaps you will remember my face the next time we meet," she said, intending it as a rebuke, though he showed no recognition of it.

She hadn't expected to see him again so soon. Doffing his hat, he dismounted with a grace that left her regretting the need to sell her horses. The larger, eastern-bred mounts were accustomed to eating grain and would only be a burden on the trail.

"Can I help you get something, ma'am?" The scout's helpful attitude evaporated with one look in the back of the wagon, his dark eyes growing wide. "Maybe I better wait here, in case you get lost."

Annabelle understood his hesitation. The wagon was big as a boat and cluttered as an old barn. Heavy wheels, set wide and constructed of a wood that resisted shrinking in a dry climate, supported the deep bed divided into two floors. The lower, reserved for provisions, stored things that were not needed each day. The upper, for clothing and bedding, doubled as a lounging place during the day and a bedroom at night. The running gear was removable so that the wooden wagon box, sealed watertight with pine tar, would float while fording a river.

"My challenge is trying to find a place to store these boxes without removing half of what we've already packed," she said.

Josey Angel extended a hand, but Annabelle ignored the offer. She'd been climbing in and out of the wagon for days while helping to pack provisions. The wagon had an arched, canvas-covered roof, with the hickory bows stretched high enough so a child could stand under them. Annabelle hunched over and narrated her progress as she made her way into the wagon.

"This first big box is packed with bacon, salt and other things we need often." She stepped past huge linen sacks of flour and corn meal, smaller sacks of beans, rice, sugar and green coffee beans that they would brown in a skillet. "This old chest has clothes and things we will want to wear and use on the way. Then there's the medicine chest." She moved farther back, opened the box and recited its contents. "Brandy, quinine for malaria, hartshorn for snakebite, citric acid for scurvy."

She kicked at a metal cleat fastened to the bottom of the wagon. "These are for ropes to hold things in place." She moved on, pointing to another box, nearly as high as the chest. "That has a few dishes and things Mother will want once we arrive." Seeing his reaction, she said, "You don't carry a tea set on the back of your horse?"

Making her way back, she described items gathered along the sides: ax, shovel, handsaw, auger, rope. In one corner stood a ten-gallon keg for water and a churn. "That's where the sheet iron stove goes when we aren't using it," she said, pointing to the other corner. "See how the lunch basket fits into the tub?"

He pointed beside her. "Whose chair?"

"That's Mother's. We'll turn it down at night, level things out with the sacks and pile the bedding and comforters on top to sleep."

"You'll sleep here with your parents?"

"A gentleman wouldn't ask," she said. Seeing that hint of a smile on his smooth face, she added, "We'll hang a sheet between us for privacy."

Annabelle sprang down from the wagon to stand beside him. "That's a washtub," she said, sniffing the air loudly. "I suppose you cowboys wouldn't know about those."

He stood back to allow her to pass.

"I suppose I better check on Father before somebody gets hurt," she said, leaving him by the wagon. She wondered if he would follow her and wasn't surprised when he called after her. "Weren't you going to store these boxes someplace?"

She turned to see him nudging the candles with a boot.

Oh, blazes. Annabelle trudged past him, avoiding his gaze. She sighed as she looked in the back of the wagon, still uncertain where the boxes would fit.

Josey Angel hovered, like some kind of sad-faced puppy. "I guess I best be going." Annabelle didn't even bother to look at him. "The Colonel wants to be in town when the general returns."

"General?" Annabelle's stomach fluttered.

"That's right. He's due back from his inspection of the forts. I think he's staying at your hotel. There's a party planned for him tonight, and the Colonel hopes to hear news about the trail."

Annabelle didn't hear anything more the scout said. She steadied herself against the dresser in the wagon, her head spinning at the prospect of what his words suggested. There had been one Union soldier Southerners despised even more than the devil himself. Though she already knew the answer in her heart, she had to ask the question.

"Which general?"

"Why, Sherman, of course."

CHAPTER TWELVE

Josey stood just inside the Herndon House dining room wishing he were somewhere else. He would have preferred to remain in camp with Lord Byron, but he couldn't leave the Colonel to ride back late from town alone.

For the past hour, Josey had pretended to study the elaborate wood molding and pilaster-framed doorways of Omaha's finest hotel. He kept to the fringes of what he heard described as the social gathering of the season. The swirling motion of people and their clamor reminded him of a battle.

The hotel staff created a field by removing the imported furniture from the dining room. A mirror hanging over the large fireplace reflected the light of the gas lamps lining the far walls, making the room appear large enough for a battalion. Waiters in dark broadcloth suits moved about like messengers. Instead of officers' orders, they delivered trays crowded with flutes of sparkling wine.

The important men of Omaha wore uniforms of Sunday-best suits tailored to conceal expanding paunches. They maneuvered individually or in small groups, more like guerilla fighters than a unit. Sherman's junior officers, tall, straight-backed men with clean uniforms and shiny boots, opposed them. They guarded their commander's flank, quick to block any unwanted incursion or to rally to his support in an engagement.

Josey tried to distract himself with different thoughts, yet too often his mind turned to Annabelle. He was a fool for not anticipating her reaction to the news of the general's arrival. The brutal campaign through the South had been necessary to end the war, yet many Southerners would never forgive or forget Sherman's march. Maintaining his distance from the fiery woman would be smart, but he couldn't forget how she looked facing down those fools in the street or how she smelled standing close to him.

Thinking of Annabelle brought back memories he preferred to bury. The bad days in Kansas. The little farm along the border. The woman with straw-colored hair who lived there.

Josey had been hunting that afternoon, seeking something to add to the stew pots in camp. He heard her cries before he saw her. He saw the men first. They were bummers and dressed for the part, scavenging for supplies. Their disheveled uniforms made it difficult to determine which side they were on. One carried a squawking chicken upside down by its legs. Two others held armfuls of sacks. The fourth, a sergeant, held the woman, her arm twisted behind her. He released her with a shove, and she fell to the ground. Her light cotton dress tore at the shoulder, revealing smooth skin tight against sharp collarbones. The men stopped when they saw Josey.

"What's going on, Sergeant?"

The sergeant was a burly man with a stomach that hung over his belt and a mustache so thick and long he must have tasted it at every meal. "Just following orders, sir."

"Your orders include mistreating women?"

The sergeant scowled, his manner betraying his resentment for cavalry. "Orders were to get what we can to feed the battalion. These Southern bitches will hide everything." He pointed to a box by the door of the house that held a collection of candlesticks and flatware. "We found that buried behind the barn."

"Soldiers can't eat silver."

The sergeant stared at Josey, his breath coming in heavy puffs that stirred the hairs of his mustache. They both knew the silver wasn't going back to camp. Bummers who stole household goods shipped them back home as plunder. The sergeant wore a gun belt with a pistol in a covered holster. He moved his hands to his waist and looked to either side. With their hands full, the others wouldn't be much help, and they didn't appear in a hurry to make themselves targets. They seemed plenty aware of the two guns Josey wore on his waist and the rifle in its saddle scabbard at his side.

With a heavy sigh, the sergeant said to the others, "We've gotten enough here. Let's move on." He looked back at the box of silver but made no move toward it.

The woman looked up at Josey. Even with a dirt-streaked face and pain-dulled eyes, she was pretty. Josey wondered what else the sergeant might have taken if he had not come along. "They've left me with nothing," she said. "I'll starve."

Josey looked away. "I can't help you, ma'am. An army's got to eat."

The sergeant smirked as he led the bummers away. Josey dismounted, offering a hand to the woman. She ignored it, rising on her own with a grimace. She limped to her house, stooping to drag the box of silver inside, then closed the door.

It should have been the last time Josey saw her. He should have never returned to the cabin, and over the last two years he'd lost track of how many times he wished that had been true.

A commotion from the other side of the room drew Josey's attention back to the party. A haze of cigar and pipe smoke hung over the room like a cloud of black powder. A cacophony of countless conversations assaulted his ears. Banalities about weather. Women's gossip about the marriage possibilities for the plain-looking daughter of a merchant. Soldiers' tall tales of valor. Mingled with the party noise, they sounded like battlefield commands. His throat tightened. His breath came in quick gasps. He put his back to the wall. Scanned the field for a line of retreat.

The Colonel's light touch on his arm jolted him. "Everything all right, Josey?"

Josey swallowed. He breathed easier in the space created when a circle of admirers closed around Sherman on their side of the room. "Let's take a minute," the Colonel said. "We'll wait until the crowd clears before talking with the general."

Before that happened, Sherman lost his position as the center of attention.

A young woman in a black dress commanded the notice of every man in the room. Just as quickly, every woman studied the newcomer's dark hair, tied up in ribbons to match her dark dress, and appraised the low cut of her gown. She spurned the hoops worn by the other young women so that the material clung to her slender figure. With her shoulders held back, her head high, the woman glided across the room.

Directly toward Josey.

CHAPTER THIRTEEN

Annabelle began dying her dresses black after her brothers' deaths nearly four years earlier. The subsequent loss of her husband left her no reason to alter her wardrobe. Her mother occasionally inquired when the mourning period might end. She still dreamed that Annabelle would remarry and make her a grandmother. The truth hurt too much, so Annabelle told her she felt no need to move on.

"Black is a forgiving color for a woman enduring the privations of war," she said when pressed on the matter. So long as she overlooked the sheen where the fabric had worn thinnest, the dark color concealed the wear of material too scarce to be replaced.

Standing before a mirror in her room at the Herndon House, the sounds of the merriment downstairs drifted in from the hallway. Annabelle rethought her plan to confront the man responsible for so much grief to the South.

On returning to the hotel late that afternoon, she found a crowd gathered. Blue-coated soldiers moved with purpose across the hotel's wooden boardwalk and under the awnings that covered the first-floor windows of the Union Pacific Railroad office. The place resembled a camp quarters more than a luxury hotel. Townspeople in business attire turned out to watch in hopes of seeing the great man.

William Tecumseh Sherman.

The news staggered Annabelle. In the last months of the war,

Sherman's approach terrified all of Charleston. It was a relief when he marched instead on Columbia. On hearing how Sherman's troops razed that city, Annabelle's guilt at drawing comfort at others' suffering transformed her fear into hatred for the man leading the marauding bluebellies. She wished then that Sherman *had* come to her city. She would have faced him herself.

Now she had her chance.

Her mother helped tie her hair for the occasion, and Annabelle was pleased enough with the results, which would have qualified as fashionable even in Charleston. As for the rest . . . She forced herself to look away from the mirror. Loss of weight when food was scarce made her cheekbones too prominent, like one of the stern-faced Indian women she saw in pictures. Annabelle had altered her dresses for travel and nearly discarded this one, for the décolletage made it impractical for what she imagined life to be on the frontier. It seemed fitting for this night, even though without crinoline the dress clung to her frame in an unseemly fashion.

Entering the Herndon's grand dining room, she knew better than to be flattered by the attention. Her attire probably scandalized the women, and the reaction of the men felt no different than the attention paid by dogs at the dinner table.

As the room quieted, Annabelle realized the foolishness of her venture. *What do I have to prove? It won't matter to Sherman that I am unafraid.* Eager for a friendly face, Annabelle gladdened when a voice called her name.

As she crossed the room to greet the Colonel, Josey Angel at his side, she failed to suppress a smile. The old man possessed a charm that made it easy to forget he had worn Union blue. His eyes were kind, and he was quick to smile beneath his mustache. He reminded Annabelle of her late grandfather, who had a spritely way even in his dotage. After her grandmother died,

59

there were jokes that the widower might court one of Anna-belle's friends, a notion no one could quite deny.

The Colonel greeted her with a deep bow and gallant sweep of his arm. He had left his hat in camp and his balding head freckled with age spots left him looking older and frailer than when he sat in a saddle. "I was just telling Josey how even in mourning wear you outshine every lady here."

From Josey Angel, she received a curt nod and a soft, "Ma'am," though his dark eyes never left her. He looked uncomfortable in a dark, loose-fitting frock coat that seemed at least a size too big for him. *I wonder who loaned him that.* Without his guns and in his borrowed suit, he could have passed for a young tutor come to teach in the town's schoolroom.

"Gentlemen," she said. "Dinner clothes suit you in a fashion I would not have anticipated."

"She means we clean up good," the Colonel said to Josey with a gruff laugh. "Tell her how pretty she looks, Josey."

Whatever Josey Angel might have said was lost in another man's booming greeting.

"Marlowe."

Marlowe?

"You old warhorse. When I said I expected to see you in a rocking chair telling war stories to girls too young and too pretty for your likes, I didn't think you would start tonight."

The words came in a torrent, and before Annabelle even registered his presence, General Sherman towered over her. He looked down and laughed, slapping a hand on the Colonel's back, with a knowing wink. "Where's your rocking chair?"

The remark drew good-natured laughter from the circle of junior officers who trailed after the general, hyenas to his red-maned lion. Annabelle blushed at the implied compliment, then grew angry, whether at the man's presumptuousness or her own reaction, she wasn't sure.

Sherman was a large-framed man, bigger than Annabelle expected, and filled with an energy that accelerated the pace of everything around him. She breathed faster. Her thoughts raced. When he turned his attention to Annabelle, she felt caught in the beam of lamp light.

"Where are our manners, gentlemen. Is this fair lady one of the emigrants in your care?"

Introductions followed. Annabelle forgot the names of the junior officers attending Sherman as soon as she heard them, and she expected similar treatment from the general. Instead, he made her the focus of conversation, speaking as if they were the only two in the room.

Though just in his mid-forties, Sherman looked older, the lines of his broad forehead and face deeply creased. His hazel eyes moved restlessly about the room, even when he spoke. The constant motion made him look nervous, though he commanded the conversation and everyone in it. "I see you are in mourning, madam. Let me express my deepest sympathies for your loss."

Though perfectly mannered, the words failed to make their mark on Annabelle. "With all respect, I question your sincerity, sir, as you played no small part in the cause of my grief."

For a moment, it seemed as if all conversation in the room stopped. While the junior officers appeared horrified, she caught in a glance the tug at the side of Josey Angel's mouth she now recognized as a smile. After struggling to keep her voice from quaking, Annabelle determined to hold her ground, setting her shoulders back and returning the general's unblinking gaze.

If her comment angered him, he disguised it well. His response was spoken so softly, the junior officers had to lean in to hear.

"Would you permit, my lady, that a man can feel sympathy for the consequences of actions dutifully performed under

61

regrettable circumstances?" His pace of speech slowed, lacing his words with more sincerity, yet he still spoke too quickly to permit interruptions.

"War has existed from the beginning. Even the Bible is full of it. Some men die, while others are forced to kill. It has always been so. And while the former's loss is complete, his suffering on Earth is done. For that, it is right we mourn. But we should not discount the latter, those for whom the suffering goes on even after triumph's fifes are played."

Sherman looked past Annabelle as he spoke, and she followed his gaze to Josey Angel. Their eyes met, then his flickered away, but in that moment she saw across hundreds of miles and as many days to the source of a shared grief. She shuddered, the shiver stiffening her spine. *What could these men know of my grief? My husband. My brothers. My way of life.* She lost all of these things. Sherman knew pain, too, but war also endowed the man with fame and a sense of purpose. The general took her silence as permission to continue, though it sounded to Annabelle as if he lectured his junior officers.

The conversation turned to the logistics of their journey, the opportunities to resupply at Fort Kearny and Fort Laramie, and the expectations of a peace treaty with the Indians. Sherman confessed his initial pessimism that the warlike Sioux would treat, but his latest report from Fort Laramie's commander included news that all the tribes had agreed to talk. Annabelle interjected when he spoke of the additional forts the army intended to build along their route.

"Won't the Indians object to more forts on their lands?" she asked. "Wouldn't that incite them to violence?"

A junior officer stepped forward to guide Sherman away. The general shrugged him off. "The army can't guarantee the safety of every emigrant who crosses Indian lands, but I wouldn't send women and children into the territories if I weren't confident of what we can accomplish there." He ran a hand through his hair, leaving disheveled, spiky, red tufts. "The colonel and many of the officers charged with building the forts are accompanied by their families. I've even encouraged the ladies to maintain journals. I believe the story of their time on the frontier will prove of value to history."

The general's tone conveyed an air of finality on the topic. Still, Annabelle couldn't resist a final challenge. "If there's to be peace with the Indians, why do you need to build the forts?"

The general's accelerated speech had affected her own manner, and the words escaped Annabelle's mouth before she weighed them. The junior officers braced for an outburst, but the general's manners held. Indeed, he smiled at her, his eyes alight like a fencer enjoying an unaccustomed challenge. He offered her a quick nod. It was as close as he would come to a bow, she suspected, or a concession of defeat.

One of the other officers answered, a short, thickset man with a receding hairline and prodigious sideburns. He patted her arm as he said, "You don't think we can trust the red devils, now do you? We need the forts to make sure they stay in line."

The others hastily agreed, but Annabelle noticed Sherman said nothing. The look he gave her was anything but patronizing, and she recalled that not long ago her family feared this man even more than Indians. *How wise are we to trust our safety to his assurances?*

CHAPTER FOURTEEN

The wagons headed out the next day, moving west toward the Platte River, which they would follow until the river forked. From there, they would follow the North Platte to Fort Laramie and the shortcut promised by their guides. With favorable weather, the Colonel estimated it would take six weeks to reach the outpost. Annabelle found it beyond her imagining that they could travel for so long and still not even be halfway to their destination. Yet the Colonel said they would need another two months from that point to reach Virginia City.

On leaving Omaha, Annabelle's apprehension in abandoning everything she knew gave way to wonder at what she discovered. After weeks in town, everything smelled fresh. Even the air seemed lighter, bringing a crisp clarity to her vision as in moments after a rain. In one spot where the new telegraph line stood like a final tether to civilization, she counted more than a hundred poles. She tried calculating how many it would take to traverse the plains, but the numbers swirled in her head like driftwood bobbing among waves.

Walking behind the family's wagon, Annabelle's thoughts turned to the sea more than once. The tall grass that surrounded their path rose and fell in the breeze like ocean swells. Just as waves' peaks and troughs reveal themselves only once a boat is among them, the seemingly flat land unveiled a contoured terrain of rolling hills, thorny bushes and wildflowers as the wagons passed.

When they stopped at midday for a meal and to rest the stock, Annabelle and her cousin Caroline collected flowers to press in a book. Annabelle couldn't remember the last time she'd pressed flowers. She must have been a child. Back then, she treated her younger cousin like a living doll, dressing Caroline in hand-me-down clothes, forcing her to sit still while she brushed her straight, blonde hair, making her learn her letters. Though no longer a child, Caroline's youth eased her adjustment to their new environment in ways Annabelle envied.

The first evening in camp, the Colonel showed the ladies what he called an old Indian trick—ridding blankets and bedding of lice and fleas by spreading them over anthills. Annabelle smiled to imagine the horrified reaction among the ladies of Charleston on learning the necessity of such a chore. Yet that wasn't the last challenge to Annabelle's sense of decorum.

Plainly put, there were no privies on the trail. Annabelle had known this, of course. What she hadn't counted on was how the damnably flat and treeless terrain denied any sense of solitude. Annabelle hoped a solution would present itself, but nature conspired to put the matter forefront in her mind as the first day trudged on.

Just before dinner, with everyone in camp occupied by the evening's chores, Annabelle slipped away with a sheet of Gayetty's medicated paper, waiting like a child at a cookie jar until certain no one watched.

Discreetly separating from a camp of so many people proved no easy task. Annabelle came across a copse of prickly bushes growing near the banks of a stream. Squatting behind them, she felt confident enough of her solitude to relax. The ridiculousness of her position brought on a fit of laughter she stifled for fear of drawing attention.

From Caroline, less inured by the inhibitions of propriety, she learned not to be so troubled by the chore. Annabelle watched with amazement one morning as her cousin walked not twenty paces from the wagon and squatted, her dress spread around her as a natural screen. She lingered but a moment before bouncing up as if completing a dance step and leaving the daintiest of puddles on the sun-scorched dirt.

Proof that youth had its advantages in these matters came in the example of Annabelle's mother, whom she suspected had not fully relieved herself for days after leaving Omaha. As willful as her mother could be, Annabelle wondered if she intended to reach Montana in her constipated state.

Then one night the sounds of her mother rising in the hours before daybreak awakened Annabelle. She smiled to realize her mother had stowed a sheet of medicated paper where it would be handy upon a nocturnal departure. Her father never stirred on her mother's return. Annabelle remained still, preserving her mother's sense of privacy.

CHAPTER FIFTEEN

Josey and Lord Byron rode to the meadow where the stock grazed, maneuvering around the herd to steer them to camp. Good grass wasn't hard to find this early in the season. While there was little to fear from Indians here, the oxen and cattle were safer within the wagon corral, where the men took turns standing overnight guard.

After an afternoon in the field, the cattle were contented and docile. The sounds of barking dogs and the clatter of tin plates and iron cookware carried from the camp as they approached. The waning sun brought a breeze that dried the sweat on Josey's back and carried the sweet smell of frying bacon from the cook fires. His stomach rumbled.

The men worked without speaking. They could ride all day while hardly exchanging a word, and then, when they did, not even finish a sentence before one understood the other's meaning. This habit drove the Colonel to distraction. When the three of them rode together, the old man maintained a running monologue to fill the silence and then cursed the other two for not interrupting. Sometimes Josey remained silent longer than he naturally would, just to wind up the Colonel. He suspected Byron did the same, though they never spoke of it.

The big man's silence came from a different place than his own. Byron had suffered not just through the war but all his life. He bore the scars of savage and repeated beatings that made Josey's battle wounds look like scratches. Years before the war, the man they first knew simply as Hoss had been taken from his wife and children. They died without him, and Josey knew his friend prayed for the souls of his family every night. Then he slept.

Josey envied the peace of mind that permitted such easy slumber. He tried prayer, too, but talking to God only stirred him up. As they settled in one night Josey asked Byron how he fell asleep so easily.

Byron must have thought the question a joke. Josey rarely japed, so he was eager to hear the rest. "I just close my eyes and breathe."

Josey wondered if counting breaths would steer his mind from darker thoughts. "Do you think about your breathing?"

"I don't think of anything." Byron's deeply lined forehead creased with concern. "What do you think about?"

"Things I've done. Things I've seen."

"Why would you do that?"

Now Josey wondered if Byron was joking. "You're a stronger man than me if you can keep from thinking on what was done to you."

Byron held quiet a moment. When he spoke, his voice rumbled like far-off thunder. "Things they done to me, they can't do to me no more, so I don't think on them."

Josey waited for Byron to say more but soon all he heard were his friend's steady breaths. It was like Byron to leave unsaid what Josey already knew. *I think of the things I've done because I fear I will do them again.*

With Josey lost in thought, Byron rode ahead, turning one of the oxen that had strayed. He rode well enough for not having grown up with the skill, but there was a stiffness to him in the saddle that left him sore after a long day. That was why Josey did most of the hard riding, ranging ahead of the wagons, watching for trouble and scouting good campsites.

He often came across other wagon trains headed west and sometimes travelers turned the other way. They were eager to see a fresh face and generous with news about what they had seen. There were no strangers on the trail, the Colonel liked to say. Even Josey could be sociable long enough to pick up news from fellow travelers. This day had been different.

"I saw riders," he said when Byron returned to his side. "On that ridge to the north, when I came back from scouting."

"I didn't see them." Byron satisfied Josey's curiosity without being asked.

"I don't think they meant to be seen. They rode off, headed north, as soon as I came into view."

Josey circled back, guiding a pair of milk cows that belonged to the New York families. It took a few minutes before he and Byron were close enough to speak, and they resumed the conversation as if it had been uninterrupted.

"Indians?"

"No. Weren't soldiers, either." Josey turned over in his mind something in the way the riders moved off. "Might have been once, though."

"You ain't seen 'em before?"

Josey shook his head. So many wagon trains left Omaha they were bound to bunch together. Sometimes they saw wagons on the south side of the river, their canvas tops gleaming in the sun. At night they might see campfires twinkling on the horizon. No one had cause to hide.

Not unless they did.

The cattle were quiet. From the sounds at camp, he knew dinner would be ready soon, but neither man moved. Josey didn't like mysteries. They pricked at his mind like a sandspur on his trousers, rubbing with every step.

"I expect we'll see 'em again."

Chapter Sixteen

Exhausted by long days on the trail, slumber should have come easily. Yet even after almost a week, the sensations of sleeping in the wagon were still too new. Annabelle lay awake beneath her blanket, her bones sore, muscles leaden, unable to get comfortable no matter which way she turned. Even once she found her ease, sounds that went unnoticed during the day clamored in a discordant jumble to a restless mind. Squawking chickens. Lowing cattle. Barking dogs answering howling wolves. Whispered conversations carried by a wind that set loose canvas flapping and leather harnesses creaking.

Finally smothered in blessed sleep, Annabelle awoke with a jolt, her heart racing like after a hard ride, her nightgown sticky with sweat. She lay still a few moments, disoriented in the dark by the dream, a subject she thought she had put behind her, if not literally buried. The white canvas wagon cover looked just enough like the canopy of her marriage bed to confuse her addled brain and leave her grasping to determine what was dream and what was real.

Not wishing to wake her parents, Annabelle crept from the wagon, flinching every time the wood creaked. Crawling from the wagon, the fair light cast by the silver half moon and millions of twinkling stars reassured her. Two nights earlier a storm as ferocious as any hurricane she had seen tore at their campsite. Great billows of dark clouds rolled in. Lightning played over them like holiday fireworks. The breeze whipped into a gust, washing over them the fresh smell of rain. The skies darkened as a moonless night, and the rain came as the men unhitched the teams.

They scrambled to secure the oxen and cows. A couple of the miners had set up a tent, and it blew over despite extra lines meant to hold it in place. Her father and uncle drove stakes into the ground to anchor the family's wagons while she and her mother took shelter within. Even with the anchors, the wagons rocked like wave-tossed boats. Rain blew sideways into the openings in the canvas, soaking nearly everything.

Few slept that night. They rose to a dreary morning, their camp practically in ruins. They might have lost all the stock but for a cow that wandered into camp to be milked. The scouts followed its tracks to find the rest of the herd.

Thick mud made the road nearly impassable, sucking at the hooves of the oxen. Damp seeped into everything. At the midday break, Annabelle and her mother spread out their bedding to dry in the sun. They wiped down everything inside the wagon with a water and vinegar mix to prevent the spread of mildew. They hung sodden clothes from the wagon's canvas to dry in the wind.

Two days later, it was so dry wagon drivers raced to move out first and avoid swallowing the dust of the wagons in front. The emigrants prayed for a light rain to tamp the trail and break the midday heat, but it seemed nothing came in half measure in these western lands.

Except for sleep. Annabelle believed a good night's sleep was a palliative for nearly any adversity, and she remained confident she soon would adjust to her new environment. Hoping the cool air would aid in recapturing sleep without any cursed dreams, she carried her blanket, pillow and an old quilt to spread on the ground. Her eyes sharpened by the darkness, she maneuvered easily in the night. As she sought a soft spot near the wagons, the discreet rumble of a man clearing his throat startled her.

"If you're going to sleep outside, lie under the wagon. It's safer."

The Colonel reclined on the ground beside the orange glow of the cook fire. Annabelle wasn't sure whether she recognized him by his lean form or the harshness of his Yankee accent. She shuffled forward, wrapping herself more tightly in the blanket and quilt.

He must have registered her confusion as she considered the unseen danger his advice implied. "The stock." He nodded in the direction of the animals. "If anything should startle them into a stampede, you'll be safer under a wagon."

"Wonderful. Another worry to keep me awake. The wolves and rain storms weren't enough."

He tipped his hat. "All part of the service, ma'am."

"At least it's a lovely night." She found a spot near the fire to lay her quilt.

"You've had trouble sleeping?" The Colonel lit his pipe, his face hidden behind the flare of the match.

"I don't think we slept a wink the first night. Father discovered an ax next to Mother's side of the bed. She is terrified of an Indian attack. Father was more afraid of Mother waking from a wolf or coyote howl in such a state that she might dismember a limb—his or hers—before she knew what she was doing."

The Colonel stifled his laughter to keep from waking the others, his amusement prompting a hoarse cough.

"Why aren't you sleeping?" she asked. "I can't believe you're unaccustomed to sleeping outdoors."

"Old men like me don't need to sleep much." In the glow of his pipe she saw his mustache rise into a smile. "Which is a good thing given how many times we have to piss in the night."

A look of alarm passed over his face. "Excuse my language, ma'am. I've been living among uncouth soldiers for too long."

"Your language is not alien to me." Annabelle liked how he called her "ma'am" even though he was older than her father. His manners reminded her of Southern gentlemen. "Once I can sleep better, I think I might come to enjoy our travels."

"Is it bad dreams that bother you?" the Colonel asked.

Annabelle shifted. "Why would you think that?"

"They are common enough these days."

She wondered if he spoke of the war in general or Josey Angel. Annabelle rarely saw the young scout among the wagons. He usually rode ahead and showed up only to report to the Colonel before riding away again. His long absences did not remove him from Annabelle's mind, but she resisted asking the Colonel about him. Instead she asked, "Do bad dreams keep you awake?"

"Me?" He chuckled. "When you reach my age, you stop worrying about your dreams. You're just grateful to still have them."

Annabelle stretched, feeling refreshed despite her abbreviated sleep. The camp would stir soon. Light appeared long before the sun, and the emigrants took advantage of every minute in the cool morning. Rising from her seat by the fire, she bid the Colonel a good day. "I may as well start getting dressed."

"I should go, too." He tipped his hat and rose with some difficulty on knees that seemed to waggle.

Shaking the dust from her quilt, Annabelle watched distant lightning strikes flash on the horizon. She hoped the sight didn't portend another storm. The lights reminded her of the shelling in Charleston, carried her back to another time. It had been months since she last dreamed of her husband. Richard had been so angry in her dream. She wasn't sure why. *For selling the family land? For giving him up for dead?* There were too many possibilities, some she even blocked from her mind.

Annabelle remembered the day he left, so handsome in his

uniform, his wide shoulders gilded with fringed epaulets, a plumed hat making him look even taller in the saddle. He wore a red sash about his waist and carried his father's sword and pearl inlay revolver. The sun shone and he looked the very image of Southern gallantry.

Yet it wasn't until he disappeared from view that Annabelle permitted a smile. *Couldn't restrain it, really.* If she'd been troubled by guilt at the moment, the feeling disappeared in the relief at his departure. She might have felt differently if she'd known he wasn't coming back. That moment of pleasure left her no defense against his anger in her dream.

"You never came home," she said in the dream.

"I've been here all along," her husband responded. He reached toward her in the dream, and she pulled back, tripped, her leg jolting for balance with a sudden movement that woke her.

It's better to be awake if that's what sleep brings. That he should hold such sway over her after all this time proved how deeply he wounded her. He had been dead nearly two years now. She would never know precisely how long. The uncertainty made her envy widows who received accounts of their husband's deaths. As difficult as those letters were to read, at least they delivered a sense of finality. The women grieved and moved on. Annabelle never had that. She imagined Richard's death a thousand ways, sometimes, in her darkest moments, wishing him the pain in death he had thrust on her in life.

Such thoughts always wracked her with remorse and left her more vulnerable to the nightmares. He had come to her, angry, his comely face twisted into a mask of hatred she had never understood.

No. That wasn't right. She understood why he hated her. Perhaps the mystery was in how much. *Where was the forgive-*

ness? Where was the healing of time? She feared she would never understand that.

CHAPTER SEVENTEEN

The wagons typically stopped late in the day, depending on where the scouts found a good campsite. They had left behind Fremont, a settlement of maybe two hundred souls. Two weeks out from Omaha, the scouts brought back word that they'd passed the westernmost point of the Union-Pacific railroad construction site. They were still at least a week away from Fort Kearny. The monotonous routine and vast distances sobered Annabelle, like crossing an ocean in a rowboat with only a vague faith that land waited on the other side.

Yet the journey brought its own pleasures. Evenings were Annabelle's favorite time. While the men unhitched the wagons and moved the stock to graze, the women and children gathered fuel and started cook fires. Trees were still plentiful near the river when they first left Omaha, but they began to see fewer, then hardly any. Earlier travelers had cut down what few trees there had been, the Colonel explained. Before that, great herds of buffalo ate or rubbed down whatever shoots came up long before they grew into trees.

A stream of emigrants with rifles had run off those herds, yet plenty of evidence remained of their migrating through the area between seasons. When dry, great piles of dung could be burned, putting off enough smoky heat for cooking. The boys in particular enjoyed gathering the dried buffalo chips, even if they spent as much time flinging them at each other as adding them to their cart.

Each evening, her father and Luke took the end board from one of the wagons and placed it across two provision boxes. The women set the "table" with tin plates and cups. Without chairs, most sat on small boxes. After supper, while the women cleaned up, the men oiled harnesses and saw to repairs. Later, they played cards or got out their dice to play chuck-a-luck. Sometimes they visited with other families. On fair nights, the emigrants came together at one fire. They talked of family and loves left behind or spoke dreamily of their hopes for the new land.

One warm night when the mosquitoes were scarce, they made music. Caroline had a beautiful voice and, despite her youth, played the best fiddle among them. Others improvised instruments from washboards, spoons and kettles. Some of the couples managed to dance a few steps in a dusty clearing near the fire. The Colonel sat to the side, tapping his knee in rhythm with Luke's spoons. Caroline asked if he knew a song.

"I best leave that to you, pretty lady," he said, drawing a blush from the teen. "If we come across some hostile Indians, maybe then I'll try a tune. The sound is sure to drive them off."

Josey Angel and Lord Byron never joined them on these evenings around the cook fires. They always took the first shift of guard duty, with the rest of the men taking turns on the overnight shift. The guides would fill plates of food and disappear to eat in darkness with the animals. It wasn't clear to Annabelle if they wanted to eat by themselves—or if they assumed that to be the preference of the others.

Quick to warm to an audience, the Colonel enjoyed company. Once Caroline finished her song, Annabelle asked him about Indians. She knew his opinion that sickness and travel accidents posed a greater threat and didn't want his joke about hostile tribes to alarm her mother.

"Indians are a concern." His measured words sounded as if

he hoped not to frighten the women without giving the men reason to feel they no longer needed the guides' services. "That being said, the Indians along the Platte are mostly peaceful now."

"You mean they've been put in their place," one of the Daggett boys said. Annabelle couldn't yet tell them apart.

The Colonel chewed on the stem of his pipe. "The tribes aren't what they used to be. Some lost more than half their people to cholera, smallpox, measles. One of the many gifts we've brought to the land. Now, so long as the white men stay on the trail and avoid trouble, the Indians in these parts usually keep their distance."

"Unless they're out begging or stealing," the other Daggett said.

"A lot of them beg," the Colonel confirmed, "but that's not always the case. Many Indians have a custom of giving a token to strangers—and they expect something in return. That can seem like begging if you don't know better. But when there's trouble in these parts, it's not always the Indians' fault."

"What do you mean?" Annabelle's mother asked.

The Colonel never needed much encouragement to tell a story. "We passed a shallow stream not long after leaving Omaha—you probably didn't take much notice. It's just a little thing the locals call Rawhide Creek."

Interruptions were rare once the Colonel started a story, but he liked to pause for effect. He took a moment to brush his mustache with his fingers, clearing any trace of dinner that remained.

"Some years back, during the gold rush to California, a young man set out all full of himself and sure as blazes the only good Indian was a dead Indian. He swore to anyone who listened he'd kill the first Indian he saw."

"What was his name?" Caroline asked when he paused to

78

draw on his pipe.

"Hush. Don't interrupt," her mother said.

"That's all right," the Colonel said, a pleased look on his face. He had a sweet spot for Annabelle's light-haired cousin. "I believe his name was Davey."

She nodded as if that sounded right. "Davey."

After a puff of smoke, the Colonel continued. "Even then, there weren't many Indians along the trail. It wasn't until he got to the creek that he saw his first Indians . . . a squaw and a little girl sitting on a log by the water."

Annabelle didn't like where she thought the story was headed.

"One of the men in the train sees this and teases the braggart. 'Here's your chance, Davey.' Of course, this man never thought Davey meant to kill a woman or a child. He was just having fun. But wouldn't you know it—Davey pulls out his rifle, and as his wagon draws near the Indians, he shoots the woman dead."

Everyone had drawn closer around the fire. No one spoke. Annabelle wasn't sure anyone breathed. Even the mosquitoes seemed to quit biting.

"The settlers were so shocked, no one knew what to do. They were more afraid of Davey than Indians at that point. So they rolled on, ignoring the cries of the child with the dead woman, treating the incident no differently than if Davey had shot a wolf or wild dog." He drew deeply on his pipe, holding his breath a moment before slowly exhaling. Annabelle smiled. *He enjoys the attention as much as the tobacco.*

"Their attitude changed that night when a tribe of Pawnees surrounded their wagons. The little girl was with them and recognized Davey right off. He wasn't so full of sand face to face with a whole pack of braves."

"What did the other settlers do?" little Jimmy asked. Too late,

Annabelle wondered if her younger cousins would sleep that night.

"They just stood aside," the Colonel said, sweeping his arm as if inviting guests into a parlor. "No one was going to risk his life to protect Davey after what he'd done. They watched while the Indians dragged him off."

The Colonel sat back. The silence lingered, and in the soft glow of the fire Annabelle saw a twinkle in the old man's eyes as he measured the moments and waited for their patience to run out. Annabelle's aunt Blanche gave in first, practically bursting out, "Well, what did they do to him?"

The Colonel leaned forward, his voice barely a whisper over the crackling fire. "I'm not sure I should share the rest in mixed company."

"You *have* to tell us," Mark and Jimmy sang out together.

"Maybe he shouldn't," Annabelle's mother said, pulling her blanket tighter around her shoulders.

"Please," Caroline said, adding her voice to the boys.

"It's not a pleasant ending," the Colonel warned, trying to sound stern, though his mustache had curled into a smile.

"Go on." This time it was Annabelle's uncle Luke encouraging him.

The Colonel nodded. "They dragged Davey away from the camp and tied him to a tree near the creek. Then they took their sharp knives and set to work."

"Doing what?" Mark asked, his eyes big as gold dollars.

The Colonel leaned toward the boy. "You ever peel an apple with a knife? That's what the Indians did to ol' Davey. They peeled him like an apple."

Both boys and their sister squealed in the delighted disgust only children can muster. Annabelle felt ill.

"They say the screams went on for hours. Nobody slept that night, even once the screams stopped. By sunup, the Indians, and most of what was left of Davey, were gone. But Rawhide Creek got a name that's stuck ever since." The Colonel sat back, looking pleased.

Annabelle looked toward Caroline and the boys. She needn't have worried about them. The children's eyes were aglow. Caroline would probably have a song composed about the story before Sunday. Annabelle's mother looked pale, even in the amber glow of the fire. Annabelle's plan to put her mind at rest had backfired, but she didn't mind. A smile crossed her face as she watched her family and new friends. Even without walls and a roof, there was no place else she would have rather been.

This world possessed a simplicity that appealed to her. So many things weren't the way she imagined them when she lived on a cobblestone street lined with houses, a place where Indians seemed no more real than Amazons or centaurs. The world seemed small then. Now she lived in a place where the sky stretched forever, where it seemed she could walk in any direction and never reach an end, where even the most fantastical story sounded more real than the news in the papers at home. Anything could happen.

The Colonel watched her from across the fire, a grin behind his pipe as if he read her mind and agreed. He was probably just pleased to see his story well received, but Annabelle smiled to imagine someone understood.

CHAPTER EIGHTEEN

Walking alongside her family's wagon, Annabelle envied the guides on their horses. She and her father had sold their horses before setting out, knowing they couldn't properly feed animals raised on oats while on the trail. Her father consoled her with the belief that horses were one thing they would find in ample supply in Montana. Of course, he spent his days driving a wagon. Perched in the only seat equipped with springs, it was easy for him to think a horse an unnecessary luxury.

On dry days when the wind didn't blow too fierce, Annabelle preferred walking to riding in the wagon, which jostled so much her stomach grew queasy. Her mother spent the better part of her days reading in the back of the wagon, but more than a few minutes made Annabelle ill. On a bright, cloudless day, she led the family's cow by a rope, the Colonel having instructed her in the best methods for training the animal to follow the wagons.

He rode up alongside her, tipping a hat in greeting. The Colonel and the scouts rode Indian ponies that were accustomed to foraging on grass. They were smaller and not nearly as handsome as the riding horses Annabelle had known, but they were sure-footed and appeared tireless despite their diet. Recalling their meeting with General Sherman, she couldn't resist a gentle tease.

"May I call you Marlowe?"

"You may *not*," he said, though she detected a hint of amusement in his gruff manner. "I've never liked that name. My mother thought to make me a poet. It didn't take."

"I don't know," Annabelle said. "There's a poetry in the stories you tell."

"Those are just things I've heard. The best ones I can't tell, not with such a delicate audience," he said, looking to her.

"You forget I was a married woman. I'm no blushing maiden."

He ignored her teasing. "Josey's the one who should have been named for a poet."

"Josey?"

The Colonel cut a glance her way, as if taking measure of her curiosity. "When I first met him, he used to scribble away in a notebook nearly every night at camp." From his tone, Annabelle knew he spoke of their time in the war. "He had some dog-eared books he would read by the firelight."

"Does he still have them?"

The Colonel shook his head, his gaze far away. "One night he tore the pages from his books, one by one and burned them in the fire." He must have seen the look of confusion on her face. "He never told me why."

Just like a man not to ask. "What a loss," she said.

"Nothing lost," the Colonel said. He pointed to his head. "It's all up there. He read those books so many times, I don't think he forgot a word."

Annabelle tried not to sound miffed. "He told me he has a terrible memory."

"He does for some things. Can't play a hand of cards worth spit. Forgets names and faces. Loses track of conversations like he's drifting somewhere else."

Afraid to ask where, Annabelle was pleased the Colonel continued. "We had this fellow who rode with us a spell in Georgia. He was an artist from *Harper's Weekly*. They sent him to draw pictures so people in New York and such would know what the war was like."

Hoping to encourage him, Annabelle said, "I've seen drawings like that."

"Josey wasn't much for conversation at that point. The rest of the company kept their distance, all but this artist from *Harper's.*"

Annabelle couldn't imagine a time when Josey *was* much for conversation, but she didn't interrupt. A terrible cough left the Colonel's voice hoarse. "All this dust isn't good for my throat," he said, taking a sip from his canteen and leaning down from his horse to offer her a drink. "I might have to move back to the front of the line just to breathe."

"Finish your story first," she pleaded, handing the canteen back. "Why did Josey talk to the artist if he wouldn't talk to anyone else?"

The Colonel hocked and spat, a hint of laughter in the sound. "I don't think the artist gave him much choice. He pestered after him like a mosquito buzzing in his ear. The artist was good—he sketched enough of what he saw to fill in the rest later. But, Josey never forgot anything he saw—or did. The artist called it Josey's gift."

"That's remarkable."

"Josey never saw it that way." The Colonel's voice grew soft. "I suppose it was a gift he gave to the artist. Because after the artist sent off his drawings to be engraved and published the next month, he forgot what he had drawn. Josey couldn't. I don't think he can yet."

They moved on in silence, and Annabelle regretted putting the Colonel in poor spirits.

Hoping to brighten his mood as he rode off, she said, "Well then, I shall call you Marlowe only when we are alone."

That won her a bushy grin before he galloped off. Over his shoulder he called back, "Then you shall be left alone by me."

By the end of the day, the cow followed the wagon with nothing but a long tether, and Annabelle walked beside it. Her mother had warned about her fair skin burning in the sun, but the fresh air invigorated her. Her feet grew sore and her legs stiff, but she walked farther each day.

The wagons in the lead had started pulling into a corral when the Colonel rode back to her. From the mischievous glint in his bright eyes, she sensed a test. After he greeted her, she responded with emphasis, "Good afternoon, *Colonel.*" Their friendship was sealed.

He began sharing news from the other wagons when another bone-rattling coughing fit interrupted him. His horse turned in a circle while he struggled to catch his breath.

"Are you all right?"

"It's nothing." He cleared his throat and spat. "Excuse me. These old bones aren't as suited to sleeping outdoors as they once were. It's usually mornings that are the worst."

"Mother has some honey and vinegar for a cough. You should see her about that."

The Colonel tipped his hat. "You're kinder than an old goat like me deserves, Miss Rutledge."

"It's Holcombe," she said automatically. "My married name, that is."

The Colonel looked stricken. "My deepest apologies, ma'am. I had forgotten."

Not wishing for things to be awkward between them, she quickly added, "Call me Annabelle, please, and we will be spared any future confusion."

His weathered face crinkled into a smile, not unlike the way her grandfather had smiled at her when she was a little girl. He moved off when Josey Angel rode up, stopping far enough away that Annabelle couldn't hear what they said. They exchanged only a few words before Josey Angel rode away. She watched with envy how the horse's flanks lunged with each powerful stride, Josey crouched forward, seeming to move as one with his horse.

"I wish I could ride like that."

The Colonel drew up beside her. "No reason you can't learn."

Annabelle rolled her eyes. "Don't mock me. I couldn't ride like that even when I had a proper saddle."

"So don't use a proper saddle."

"I could hardly ride like him in this," she said, looking down at her black dress.

"A change of wardrobe might suit you, Annabelle." The Colonel tipped his hat and rode ahead before she could ask what he meant.

CHAPTER NINETEEN

It irked Caleb that the Union officers and their Sambo should feel so welcome at the Southern wagons. The scouts did enough work that they weren't expected to cook or wash clothes, taking their meals in turn among all the wagons. Yet it seemed they preferred Southern cooking. *Or at least the company of Southern women.*

Fools hung on every word the Colonel said, like he was Jedediah Smith himself, back from the Rocky Mountains. Josey Angel didn't say much, but after he returned to camp with an antelope for the farmers to butcher, they acted like he was Daniel Boone or Davy Crockett.

Not that Caleb was above accepting a bowl of antelope stew when offered. He settled in next to the Daggett boys, hoping to put his mind on something else.

"Boys, we'll be eating even better once we reach Dakota territory," he said. "Venison, grouse and pheasant, wild geese and ducks with enough feathers to fill a new bed, with extra for your pillows."

"Not if you're counting on Clifton to shoot anything," Willis said, nudging his brother so hard he nearly fell off the crate he used as a seat.

Clifton scoffed. "How do you know what we'll find?"

"Heard it from a mountain man outside Omaha," Caleb said. "Montana's not like this dusty prairie. They've got plenty of timber to build houses, and so much wild game no one goes hungry."

"If it was so great, why'd the mountain man leave?"

"To sell his skins. He told me he killed twelve buffalo in one day. The tongue is the best-tasting part, he said. Can you believe that? They got beaver in all the rivers. And bears, some so big when they stand they're tall as two men, one sitting on the other's shoulders. A bear that big will have a hide that would cover a bed, and enough oil to make soap for a year of washing."

"A year?" Clifton sounded skeptical. "Maybe with as much as you wash."

Willis laughed so hard their conversation drew the notice of the others around the cook fire. Caleb enjoyed the attention. "Shows how little you know, you cockchafer. They said one bear has enough oil to fry all the potatoes and make pie crust for at least six months."

"That may be true, but only a fool would try to find out."

Caleb and the Daggetts turned to see the Colonel standing over them, a bowl of food in his leathery hand. Caleb resented giving up his audience. "What do you know about it, old man?"

If the Colonel took offense, he gave no indication of it. "I've seen a bear as big as you say, and I can tell you, killing one ain't no easy thing."

The Colonel turned toward the others, who were listening to *him* now. Annabelle, in particular, had her dark eyes locked on the codger. While she still wore her black dresses every day, she had lost her bonnet. Her dark hair hung loose about her shoulders, making it hard for any of the younger men to look anywhere else.

"Nobody fools with a grizzly bear," the Colonel continued. "Even Indians, if they kill one, can claim the same honor as killing an enemy in battle. They count coup just for touching it."

"What's coo?" one of Annabelle's whelp cousins asked.

The Colonel smiled at the boy. "It's how an Indian brave tests his courage. Courage is easy at a distance. You have to be brave to get close enough to your enemy to touch him. To some Indians, that's a greater feat than killing a foe."

"Did you count coo with the bear?" the boy asked.

The Colonel choked back his laughter. "Never even thought to try," he managed. He remained standing while the rest sat around the fire. He took a step toward the boy, handing him his bowl and raising his hands over his head. "It towered over us, like this," he said, adding a roar for the benefit of the children seated near Annabelle. A coughing fit forced him to pause.

Caleb rolled his eyes and started to say something to the Daggetts but Willis shushed him as the Colonel recovered his breath. "We had been stalking a deer, Josey and me. Never thought to see a bear, certainly not one that big."

"What did you do?" Annabelle asked.

"Lucky for us, the bear didn't charge. I think it meant to frighten us away. That gave me time to take aim. I had picked out a spot right between its eyes." The Colonel extended his arms, as if holding a rifle, one eye closed in pantomime. "I cocked the rifle and held my breath to steady my hands."

"Then what?"

The Colonel dropped his arms. "Josey knocked down my rifle."

"What?" The boys didn't believe it. "Why?"

"That's what *I* said," the Colonel told them. "We backed off, giving the bear a wide berth, and once we were away I asked him. Then Josey, he says to me the meanest thing he's ever said, at least to my face." As he told this part, the Colonel laughed. "He said, 'I wasn't sure you could kill it before it got us.' He didn't think one bullet would be enough, no matter where I hit it."

"Coward," Caleb said, though no one paid attention.

"I told him, 'Well, you could have finished him off.' But Josey just shook his head. He said killing a bear wasn't like killing deer or a wild bird. Bears have a soul, he said."

"But he's killed *men*," Annabelle said, her face pinching into a frown. "I don't know about bears, but I know men have souls."

The Colonel nodded. "I think I said nearly the same thing." He took back his bowl from the boy. "You know what he said to me? 'Yes, but most men got it coming.' "

As he finished his story, another coughing fit overcame the Colonel, this one so bad he couldn't breathe. Annabelle rushed to him.

"He's burning up," she said to her mother.

Others came to help. The old coot could barely stand. Annabelle sent one of the boys running for Josey Angel. Her aunt tried to get the Colonel to lie down while Mrs. Rutledge ordered the men to put him on a bed in their wagon. Having regained his breath, the Colonel wouldn't have it.

"A good night's sleep is all I need," he said, his voice hoarse. "It's only the ague."

Backing away along with the Daggett boys, Caleb hoped he was right. More than once the old man had warned them disease was a greater threat than Indians. Caleb didn't mean to find out.

CHAPTER TWENTY

The old man was sick.

Josey saw it coming but couldn't stop it. He told the Colonel to rest, to ride in a wagon or hold the emigrants in camp an extra day. They might have blamed it on a need for repairs or rest for the stock. The Colonel's pride wouldn't permit it. He didn't want to let on that he felt poorly.

There was no hiding it now. The first glow of morning bleached the sky and Josey saw his friend wouldn't be rising with the sun. The Colonel slept fitfully. His clothes and hair were damp from fever, and he looked wan and weak. Josey felt the heat pouring off the old man even before his hand made contact with his papery skin. Lord Byron kneeled beside Josey. His furrowed brow reflected everything Josey thought.

"We should get him into some dry clothes and a clean bedroll when he wakes," Josey said.

Byron nodded, and Josey noticed the clothes on the ground behind him. He should have known Byron was a step ahead of him. "Best be getting to the wagons," Byron told him. Josey smiled, realizing he'd been dismissed.

It had been a restless night for both. The old man shivered when they put him to bed. Byron stirred the fire to life and fixed the bedroll. Josey lay beside the Colonel, wrapping him in his arms to still the shakes. When the Colonel slept, Josey rose without disturbing him and sat beside Byron, who handed him a tin cup. Like most Union soldiers, Josey had practically lived on coffee. He gave it up on the march through Georgia, where the blockade made it impossible to find real beans and the bitterness of the roasted rye and sweet potato blends the rebels ground as a substitute put Josey off the stuff for good. Yet he accepted the cup from Byron, knowing neither would be sleeping.

All had suffered the ague that winter, one of the coldest anyone remembered. Ague left a man feeling like he'd been dragged behind a wagon for a day and a night, but he would rise eventually. Byron and Josey recovered quickly, but the illness lingered in the Colonel. He possessed such vigor, Josey forgot that most men his age spent their days rocking on a porch somewhere. Josey figured the Colonel had suffered a relapse, but until they knew for sure, he had to keep the Colonel away from the others, especially the children.

A wagon train left little time to care for the sick. Cattle needed fresh grass. Provisions were limited. If the Colonel didn't recover quickly, they couldn't ask the others to wait. Byron knew this as well as Josey. He said simply, "He won't be well enough by morning."

"We can rest a day. Tomorrow is Saturday. We would have stopped on Sunday, anyway." Byron didn't speak. A tilt of his head was question enough. They stopped on Sundays, in part, so the faithful among them could honor the Sabbath. "We won't give them a choice," Josey said.

That would buy them a day. A sick man might ride in the back of the wagon, but they would have to bind the Colonel with every rope they had to keep him still. It would be a painful ride. The Colonel might regain his strength faster by staying put.

"If it comes to it, I'll stay with him," Josey said. "Give him another couple of days to get strong. On horseback, we'll catch the wagons by the time you reach Kearny. It's at least another month before we reach Bozeman's cutoff." Josey didn't want to think about what it would mean if he didn't catch the wagons by then.

"You'll have to go ahead with the train," Josey told Byron. "Just in case."

Byron rose without speaking and stepped away from the fire's light. The sound of his heavy footfalls carried from where Josey had hobbled the horses. They snorted and stamped at Byron's approach. He couldn't have shown his displeasure with Josey more clearly by shouting it in his face. Josey followed and found him rummaging through their gear, collecting extra canteens. The Colonel would need water in the morning, and it was just like Byron to anticipate the old man's needs. Josey put a hand on his thick shoulder. "I'm sorry, Byron. I—"

"He means as much to me as you." Byron loomed over him, a good half a head taller and broader through the shoulders by a third. In the darkness, the whites of his eyes glowed like lamps, and they were moist with emotion. "I can care for him as well as you."

"Better, I would say."

Byron was missing a tooth and the black gap showed in the flash of his smile. He handed one of the canteens to Josey as they walked toward the fire. "It's not easy being the only black man in this company," he said, a smile allaying some of the sting of his words. "You feel like a roach in another man's rice."

"Any of those boot-lickers mistreating you?"

Byron shook his head. "It ain't like that."

"They been tellin' you how nice they treated their negroes?" It was a joke between them. Every Southerner they met, at least the ones who weren't outright hostile to a black man, felt compelled to share how kindly they'd been to their slaves. After a while, Josey and Byron figured every Simon Legree must have thrown himself in front of the Union rifles on principle because only the big-hearted graybacks who'd read *Uncle Tom's Cabin* seemed to have survived the war.

"They nice enough," Byron said, "but you know those white folks won't follow a black man."

In the morning, when they found the Colonel still wracked with fever, Byron stayed with him. Josey went to the wagons where the men were hitching the teams. He spoke of the Colonel's condition and his plans to rest that day.

"But tomorrow is the Sabbath," said Alexander Brewster, a New York farmer who had attended a seminary for a spell and assumed the duties of camp minister. On Sundays he stood at the center of the corral and read aloud from the Bible while the women saw to washing clothes and baking bread, the men to mending harnesses and yokes and shoeing the animals that needed it.

"If the Sabbath is that important to you, then I expect you will welcome the opportunity to display Christian charity," Josey said, looking the larger man directly in the eye. "And I thank you for it."

Ben Miller, the oldest of the bachelor miners, protested a delay of any kind. "At the pace we're going, the gold will be gone by the time we get there," he said, scratching at the sunburn on his neck.

Rutledge spoke up. "We're making a good pace, a pace that will get us there without breaking down. That's the thing you should concern yourself with." Turning to Brewster, he said, "We will make today our Sabbath, and the Lord will reward us for it."

Luke Swift, Rutledge's brother-in-law, and the others agreed. Josey left them to work out the details of unhitching the teams and moving them to a fresh grazing area.

By the time he returned, he found Rutledge's wife, Mary, and Annabelle with Byron and the Colonel. Seeing mother and daughter working together, Josey realized how much they

favored each other, Mrs. Rutledge's touch of gray doing nothing to diminish the strength of her features. They would need strength, given their patient's mulish disposition. Now awake, the Colonel looked more grumpy than frail.

"I brought tea," Mrs. Rutledge announced, leaving no doubt who was now in charge of the Colonel's care. "I gave him a honey and vinegar mix for the cough. We need to get liquids in him—and I don't mean spirits," she added, glancing to the Colonel.

"He won't drink any more water," Byron said.

"I would rather die from fever than from you drowning me." The Colonel cursed in a hoarse whisper until Mrs. Rutledge silenced him with a cup of tea. Josey took the old man's fractiousness as a good sign. Had he been suffering cholera, the Colonel would have been a more docile patient.

CHAPTER TWENTY-ONE

When Annabelle returned that afternoon with more tea, she found the Colonel and Byron dozing beneath their makeshift tents while Josey Angel and her mother sat together beneath a canvas tarp he had rigged for shade and a windscreen.

The sight of Josey Angel speaking to her mother like they were kin stopped her. The windscreen blocked their view of Annabelle's approach, yet she heard every word.

"He's like a father to you," her mother said. She watched Josey eat as if he were one of her boys. They would have been close in age. As loud and lively as her brothers had been, Annabelle didn't see much of them in Josey Angel. They did have the war in common, and Annabelle would never know how it affected her brothers. She wondered if Josey had always been as he was now. *Would* his *mother recognize him?*

Josey Angel said something between bites of biscuit. Feeling guilty for listening, Annabelle thought to call out, but then her mother asked about his parents.

Annabelle crouched to her knees.

"They're good people." Josey bit into another biscuit.

"When did you last see them?"

"When I left for war."

"Did you part on bad terms?"

"No."

Her mother had a way of using silence to make a person say more than they intended. The trick had always worked better on the boys than it had on Annabelle. After a pause when it seemed Josey Angel would say no more, he added, "It's been so long, I almost forget what she looks like."

I should bring the tea before it gets cold. Josey and her mother sat without speaking, and Annabelle lingered another moment, listening to the music created by the rush of the wind across the tarp and the flute-like call of an unseen meadowlark.

As they returned to the wagons, Annabelle confessed her eavesdropping to her mother. They hadn't stayed long, wanting to give Josey Angel opportunity for a nap while the Colonel slept. He spoke of his plans to lead the train the following day, and not even her mother could object to leaving the Colonel and Byron once he explained his reasoning.

If she hadn't heard it, Annabelle wouldn't have believed how freely Josey Angel spoke with her mother. She remembered a stray cat that used to come around their house. Just children then, Annabelle and her brothers tried to feed the cat, but they were too boisterous to lure it close enough to be petted. The cat sensed danger even in their good intentions and maintained its distance.

On a day when the boys were away, Annabelle spied her mother feeding scraps to the cat. Through a window, she watched her mother squat on the porch, a morsel of chicken pinched between her fingers. The cat took a step toward her and stopped. Then another silent padded footfall. The cat crept closer, its body tensed for flight, but her mother held her place, long past the point her knees must have ached, until the cat came to her, took the food from her fingers and, as it chewed, allowed her mother to scratch the fur between its ears. A few more bites and the cat rubbed its bristled face against her mother's hand.

She never reached to it. Her mother accepted only what

intimacy the cat permitted. Her mother laughed when Annabelle told her Josey Angel reminded her of the cat.

"It's not the first time I've had a secret rendezvous with our young guide," she said, enjoying Annabelle's reaction. "I was as surprised as you look now," her mother said, explaining their first meeting had come before daybreak one morning when her mother had been unable to sleep. Just as Annabelle had once found the Colonel, her mother found Josey Angel stirring up their cook fire.

"Would you have guessed he prefers warm milk to coffee? The Smiths permitted it to him, so long as he milked their cow."

"Mother, get on with the story," Annabelle said, resisting an urge to shake her. "What did you talk about?"

The joy fell from her mother's face. "We talked about the war, of course." Annabelle had to coax the rest of the story from her mother, who confessed she couldn't look at Josey Angel without seeing her boys.

Annabelle thought to change the subject. Her mother almost hadn't recovered from their deaths. The oldest, named Langdon after her father, had died from fever on a hospital sickbed nearly four years earlier in a little town in Maryland. Her brother Johnny wrote the letter home. For four days, her mother's only comfort on receiving the news of one son's death was the belief that the other still drew breath and would return to her. Then they read in the newspapers about the battle at Sharpsburg. They found Johnny's name in the published list of dead. A soldier's letter followed, assuring them Johnny had "a good death," but it proved no comfort to her mother.

Their walk brought them near the campsite. Annabelle led her mother to the edge of a creek that fed into the river. They found a round boulder by the water's edge big enough to serve as a seat for both.

It struck her that she and her mother never talked about their grief. They didn't talk about so many things. Each carried so much pain, sharing with the other felt like you were adding to that person's load. It was easier to hold it in. Yet hearing her mother talk now didn't add to Annabelle's grief. If anything, it lessened the burden, like two oxen yoked to the same cart.

"I knew *everything* about those boys, at least until the end. *I* nursed their first wounds. *I* taught them their letters. *I* brought them to peace when they fought."

Annabelle remained silent as her mother explained her frustration. Letters from the boys were filled with queries about the most trivial news from home and empty reassurances about their well-being.

Their last time home, on leave the year before they were killed, they went with their father to his study to discuss the war, as if their mother were an Eve in the Garden to be shielded from knowledge. "I nearly burst in on them, calling them out as imposters, those *gentlemen* who not so very long before had come bawling to me when they lost a game to their sister."

Her mother drew a deep, shuddering breath. "Until the end, there wasn't a day I didn't feel a part of the boys' lives. I knew that wouldn't last, but I looked forward to seeing my boys grow into men. Husbands. Fathers."

Her mother never knew what manner of men war made her boys. Nothing in her imagination helped her understand a war where so many died or came home mangled. The casualty figures reported in newspapers seemed unfathomable—twenty-three thousand killed or wounded or missing at Sharpsburg, a figure equal to at least half the population of Charleston. Annabelle tried to picture the city with half its people gone, but it was beyond her imagining.

That failure to understand prompted her mother's question to Josey Angel the morning they talked by the fire. "Why do men feel they must protect women from a knowledge of war?" She expected him to evade the question. Instead, perhaps because he wasn't her son, he spoke to her with a candor her sons couldn't.

"Are you certain it's you they protect?" he said, staring into the fire as if an answer lay amid the ash.

"I don't understand."

Josey Angel raised his head, looked at her mother as he spoke. "I went to war expecting excitement, memories that would sate my pride in my old age. Now I can't escape them. I'll never be rid of them."

The camp stirred. He made to rise but stopped even before her mother bid him to stay. "There's this, too," he said, seeming to stare past her. "So long as you don't know the things I've done, in your eyes, at least, I'm still the boy you knew."

As Annabelle listened to the story, she thought at first her mother misspoke. *Did Mother hear the words as her Johnny might have said them? Or did the Union soldier speak them as he would to his mother?*

"He's a good man, Anna. I can see that in him."

Her mother rose to leave, her long legs quickly covering the ground to camp. Annabelle followed, turning over the conversation in her head. Her mother's grief had always been greater than her own, and Annabelle feared her mother saw a son where another man stood. That man was a killer, their well-being in his hands. Annabelle hoped her mother was right.

CHAPTER TWENTY-TWO

Caleb halted his team with a sharp call and a crack of the whip. The oxen were more than accommodating. Big brutes never moved faster than a man could walk—but they did it while pulling a six-ton wagon across almost any terrain.

Driving a prairie schooner pulled by three yoke of oxen wasn't the same as a stagecoach or buckboard. Wagons were easy on roads with a team of horses. Occasionally travelers in a stage or converted farm wagon drawn by horses passed their train. Caleb had even seen a couple of handcarts pushed by Mormons headed to the Great Salt Lake. They could travel like that on the emigrant trail. After decades of use, Caleb had never seen a better natural road.

The land was level, the ground hard and the road nearly as straight as what a city planner would draw on a map. One of the Yankees had a viameter, which ticked off each revolution of a wheel and calculated the distance traveled. They averaged twenty miles on good days. They wouldn't make that much once they left the plains and headed into the mountains or when they crossed badlands with scarce water and little grass. Caleb wouldn't want to be pushing no handcart then, though at least that would be better than a broken coach or a wagon with worn-out horses.

With the oxen stopped, Caleb threw the brake lever and went to find out what caused the delay. A wagon train is a frustrating mode of travel for a man in a hurry. Wagons can only go as fast as the slowest among them. The miners spoke often of going off on their own. The only thing stopping them was the guides' promise of a shortcut. No matter how fast they traveled, the miners wouldn't beat the farmers and shopkeepers to Virginia City if they had to cross the Rocky Mountains.

As he strode toward the front of the line, Caleb saw Josey Angel riding by on his gray Indian pony. *Come to play the hero.* With the old man gone Company Q and the cuffy playing nursemaid, Josey Angel acted like the settlers couldn't yoke their oxen without his telling them how. He still rode ahead some to check their path, but then Caleb would see him riding alongside the wagons, keeping everybody on pace, tossing orders like he knew something. The boy probably didn't know the first thing about wagons. *I would like to see him drive a team.*

Josey Angel dismounted and joined a cluster of men around the back of Willis Daggett's wagon. Rutledge was there with his brother-in-law, the Daggett boys, Smith and Brewster. The crowd obscured Caleb's view, but the wagon tilted to the side so badly he didn't need a wheelwright to figure the problem. *Ah, hell. This ain't good.*

Rutledge saw him coming. "Oh, good, you're here." Caleb liked that, adding in his mind, *Finally, someone who knows what he's doing.* "Can you fix it?"

The wheel was busted up. A couple of the spokes had shattered, others fallen loose and the wooden rim had come apart from the iron tire. Caleb wasn't surprised. Even with the hardwood used for wagons and wheels, the wood shrank in the dry air. Caleb had told Rutledge the drivers should soak the wheels in the river every couple of days to protect against shrinking. If the wagon master knew anything about wagons, he'd be telling everyone that. Caleb looked down at Josey Angel, his face as smooth as a woman's, and wondered if the others were smart enough to realize this was his fault.

"Fix it with what? You got an extra wheel lying around?" Caleb already knew the answer. He had told Rutledge they should bring extra wagon parts, but the moneygrubber didn't want to take up valuable cargo space on stuff he couldn't sell in Montana. He brought one extra wheel—which he had sold a few days into the journey when a wheel on one of the Yankee's wagons gave out. Rutledge had been quick to turn a profit when he had the chance, leaving Caleb to wonder what that wheel was worth now that one of Rutledge's wagons had broken down.

Rutledge turned to Josey Angel and asked about Fort Kearny. "Might there be a wheelwright there or at least a smith with extra wheels for sale?"

"I'm sure there's something." Frowning, Josey Angel removed his hat and wiped the sweat from his head with his sleeve. "We might be a couple days out still."

"You're not certain?" Caleb looked to the others, making plain that a scout ought to know.

"I'm not," Josey Angel said. "I haven't been ranging as far as I normally do and no wagons have passed us coming the other way today."

"You can't fashion a new wheel from spare parts?" Smith asked Rutledge.

He can't fashion anything. Caleb stood tall as everyone looked to him for the answer. "What spare parts? We're using all the wheels we've got."

The men set in to discussing how "we" might fashion parts from extra wood. Caleb liked how they used a collective term when they meant him. He cut off the conversation before they wasted more time. "You need wheelwright's tools to do any of that. Anybody got wheelwright's tools?"

Again, Caleb already knew the answer. Josey Angel had been quiet through the discussion, more proof that he knew nothing of practical value. When he finally spoke, Caleb expected to dismiss whatever he said out of hand.

"I might be able to get you spare parts. A few hours ago we passed the ruins of a wagon. I might be able to get something there."

"I don't remember seeing a broken-down wagon," Caleb said.

"It was on the other side of the river." Josey Angel addressed the others. "Some train must have had to make a river crossing. I suppose a wagon overturned or broke down and washed up on the bank. I'll ride back and look for a wheel."

The others welcomed the suggestion, Rutledge in particular.

"Are you sure the wheels aren't busted, too?" Caleb asked.

"Won't know until I get there. Even if they are, we might salvage enough parts to fix this one."

"You could do that, couldn't you, Caleb?" Rutledge asked.

Caleb sensed he was in for a long night, and he doubted there would be any extra money in it for the work he did. But the job had never been about the money to Caleb. He was in as big a hurry as anyone to get to Montana.

Smith offered to ride with Josey. Caleb held back a chortle on hearing Rutledge suggest it would be a good idea to have as many spare parts as they found. *Wish I had thought of that.*

"Check the wheels before you come back," Caleb told them. The rear wheels were about six inches bigger in diameter than the front wheels, which helped the wagons take sharper turns. He wouldn't expect the scout to think of something like that. "Make sure you get another rear wheel."

It felt good to be the one giving orders for once.

Josey Angel would be gone for hours looking for a wheel, and Caleb enjoyed the attention that came with being the man of the moment. Walking among the wagons, he offered the other drivers his wisdom on the upkeep of their equipment, whether or not they seemed to welcome it.

Still feeling full of himself, he saw Annabelle walking toward the wagons with her pretty cousin. The younger girl was turning into quite a cherry with her long, blonde hair and pert face. To look at her from the neck down though, she still had the figure of a twelve-year-old boy.

Caleb's eyes rolled past her to Annabelle. She was changing, too. The time outdoors had ruddied her complexion. Gone was the Charleston society lady with porcelain skin. Instead of tying back her hair and covering it with a bonnet, Annabelle had taken to letting her long, dark curls fall loose, the way a girl might. All that walking had changed her body, too, made her leaner, stronger. It wasn't the look a gentleman might fancy, but it suited Caleb fine. He admired the way her long strides pulled the dark dress tight against her thighs. She looked less like a doll to be put upon a shelf than a woman who appreciated the value of a day's work in a man—and might know just how to reward him for it.

The girls were talking happily and didn't notice Caleb's approach until he called out a greeting. Caroline showed him a handful of yellow flowers they'd gathered.

"They grow on the prickly pear," she said. "Such a pretty flower for such a nasty plant."

Caleb admired them. "I would be happy to help you find more."

"I think we've got all we need," Annabelle said. "We're going to press them into a book Caroline's been keeping."

"That sounds nice," Caleb said, afraid he sounded like a fool. *What did gentlemen talk about with ladies?* Nothing sounded right. So he explained how he was waiting for Josey Angel—saying the name as if identifying a truant schoolboy. He sensed from their reaction they failed to grasp his importance to the company. As they made their farewells, he hastened after them. "You should ask me to go with you the next time you go hunting wildflowers."

"Oh," Annabelle responded, "we couldn't trouble someone like you with such a little thing."

Caleb wasn't sure he liked her tone. "It's dangerous for two such pretty girls to go off from the camp." Caroline blushed a little but Annabelle gave no sign of acknowledging the compliment. "You might come across Indians or bears."

"I wish we would see an Indian," Caroline said. The only Indians they'd seen had been in towns or near settlements, dressed almost like white men in store-bought shirts and pants without a stripe of war paint. "I'm beginning to think there aren't any left."

"You wouldn't wish that if you were alone, with no man to protect you." Caleb smiled at Annabelle, but she didn't return the good humor. Her face had darkened.

She looked like she might say something when a child's shrieks jolted them. A woman's anguished cries joined the screams from the direction of the wagons. The girls moved that way, but Caleb outpaced them. The sounds came from a wagon near the back of the line. Caleb recognized it as belonging to the Brewsters, one of the Yankee families. The sound seemed to come from inside the wagon.

Or under it.

CHAPTER TWENTY-THREE

Caleb stopped short of Brewster's wagon. A tow-headed child, barely more than a toddler, sat in the dirt beneath it. Curled before him was the biggest rattlesnake Caleb had ever seen. Coiled to strike, it looked to be taking the bawling child's measure. The boy's mother stood frozen beside the wagon, compensating for her inaction with screams for somebody, anybody, to do something.

I should do something. Caleb had been the first man to arrive. Mrs. Smith and Mrs. Chestnut held back the mother. "Stay back," he said, in case they needed to hear it from a man.

Annabelle came to his side. "Where's your gun?"

His gun. *Good idea.* The sight of the snake transfixed him. *Sweet Jesus, it's big.* Coiled like that, Caleb couldn't tell how long it was. Green and gray with brown blotches across its back, the monster looked engorged. It would have taken both of Caleb's hands to encircle it, not that he intended to try. Neither snake nor boy moved, a noisy standoff, the faint whirring of the coiled snake's rattle nearly drowned out by the purple-faced boy's howls.

Brewster, the boy's father, came with a pickaxe, but he hesitated on seeing the snake. *Brother, you're going to need a bigger pick.* Brewster looked to be judging how best to strike, but the snake's position under the wagon presented no clear trajectory, even if he were confident of his aim.

"Your gun. Go get your gun," Annabelle urged, her hand

107

pulling on Caleb's arm.

Yes. That's right. Caleb stepped back toward his wagon, his eyes still fixed on the snake. *I'll be a hero if I kill that monster.* Annabelle would like that. He had killed a snake not long ago. *What if I miss?* It wasn't such an easy thing to hit a snake with a bullet, especially with so many people around and a child so near and screaming like a banshee. *Better get the rifle.*

"Go on," Annabelle said, both hands on his arm, tugging him away from the wagon. Others arrived, crowding the area between the boy and the other wagons.

"Let me through," Caleb announced, "I'm going to get my gun."

"I've got a gun," one of the other men said.

I want mine. The idea of missing the shot was still in his head. Better he take the shot with a gun he knew. More people ran up, shouting questions and conflicting commands over the boy's shrieks and the mother's screams.

The sound of pounding hoof falls added to the cacophony. Caleb turned in time to see the snake fly up as if launched by springs. In the same moment, every emigrant flinched at the sound of thunder, and the heavy-bodied snake fell to the ground, limp as rope.

Caleb looked up to see Josey Angel, still on horseback, his revolver already holstered. With a light-footed leap, he was off the horse and had scooped the boy in his arms even before the sound of the shot stopped reverberating in Caleb's head. Annabelle and the boy's mother rushed forward. Caleb followed, still a little stunned. Taking the boy from Josey Angel, Mrs. Brewster looked to be washing him in her tears, holding him so tight no one could see the boy's wounds. Josey Angel gently pried the boy loose as Annabelle wrapped her slender arms around the mother.

"It's his hand," Josey Angel said.

There was already reddening and swelling around the puncture wound. Josey Angel tugged the kerchief off his neck and wound it over the boy's hand above the wound. "His heart's racing. Keep him calm, if you can," he said to the mother. "We should wash this."

"Shouldn't you suck out the poison or cut it or something?" Caleb had heard that once.

"That won't help," Josey Angel said, never taking his eyes off the boy.

"We have some hartshorn," Annabelle said.

"Go get it." To the mother Josey Angel said, "We'll have him drink a little."

Before Annabelle rose, Mrs. Fletcher called out, "We have hartshorn. Our wagon's right here." She ran off.

The entire wagon train had turned out. Mrs. Smith and Mrs. Chestnut guided Mrs. Brewster, still clutching the boy, while the men ran off to get fresh water. The Chestnut boy and Annabelle's cousins, Mark and Jimmy, gathered around the snake.

"Stay back," Josey Angel commanded, in a voice that brooked no disobedience. "Even a dead snake might bite."

The children backed away, creating a circle around the snake. *I should cut off its head.* But the image of a dead snake reflexively biting him rooted Caleb to the spot. Annabelle sat beside Josey Angel. "Is he going to live?"

"I don't know." Josey Angel pulled a large Bowie knife from his belt and with an arc of his arm quick as a finger snap he cut clean the snake's head. He pointed to the engorged body with the knife. "Looks like it just ate. Maybe the boy didn't get a full dose."

"He must have come across it while playing," Annabelle said. Caleb saw tears in her eyes.

"It might have been sharing a prairie dog burrow there under the wagon," Josey Angel said. "Just bad luck."

"Bad luck," Annabelle repeated. Her body shook slightly with the tears she had been fighting back.

I should go to her. Comfort her. Caleb stepped toward Annabelle just as Josey Angel stood and extended his hand. She took it and rose beside him, nearly as tall as he. "Thank you," she said to Josey Angel. Seeing Caleb as he turned, Josey Angel kicked the snake's body a safe distance from its severed head. "You can feed that to the pigs."

CHAPTER TWENTY-FOUR

The Brewsters' boy was recovering the next day when Annabelle went to call on the family. She and her mother had brought food the night before, knowing Julia Brewster would be in no condition to cook. It seemed every family in the wagon train had the same idea. Sara Fletcher had even baked a pie using jarred peaches. The bachelor miners saw to unhitching the family's team of oxen so Alexander Brewster could pray over his son while some of the other men tended to his wagon.

The boy, David, lay wrapped in blankets in a bed in the family's wagon. His mother, Julia, sat beside him, looking drawn and hollow-eyed after a long night. "He's finally resting," she said, describing a night of pain and nausea. "We struggled to keep him calm. His sleep is the greatest blessing we could have."

Even in their anxiety, the Brewsters had been so grateful for the kindness of the other emigrants, so welcoming to their visitors that Annabelle regretted not calling on them sooner. The Brewsters were from a small town in New York, and they tended to sup with the other Yankee families, just as Annabelle and her family socialized more often with their fellow southerners. An uneasiness lingered after the war, like a wound sore to the touch. Now Annabelle realized she hardly knew these people. Little David looked no different than children she had known in Charleston. His parents spoke the same language as she, even if their pronunciation sounded somewhat different. Annabelle noted that Josey's kerchief was still tied around the boy's swollen hand.

"It was worse last night," Julia said, smoothing out the blankets beneath her boy's hand. "Alex said it looked like a cooked sausage about to burst."

After the Colonel's illness and losing a day of travel because of the broken wheel, the travelers gathered around their campfires the previous night welcomed the news of David's recovery. As they prepared meals to share with the Brewsters, Mr. Smith made the rounds of the camps, eager to tell the tale of his afternoon with Josey. The burly farmer sounded proud as kin as he described how Josey swam his horse across the river and retrieved two wheels and parts from two others, using a rope to float them across when he swam back. With parts from the wagon, they fashioned a travois to drag the equipment and were nearly back to the camp when they heard David's cries. Josey cut loose the travois and galloped the rest of the way.

Recalling his gentleness with David, Annabelle might have thought it was a different man in Josey's clothes who tended the boy. He'd never given an indication he cared a whit for any of them—until it had been necessary.

Was Mother right about him? No one she knew had come back from the war the same. The ones who'd seen the most fighting had been blanketed by sorrow and suffering for so long that all joy and lightness seemed smothered from them. Annabelle wondered if the war killed the capacity for joy in them—or merely covered it beneath heavy folds of mourning. Annabelle knew about mourning, but hers had been focused outward, toward those she had lost. *What might it be like to mourn what you had done as well as what you had lost?* There might be sadness in that at least as great as her own.

Taking David's good hand, Annabelle stroked the boy's delicate skin, noticing how impossibly small his fingers seemed.

It amazed her that such tiny, perfect beings grew into adults. Julia watched her with a look of contentment, like someone nestled before a fire after venturing into a bitter cold. "You were widowed before you had children?"

"Yes, I—" Annabelle had been asked such questions before and had a prepared answer. Studying Julia's face, seeing her pale blue eyes filled with compassion rather than judgment, Annabelle stopped herself. "I lost my baby," she said, so softly she almost couldn't hear the words.

Julia came to her, moving across the cramped wagon with practiced ease, arms around her like a sister. Now Annabelle cried. Julia held her until she sensed Annabelle was cried out, saying the sort of things mothers say to soothe their little ones. Feeling ridiculous, Annabelle pulled back to wipe her eyes, Julia offering a handkerchief from the pocket of her calico dress. "I'm being silly. You are the one with reason to shed tears."

"You are still young," Julia said. "You will marry again and—"

Annabelle shook her head, swallowed back tears. "The doctor said . . ." She choked on the rest, unable to voice the diagnosis she had shared with no one, not even her family. Her mother believed Annabelle showed no interest in another husband because she still mourned the first. Annabelle couldn't bring herself to tell her mother the truth, knowing no man—at least none worth having—would want a barren woman.

Julia embraced her again. "I'm so sorry."

CHAPTER TWENTY-FIVE

At camp that night, Josey filled his plate at their cook fire and tried to slip away as he usually did.

Annabelle's mother wouldn't have it.

"Josef, you can't imagine you've fulfilled your duties as wagon master if you think you can run off into the darkness like a thief."

Josey looked so much like a boy caught stealing cookies from his mother's kitchen that Annabelle burst out. She needed a good laugh after her talk with Julia Brewster. Josey mumbled something about watching the stock, but her mother told him her father had put the Daggett boys to the task.

"We can't have you so tuckered out tomorrow you don't know which way is west," Annabelle's aunt Blanche chided.

"Besides," her mother added, "it's part of the wagon master's duties to entertain us. The Colonel always tells us a story."

From Josey's reaction, Annabelle figured facing the whole Sioux nation presented a more appealing prospect. Before he objected, Mark and Jimmy called out their assent. The Colonel's stories, even those about torture and murder, were too bloodless for their tastes. They hoped for something more ghastly from a notorious gunman.

"I'm no storyteller," Josey said.

Caroline chimed in. "You can always give us a song."

Josey looked more ready to face the Sioux *and* the Comanche than fulfill that request.

"Maybe you can read us some Shakespeare," Annabelle said. The boys made known their dissatisfaction with this suggestion.

"Do you have a book?" Josey asked.

Annabelle shook her head. "Guess you will have to sing after all."

Everyone had filled their plates and found seats around the fire, all looking at Josey, who shuffled his feet in the dust. The men had been passing around a bottle. Annabelle's uncle Luke offered it to Josey, who sniffed it and passed it on.

"For goodness' sake, somebody find him a seat," her mother said.

Luke gave up the box he had been sitting on and went to find another. Josey sat down gingerly, as if he expected to find a scorpion coiled on the wood.

"Please, Josey, tell us a story," Jimmy urged.

Mark picked up the thread, his eyes alight. "You were in Kansas, weren't you? Bleeding Kansas?"

"I won't tell you about Kansas." Josey fell quiet a minute, his eyes drawn to the fire. About the time Annabelle thought the boys had silenced him for the night, he cleared his throat and spoke so softly she wouldn't have heard him if she hadn't been holding her breath.

" 'She walks in beauty, like the night,' " he said quickly, as if embarrassed by the sound of his voice. His eyes cast toward the ground, he continued.

" 'Of cloudless climes and starry skies;

" 'And all that's best of dark and bright

" 'Meet in her aspect and her eyes.' "

Jimmy groaned. "Is this a *love* poem?"

Before he finished the first stanza, Annabelle recognized it and smiled. Josey looked at her, his coffee eyes warm in the fire's glow, and she looked away. He lost his voice a moment, then resumed.

The others remained quiet. Only the boys, bored, continued eating. Caroline sat with her mouth hanging open so that Annabelle feared her cousin might catch a mosquito along with her meal. Her parents, Luke, Blanche and Caleb had different reactions. Annabelle noticed them looking between her and Josey, as if watching the flight of a ball between throwers. Annabelle shifted in her seat, trying to ignore them. Josey gazed into the fire, as if the words lay there, hidden among the embers.

He looked up when he recited a line about "every raven tress," his eyes meeting Annabelle's. Feeling her face flush, Annabelle looked to her feet, but she knew the others were watching.

On completing the poem, Josey bowed his head as the women applauded and a few men whistled their appreciation. "Is he done yet?" Jimmy asked, drawing a rebuke from his mother.

Annabelle clapped politely, careful not to look Josey's way. She heard her mother say, "That was beautiful." Blanche agreed. "I know I've heard it before, but I can't place it. Who is the author?"

"Lord Byron," Annabelle answered.

"The *Sambo* wrote it?" Caleb blurted.

Annabelle laughed, the tension she had been feeling released. "No, the *English* Lord Byron."

"Oh," he said, his thick features twisted in confusion. "That's quite a coincidence."

Annabelle enjoyed her laugh and didn't even mind when she looked up from the flames to see Josey watching her. This time there was no doubt: the blank-faced boy she had first seen was smiling, whether from relief or joy didn't matter in the moment.

Willis Daggett called out Josey's name, breaking the spell. In a moment he came among them, breathless and wild-eyed. "You better come," he said between pants. "Riders coming."

Josey was up in a moment, his rifle in hand, though Annabelle hadn't even seen it near him. "How many?"

"Two. I think. It's awful dark."

Annabelle's eyes found Josey's. *Two?* He allowed himself another smile, and Annabelle shared it. Clifton Daggett arrived a moment later to confirm her suspicion. "Lookee who I've found," he said, walking in ahead of the shadowed riders.

A cheer from everyone around the fire quickly drew the attention of the other wagons, and in a moment well-wishers surrounded the Colonel. He still looked pitifully weak, especially after what must have been a long ride.

"Your campfires guided us in," he said over the clamor. "Nice of you to wait up for us."

It seemed twenty different people started in on twenty different versions of the news from the last couple of days. If not for her mother finding him a place to sit and a plate to fill his hands, the Colonel might have collapsed again. Almost forgotten in the shadow of the crowd stood Lord Byron, his gaptoothed smile beaming through the day's dust. Josey went to him, a hand on his shoulder the only demonstration between them. Annabelle hung back a step, not wanting to intrude, but Byron's deep bass carried to where she stood.

"Them riders are back. Think they was following us."

Annabelle wanted to ask what they were talking about, but Josey's tone held her back.

"They're coming for us," Josey said.

"They ain't leaving."

"Maybe we should go see them first."

Chapter Twenty-Six

Morning broke with a golden light on the horizon as Annabelle and Caroline carried buckets and the breakfast dishes to a stream feeding clear water into the Platte. While Caroline squatted behind a shrub to relieve herself, Annabelle paused, squinting against the day's first brightness. The grass grew thick near the water, and each blade glittered with dewdrops, transformed by the sun into an endless paradise of diamonds.

Caroline, who always had a streak of poetry in her, seemed to read her thoughts. "Look, Annabelle. It shines so prettily, it's as if every sorrow is behind us."

Annabelle agreed. She had never considered herself especially attuned to the natural world, but the more she traveled, the more she became aware of it, whether it be a kaleidoscope of wildflowers or a field of grass vast as an ocean. She relished the prospect of seeing mountains so great they were capped with snow even in summer.

Having traveled almost a score of days, they were nearing Fort Kearny, their last chance to get mail, buy fittings for broken wagons and other supplies before reaching Fort Laramie. Caroline stayed up late finishing letters, but Annabelle had been unmoved to do so. Her life in Charleston seemed so long ago, so far removed from her daily reality she doubted her ability to make anyone understand her new life.

As they scrubbed dishes, Annabelle heard a horse's whinnying. Caroline waved to the passing riders, and Annabelle turned in time to see Josey and Lord Byron tip their hats. She quickly returned to her task while Caroline watched them ride away. "Do you think he's handsome?"

"Who?" Annabelle said, not trusting the question.

Caroline giggled. "You know who." Her hands were busy, but she motioned toward the riders with a nod of her blonde head.

Locking her eyes on the tin plate, Annabelle hoped Caroline couldn't see her face. She scrubbed harder. "I don't know."

"You've got eyes, don't you?" Caroline giggled again. "I used to not think so. He frightened me."

Annabelle stopped washing. "What did he do to frighten you?"

"Oh, he didn't do anything. It was just the way he looked. How he never smiled. I told myself he doesn't have a song in his heart, and that frightens me, especially in a man."

Caroline *would* think of him in terms of a song. Annabelle had never known anyone, especially a woman, who imagined music and could give voice to it like Caroline. "You don't think that now? He wouldn't sing for you last night," she reminded.

"Seemed to me he was singing for you."

Annabelle splashed water at her cousin, drawing a girlish shriek. *She's not such a child anymore.* "So you think you misjudged him?"

"He has a song in his heart," Caroline said. "It's just that it's a sad song."

Annabelle studied her cousin, wondering at Caroline's meaning. What she saw was just Caroline: bright, pretty and happy, nothing to hide. She would probably start humming a new song any moment. Yet for all her girlish ways, Caroline was starting to see with a woman's eyes. Annabelle wondered if her young cousin didn't see clearer than she.

CHAPTER TWENTY-SEVEN

Finding the riders' camp proved easy. They hadn't expected anyone to come to them. What took so long, once Josey and Lord Byron figured where they were, was riding wide enough of the pickets not to be noticed.

Josey never minded a long ride, especially when he was alone. Riding with Byron wasn't much different. Josey appreciated a man who didn't feel the need to express every thought in his head. He made an exception for the Colonel, who at least usually said something worth hearing. Most men talked just to hear the sound of their voice.

Josey couldn't recall when he realized he disliked most people. He hadn't grown up that way. He had loved his mother and father. He had loved the brother who died of fever when both he and Josey were children. He had friends he loved, though they never expressed it as such. There was a girl he thought he loved before he went to war.

Then things changed.

After watching so many friends die, from sickness or in battle, it was safer not to have friends than mourn new ones. It surprised him just how simple that was. The Colonel called him a misanthrope, a diagnosis Josey didn't dispute. The label was readily reinforced every time someone shot at him. It made rationalizing the killing easy. It was war. It was self-defense. In at least one case, when the men wore the same uniform, the bastards deserved it.

Josey never much questioned the morality of the killing because he never expected to outlive the war. The way he saw things, a number needed to die before both sides lost their taste for it. He didn't know the number. He expected it differed for every war. He never figured the number would prove so high or that he would play such a part in seeing it achieved. Believing himself no different than a bee in a field of wildflowers, Josey stopped questioning his role.

He came to this view because of a book his mother had given him as a boy. He had been stung, and bees frightened him. One day on the porch while his mother snapped beans, a bee floated overhead and Josey swatted at it with such energy and anger she stopped what she was doing.

"Josef, did you know without bees there would be no flowers in the field?"

"No, Mama."

"Do you like flowers?"

He shrugged. "I don't like bees."

"I like flowers, Josef. I think the world would be a sorrier place without them."

"Yes, Mama." He stopped swatting, but his contrition didn't spare him a sentence of reading the book about insects she gave him. He never forgot the lesson, learned more at his mother's knee than between the bindings of the book: Bees were necessary to make flowers. That's what bees did. Then, when summer ended and the flowers were gone, the bees died.

All things had a season, and Josey's role in the war seemed as simple as that. It was the only way to make sense of everything he had seen. Once he came to view the war in those terms, he stopped mourning what he had become. He was as necessary as the bees. He tended his flowers, resigned to the idea that when his task ended, his end would come, too.

What would become of a bee that outlived the summer flowers?

Once the war ended, Josey discovered the qualities that made him an effective soldier didn't translate to civilized society. On receiving their discharge papers, the Colonel spoke of securing homesteads for themselves, so they headed west. With nowhere else to go, Byron tagged along. Mostly, they just wandered. Josey had some trouble in Kansas and again in Montana, but they left it behind by staying on the move.

The constant movement suited Josey. He preferred not having to explain himself, and riding with the Colonel and Byron allowed him to avoid most people. With no one to bother him, he studied how the grass changed from dark to light as the sunlit blades bowed to the wind. He watched clouds hover over distant hills as if tethered by invisible wires. He viewed jagged mountain peaks protruding dark against a snowy backdrop, trees covering their lower hillsides like a piney shawl. He found solace in these things. The world of people had brought him nothing but fear and pain.

He and Byron approached the riders' camp from the north. Set on the far side of a ridge, it provided the riders with a view of the road and the river to the south but left them blind in the opposite direction. Josey and Byron ascended the ridge before anyone noticed.

From the size of the camp, Josey judged there to be about a dozen men, but he didn't expect trouble. Road agents weren't common on the emigrant trail, where most travelers were too poor to make the effort worthwhile. If these riders had any salt, they would be working the roads closer to the gold fields. They were vultures, preying on the weak or the stupid. Once they knew the wagons would be prepared for them, Josey figured the riders would go off in search of easier pickings.

A group of four men, none of them heeled, came forward. They didn't look happy to see visitors. "Where do you boys think you're going?"

"Just paying a visit," Josey said. As they drew near, he recognized the man who had spoken.

After nearly three weeks on the trail, he didn't look as fresh as he had in Omaha. Josey felt the hollow pang that came on anytime he realized he'd made a mistake. Something had brought these men out this far, and Josey couldn't figure what it might be. He only knew it couldn't be good.

Chapter Twenty-Eight

"Harrison, isn't it?"

The man who had confronted Josey on the streets of Omaha had traded his white shirt and gambler's vest for a loose, cotton work shirt. His mustache was trim and the rest of his face clean-shaven. *Still the dandy.*

"Josey Angel. Didn't expect to see you again so soon."

Josey also recognized the tall man in the Confederate coat who had been with Harrison in Omaha. The other two he didn't know, one an older man with a gray beard, the other a mulatto boy no older than Annabelle's cousin. Josey didn't bother to pretend his visit was an accident. "You in charge?"

"So far as you need to know."

That means no. Josey dismounted. "I came to see who's in charge."

"Not with those," Harrison said, nodding toward Josey's guns. He held his hands wide to show he didn't wear a gun belt. "Nobody comes to camp heeled. We wouldn't want any accidents."

Slipping off his gun belts, Josey handed them to Byron, who remained mounted. "You better stay here with the horses." He wouldn't have to tell Byron having a well-armed man at his back would be a comfort if anything went wrong.

Harrison led the way along a path down the ridge to a clearing where a cook fire of buffalo chips threw off an acrid smoke. The mulatto boy ran ahead to a man lying prone by the fire, using his saddle as a headrest, his eyes covered with a wide-brimmed hat. The boy fell in beside the man and whispered something in his ear. The news proved important enough for the man to fix his hat but not so important he felt a need to rise.

"Captain, I give you Josey Angel," Harrison announced.

The man sat up and smiled broadly. He was slick-looking, too, handsome in the way of cardsharps or actors, with a pencil-thin mustache like a gabled roof over his mouth. Even seated, his clothes fit a little too well, his dark hair just so beneath a hat too new to be broken in.

"Were you really a captain?" Josey asked.

"Confederate States of America," he said. Then, less proudly, "You'll forgive me if I don't salute."

"You got a name, captain?"

He waved his hand as if swatting away a mosquito. Then he paused to study the nails on his hand, picking at a hangnail. "Names, ranks. They don't mean much out here."

"Where did you fight?"

The captain rolled his head. "Here, there." To Harrison he said, "If he's going to ask my life story, shouldn't he buy me a drink?"

"You were a guerrilla."

"He says that like it's a dirty word." The captain still talking to Harrison.

"Did you keep raiding after you deserted?"

That got his attention. His eyes narrowed and the smile left his face. "Do you blame me?"

"For raiding." Josey nodded. "Not for deserting."

The captain laughed, his arched mustache flattening when he smiled. To Harrison, "You didn't tell me he was funny." To Josey, "Harrison told me you were taciturn."

"That what he told you?"

"Would you like me to explain what it means?" the captain said. The boy giggled.

Josey stepped toward the fire and crouched across from the captain. A kettle was heating, but the fire had only recently been set, a circle of small river stones piled around it. Josey picked up a stone, feeling its heat, then passed it between his hands like a potato.

"I think I've hurt our guest's feelings. Now he's brooding," the captain said to his audience. He looked to Josey. "Mr. Anglewicz," he said, pronouncing it correctly, "please accept my apology. I get carried away sometimes. We should be friends, you and I."

"Friends?"

"We have more in common than you might imagine. Let me ask you, what would you have done if you'd been born in South Carolina instead of—was it Illinois?"

Josey nodded absently. "Done about what?"

"Well, the war, of course. It is clear you object to slavery, so as a man of enlightenment it was convenient you were born in a northern state." He reached out beside him, gently cupping the boy's chin in his hand. "What about me? It was merely by an accident of geography that I was born in the South, bred to be a slave owner, consigned to an army intent on defending an institution to which I found I objected." The boy smiled at him, and the captain petted his head like a dog.

"So you are a 'man of enlightenment,' too?" Josey asked. The captain held his hands wide as if the answer were evident. The conversation had taken paths Josey never anticipated. The stone in his hands grew cold. "So why are you following us?"

He gave a look of surprise. "Following you? We're just going in the same direction." To Harrison, "This is the road west, is it not?"

Josey was losing patience. "Why are you going west?"

"Looking for gold. Same as you. Found any yet?" The slick spoke like he was delivering lines to an audience. His last question sounded different. Josey felt himself studied for a reaction. *Coming here wasn't a good idea.* The moment passed, and the captain shrugged. "No? I guess we will have to wait until we reach the mountains."

As they talked, the other two men who had greeted Josey and Byron came to the fire. Josey noticed they now wore gun belts. The old soldier stood over his captain, while the graybeard took a position beside Josey.

"I had wanted us to be friends, Mr. Anglewicz. But now I fear you will only be in my way," the captain said, a mournful note in his voice as he nodded to the old soldier. "Call it an unfortunate accident of geography."

The gray-coated man reached to his holster—but he never got any farther.

Quick as a snake, Josey stood and hurled the stone, catching the gunman full in the face. In the same motion, he grabbed the kettle with his free hand and whirled toward the graybeard, bashing him on the side of the head with a blow that sent him sprawling. Josey had the old man's gun almost before he hit the ground. In two strides, he stood over the fallen soldier. Blood poured from the man's nose, and he never saw Josey take his gun.

Holding both guns, Josey looked across at Harrison, unarmed and slack-jawed on the opposite side of the fire. The captain had turned to watch Josey, his arm around the mulatto boy. "Did you see that? I was right about him."

Josey kept all three in view as he backed away. *I could stay a year and not understand any of this.*

"Thank you for your hospitality, but I would appreciate no more accidents of geography," he said, waving one of the guns

127

toward Harrison, "or I'm afraid I might have an accident with one of these."

CHAPTER TWENTY-NINE

The Colonel and Josey stood at the edge of the Platte early the next morning, Josey watering the horses while the older man stuffed his pipe for an after-breakfast smoke. Whips cracked and oxen bellowed behind them as the emigrants yoked the teams. The smell of coffee and bacon lingered on the breezeless air. Josey squinted against the light as the sun's first rays pierced the horizon. The Colonel closed his eyes and managed to breathe deeply without coughing.

"I tell you, this is beautiful country, too," he said. "A man could settle here and live a right good life, I expect."

"Awful flat."

The Colonel fell into a coughing fit. He raised a hand when Josey took a step toward him. "That's downright poetic, Josey." He leaned over to spit a wad of phlegm onto the rocks beside him. "The mountains spoiled you. You want a landscape pretty enough to put a frame around and call it a picture."

They had talked through Josey's meeting with the road agents the previous night. The Colonel concluded the riders wouldn't harass them now that they knew the wagon train was prepared. Josey wasn't so sure. He'd turned it over in his head more than once, wondering if he'd been right not to kill the strangers when he had the chance. A few weeks earlier, he would have killed them, their deaths bothering him no more than shooting a wolf on sight. Even if the beast wasn't attacking your stock that moment, it was only a matter of time.

Something had stayed his hand. He didn't know what danger Byron might be in or where the other men from the camp were. Even if Josey had finished off those around the campfire, he couldn't be certain he and Byron would be safe. He told himself that was all there was to it.

Feeling stronger after some hearty meals and a good night's sleep, the Colonel wouldn't have his mood spoiled by an unlikely threat. Still, he had asked Byron to scout ahead today, leaving Josey free to sweep their flanks and rear just in case the riders repaid the visit.

"You get older like me, you learn to see the beauty in what you've got. You appreciate the moment more. Even the flat lands."

"Is that why we spent the last year crossing the country back and forth?"

"Don't sass me." He struck a match and lit the pipe, taking a few quick breaths to fire up the tobacco. "If I was your age and had me a good woman, it wouldn't matter where I lived. I'd live in peace, work hard and declare every sunrise the prettiest I ever saw."

Josey filled his canteen in the clear stream. "Maybe you'll find someone to watch sunsets with in Montana."

The Colonel coughed. "Fat chance of that. The only women we saw in Montana were wives or whores or indistinguishable from grizzlies. Which would you pick for me?" He drew deeply on the pipe. "Don't answer that."

The sun shimmered, a full red ball low in the sky. Thinking the subject dropped, Josey took in the view.

"That Annabelle, she's a fine looking woman."

"Too young for you," Josey said, a little quicker than he intended. He moved off to retrieve the saddles from the riverbank.

The Colonel laughed so hard he nearly choked. "You suppose, eh? Do you suppose that's a sunrise we're watching in the east?"

Josey dropped his saddle on his spotted gray pony and tightened the cinch, trying to ignore the amused glint in the Colonel's eyes.

"Even the rainy mornings would be beautiful if you had a woman like that waking up next to you. She's almost *too* beautiful. A too-beautiful woman will rob a man of all ambition, once he has her at least. Next thing you know—"

"What do *you* know about it?" The horses lifted their heads from the stream, ears perked at the sharpness in Josey's voice.

The old man only laughed more. "I know a hell of a lot more than you'll ever know if you don't talk to the woman." Josey stooped to pick up the Colonel's saddle. "That's it. Pretend you don't hear me. But know this: It's a long way to Montana, but we will get there one day. What will you do then? If you're still watching sunrises with this old coot, you'll be a sorry excuse for a man, and a bigger coward than I would've figured."

The old man meant well, so Josey bit back the anger rising inside him. Overhearing the settlers talk about their plans, Josey daydreamed, too. He knew a place, a little valley along the Madison River between Bozeman and Virginia City. It hadn't been settled much yet. If Josey could get enough land there, a few good men might drive cattle up from the south. It would be good business feeding the miners and all the folks who had moved into Virginia City now that it was the territorial capital.

Sometimes he wondered if Annabelle would like his valley. She was as beautiful as the old man said, and Josey sensed a strength in her that drew him like no woman he'd known.

Yet he put her from his mind. She stirred memories too painful to recall, and he recognized his daydreams as nothing but a pleasant fantasy. Annabelle and her family needed him. They were frightened in a strange and wild place, and they would hold a dangerous man close so long as he made them feel safe. A big dog kept near the chicken coop to run off foxes and coyotes but never allowed in the house; that's all Josey was to them. Once they reached Virginia City, once the women felt safe and civilized again, the dog in the yard would be the biggest threat in their lives. Josey would have to go. The stain of death on him was too deep to be washed away.

Josey stood with his back to the old man. "You don't understand."

"I understand enough. I understand if you don't talk to that woman, she will haunt you every day you draw breath. You've had enough of that already, enough for two lifetimes, likely."

The Colonel stood from his perch on the bank, waited for Josey to face him. "If you talk to her, maybe she will turn away from you. Can't blame her if she did. But maybe she won't. I think you've got a feeling maybe she won't. And if she don't, well, maybe she can help you forget some of the bad and learn to forgive yourself for things that weren't your fault."

The Colonel didn't look like he'd expected an answer, so he wasn't likely to be disappointed. "That's enough lollygagging for one day." He hiked up his gun belt and ambled from the river. "I feel like I could piss like a horse, but I would bet four bits I can't dribble enough to wet a stone."

CHAPTER THIRTY

After weeks of worry mixed with curiosity, the first time Anna-belle saw what her cousin would call "real Indians" proved a disappointment.

They came into camp on foot, more than a dozen bedraggled men whose only resemblance to the noble savages of Anna-belle's imagination was a ruddy complexion. There were no feathered headdresses. No buffalo skin robes. They wore clothes not unlike the men in the wagon train, but they were so dirty and smelled so foul Annabelle recalled tales of emigrants hiding gravesites of loved ones so Indians wouldn't dig them up and steal the clothes.

The Indians were unarmed, but they created as much of a stir as if they had ridden in wearing war paint and launching arrows. The Colonel and some of the men greeted the strangers, who moved about the wagons like customers in a store, finger-ing merchandise and casting an appraising eye everywhere. A handful of dogs followed them, their barks and furtive move-ments alarming the oxen and camp dogs. She noticed Josey, rifle in hand, maneuvering in a way that kept the campfires and the emigrants at his back.

Her father strode past Annabelle, pulling on a coat as he left the warmth of the fire. "I had finally convinced your mother to put away her ax," he grumbled.

He intended to put her at ease with the joke, but Annabelle felt more pity than fear. The Colonel had told them how poor the tribes along the Platte were. The cholera epidemic that ravaged the trail more than a decade earlier wiped out so many Indians that in some villages those who remained had to move on or die. Government treaties that guaranteed safe passage for the emigrants were supposed to provide for the Indians. The promised goods were delivered for a few years but stopped or were stolen by government agents once the Indians grew too weak to pose a threat.

Through hand gestures and a smattering of broken English the Indians made clear they wanted something to eat. George Franklin, a Yankee Annabelle's father compared to Scrooge for his miserly ways, objected. "If we feed them, we may never be rid of them," he said.

Her father took the opposing view. "It might be wise to engender some goodwill among the natives."

Her father had to be as disappointed as she. Despite her mother's misgivings, he looked forward to trading with Indians. But it didn't look like these people had anything worth bartering. There wasn't a young brave among them. One or two looked to be boys, no older than her cousin Mark. The rest looked to be her father's age or older. The oldest among them had a head of white hair and a face like desert baked and cracked by drought. Around his neck, he wore a necklace of animal teeth—at least Annabelle assumed the teeth were from an animal.

"Look at them. They're no better than stray dogs," said Ben Miller, the grubby miner whose hygiene wasn't much better in Annabelle's view. "We've got nothing to fear from them."

Josey remained silent, his eyes never leaving the Indians, who seemed just as aware of him. He didn't look so young or small holding that rifle. The Indians had been watching the men debate, but they kept looking to Josey. *He makes them as nervous as they make us.* Annabelle failed to suppress a smile.

"If you don't agree to feed these men, I'll do it myself." Her mother, so terrified of Indians when the journey started, pushed past the men, scattering them like ninepins.

"We'll handle this, Mary," her father said. "Why don't you go and see what food all the camps can spare."

Mollified, her mother turned back while the Colonel addressed the Indians. Every group of wagons brought forward some food. It seemed more than enough to feed a dozen Indians, though after watching them wolf down what was offered Annabelle figured they could have eaten twice as much. They walked out of the camp as soon as they were fed, with neither a word of thanks, nor threat, nor request for more.

Despite the Indians' haggard appearance, a new tension ran through the camp, and if her mother brought the ax to bed, her father didn't complain. Some of the men laughed off the fear. The Indians had looked so pathetic, Clifton Daggett said, surely they posed no threat. Annabelle heard such sentiments repeated so often she recalled Shakespeare and a lady's protests.

Caleb Williams warned that the Indians' appearance had been a ruse, intended to lull the camp into complacency so the braves could sneak in and kill them in their sleep. The burly handyman was shushed by the others.

Whether from fear or prudence, the camp doubled the guard around the stock while others took turns patrolling the wagons. Some of the emigrants who had been sleeping in tents remained in their wagon. Not many of the men slept at all.

The camp rose early the next morning. The guards reported that none of the stock had been disturbed. Everyone relaxed as water boiled for coffee and bacon sizzled. The Indians soon returned. They came just as they had the night before, unarmed, leaving their horses outside the camp. They were hungry again.

"Didn't I tell you?" George Franklin said.

135

More than a few of the emigrants looked to Annabelle's mother. She had made her point the night before that they weren't afraid of the Indians. To capitulate to new demands might suggest otherwise. She smoothed out the folds of her dress and tucked a few stray hairs beneath her bonnet as she stood.

"Tell them we're not running an Indian hash house here," she said.

Again, the Colonel handled the communications. The Indians didn't seem pleased with his message but rather than argue they gestured, making it clear they hoped to leave with one of the cows that had been trailing behind the wagons. The Colonel refused, and the Indians gave up rather meekly. Annabelle couldn't see Josey, but she knew he would be nearby, rifle at hand.

They finished breakfast even faster than usual. The women packed and the men yoked and hitched the animals with no idle chatter or dawdling. As the wagons pulled out, Annabelle looked back with a mixture of emotions.

These Indians, who had stirred so much concern among the travelers when they set out, seemed more pitiful than fearsome. Yet the image of the white-haired Indian who appeared so ancient to Annabelle the previous night stuck with her. Watching him go to where they had left their horses, she marveled as he sprung to his pony like a young buck. Galloping off, he looked more centaur than man and horse, and it sent a shudder down Annabelle's back. *If the old men ride so well, how dangerous must the braves be?*

CHAPTER THIRTY-ONE

After a brief layover for repairs and mail at Fort Kearny, they found the road changed. The wagons passed over some steep, sandy bluffs that made for hard pulling, even for the oxen. On more than one occasion, the women and children left the wagons and walked for miles in the sand while the men cursed and sweated, doubling up the teams at times to get the wagons across.

Tired as he was, Caleb took his pistol out that night to clean it while the women cooked dinner. He shut their gay chatter from his mind. *Josey Angel this. Josey Angel that.* They treated the man like some kind of hero after he showed up with a big buck draped across the saddle of his pony. A few of the farmers butchered it, and everyone anticipated fresh venison stew. Josey gave the antlers and skin to the Georgia banker, Stephen Chestnut, the one man in camp who belonged on the frontier even less than Rutledge.

Chestnut, a small-boned man with a wispy mustache and rheumy eyes, determined to make himself over as a mountain man. He wanted buckskins like Kit Carson wore in the dime novels and planned to mount the antlers over the fireplace in the log cabin he would build in Montana.

The asswipe didn't even understand the antlers a man hangs in his home are supposed to come from an animal he shot himself. Didn't matter to Chestnut. Even worse, now he talked of Josey Angel as if they were bosom friends. Caleb doubted Josey Angel had spoken two words to Chestnut before he handed over the antlers.

Caleb didn't understand. Chestnut, who lost his bank and nearly everything he owned when Sherman's army swept through Georgia, ought to be the last man to curry favor with that bluebelly. Southerners swore they would never forget. Well, Caleb hadn't forgotten.

"I sure hope they're going to fry up some steaks with that buck. It's been too long since I've had a good steak," Willis Daggett said. Having seen Caleb, he and his brother got the idea to clean their guns, too.

"Big as it was, I'm not sure there's enough for steaks," Clifton said. "Just wait 'til we reach Wyoming. I bet Josey will come back every night with *two* deer."

"I wish you two would shut up about it," Caleb said as he peered through the Navy revolver's six empty cylinders to make sure they were clean. The pistol hung heavy on his hip and got in the way while he drove the wagon, so he had packed it after a few days on the trail. The only time he'd thought to get it was the day the snake bit the boy. The run-in with the Indians reminded him it probably needed cleaning.

"Don't you like venison?" Willis asked, not understanding Caleb's foul mood. "If you don't want yours, can I have it? You can have my biscuits."

"Keep your paws off my stew, fat boy," Caleb said.

The brothers ignored him. "Josey told me he cleans and loads his guns before every breakfast and supper," Clifton said, sounding like he repeated the gospel of Jesus Christ.

Willis seemed jealous. "When does he talk to you?"

"All the time, you fool. He says any man who tends himself before his guns isn't worth much. I'm going to start doing that, too."

"How often do you idiots need to shoot?" Before either

Daggett answered or made any more noise about their hero, Caleb cut them off. "I just don't see what all the fuss is about. If we spent our days riding all over the country, we would come back with something even better than a deer, like a buffalo or a bear."

"Josey Angel told me they's too heavy to carry back to camp," Willis said. *So now he's having private conversations with Josey Angel, too.* "You'd have to skin it and butcher it where you killed it. Be better if we shot antelope or deer like Josey."

Clifton snorted. "Willis, you ain't no crack shot like Josey Angel. You couldn't hit the ground if you fell out of your wagon." He laughed at his joke, leaving him unable to fend off an assault from his larger brother, who landed a punch that left him rubbing his shoulder.

Caleb was about to yell at the boys to shut up when he noticed, almost lost in the gray and brown of the chaparral, a good-sized jackrabbit poised on its hind legs, its nose twitching in curious study of the three men. The boys noticed it, too. "You loaded?" Willis asked his brother.

"Not yet."

Caleb looked to them. They exchanged grins. The race was on.

A powder flask lay at Caleb's feet. He tapped it against his knee to loosen the contents, then poured what he judged to be the right amount into a chamber—no time to measure—then slipped the ball in and pulled down the loading lever to pack it securely. In his haste, he left the other cylinders empty. He added the percussion cap, careful not to set it off in his hand. He sensed the others moved just as fast, so he raised the gun and sighted quickly. The explosion in his hand echoed immediately with two others, the sound so great his head throbbed. Through the haze of smoke, the rabbit disappeared.

"Damn."

"Did we hit it?" Willis asked.

"What do you think, you ignoramus."

They stood for a better look, just as nearly every man in camp appeared around them, armed and cocked and ready to go off at the first sight of marauding Indians.

"What's happened?"

"Is anybody hurt?"

"Where did they go?"

It took a moment to explain and calm everyone, and then they heard another shot from the other side of camp. "Now what?"

Rutledge was spitting mad. "Fools. With everyone so wound up over Indians someone might have died of fright."

Caleb almost laughed at the man's vexation. *You would be the first to go.* Then he saw Annabelle, who had come with the other women to see about the commotion. Her hair hung loose and wild around her shoulders. Something was different about her, though Caleb couldn't place it. He felt a fool now for missing his shot. He supposed Josey Angel never missed, at least not that anyone witnessed, and now he and the Daggetts couldn't hit a jackrabbit with three shots among them.

"Everything's fine. Nothing to worry about," Rutledge called.

Mrs. Rutledge approached her daughter and handed her a ribbon for her hair. As Annabelle turned and walked toward the wagons, Caleb realized what was different. Instead of black, she wore a gingham dress of white and faded-blue checks.

Before Caleb could figure what that meant, little Sarah Chestnut raced to the group, breathless and red-faced. She was a tiny girl, all elbows and knees, but the family features that served her father so poorly made a more comely impression on her. Later, Caleb would have time to reflect on the strangeness of having Stephen Chestnut in his thoughts just moments before tragedy struck. In the moment, though, all eyes were on the girl as she spoke between great gulps of air.

"Come quick. My brother's been hurt. Bad."

CHAPTER THIRTY-TWO

In the morning, they had a body but no coffin, no grave and no clergyman.

Josey had been so intent on protecting these people from road agents, wild animals and Indians he never stopped to think of the everyday places where danger lay.

Stephen Chestnut had no experience with guns, but he thought it necessary to have one to protect his family. His teenage son, Burton, had even less experience in handling the weapon. He probably didn't know his father had left the rifle loaded after encountering the Indians. Josey imagined the boy's death almost as if he'd been there: Hearing multiple shots on the other side of camp, the boy feared the wagons were under attack. He must have triggered the gun when he grabbed it. The shot tore away half his face. No one could do anything for him.

In their shared grief, the wagon train came together. Annabelle, wearing black again, cleaned and wrapped the body with her mother and aunt. The rest of the women took on extra cooking and cleaning to help the family. Ben Miller led the miners in digging a grave. Fearing wild animals might dig up the body, no one liked the idea of a burial without a coffin. George Franklin came forward with a solution. The Yankee known for his frugality had a double floor in his wagon. By repacking things, he removed the wood used to construct the second level. Caleb Williams and the Daggett boys used it to build a coffin. Langdon Rutledge and his brother-in-law formed a marker in the shape of a cross from extra pieces of wood. Alexander Brewster prepared a eulogy.

Frontiersmen might be quick to condemn city folk who seek to make their way in the west, he told the grieving parents, but it takes a special kind of bravery for such men to strike out into a new world.

"Burton Chestnut's final thoughts had been for the safety of his family and friends," Brewster concluded. "He may have been afraid, but he didn't let his fear stop him from taking action."

Josey thought it a fine eulogy. There wasn't a dry eye among the women—and many of the men as well. He helped place the coffin into the ground. As soon as they covered the coffin, the families prepared to move on. They couldn't stop to mourn, even for a day.

Before dawn the next morning Josey lingered over a cup of warm milk when Mary Rutledge joined him by the fire. He listened as she spoke of the funeral, realizing she'd been unable to bury the two sons she lost.

"I suppose you get used to funerals in the army," she said.

"Not really." Josey recalled fields that appeared carpeted with corpses. Dead buried in mass graves. Grave diggers dumping bodies into a hole. A man leaping on top, compressing the pile so more bodies would fit. "War doesn't leave much time for proper mourning. I expect it's harder on those at home. Your sons. Annabelle's husband." He watched her as he said the last but saw no reaction. "She must have loved him dearly, to mourn so long."

"I'm not sure she ever loved him."

Josey's pulse quickened at her response. More questions popped into his mind, but he feared asking might appear unseemly. He relaxed when Mrs. Rutledge continued without prodding.

"I blame myself for permitting the match. Richard was a strange man. He was handsome, came from a good family and could be charming as the devil. But I don't think it was in him to give himself to another. He married Annabelle for Langdon's money and to appease his own father more than anything she meant to him. Annabelle and I have never talked about it, but after Richard's father died and his inheritance was secure, I don't think he cared to be married any longer."

"But she is so beautiful, why—" Josey stopped as Mrs. Rutledge looked to him, her eyes alert to his curiosity. In the first hint of a smile, he saw Annabelle in her mother's lean face. Mrs. Rutledge—Mary—would have been just as beautiful once, was still beautiful, in truth.

Mary cocked her head as she looked at him, leaving Josey with the uncomfortable sense that he was being judged. "Have you ever been married?"

Josey nearly choked on his negative response.

"Ever been in love?"

He squirmed under the woman's gaze, unable to recall when he'd last been so uncomfortable. She waited, one eyebrow cocked in anticipation. He didn't see an alternative but to answer. "There was a woman."

"That's not what I asked."

Even with the passage of almost two years, the answer was complicated in Josey's mind. When Josey met her, the woman lived alone near the border between Kansas and Missouri. He'd never been clear about which side. She was older than Josey, and she was married. Or had been married. Josey never asked. "I cared for a woman."

Mary Rutledge watched him closely. "You must have cared a lot."

"I don't think there was enough time to call it love."

"Love can happen fast."

"How do you know?"

She merely smiled at him.

CHAPTER THIRTY-THREE

The woman lived on a small farm, little more than a cabin with a barn and a field. After Josey ran off the bummers who harassed her, he should have never seen her again.

Yet she occupied his mind that afternoon when he took aim at the deer. Even as he shot, he knew it had no more chance of filling the army's larders than the silverware the soldiers had intended to steal from her.

The woman greeted him at the door with a flintlock pistol pointed in his face.

"What do you want?"

"Nothing. Want to give you something." He returned to his horse. She stepped onto the porch to watch him. He hoisted the buck onto his shoulders. "Somewhere I can hang this?"

She motioned with her head toward the barn. "Out back. There's water and a tree." She turned and went into the house, closing the door.

It was dark by the time he finished and knocked on the door. The pistol was gone. Her straw-colored hair was dark around her face where she had washed. She wore a clean dress, white with a pattern of flowers on the cloth. Josey figured she didn't wear it much.

"You should let it hang for a few days—" The look she gave cut him off. She knew how to butcher a deer.

"I'm sorry about before," she said, not meeting his eyes. "It was kind of you to come back. I guess I'm not accustomed to kindnesses."

She invited him in. Her soft voice carried a hint of accent that made Josey think she must be from farther south. They stood in a large central room. A doorway in the back led to a darkened bedroom near stairs to a loft. He expected she had a husband and children but saw no evidence of anyone else. She stood close enough he could smell fresh soap and something else, like flowers, maybe lavender. His hands fidgeted, and he crossed his arms to still them.

She moved past him toward a stone hearth where a kettle hung over a fire. "I've started a stew," she said, lifting the lid and stirring. "It's nothing much, but I managed to keep some things from your friends."

"They weren't my friends." His stomach rumbled at the smell of the stew. "I should go."

"Your stomach disagrees." Her laughter melted some of his awkwardness. She studied him a moment, then looked away. "There's a bath behind the screen. The water's no longer hot, but it's mostly clean."

He took the hint. He watched over the top of the screen as she sliced bread, humming softly as she worked. He undressed slowly, feeling exposed even with the screen.

As he bathed, she called from the other side of the room. "I brought you some clothes. They may be a little big, but they will be more comfortable than that dirty uniform." He laughed at the sight of her clean white hands reaching blindly around the screen to leave the clothes. "Don't be rude," she said, a note of gaiety in her voice.

The clothes were too big. *Her husband's?* Like a child in his father's flannel shirt, he rolled up the sleeves and tucked the extra folds into the pants. She managed not to laugh as she gave an appraising look. "How long have you been growing that beard?"

Josey shrugged, moved his hands over the patch of whiskers.

"I think it's time you gave it up." She smiled so the words wouldn't offend. "Will you let me? We have time while the stew cooks." She set him at the table and covered his clean shirt with an apron. "I've been warming water for tea." She slipped a hot, wet cloth over his face. "This is more important."

As she soaped him, Josey saw her in glimpses, like pieces in a puzzle. Her eyes were a cornflower blue. Her long, narrow face probably gave her a gaunt look even when food wasn't scarce. A few strands of gray stood out in the hair pushed back behind her ears. A simple silver band adorned one finger. The skin on her hands and neck was sun-darkened, but when she leaned over him with the straight razor, her dress fell forward enough for him to glimpse the pale skin and a splash of freckles beneath. She did not speak as she worked. Her hands were steady—she had done this before—and Josey's breath grew irregular as she leaned against him.

"Don't move." Her voice whispered against his ear. The razor scratched against his neck, but he barely felt it move. She finished too fast. Josey could have sat there all night.

Leaning before him, she seemed pleased with her handiwork. "It's as I thought: You're much too handsome for a beard." Her hands traced the contours of his face, feeling for stubble. He wanted to pull her toward him but feared moving. She leaned closer. Watched his eyes. Their mouths met and she fell against him.

The rest of the night was a blur of twining limbs and fevered thrashing. It struck Josey as a cruel curse that he recalled skirmishes in painful detail but remembered only stray moments from the happiest night of his life. He couldn't say how they got from the chair to the bedroom or almost anything of what happened there. At some point, spent, they went to the table and ate. She talked. He listened. She asked questions. He answered. They talked of so many things, but he remembered best what they didn't talk about. She never spoke of her husband. He never spoke of the war.

After eating, they went back to bed, and eventually she slept. He watched how her body moved with each breath, her head against his chest as he matched his breaths to hers so as not to disturb her. As dawn spilled into the room through the open doorway, his chest filled and he drew her in. No matter how tightly he held, he couldn't feel close enough.

He saw his life stretch before him, like chapters in a book already written. He would plow fields, milk cows, raise chickens and pigs. If he failed at that, he would start a store, like his father. He would tend its shelves and sweep its floors and everything else he had once pronounced too banal to hold him. A year at war had cured him of any boyhood illusions that life needed to be exciting. This was life, in this room, with this woman, and it was all the excitement he would ever need again.

"Are you all right?"

He hadn't meant to wake her, but the harder he clung to her, the weaker his grip on the moment became. He wanted to stop time, to never again feel the emptiness of life without the promise of her body pressed to his. He opened his mouth to tell her this, but all he managed was, "I love you."

"Oh, you sweet boy." She rose from his grip and kissed his forehead.

The response deflated him, but as she moved, her breasts pressed against him. He lowered his head and kissed the nipples, one after the other, then turned her onto her back and kissed some more. She repeated herself, but the words sounded different and carried a new meaning the second time.

"Oh, you sweet boy."

★ ★ ★ ★ ★

Josey had been a boy that morning in the woman's farmhouse. A silly boy, she might have said, though the woman was too kind. As he shifted on the packing crate, aware of Mary Rutledge watching him, he imagined her capable of reading minds.

"What's the matter?"

He shook his head, but he knew she wouldn't let it go. He should make up an excuse to leave, but he couldn't move. He was accustomed to not sleeping much, but his legs were leaden, his head so heavy he couldn't even look up.

"You lose something when you bind yourself to another." He risked a glance. Sadness pinched her features.

"Oh, but you can find so much more."

Pain. That's what you find. Loving someone was like standing in the open during a firefight. Men in formation ramming their rifles while everyone around them fell. You bared your chest and waited for love to take a shot at you.

"What happened to her?"

Josey didn't know where to begin. The story included more than a woman needed to hear, more than he wanted to hear. He said simply, "She died."

He rose. "I need to go." His voice sounded strange.

"Wait—" Mary Rutledge wanted to say something. Something motherly and wise. Maybe something poignant about a generation who knew more of mourning and hurt than of love and hope. But there was nothing to say. He saw that. So she remained silent, and it was Josey who spoke.

"I never even knew her name."

CHAPTER THIRTY-FOUR

For twenty minutes Josey rode past the Rutledge wagon, waiting to catch Annabelle alone. Finally, he saw her carrying a bucket to the creek. Her strength always surprised him. She wore what looked like a new dress for her, white with blue patterns and a calico apron. He rode up on his spotted, gray pony, leading a smaller paint pony on a rope.

"Evening, Miss Annabelle." He had never had cause to call her by name and it sounded foreign on his tongue.

She replied with a curious smile. "That's a pretty horse you have."

"I'm pleased you think so." In truth, the paint looked scraggly compared with the well-bred horses Annabelle would have ridden back east, but Josey knew the mustang could run all day eating nothing more than prairie grass, and it would prove as sure-footed as a mule in the mountains. "It's for you."

Annabelle's look of shock wasn't the reaction he sought. "Well, I'm sure I don't know what to say," she stammered. A flush came over her face, and she turned to the wagons as if seeking reinforcements.

Josey couldn't figure what he'd said wrong, and his temper started to get the better of him. "You could start with, '*Thank you.*'"

"This gift is too rich." She covered her face with her hands. "I can't accept it."

Sensing the change in mood, the horses grew skittish. Josey

dismounted to keep the paint from bucking. He led the pony closer to her. *Does she think it ugly?* Small and black with milky splotches, the horse had a white mane that made him look prematurely old. "It didn't cost much. I got a good swap at an Indian village."

Annabelle stepped back from the horse. "That's really not the point. It simply wouldn't be appropriate."

Josey fought the rage coming on. *Damn you, Colonel. Why did you put me up to this?* "The Colonel told me you wanted to learn to ride." He swallowed back the anger, hoping the woman would see sense. "I thought you should have your own horse." The color had risen in her cheeks. Her skin, tinted by the sun, looked even prettier than usual, offset by the soft colors of the dress. His anger leeched away. "I didn't mean anything by it."

The words had sounded as good as an apology to his ears, but she seemed unmoved. "You shouldn't have troubled yourself then," she said with a sudden anger he found as baffling as if she had spoken in Chinese. "For one thing, I already know how to ride. For another, I guess you don't have to be concerned with what people will think."

What people will think? Who? He felt like two conversations were happening and neither of them heard the other. He put the rope in her hand and stepped back.

"It would please me," he said, hoping the formal nature of his speech would sound more gentlemanly, "if you would accept this token of my appreciation. You've done many kindnesses for me, washing, cooking and such. I would like to repay you for your consideration."

"Washing? Cooking?" Her voice rose to a level that threatened to spook the ponies. Josey took the rope from her and soothed the paint. "Is that what I am to you?"

She pointed a finger at him, prepared to hurl more invective. Josey flinched along with the horses, but fury overcame fluency.

Once, twice she started to speak, but all that crossed her lips were noises more akin to grunts than words. Finally, she gave up, turned on her heel and stormed off, leaving Josey alone to wonder how he would manage two horses.

"You gave her a horse? What were you thinking?"

The Colonel laughed, then laughed even harder seeing Josey's reaction. It was early the next morning. The emigrants were packing with an efficiency that came with routine. After stewing over his conversation with Annabelle all night, Josey gave up the idea that he could figure out on his own what went wrong.

"You told me she wanted to learn to ride."

"I didn't tell you to give her a horse." His laughter fit having passed, the old man's voice grew gentle. "I've known you too long to think you a fool, Josey. But you are ignorant when it comes to the ways of women."

Being unable to argue the point only made Josey more defensive. "It's a good horse."

"He ain't pretty." The Colonel stroked the paint's neck. "But he would serve her well out here."

"I tried to tell her."

"That ain't the point." The Colonel adjusted his tone, explained that the gift was too much for the beginning of a courtship.

"I'm not courting her," Josey said.

The Colonel chuckled. "Yes, you are."

"I was just trying to be kind." It didn't sound convincing, even to Josey.

"That's how it usually starts." The Colonel moved to the paint's muzzle, examining its teeth and grunting in appreciation. The horse whinnied and stamped. "Affectionate, ain't he?"

"I got the gentlest one I could."

The Colonel nodded as he ran his gnarled hands along the horse's forelegs and knees. He held the fetlock and the horse lifted its leg and he examined the sole. "What you think isn't what matters. It's what she thinks."

"Why would she think anything different? It's just a horse."

The Colonel looked up with a sigh, a teacher lecturing a particularly slow pupil. "It's not *just* a horse. A gift at the start of a courtship can't be anything a woman feels she can't repay. How would you feel if she gave you a horse?"

"I already have a horse."

"That's not the point, you dolt." The Colonel took a deep breath. "If you give too grand a gift to a lady, she might think you have expectations."

"Expectations?"

"Ideas of how she might—" he paused, searching for words that would convey the same meaning as the cruder terms in his head "—repay the favor."

Josey's stomach twisted. "What do I do now?"

"You'll figure out something." The Colonel didn't sound overly sympathetic. "If nature teaches us anything, it's that man always does."

CHAPTER THIRTY-FIVE

"It was impertinent."

Annabelle's mother agreed. "But I don't think it was ill-intended. Josey hasn't had the experience with mannered ladies that your brothers had."

Annabelle contained her reaction. Her brothers had rakish reputations in some circles of Charleston, but if her mother didn't know that, it was better she never learn. Her mother's comment suggested she knew more than she'd previously shared about a topic of far more interest to Annabelle.

"What do you know of Josey's experience?"

"Not very much, I assure you." Her mother looked a little flustered.

"Mother?" Annabelle felt closer than ever to her mother. At nights, they took to sitting alone in the wagon before going to sleep while her father took a smoke with the men. Her mother brushed Annabelle's long, dark hair, just as she had when Annabelle was a child. They would talk as they hadn't in years. Now her mother appeared to be weighing something in her mind. Finally, she told Annabelle of her most recent conversation with Josey.

"He's really a rather sensitive young man," her mother concluded. "A little ill-mannered, I'll grant you."

"Mother, he's killed dozens of men. Maybe hundreds. 'Ill-mannered' hardly seems a suitable description."

"He was at war, Anna. Just as your brothers were. If they had

155

lived, I wonder what strangers would think of them."

Perhaps I was too quick to be angry with him. Annabelle had been thinking of Josey more often than she would confess even to her mother. After they buried the Chestnuts' boy, her cousin Caroline had come to her, her grief deeper than anyone realized. Burton Chestnut was about Caroline's age, and he had asked to kiss her one evening while their families were gathered in the dark after sharing a meal.

"I didn't know what to do," Caroline said, burying her tear-streaked face in her cousin's bosom. "I told him no. I was just scared. I've never kissed a boy."

Smoothing her fair hair with her hands, Annabelle told the girl it was all right, but Caroline would not be consoled. She pulled back from Annabelle to look at her. "Later, when I had time to think on it . . ."

"You wished you had kissed him?"

Caroline nodded. "Now I'll never kiss him, and I feel wicked for even thinking that because he's—" She couldn't say the word.

Annabelle pulled Caroline into an embrace as she began to cry again. "We can't live like that, Caroline. Life is too short to let ourselves be ruled by regret." They talked longer, but all the soothing words sounded empty compared with the question about regret her cousin asked of her.

"Is that how you live your life?"

Annabelle considered that as her mother brushed her hair, sharing more from her talk with Josey. They speculated about the dead woman he wouldn't speak about. *We all have our secrets. We all have our regrets.*

"I suppose the pony was a noble gesture," she said as her mother tied back her hair for the night.

"Haven't you been wishing we'd kept a horse?"

"Mother."

She held up her hands in defense. "If you permit him to teach you to ride better, perhaps you might teach him better manners."

They camped the following day near a stream where the water gurgled musically as it passed over round stones in the streambed. Josey found Annabelle there with Caroline gathering water. He rode to the edge of the stream and dismounted, allowing the gray pony to drink. A light rain in the afternoon had tamped down the dust and left everything smelling fresh as spring. Caroline gave a cheerful wave before excusing herself and skipping off, leaving her bucket with Annabelle and ignoring her cousin's pleas to stay.

Turning to Josey, Annabelle said, "Only one horse today."

He wasn't sure if it was a question or statement. He had practiced what he wanted to say and didn't want to be thrown off.

"I wish to apologize for yesterday," he said, hoping the words didn't sound rehearsed. "I didn't think through how my actions might be interpreted." Annabelle watched him, as if weighing his sincerity, so he added, "I intended no offense."

"Think nothing more of it." She turned from the stream and started walking away. A slight incline with the weight of both buckets forced her to move as if limping with a bad leg.

Josey went to her. "May I help?"

"I can manage."

Returning to his horse, Josey said over his shoulder, "I have something for you."

"You think that's a good idea?"

A note of humor in her tone encouraged Josey as he fumbled through his saddlebag. "A peace offering." He brought to her a bunch of flowers with long green stems and brilliant red petals. "I've heard them called Indian paintbrushes. I thought you

157

might not have any like this."

"They're beautiful." Annabelle set down the buckets and took the flowers. The bunch filled her hands. "I've never seen any so pretty. Thank you."

Josey swallowed back the lump in his throat as he picked up the buckets and they continued toward camp. This was the reaction he had sought when he'd offered the horse. It irritated him to admit the Colonel had been right.

"You didn't have to do this."

"I didn't want to leave things like they were between us." He stole a glance. Against Annabelle's skin, the flowers glowed. He understood then why he had been moved to give her something. Josey felt a new intimacy between them, even if he didn't know what to do about it.

As they walked, she spoke of her plans for pressing a few of the flowers and sharing the rest with her cousin, mother and aunt. Josey listened, gratified for the opportunity to linger, to notice things like the delicate strength of her fingers twined around the stems of the flowers and the largeness of her dark eyes when she turned to him. He saw the slightest tint of color to her nose and cheeks. The gentle slope of her neck transfixed him, and he looked away to keep from imagining the appearance of things he couldn't see.

"I should thank you again." Her mouth tightened in a smile that didn't reach her eyes. She looked as nervous as Josey. She held the flowers close and inhaled. "They don't smell much, but they're so pretty. I would like to see them growing wild. Will we be passing near where you found them?"

He shook his head, sorry to disappoint her, then brightened with a new idea. "I could take you to see them . . ."

She sensed his hesitation. "Yes?"

"Well," he suppressed a smile, "you would need a horse."

"I can't believe you said that." She swatted him with her free hand.

Her eyes were bright and Josey's nervousness melted away. "Maybe you could do a favor for me," he said. "I have this problem . . ."

"What's that?" Her words measured as carefully as baker's flour.

"I have one too many horses, and I need someone to look after the paint when I'm ranging ahead of the train. I had it tied to Bill Smith's wagon today, but I'm not confident he can care for it properly."

"No, I would think he's too busy," she said, with feigned seriousness. "Have you thought of asking Mark? He would be delighted."

Josey shook his head. "I'm not sure your cousin is old enough for the responsibility."

"You may be right." She looked to him, and he met her gaze, an agreement dawning even if neither gave voice to it. "I suppose, since you have no choice . . ."

"I have none."

". . . then it will have to be me."

He smiled broadly, but her look forestalled any break from character as they played out the scene. He cleared his throat. "It's a lot I ask. I shall be in your debt."

"Perhaps, in compensation, you might instruct me in the proper care and exercise of the animal."

"Yes, the horse will have to be ridden, to accustom him to a saddle."

"My father has a saddle in the wagon. He had planned on waiting until we reached Montana before buying a new horse."

"Then it's a deal."

Josey extended his hand. She studied it a moment before placing hers in it, shaking his hand as a man would. Warmth spread through his arm, giving rise to color in his face as she looked to him and said, "I believe we have an understanding."

Chapter Thirty-Six

Flatlands gave way to rolling hills as the wagons continued along the North Platte. A month into their journey, the emigrants passed huge red boulders and rocky formations that resembled sculptures carved by giants. The sights were a welcome change to Annabelle after hundreds of miles of nearly featureless terrain, but the increasing slopes were hard on the oxen and drivers. Furniture lined the trail like the detritus of some shipwreck washed ashore. Oak wardrobes, finely upholstered sofas, even a spinet Annabelle imagined someone playing a final time before abandoning it as too heavy.

They camped early so the oxen would be fresh for the next climb. To Annabelle, that meant more riding time. She had known how to ride, had even considered herself a good rider, but riding with Josey in the evenings after they made camp gave her more confidence. She had named the horse "Paint" after he had told her he called his "Gray." She teased him on his originality.

"After I had two horses shot out from under me, I stopped naming them," he said, making her wish she hadn't raised the topic. "The third one I just called Brown, when I called him anything."

She almost feared asking. "Did Brown get shot, too?"

Josey shook his head. "Sold that one when I got Gray. Brown never would have made it to Montana."

"What made you want to go all that way?"

"The war was over. Didn't have anything else to do."

Josey proved a better teacher than a conversationalist, but it didn't take long for Annabelle to realize she would never ride as well or as far as he so long as she did so in a dress. Riding with her legs on the same side of her father's saddle made it more difficult to impart instructions to the horse and left her more vulnerable to a fall, especially at anything more than a walking pace.

Maneuvering Paint just past a boulder formation a good stone's throw from their camp, Annabelle hid from view of the wagons when she dismounted. The clothes she pulled from her saddlebag had belonged to poor Burton Chestnut, whose mother gave them to Annabelle. Her aunt Blanche helped her tailor the shirt and pants so they would fit better, but Annabelle still felt uneasy about anyone seeing her as she quickly changed from her dress.

"Don't you dare laugh at me," she warned Josey when he arrived a few minutes later to see her astride the horse in a teenage boy's clothes. His silence proved even more unnerving than laughter, so she prodded him. "Well? What do you think?"

She may as well have asked the Sphinx for all Josey's face showed. "I think we can take a long ride today."

The fresh air and freedom of movement invigorated Annabelle. They rode up the ridge the wagons would cross the next day, their canvas tops standing out like whitecaps on an open sea. Josey pushed on, so far that Annabelle lost track of where they were. The sky stretched forever, and if Josey had asked, she would have ridden with him to its end. They stopped near a creek to let the horses drink.

"When are you going to teach me to shoot?"

"You want to learn?"

"I saw you teaching the boys," she said of her cousins. "If I'm going to live out here, I ought to know how to handle a gun, too."

Josey offered her a pistol.

She pointed to the rifle. "Why can't I shoot that?"

He grimaced. "The Henry's not a good weapon for beginners."

She knew the rifle held special meaning to him. A gift from his father, it had been the finest rifle in the family's store. With its lever-action, his Henry could be fired sixteen times before reloading, an advantage he told her had kept him alive more times than he recalled.

"You don't trust me with it?"

"I don't trust *it*. The Henry's not the safest rifle. See here?" He showed her how the hammer was down, the lever flat against the barrel. "It looks safe. You have to pull the trigger to fire it. Unless you drop it." He let go of the rifle, stooping and catching it, quick as a cat, before it hit the ground. "The hammer rests against the cartridge that's in the chamber. If something hits the hammer, it can go off."

He handed the pistol to her. Its weight surprised her. Josey had been wearing four pistols with the rifle slung over his back when she first saw him, and he was not a large man.

"How do you carry so many?" she asked, avoiding any reference to his size. Men were so sensitive about such things.

"Whatever discomfort they cause on my hip is worth the peace they give to my mind," he said. "You survive one time wishing you'd had another gun, and you'll never mind carrying it again."

He wore only the one gun belt on this day, and he used his other pistol to show her how to fire. She flinched at the sound of his gun exploding so close even though she'd prepared for it. He motioned to a flower ten yards away. "See if you can hit that prickly pear."

Annabelle fired, again and again, shaking violently every time. She blinked with each shot no matter how hard she tried to keep her eyes open. Josey showed her how to brace her legs and hold the gun with both hands. By her sixth shot, she made the cactus move, even if she missed the flower.

He took the gun from her. "Let me reload it."

"You've got another."

"I never leave a gun unloaded if I've got time to load it," he said, as if the point should be obvious. He pulled a flask from his belt, carefully measured out powder and poured it into the first chamber. "The first thing I do every morning is clean and load my guns. Any man who feeds himself before his guns isn't worth much in my view."

After he dropped the ball in, he pulled back the loading rod, straining with the effort to force it in. "I'm not sure I could do that," she said. He had moved to the next cylinder, filling it with powder. It surprised Annabelle how long it took.

Josey seemed to read her mind. "Now you know why I carry four pistols."

After the shooting lesson, they didn't ride far before he pulled to a stop and studied the horizon with his binoculars. The fear of Indians flashed in her mind before he handed the glasses to her. "What do you see?"

Annabelle never seemed to have any luck focusing the glasses. The distant shapes might have been horses. A thrill ran down her spine as she wondered if they were buffalo, but she wouldn't embarrass herself with a guess. "Tell me."

Josey looked again. "I'm thinking antelope, though they could be deer."

"Can we get closer?"

"It's not easy. They're skittish."

Annabelle couldn't see a tree or bush higher than her horse's haunches anywhere. There was a natural slope to the land but no hill to maneuver behind. She wet a finger and held it out, something she had read in a book. Josey laughed. "Even if we approach downwind, you'd need a rifle more powerful than a Henry to get a good shot." *So much for antelope steaks.* Her disappointment must have shown. Josey walked his horse forward. "Come on. I know another way."

CHAPTER THIRTY-SEVEN

Annabelle and Josey were still a fair distance from the antelope when he leaned forward behind his horse's neck.

"They're accustomed to wild horses, but not riders," he whispered. They walked forward on their horses, their silhouette not much different than a rider-less horse. When they got as close as Josey dared, he slid off, careful to keep Gray between himself and the antelope.

Josey tied his kerchief to the end of his rifle barrel. Then he sat on the ground, patting a spot in the dirt next to him. "Come on." He lay flat, holding the rifle so it stood on its butt, the kerchief listlessly moving in a light breeze.

"Have you lost your senses?" But she followed his actions. As she lay down, she felt the warmth of his body beside hers. "If this is some kind of joke, I will slap what sense you have left out of your head."

He shushed her and whispered instructions as he moved the rifle for her to take. "There isn't much wind, so you'll have to move it a little. Not much. Like this."

Annabelle felt a fool, lying prone while moving the rifle so the kerchief danced in the breeze. She imagined Josey had somehow planned for the others to discover them in this ridiculous position. She would never hear the end of it. But Josey kept so still she matched his silence, measuring her breaths to his until she forgot how foolish she looked. He took the rifle when her arm tired.

The days were longer now, but she sensed the sun's descent as the air grew cooler and the breeze increased so the kerchief flapped steadily even without their aid. Annabelle closed her eyes, willing herself to be as still as the earth beneath her.

She might have fallen asleep, for Josey's voice, light as the breeze, brought her eyes open with a shudder. "Look to your left."

Annabelle tried to look without turning her head, but the effort strained her eyes. Ever so slowly, she tilted her head by single degrees—and gasped. The antelope looked humungous from her vantage beneath it. Its white-furred chest and belly nearly obscured her view of its dark face and eyes as it studied her as curiously as she gazed at it.

"Is this close enough?"

She had forgotten about the rifle or her hope to provide steaks for supper. Instead of startling the animal, Josey's whisper set off its pointed ears, creating a quizzical expression. Annabelle stifled a laugh. The curious animal's eyes as it studied her struck her as nearly human.

"I can't shoot it. Not now." Annabelle extended a hand, fingers splayed, and the antelope's snout flickered in response to the smell. It stepped forward on impossibly slender legs, lowering its head so that they nearly touched. Annabelle leaned forward, extending her fingers a few inches more. The antelope skipped away. Annabelle sat up and it bolted, bounding off with the rest of the herd, like birds in formation, first left, then right, their white tails wagging mockingly.

"I'm sorry," she said, though she didn't feel regret.

Josey rested a hand on her shoulder. "I've never been able to shoot when they're like that, either," he said. "The only ones I've hit have been at a distance. Pulling a trigger's always easier at a distance."

★ ★ ★ ★ ★

They rode back to camp slowly to spare the horses, Josey told Annabelle, though he didn't mind prolonging their time together. Once they were at camp, they would behave almost as strangers in front of the others, their horse-riding lessons nothing more than a matter of mutual convenience. *Maybe that's all it is to Annabelle.* Josey felt safer thinking so.

Looking at her reminded him of the first time he had seen the western mountains: beautiful and formidable. He had spent a morning once watching a mountain slowly emerge from the murk of night, light descending its slopes like a fleet-footed climber. First a fiery glow on snow-capped peaks, then a peeling back of shadow over rocky crevices and piney slopes, the mountain reluctantly relinquishing its secrets.

Josey led their horses up the ridge overlooking the wagons, corralled in a good spot by a stream with clear water. A drop of sweat rolled down Josey's back, giving him a chill despite the lingering heat of the afternoon. Annabelle looked at him curiously but sensed his need for quiet. He liked that about her. Talking with her was never boring, but she didn't mind quiet, either.

Something in this quiet felt wrong. He dismounted and examined swirls of dust in the ground. Plenty of hoof prints. An Indian might make sense of them, but Josey couldn't. He held his hand over a pile of horse dung nearby. No warmth, but it looked moist. In the dry heat of early July that had to mean something.

"What is it?"

He was making Annabelle nervous. "I don't know. Maybe nothing."

Focus. His mind wandered when he and Annabelle were alone, like time didn't exist. He returned from an hour-long ride feeling like only a minute had passed. When he was with her, something turned off in his brain, a welcome respite from worry, regret or memories he would rather forget.

With Annabelle, he thought only of the moment—no, thought wasn't it. He *lived* the moment. The only thing like it in Josey's experience was battle. If you didn't live the moment in battle, you were dead. Josey imagined the Colonel's advice: It was good to *loose* his mind with a woman, making a joke, loose or lose all being the same in love. Yet standing on a ridge overlooking the emigrants whose safety was his responsibility, a mounting dread pricked at him, like a man who remembers too late a forgotten task.

Josey jumped back on his gray pony and fetched his binoculars. He almost missed it. The ridge sloped into a gully carved by the stream near the campsite. Josey couldn't see into the gully as he trained the binoculars there. Waves of shimmering heat rising from the ridge played tricks with his eyes. He blinked twice to clear them. The dark smudges on the rocky outcropping near the gap were probably just the shadows of odd-shaped boulders. Three birds took flight from the gap, and he held his gaze on the spot, wondering what stirred them.

"We need to go," he told Annabelle. "Now."

CHAPTER THIRTY-EIGHT

At the end of every day the drivers formed the wagons into a large ring, chaining the tongue of one wagon to the rear wheel of the one in front to create a corral that held in the stock at night. After unhitching the teams and unyoking the oxen that afternoon, Caleb freed the Daggett boys to run off for a swim in the adjacent stream.

"It'll be cold," he warned. They didn't care. In a moment their bare asses gleamed like a pair of moons as they whooped and hollered their way to the water.

The sight reminded Caleb of something, like an itch in the back of his brain. The harnesses were still in his hands and he found himself twisting them so tight, the blood ran out of his fingers. He watched the boys, hearing their screams as they splashed in water that had started as snow melt.

Looking to the road behind them, he thought of a man he hadn't seen in almost two years. Jacob Cooper was tall with unnaturally long arms and so thin his chest appeared concave. A man could count his ribs through his translucent skin, like furrows in a plowed field. Yet that wasn't the most remarkable thing about Cooper.

On a day even hotter than this one, Caleb's unit camped near a secluded lake on a plantation in Mississippi after having been on the move for days. In a rare act of generosity, the officer they called "Captain Bastard" out of earshot ordered a halt so everyone could cool off in the lake.

Cooper was a funny-looking man to begin with, built more like a bird than a man, but when he emerged from the water, his dripping pecker dangling nearly to his knobby knees, one of the men called out, "Look, the sparrow's got himself a worm." Cooper didn't mind. There were worse things to be baited about than an enormous pecker.

Caleb moved to the back of the wagon, his eyes still on the road. *Cooper's out there somewhere.* He, Harrison, Johnson—they're all out there. Caleb felt it. He'd felt them since Omaha when he heard men were looking for him. He hadn't wanted to believe it. A coincidence, he told himself, but then he overheard the Colonel talking with Josey Angel about riders following them. *So much for coincidences.* Caleb didn't know how they tracked him.

With practiced movements, he set aside the boxes of supplies in the back of the wagon until he located the two small trunks buried at the bottom. He used a key he carried on a leather loop around his neck to open one of the trunks. He groped blindly, squeezing the pouches inside.

A tie had come loose and the light that filtered through the wagon reflected a glimmer like a match light. He started counting the coins once, but there were too many. He knew it totaled a fortune, more than any one man could spend in a lifetime, at least a man like Caleb.

The money was supposed to be driven through Texas into Mexico to buy guns and ammunition. Once the captain got word of it, pulling off the ambush wasn't difficult. Those men had been worried about Union spies, not a Confederate captain. Caleb hadn't even known the wagon drivers were Confederates until they were dead.

Caleb had forgotten how much the captain told him his share would be, more money than he had ever expected to see. It never occurred to him to steal from the others so that he might have a bigger share. Only now he realized it never would have occurred to the captain *not* to steal it. But not even Captain Bastard could do it alone.

They planned to sneak away under cover of a faked ambush, a night Caleb was on guard duty. His responsibilities were limited to tying the pouches together and slinging them over a pack mule. He led the animals away while the captain set off explosives around the camp. Caleb fled before anyone knew what happened.

The brilliant part of the captain's plan was the escape. They had crossed a river using an abandoned ferry the day before. Caleb led the animals with the gold to the ferry and waited for the captain. It had all seemed too easy. Then he heard gunshots and calls in the distance. Caleb had known the captain too long to betray him, so he waited as long as he dared before crossing the river.

Even once on the opposite side, he lingered, wondering if the captain might yet find his way to the river, maybe swim his horse across. Caleb knew the captain had to be dead when he never showed.

Having all the gold frightened Caleb more than it excited him. He had no idea how to explain coming by so much money. Throwing around a lot of gold coins would only make him a target, either of thieves, authorities or his former comrades. They would never stop searching for him. He started back to Charleston but realized they would look there first.

He buried most of the gold until he could figure what to do, then drifted, spending a coin here or there when he had to. The gold weighed as heavily on his mind as on his pack mule until he came across an old neighbor in St. Louis and heard Langdon Rutledge planned to lead a wagon train to Montana. Caleb couldn't recall what thoughts he strung together to arrive at a conclusion that seemed obvious only in the end. *What better place to hide a cache of gold than in a town where men were pulling big chunks of it from the rivers?*

Reassured at seeing the gold again, Caleb closed the trunks and shifted the boxes of goods and supplies to cover them. The air cooled quickly as the sun dropped. The breeze had shifted and his nose twitched at the earthy smell of the grazing oxen. He looked up at the sound of pounding hoof beats and saw Josey Angel riding hard into camp, already stirring a commotion. Annabelle trailed behind on her ugly paint horse.

Watching them, Caleb realized how his old comrades had found him. The answer should have been clear enough all along, if Caleb had been willing to believe it. *Captain Bastard must still be alive.* Caleb shivered just thinking it. *At least I won't be the only one surprised to see him.*

Chapter Thirty-Nine

The riders emerged from the gully near dusk, six horsemen silhouetted against the dying day. They showed themselves barely an hour after Josey raced into camp, but to Annabelle it felt like days had passed.

She had been bewildered and a little hurt at how quickly she had become an afterthought to Josey. His hasty return had stirred the wagon corral like a hornet's nest by the time she followed him into camp. Men loaded weapons and piled boxes of supplies to create a protected circle within the corral, providing cover for the women and children. They were preparing for battle.

By the nearest wagon, Josey talked with the Colonel, her father and a few of the other men. Josey came toward her, his face slack, eyes vacant. She wasn't sure he saw her until he stopped. "I have to go." He paused just long enough to look at her. Before she thought of anything to say, he leaped on Gray, breaking into a gallop toward the ridge from where they had come.

"Coward." Caleb Williams had been watching, his thick arms crossed in disapproval. "First time there's any real danger and he runs off. Suppose he's going back to Omaha for help."

Annabelle didn't know what to think. The next hour was a whirl of activity. She helped her mother and the other women prepare meals, which they took to the men in their positions around the corral, waiting for—what? No one would tell her.

After serving the meal, the women had nothing to do. Annabelle sat near her mother and aunt, nibbling on a cold biscuit, her leg shaking with nervous energy. The women chattered with speculation, but nobody knew anything. Annabelle's frustration with Josey grew. If only he had spoken his mind instead of riding off in such haste—all so they could sit here and allow their fears to compound. She didn't know how men waiting for battle managed it.

Surely, it's better to plunge ahead than to sit back on one's haunches awaiting the inevitable. Or was it inevitable? She'd seen Josey examine some hoof prints in the dust, stare at some horseshit, look through his glasses at—what? *Why hadn't he talked to her? Why hadn't she* made *him speak?* She had been so confused, and more than a little frightened, that she hadn't thought clearly.

"I have to see Father," she told her mother when waiting became unbearable. At least it felt good to move. Her father stood with the Colonel behind a wagon at the end of the corral nearest the gully. The rifle looked odd in his hands.

"What are you doing out, child?" She looked past the men to the stream and the slope that led to the ridge. As if reading her thoughts, the Colonel said, "That's where they'll come from."

Who? She wanted to ask, but she feared they would run her off if she made herself a nuisance. Men didn't like women around in times of conflict. They said it was for women's safety, but Annabelle wondered. Looking about, she saw miners, farmers, laborers, clerks. A few had been in the war, but none seemed particularly warlike other than the Colonel, who stood more erect and had never looked so strong, his illness seemingly forgotten. As for the others, how many would hold their ground if they came under fire?

Lord Byron hid inside the nearest wagon. He had loosened the canvas cover and peeked out from under it with his rifle. He had been a slave when Sherman's army marched through

Georgia. How often had he used a gun? Caleb Williams, the Daggett brothers, Ben Miller and the rest of the miners, family men like Samuel Fletcher, Alexander Brewster, Stephen Chestnut, still mourning the loss of his son—how well would they fight, if a fight came? Perhaps they knew no better than she, and they didn't want a woman to bear witness to their fear and doubt.

Still, she preferred sitting with the men, watching nothing happen, than sitting with the women and children, wondering when they might hear something happen. Leaning against a wagon, her fingers would begin tapping whenever she stopped thinking of keeping them still. Her father looked at her once when she failed to catch herself. She crossed her arms, pinning her hands to steady them. The Colonel stood as calmly as if he had come to enjoy a sunset. *How many battles must a man survive before he faces the next one so coolly?*

"What do you think Josey's doing?" she asked him.

The Colonel pointed to the ridge that held a commanding view of the camp and the ground around it. "He's probably grabbing a nap up on the high ground, waiting for the first shot to rouse him."

He wouldn't have to wait long. When the horsemen emerged from the gully, every man in camp with a gun trained it on them.

CHAPTER FORTY

With the sun at their back, the six riders could see into camp better than the emigrants saw them. They stopped a fair distance away. One of the men waved.

"Hellooo," he sang. "Might we share your fire? Looks like you've got the best campsite for miles."

The Colonel stepped from behind the wagon. "Best you just ride on. Find another spot."

The rider conferred with his companions. "That's not very hospitable," he called, his drawl stretching out the last word so it sounded like four. "We've got news. You'll want to hear about what lies ahead."

"You can ride up. The others stay back."

The speaker conferred with his fellows again. He rode forward, raising his hands as he drew near, his body rocking easily in the saddle, a wide grin splayed across his face. "You're not bandits, I hope," he said once stopped, no longer needing to shout.

His face and clothes were grimy with dust from the trail, which seemed ill suited to him. He looked like the kind of man who belonged in a saloon. He made no effort to hide his interest as his eyes took in their number. When his gaze came to Annabelle, his mocking grin fell away, to be replaced with a knowing smile. Annabelle looked away, feeling a shiver.

"What's your news?" the Colonel demanded. He was the only man not directing a gun at the riders, though he wore a pistol on his belt and carried himself as if he had the whole Union army at his back.

The stranger lied smoothly. "My men have had a hard ride and we're hungry. I thought we might discuss it over a meal once you saw our intentions were peaceful."

"We see nothing of the sort."

"You're a suspicious bunch." The stranger looked at Annabelle, who found his familiarity offsetting. He licked his lips, but he didn't look nervous. "A man gets hungry out on the trail. It ain't right to deny him."

The Colonel lied just as easily. "We've had some sickness, had to quarantine some folks. It's best you ride on."

"Maybe we'll just take our chances." The rider's manner gave him away. She realized he was one of the Confederates who'd confronted Josey on the street in Omaha. They'd called him Harrison. She might have recognized him sooner if not for the grime and the incongruity of seeing him on the trail. He favored her with a wolfish grin. "Maybe we'll just come in and take what we want."

"There's twenty guns pointed at you says you won't."

Harrison leaned from his horse and spat on the ground, in case the Colonel wasn't clear on what he thought of his threat. "Bunch of quim-eaters and old men from the looks of 'em. They'll drop those rifles and run at the first shot."

"You won't live to see it."

Harrison nodded his head and grinned ever wider. "You've got salt, for an old man."

The Colonel interrupted. "It's getting late. You head on now, stick to the road and you'll come to a good site before it gets full dark." He turned and walked back between the wagons. Harrison looked surprised for a moment, before the grin returned. He tipped his hat to Annabelle, pivoted and rode back to his companions.

Her father looked relieved to see Harrison ride off. Annabelle didn't share his confidence. She told him about seeing the man in Omaha as the Colonel listened.

Her father didn't want to believe it. "Are you certain, Annabelle? Why would they follow us all this way?"

She had no answer.

"I don't believe Miss Annabelle would mistake a thing like that," the Colonel said. "They probably didn't count on a hostile greeting. Maybe they thought they would get into camp, put us at ease. I expect they left a few of their number in reserve, back in that gully where we can't see 'em. They'd have come out soon enough."

"What will they do now?" her father asked.

"They'll move on, once they realize they can't ride back the way they came, not without arousing our suspicion." The Colonel turned his gaze toward the gully. "I expect their leader is back there somewhere with the rest. They'll come at us from both sides."

Sure enough, the six riders started off to the east, making a wide circle around the camp. "Maybe it's just those six," her father said, sounding more wishful than confident. "Maybe they'll just leave."

"Maybe Annabelle mistook him for that other man," the Colonel said. "But I wouldn't bet our lives on it."

Chapter Forty-One

The Colonel rallied the camp after the riders moved off. The women started a large cook fire, while he made a show of pulling the men from their posts. Only Lord Byron and a couple of others hidden in wagons remained on guard. The Colonel wanted anyone watching to think the emigrants believed the danger had passed.

"Won't that just encourage them?" Annabelle's father asked.

"Better they attack when *we're* ready—and they don't know it—than have them wear us out waiting," the Colonel said. "If they think they can surprise us, I think they'll come soon, while there's still some light. It's always better to attack when you can see who you're shooting."

They didn't have to wait long.

Another half dozen riders came charging out of the gully, and they might have come straight into camp if Lord Byron and the others hadn't opened fire when they drew near. Clifton Daggett rose up from between two wagons and fired a shot that unhorsed one rider.

"I got one," he shouted to his brother.

"Get down, you fool."

The warning came too late. The riders reacted quickly, and Annabelle looked away after Clifton was spun around from multiple shots. She looked back, hoping her eyes had betrayed her, that what she had seen couldn't really have happened. She heard more shouted warnings and Willis's anguished scream as he rushed toward his brother's body and dragged it like a heavy grain sack.

Annabelle felt untethered from the action around her. The sight of Ben Miller running forward to help Willis barely registered. Then Miller was struck and fell. The Colonel called for cover fire, but the bursting of gunfire all around Annabelle seemed muffled, as if she were far removed from it.

The riders retreated from the heavy fire, and Willis pulled his brother within the corral. Two of the young miners did the same for Miller, his cries finally snapping Annabelle from her reverie.

She went to Willis and pried him from his brother while her mother looked to Clifton's wounds. Willis fell heavily against Annabelle, his body shaking with sobs. She held his head to her chest as she looked to her mother, who shook her head and closed her eyes.

Annabelle pulled Willis tighter so he wouldn't see the two miners drag his brother's body away, the pressure of his body forestalling the numbness spreading through her. She sensed it was only his weight and the need to give comfort that kept her mind from slipping away.

She forced herself to focus amid the noisy confusion in the camp. The first six riders returned from the opposite direction, and the Colonel shouted commands to redeploy men to defend both ends of the corral. Once they realized their attempt at surprise had failed, the riders circled at a safer distance.

The attackers fell into a pattern the Colonel described as Indian tactics. A few riders at a time would bolt toward the camp, firing as they rode to force the defenders to take cover, probing for a weakness in the corral's defense, retreating before the emigrants rallied. Clifton's death made the defenders more cautious. They fended off the next two attacks without loss to either side.

As the light faded, Annabelle wondered how much longer the standstill could last. Waving a white flag, Harrison came within calling distance. He no longer grinned, though he seemed no less sure of himself. "No one else has to die," he called. "Give us the gold and we'll ride off—for good this time."

Gold? Annabelle looked to the Colonel, who looked to her father. "What's he talking about?"

"I don't know," her father said. "Truly," he added, seeing the Colonel's doubt.

"Are they touched in the head?" Annabelle's uncle Luke said. "We're *going* to the gold."

The Colonel smoothed his mustache with his thumb and forefinger. "This is a lot of trouble to go to for a few wagons. If you're carrying gold, maybe something you were saving to buy supplies, now is the time to tell me."

Annabelle's father was adamant. "We spent everything we had to outfit these rigs because the price of goods is cheaper in the east. That's the entire point of our business." He'd made his point, but he didn't like to be doubted. "The only extra money we have is the balance of what we promised to pay you."

The Colonel made a snorting sound. "You're a fair man, Mr. Rutledge, but you're not paying us enough to make all this worthwhile," he said. "What about the others. Any of them carrying gold?"

"Anyone who had gold worth stealing never would have left Omaha," Luke said.

The Colonel turned from the wagons and strode toward the cook fire. Pulling an old rag from his belt, he tied it around a stick and held it to the flames until it caught. He waved the torch overhead.

"I suppose we're going to have to do this the hard way."

CHAPTER FORTY-TWO

Annabelle wondered if the Colonel's torch was some signal only soldiers understood, but everyone else appeared as confused as she. Even the riders stopped to watch. Then one tumbled from his horse at almost the same moment Annabelle heard the echo of a rifle shot.

The fallen rider's stunned companions turned toward each other, a fatal delay. The horse of another rider reared, casting the man from its back as another shot cracked. Before anyone reacted, another horse spun wildly and fell to its side, pinning the rider beneath it.

"That would be Josey," the Colonel said with a wicked hint of mirth.

The remaining riders, unsure from where the shots came, fired toward the camp to cover a retreat. They resumed their circling, the speed of their movements making the defenders' shots ineffectual.

The circle grew tighter, the forays toward the camp, bolder. More than once a rider managed to get against the wagons and fire a shot inside the corral. They wounded the youngest of the miners, and Annabelle worried that the strain of the attack would show on the rest. The Colonel shouted encouragement.

"Give me men with family to protect over an army of mercenaries any day," he called.

A few of the riders made a run toward the rear of the camp, and the Colonel rushed to that spot, calling for Annabelle's father and Luke to follow. The attack proved a feint. The riders veered off before the counter-attack while the rest of their number rushed the side of the corral where Annabelle stood. Three men on horseback managed to reach the wagons, firing within the corral, as more riders approached. Annabelle dropped beneath the nearest wagon, hoping the riders wouldn't see her.

From underneath the wagon, the fight was a confusion of hooves as the riders sought the best way to bring the attack into the corral. The horses wheeled about at the report of another gun, a steady firing that grew louder with each shot.

A rider fell directly in front of Annabelle, clutching his neck. She rolled to get out from under the wagon. A horse fell beside her, its rider screaming as the weight of his mount crushed his leg. Caleb Williams, hiding under the wagon beside her, rose and put a bullet into the man's head.

While the other riders retreated, Annabelle came from under cover in time to see Josey. She had never seen him ride so fast, steering Gray with his knees, the reins tied short so both hands were free for his rifle. He had lost his hat with his hard charge, and his face was so grim he looked ten years older than he had that morning.

Another rider went down. Josey cast the rifle aside and drew the first of his pistols. Three of the riders turned to give chase, but Josey cut toward them.

The distance between the hard-galloping horsemen closed faster than Annabelle believed. The ground shook at their charge. In another moment, the horsemen were upon each other. One of the riders flew as if launched from a cannon, his horse collapsing beneath him. Josey rode, seemingly close enough to strike the other riders with his fists. When it seemed they should collide, Annabelle closed her eyes. When she looked again, another rider lay on the ground, and one fled as Josey dropped his pistols and pulled his last two. Gray wheeled and gave chase, but the exhausted pony slowed, and the rest of the riders escaped into the darkness.

Annabelle stared as Josey dismounted and retrieved his guns. Caleb Williams emerged from the corral, walking among the fallen to end the suffering of the wounded horses. Annabelle stood stunned by what she had witnessed. "How . . . ?" She stopped, unsure how to even phrase the question.

The Colonel scanned the darkening horizon, making sure none of the riders returned. Annabelle's confusion must have been plain. Setting down his rifle, he pulled his pistol from his belt. "This isn't much good but close up. Put a man on a moving horse, aiming at another on a moving horse and, well, most men, they may as well be throwing stones at each other."

Annabelle nodded, as if that explained everything, though she felt no closer to making sense of what she had seen. "Josey didn't miss."

"Josey ain't most men."

They buried Clifton Daggett in the dark and were on the move again before first light. They didn't even build a coffin. No one complained at the haste, not even Willis Daggett, who wept as they laid his brother in a hole Caleb feared wouldn't prove deep enough to stop the wolves. No one said anything. The emigrants were eager to be gone from the place, as if danger were inherent to it. Knowing better, Caleb visited the other wagons, curious what folks said—and what they might suspect.

He overheard Mary Rutledge tell her husband, "They were *white* men. All this time I've been afraid of Indians. I never thought we had to fear white men with the war over."

"The Colonel called them road agents," Rutledge told his wife. "He said they've been a problem near the gold fields, but he's never heard of them on this part of the trail. It doesn't make any sense to rob a train headed *to* the gold."

"Why would they attack us?"

"I don't know. Desperate men will do desperate things."

No one saw Josey Angel that night, and no one seemed to mind. Sitting by the cook fire as Constance Smith stitched up a wounded Ben Miller, Caleb listened to Bill Smith speak with wonder. "He must have killed half a dozen men."

"There weren't that many bodies," Miller said between gritted teeth.

"Well, he killed at least four," Smith replied.

"A good thing," his wife added.

"Until tonight," Miller said, "I'm not sure I believed those stories people told about him."

"I did," Smith said.

No one remarked on how there were no survivors among the men they left in the field for the wolves. For once, Caleb didn't mind the legend of Josey Angel, as everyone assumed every shot he fired was lethal. Maybe those who knew better preferred not to say anything, relieved someone had the stones to do what needed to be done. They weren't equipped to handle prisoners. As Caleb walked among the fallen with a pistol, nobody noticed or cared that it wasn't just horses he put out of their misery. Well, that wasn't exactly true.

Jacob Cooper noticed.

He had been trying to crawl out from under his horse, his bony legs not quite skinny enough to squeeze his way free. He looked relieved to see Caleb.

Until he saw the Navy revolver.

"Please," he said. It wasn't much for a last word.

The memory of Jacob Cooper bothered Caleb. What he didn't find bothered him more. No Johnson. No Harrison. No captain.

As the wagons pulled out and headed toward Fort Laramie, Caleb stole a glance east. The sharp rays of the rising sun

186

blinded him to what lay that way, but he didn't need to see to know. They would come again.

CHAPTER FORTY-THREE

Annabelle dismounted and followed Josey's example in tying a loose tether to a picket pin so Paint could forage among the buffalo grass. Josey led her up a narrow game trail along a butte that overlooked the river, and she found the climb much easier in pants than a dress.

After five weeks on the trail, the flat plains had given way to sandy bluffs and peaks. They rose majestically over the flatlands, though Josey told her they were but bumps in the road compared with the mountains they would see as they neared Fort Laramie and the land some people were calling Wyoming.

The most impressive sight the previous day had been Chimney Rock, a towering spire rising from a mound of sandstone. The Colonel teased the ladies, hinting broadly that its Indian name referred to a particular part of elk anatomy. The English name seemed apt enough. To Annabelle, it resembled one of the burned-out farmhouses left by Sherman's army, when only a brick chimney remained standing. She kept this observation to herself.

The emigrants saw little of Josey in the days after the bandits' attack. The Colonel explained he swept the trail behind them to ensure they weren't followed, but Annabelle suspected that Josey needed to be away from people. She missed their rides but found the time away from him a relief. Watching him charge so heedlessly toward those riders scared her, though she wasn't sure what frightened her more: what he had done or the risk he had taken.

When Josey returned that afternoon with an invitation, Annabelle couldn't resist. Reaching the heights, he led her to the south side of the butte, where she saw the river laid out before them, a wide expanse of badlands beyond that, and a breathtaking wall of sand and rock, much larger than anything they had yet seen, with a symmetry that made it look as if it had been sculpted.

"Scotts Bluff," he said.

"It's magnificent."

It rose several hundred feet, a fairy vision of high walls and battlements so big the juniper and pine trees that clung to the cliffs appeared as little shrubs. As she stared, Josey told the story of Hiram Scott, a fur trapper in a party of explorers who were lost and starving in the wilderness when he fell ill. Coming across tracks from another party, Scott's companions abandoned him and were eventually saved. Some returned the next year and discovered bleached bones and a grinning skull near the bluffs.

"They realized it must be Scott from scraps of clothing," Josey said. "He managed more than fifty miles—some say a hundred—before he succumbed at the foot of those walls. His comrades felt so guilty they named the bluffs for him."

They stood silent, Annabelle breathing in the sweet pine on the breeze, counting time in the crawl of shadows stretching from the heights. "They look like the walls of an ancient fortress," she said.

" 'Three times they raced around the walls of Illium.' "

"Homer?" He nodded. "How perfect. I could see you there, Hector guarding the gates."

Josey shook his head. "I would be Achilles."

She smiled, assuming he spoke from pride. "Of course, Achilles defeats Hector. But I liked Hector. He loved his wife. He loved his son and father. Achilles loves his friend Patroclus but not as much as he loves himself." She nudged him with her shoulder. "Should it disturb me that you prefer such a man?"

"I didn't say I prefer him." Josey took off his hat and wiped his face with a sleeve, exposing a funny pale line across his forehead where the hat shaded him. "Every time I read the poem, I wish for a different outcome. Hector could never win. Achilles was made for war."

"Hector fights for his city and home. He fights for love. Shouldn't that make him stronger?"

Josey replaced his hat. "It makes him weaker. Because he has so much to live for, Hector fears death."

"Any sensible man should."

"Achilles was not a sensible man."

Annabelle studied the man beside her. She could feel so close to Josey one moment and then see him as a stranger in the next. *It's like he's two men.* The thought reminded her of their first meeting, when she wondered if he were named for a dark angel or an angel of light. *The answer is both.*

"It's like that poem you recited," she said, more to herself than aloud. "The best of dark and bright."

"That poem was about a woman."

"Was it?" She faced him. He had looked drained of emotion when she first saw him, and he still seemed that way at times. That didn't mean he was without feelings, just that he hid them—or hid from them—like pulling dark curtains across a window.

"More than a woman, a man needs both," she said. "Hector was full of light. He didn't have enough dark in him to kill Achilles."

★   ★   ★   ★   ★

Back in camp, Josey helped Annabelle unsaddle her pony. He was brushing down Gray when he noticed her staring. With the sun behind him, she squinted as she looked, moving so his head shielded her eyes against the brightness.

"Do you not have to shave?" she asked.

"I shave."

"Every day?"

He moved to brush Gray's other flank. "Not every day." Sadness filled him as his mind drifted to another place, another woman. Josey swallowed it back.

She came to him, extending a hand. "May I?" He held still, feeling like a horse submitting to being petted. She cupped his chin in her hand and stroked her thumb across the skin. He heard the roughness of whiskers against her finger even if she couldn't see them. She laughed with surprise. "How long, if you didn't shave, before we would see it?"

"You would not like what you saw." Josey returned to brushing the horse. Talking with Annabelle usually felt like two neighbors standing on either side of a fence. Without that barrier, he felt exposed, uncertain of his footing. He understood their time together meant more than riding lessons. But he avoided thinking on it too much, afraid that defining what was between them risked bringing it to an end, a dream that evaporates like dew with the sun's rising.

The flirtatious smile slipped from her face. "How many men have you killed?"

There it is. She had to ask. "Don't ask me that."

"A lot?"

Don't tell her. She will never look at you again the way she just did. "You don't want to know." It wasn't just the number, even if he knew it. She would want to know how he felt when he pulled a trigger, what it meant to watch a man fall and know

191

you were the cause of it; answers he could never share with her.

Annabelle moved closer. "You can tell me, you know. I wouldn't judge you. Not for that." She stood so close they would touch if he leaned forward. She smelled of horse and sweat and pine. No flower had ever smelled so good to him. She looked at him expectantly. He saw himself reflected in her eyes and turned away, revolted by what he saw.

CHAPTER FORTY-FOUR

Reaching Fort Laramie meant the emigrants had traveled more than five hundred miles from Omaha. The others were giddy to view stately Laramie Peak to the west. Annabelle saw the mountains as a reminder that the second half of their journey would be more difficult. Eventually, they would reach Virginia City, and . . . *then what?*

Annabelle avoided Josey after the night of their ride to Scotts Bluff. She had been certain he meant to kiss her, and then he turned away as if disgusted. She didn't know why she should care what he chose to do after they reached Montana, yet she found herself wondering more and more. *Surely, he can't intend to wander the rest of his life?*

With no walled stockade as she had imagined, Fort Laramie looked more like a village in the wilderness than a military outpost. Around the field outside the sutler's store stood real houses with siding painted white, even a stone church. The barracks and officers' quarters might have passed for hotels if not for the lofty flagpole on the parade ground, where soldiers trained with wheeled mountain howitzers.

If she hadn't known better, Annabelle would have thought Indians had the place under siege. The peace treaty had been signed at the end of June a couple of weeks earlier, and many of the Indians lingered near the fort to swap or beg from soldiers and travelers. On their way to the fort, Annabelle traded a pair of old, black, cotton dresses for new moccasins and buckskin leggings she thought ideal for riding. Her father told her she could negotiate a better deal, but she already felt like she took too much for her threadbare offerings.

She found the Colonel enjoying a smoke in the shade of the porch that wrapped around the side of the store. She greeted him and took the chair beside his, swapping news of their activities at the fort. Annabelle's curiosity about Josey felt like an itch that finally got the better of her, and she turned the conversation to the wayward scout. "Do you know much about Josey's family?"

The Colonel took out his pipe and looked at her, not bothering to hide his amusement at her question. "I've never met them, if that's what you mean. Josey doesn't talk much about them."

"He doesn't talk much about anything."

"He's a good listener."

"He told my mother he hasn't seen his family since the war. They must think he's dead." The Colonel said nothing. "Doesn't that make you sad?"

"There are worse things."

Annabelle couldn't know what the Colonel and Josey had endured, but she knew better than anyone what it was like to not know the fate of a family member.

"My husband stopped writing to me long before I learned he'd been killed. People would tell me how hard it must be to mourn without a proper burial. I never told them the hard part was knowing I had lost him already. No widow should feel that way. No grieving mother, either, I expect."

Having said more than she intended, Annabelle wondered if the Colonel would abandon the conversation. He had been spending much of his time with the fort commander, discussing conditions on the trail. Instead of offering an excuse to leave, he cleared his throat. "It's not my place to speak to another man's motives, even a man I know as well as Josey."

Annabelle knew well enough when the Colonel warmed to a story, and she settled in as he told her about riding with a posse during their time in Montana. While in pursuit of a band of horse thieves, they caught a young man, almost still a boy.

"He admitted to it, even before anyone tried to beat it out of him. After all that hard riding, more than a few looked forward to that rough brand of entertainment."

"Did he say why he took the horse?"

"He wanted to go home. He was done panning for gold, I expect, and had run through whatever money he had. He just wanted to go home."

Annabelle shuddered to imagine the young man's desperation. "What did you do?"

"I didn't do anything. Neither did Josey. The other men we were with, this was their town. Their laws. They were determined to hang the boy, to set an example."

While the posse fixed the rope, the Colonel asked the boy if he wanted water or something to eat. He requested only pen and paper to write a letter to his father, explaining what had happened and asking his forgiveness. He finished the letter before the posse found a suitable tree.

"I told him he had more time, but he handed over the letter and asked that it be sent to his father. 'I'm ready,' he said. Can you imagine?"

Annabelle wasn't sure she wanted to hear the rest. "You didn't hang him, did you?"

"It wasn't my place to decide, I told you." A hint of temper betrayed the rawness of the Colonel's feelings. "I think if that boy had begged for his life, the posse would have banished him from the mining camp and he would have lived to ask for his father's forgiveness in person." The Colonel grunted at a new thought, breaking the tension in his voice. "I heard of one posse that banished a man so penitent they were moved to each contribute a few dollars to send him on his way. When I think of that boy now, I wish that's what we had done." He swallowed. "He never begged. Never asked for mercy. His expression never changed. We were all so dumbstruck it never occurred to anyone to do anything different. A minute later, he was dead."

"Did you see the letter?"

The Colonel shook his head. "Never did. Those who did, well, I think we all felt bad enough. We buried him under the tree. Then we went back to camp. No one had the stomach to chase after the other men who had been with him."

Recalling the story began after a question about Josey, Annabelle asked, "Do you think his father found comfort in his letter?"

"I can tell you for certain he did not."

"How would you know . . . ?"

"Certain members of the posse believed it would be crueler to send the letter."

Annabelle sat up abruptly. "That's terrible."

"Is it?" The Colonel faced her, his mustache drooping like a frown. "I won't pretend to know that it was kinder to spare the father from the knowledge his son had become a horse thief. But that's what Josey believed. I don't recall all he said, but it convinced those men to leave the poor boy's father in blissful ignorance."

Annabelle wanted to argue the point, but they were interrupted. A uniformed private offered an uncertain salute to the Colonel and handed over a written message from the fort's commander. The Colonel looked more than a little grateful to break off their conversation as he stood and opened the letter, pacing as he read it. The private, a splotchy faced boy who didn't look much older than Annabelle's cousin Mark, stood waiting.

Finishing the letter, the Colonel stopped in front of him. The drooping gray mustache always gave the impression of a frown, but on this occasion the rest of the Colonel's features matched.

"What's wrong?" Annabelle asked.

"We need to hurry, I'm afraid." To the private he said, "Tell the commander I'll be right there." Then he turned to Annabelle. "It seems the peace treaty everyone's talking about doesn't mean as much as the government men from Washington have been letting on."

"What do you mean?"

"I mean all these soldiers may soon find themselves at war—and if we don't hurry, we may wind up in the middle of it."

CHAPTER FORTY-FIVE

Josey led his gray pony to the river and left him to drink his fill. From his saddlebags he pulled out and unwrapped a parcel of purchases from Fort Laramie. The pants were stiff and smelled vaguely of medicine. Better that than the cowboy sweat that clung to his old clothes no matter how many times they were washed. The new flannel shirt smelled better and felt nicer, too.

The days were still hot, but that wouldn't last. The Powder River country they would soon enter stretched from the North Platte to the Yellowstone River, between the peaks of the Bighorns to the west and the Black Hills to the east. Even in summer, cold breezes slid down the snow-capped mountains. Within moments, a man who had been sweating in the thinnest of shirts would be grabbing for his coat.

Josey carried the parcel toward the water, chiding himself for wondering what Annabelle might think of the shirt. He hadn't seen much of her in the past week. He'd spent most of his time at the fort talking with soldiers about the peace treaty. Officially, the talks were declared a success. The Indians had signed, and the bureaucrats from Washington went home to bask in the success of guaranteed peace.

From the soldiers, Josey learned that at the time the diplomats were negotiating, Colonel Henry Carrington and his regiment from the Eighteenth Infantry arrived at Fort Laramie on orders from the war department to build and fortify a trio of outposts along the Bozeman Trail between Fort Laramie and the Montana Territory.

The inconsistency of these separate endeavors wasn't lost on the outspoken Sioux chief Red Cloud. Following Carrington's arrival, Red Cloud left Laramie. His final message to the peace commissioners made the rounds of the soldiers.

"The Great White Father in Washington sends us presents and wants a new road through our country while at the same time the white chief goes with soldiers to steal the road before the Indian says yes or no."

The Indians who remained to sign the treaty were the same "Laramie Loafers" who had been living off handouts from the fort for months. It was akin to Grant accepting surrender at Appomattox from a gaggle of old men and widows while Lee rode on Washington.

Following Red Cloud's declaration, the Laramie commander sent word to the Colonel that he would be stopping wagon trains at the fort until they were sufficiently large to protect themselves. The Colonel persuaded him to permit their train to hurry ahead in hopes of catching a military transport that soon would leave Fort Reno, the first outpost along the trail. If the emigrants accompanied the soldiers through the disputed Powder River territory, they should have nothing to fear from Red Cloud.

Josey saw no better alternative. Once they reached the disputed land, the emigrants would need to increase their nightly guard, and Josey planned to range farther ahead than usual to scout the safety of the route.

Keeping busy enough to distract himself from thoughts of Annabelle seemed a good idea, but that didn't make it simple. He had her in mind when he bought the clothes, wondering if she would like them. Josey longed to see her. Her smell filled his head when he recalled the night after their long ride. His body ached to imagine holding her. He had wanted to kiss her, but when he looked into her eyes he saw how it would end. How it must end. The big dog in the yard. She didn't see it now because she needed him. Once she felt safe again, she wouldn't want him around. He had survived the war but doubted he could live with that pain.

He found a large, flat rock that provided a natural drop where the river ran deep. The snow-fed water would be cold. No sense drawing it out. It would have been a waste to put new clothes on a man who smelled more horse than human, so Josey looked around a final time to ensure he was alone, then quickly stripped and leaped in.

Annabelle hadn't been looking for Josey when she left camp for a ride. That's what she told herself. The wagons stopped early for the day near Bridger's Ferry. With other wagons already waiting to cross, their turn wouldn't come before morning. Annabelle missed her long rides with Josey. When she didn't see him in camp, she headed out on her own. Finding him swimming in the river was a coincidence. She would swear to it.

Tethering her horse near Josey's, Annabelle perched on the stone where Josey had piled his clothes. He moved briskly against the stream and didn't see her as she admired his purchases.

"New clothes. How nice." He spun around toward the sound of her voice so fast, she smiled to see him startled. "Don't worry, it's just me. Not a band of Sioux."

"The Sioux I could handle," he said, crouching to keep his body below the waterline.

"I wasn't spying on you."

"Then why do you feel the need to say so?"

He joked so rarely Annabelle couldn't take offense. "I'm not going to answer that." She stood with her back to him. "I'll look away until you get dressed. You must be freezing."

"The water's not so bad if you keep moving. You should try it."

She feigned anger. "A proper lady doesn't bathe in the river."

"I don't know why not. It's faster than washing one part at a time with your underclothes on. It feels good, too. Besides, a proper lady doesn't wear pants or ride like a cowboy, either."

Though she wouldn't give him the satisfaction of admitting to it, Josey had a point. Every time she did something that would have seemed improper at home, she found she liked it. Looking around, Annabelle reassured herself of their isolation from camp. No one would be likely to stumble across them. Still, some lines shouldn't be crossed.

"I won't look." Josey seemed to be reading her thoughts. He turned from her, struggling slightly to keep his balance as he hunched in the water.

"How do I know you won't peek?"

"You have my word as a gentleman."

"I'm not sure how much that's worth."

"Only one way to find out."

The water looked refreshing. Annabelle had assumed the blistering heat of the prairie would give way to something more comfortable as they neared the mountains, but that hadn't happened yet. The thought of dunking her head in the water to wash away days of dust appealed to her, and the notion of fully immersing her body won her over. She hadn't had a proper bath since the last night in Omaha. Plus, she carried a luxury item purchased in Fort Laramie: a bar of Castilian soap.

"I'm holding you to your word." She loosened her hair and began to unbutton her riding shirt. "And you better keep your distance once I'm in there."

"You won't even know I'm here." He moved upstream from her.

"Don't go too far." Privacy was one thing, it was quite

another to be *alone* so close to Indian country.

She fetched the soap from her saddlebag and started to pile her clothes next to his. She had intended to leave on her undergarments, but it occurred to her she would be unable to put on her shirt and pants if her drawers and chemise were wet.

The sun warmed her bare skin, yet she shivered with a frisson of wickedness as she stripped. Her skin prickled at the slightest movement of air. With no intention of leaping in, Annabelle stepped tentatively onto a dry rock where the water eddied into a calm pool. She moved slowly, her eyes shifting from the rock to Josey to be sure he kept his promise. He had stopped swimming but kept his back to her.

"Aren't you in yet?"

"Be patient."

"It's better if you jump."

Annabelle dangled a toe toward the water, still watching Josey as she leaned forward. With a slight drop from the rock to the river, she balanced herself on one bended knee. The cold water sent a shock through her leg, as if she'd stuck her foot into a campfire rather than a stream.

"That's *cold.*"

With a jolt, she pulled back her leg, losing her balance. She had misjudged the depth of the pool, and her leg went into the water to just past the knee, her foot sinking into squishy river bottom. She shouted again and tried to leap from the frigid water, turning as her wet and muddy foot slipped on the rock. Annabelle's arms spun like a windmill, seeking something, anything, to regain her balance.

There was nothing.

For the briefest moment, Annabelle viewed the perfect blue sky as if it stood before her on a painter's easel. Before she had time to consider this unnatural perspective, she went under.

The shock of the cold made Annabelle want to scream, even

as the impact with the streambed forced the breath from her body. Water rushed over her. She heaved for air—too late. Droplets tore at her throat like swallowing shards of glass. She flailed, convinced she was drowning, becoming aware only gradually that something had her, lifting her body and turning her as she coughed and fought for breath.

The coughing and wheezing probably lasted only a few seconds, though it seemed an eternity before Annabelle regained her wits. She hovered over the water, across Josey's knee so the pressure on her stomach forced out the water. He brushed her hair from her face with his fingers, saying something, the sound soothing even if the ringing in her ears precluded understanding. She coughed her throat raw. She moved when the pressure from his knee made it difficult to breathe.

"You all right?"

She nodded, her breath coming in short gasps. She had fallen to her knees, the water nearly to her navel. He was behind her, his arm around her waist. He shook slightly, but not from the cold.

"Are you laughing?"

"No," he insisted.

He drew back before she swung at him. The motion reminded her of their nakedness. She averted her eyes. "Oh." She sank to her bottom so the water reached her shoulders.

"You should have let me drown." She failed to stifle a laugh. "I suppose you will never let me forget this." Her voice rasped from the coughing. "And I suppose you looked, you devil."

"I *wish* I had been looking, but I only turned around when you started shouting. I thought that Sioux war party had come after all."

Laughter brought on another coughing fit. From behind, he enveloped her in his arms. She didn't object. His body warmed hers, and he held her until the coughing stopped. She turned to look and felt she was falling again, into his eyes, big as saucers, brown like sugary coffee. He wanted to say something but before he drew a breath her lips sealed his.

The kiss ended quickly, but there was no denying it happened.

"Why did you do that?"

"Because I knew you wouldn't."

He offered no argument. His eyes looked even bigger as he leaned into her and lifted her chin so her mouth met his.

"You won't need to think that again."

Chapter Forty-Six

"War leads to lovemaking."

That's what the old woman had said. The ladies were taking tea on the piazza overlooking the garden, where a profusion of ivy, vines and roses shrouded them from the foot traffic on the street. A gentle breeze found its way from the battery, carrying the fragrance of magnolias in bloom. Annabelle could almost forget the war on such a glorious June day, if only there had been anything else to talk about.

Mrs. Huger, their hostess, was in a philosophical mood. A large woman, she had the unfortunate habit of choosing short-sleeved dresses, leaving exposed fleshy arms that dangled like chicken wattles whenever she raised a hand to make a point.

"Soldiers do more courting here in a day than they would do at home, without a war, in ten years."

Some of the younger women giggled. More than a year after the fighting had begun, Annabelle held no more illusions about war than she did of love. She kept her silence for the benefit of her young friend Rebecca, whose reading of a letter from her beau inspired Mrs. Huger's philosophical turn. The ardent young man served alongside Annabelle's brothers in Virginia. He wrote to Rebecca as if she had just come from a convent. *To hear his letters, he must think she had never flashed her innocent blue eyes on a man before he came along.* Annabelle knew her brother Johnny could dispel him of that notion, but she kept silent on that point as well.

With so much mourning in the world, Rebecca's letter was a harmless distraction, and Annabelle urged her to continue. "I'm not sure I should," Rebecca said, her face growing as crimson as one of Mrs. Huger's roses.

"That's the part you *should* read," Cassandra McLean said with more than a hint of naughtiness. The other girls pleaded, and Rebecca made a show of appearing reluctant before she continued.

"My dearest Rebecca, my love for you burns so hot within me that I feel I am waterproof. The rain may fall, but it merely sizzles and smokes away, no more dampening my clothes than my ardor for you."

Oh, good Lord. Annabelle focused on her knitting. She was not as gifted a seamstress as the other ladies, but she had vowed to knit a pair of socks every day for the soldiers.

After the women finished tittering about Rebecca's letter, Cassandra asked if Annabelle had anything to read. It was just like her to stir up trouble. Cassandra had been Annabelle's chief rival for Richard. If she felt outclassed by that setback, her subsequent marriage and the birth of two sons were ample compensation. *It's too bad growing bottom-heavy after the birth of her boys prevents her from being charitable about her good fortune.*

"I fear I don't," Annabelle said, careful not to sound irritated by the question. "You know Richard is in the west, and the mail service is not reliable since New Orleans fell."

Cassandra acted surprised, but it was always the same. Richard only wrote at planting or harvesting time. He would be furious to know Annabelle ordered the men to plant crops they could harvest to feed armies and besieged cities. She told herself she wasn't defying her husband so much as relying on her judgment during his absence. He lacked the perspective to understand the impracticality of cotton so long as the Union blockaded the harbor.

Disputes over planting were the least of Annabelle's problems with Richard. She remembered when she had been like Rebecca, starry-eyed and in love with the idea of being loved. Richard was quite the prize: a handsome man with a respected name and heir to one of South Carolina's largest plantations. He hadn't pursued Annabelle with the poetic fervor of Rebecca's beau because he didn't have to. Richard Holcombe was accustomed to getting what he wanted.

They hadn't been married long before Annabelle realized Richard's ardor had been motivated less by her charms than her father's money and a wish to secure his inheritance. Until the marriage, Richard had debts that would have shamed him in his father's eyes. Annabelle convinced herself their relationship would be different once she gave him a son. Yet he grew cooler toward her once his father died, even after she became pregnant.

The riding accident made for a complete break between them.

Richard warned Annabelle not to ride, but it was one of her few pleasures and her doctor assured her the exercise would be good for her and the baby at that early stage. Harry, the slave boy who worked in the stables, must not have secured the balance girth that day. He was usually so careful about such things.

The fall would have been nothing if not for the baby, more like slipping from the horse's back than falling, she told Richard later. She felt no ill effects, but he insisted she take to bed. He never left her side over the long days that followed and spared no expense in seeing to her care, sending off for a specialist from Savannah. The baby seemed fine at first. Only later the doctor explained how the fall caused irreparable harm to the child, making the miscarriage inevitable. With Annabelle in a laudanum fog, Richard told her the doctor's damning verdict: because of her injuries, she would never conceive.

From that day, Richard looked at her as if she were a murderer. Where he had been indifferent before, he grew practically hostile. Worst of all, Annabelle couldn't blame him. It *was* her fault. For a moment, while bedridden, when Richard held her hand and whispered reassurances, she'd been *glad* for the fall. She still expected the baby would be fine, that the bruises and wound to her pride would be a small price to pay for the demonstration of Richard's feelings. After losing the baby, she couldn't look at Richard without seeing an accusation in his eyes, guilt cutting through her like a rapier.

She'd been unable to tell her parents any of this. Richard had urged her not to tell them of the pregnancy until she was showing. The fall happened before that, during the harvest when her parents were away from Charleston. Even afterwards, Annabelle couldn't share the news with them. She was the smart one. She was the gifted one. She was the pretty one. She was the *perfect* one. Her brothers got into trouble and came away even more loved for it. Annabelle's way to be sure of her parents' affections, especially her father's, was to never disappoint them. It was bad enough that Richard blamed her. She couldn't bear their disappointment as well.

Intelligence, strength, beauty—none of it mattered if Annabelle did not give her husband a son, or at least a daughter to whom he could bequeath his family's land. Within months, Richard spoke of selling the plantation and moving to Europe. Annabelle learned of his plans from her father, who heard it from business associates. She acted with her father as if she knew, as if part of Richard's schemes had been her idea, so that her father wouldn't suspect what she did: that Richard planned to leave her.

The war came upon them before sale of the land progressed beyond talk. Richard fulfilled his patriotic duty in raising a regiment of volunteers and riding off. It was going to be a quick war, everyone said, and Charleston would prosper even more as the business capital of a new Southern nation. With Richard gone, Annabelle proved capable of carrying out his affairs, perhaps even better than he, for no detail was unworthy of her attention.

When Caleb Williams brought back news of Richard's death, Annabelle did not grieve. She'd been mourning for her brothers, whose loss she felt keenly. Richard's death represented something different, something she dared tell no one, in particular the ladies at tea parties. Richard's death marked *her* emancipation. If the war hadn't gone so badly, she would have lived out her days contentedly. The last thing she needed was a man, and she'd been unable to tell her father or mother why no man—at least no man worth having—would want her. *Damaged goods.*

Annabelle's bitterness toward sharp-tongued Cassandra McLean that day in Mrs. Huger's garden would be forgotten. Within three years, Cassandra would lose her husband on the battlefield and both boys to the sickness that swept through the city in the war's final year. Cassandra soon joined them, a death Annabelle's mother attributed to heartbreak.

They buried Cassandra in the white frock she wore at her engagement in a churchyard beside her husband and sons. Just before her death, as she lay wasting away, Cassandra spoke to Annabelle of her joy when her first son was born. It was before the war. Her husband was with her, and the idea of the lives that stretched before them in that moment created a sense of what she called "a perfect happiness."

Annabelle mourned Cassandra's passing, but she did not pity her onetime rival. *How many people ever know a perfect happiness?* Annabelle never had, and on the day they buried Cassandra she expected she never would.

CHAPTER FORTY-SEVEN

Annabelle and Josey lay together afterwards on a grassy spot where the bank rose steeply, shielding them from any prying eyes that might pass. Not that Annabelle worried. Her mind had been blessedly empty when Josey swept her in his arms and carried her from the river. There had been no time to think, only to feel, to react to his urgent need, a need she found rising within herself as well, as unexpected as it was welcome.

She smiled as she nestled her head against him. The sun dried their bodies, and the high grass protected them from the breeze that ran along the stream. Josey felt so warm against her and was so still she wondered if he slept. It amused her to think he could sleep while her mind buzzed like hummingbird wings.

She had never expected to be intimate with Josey. She had thought her fear too great to allow anything to happen. The darkness in Josey frightened her, especially when she thought of herself vulnerable to him. Yet there was a thoughtfulness to him, too. In all her flailing about in the water, he had even managed to save her precious soap.

Something shifted inside Annabelle when Josey carried her from the river. He had been hungry, *eager* for her, yet he acted with a gentleness she had never known with Richard. She responded to Josey's touch as she never had with her husband, so that *she* urged *him* on. His eyes as he entered her were filled with a tenderness she didn't know a man could possess. The painful thrusts she had come to expect from her husband, with

Josey were like a gentle rocking, a motion as natural as waves lapping at the shore, filling her rather than penetrating her, his arms around her, his body against hers, enveloping her in warmth, comfort, *love?*

Then, a new urgency, not violent, but no longer gentle. Their movements faster, like racing heartbeats. Her back arching to meet him, her arms pulling him to her again and again, feeling him grow inside her in a final burst of pleasure.

It might have been a moment of perfect happiness if Annabelle could have kept her mind from wandering to the past—and what that might mean to her future. She stroked his hair, and he turned toward her, kissing her hand.

So he was lying there, just like her, his head filled with thoughts . . . *of what?* She feared asking. The poets never spoke of how fraught love could be for a woman. One moment Annabelle had been afraid of being with Josey. Now she feared being without him. *What if he doesn't feel as I do?* Perhaps he only wanted her body for what soldiers called "horizontal refreshment."

Worst of all, he might really love her—until he learned she couldn't give him children. The thought terrified her. Rising on an elbow, Annabelle studied him. He looked younger without his clothes, his body as white as hers but harder, his bones and muscles creating sharp angles where hers curved. "Did you sleep?"

"Almost. I couldn't." He turned to her. "I have to ask you something."

He has to ask me *something?*

"You don't regret what we've done?"

She almost thought he was joking. "Should I?"

Josey leaned on his elbow. With his free hand, he touched her shoulder tentatively, like reaching for a butterfly. "I hope not. I don't know what I would do if you regretted this."

She sighed heavily, her relief confusing him, so she added, "I'm delighted this happened."

It was his turn to sigh. "This changes things."

She nodded. *I should tell him now.*

"The war changed me," he said. "I can't be the man I've been and be with you."

She wasn't sure she understood. Wasn't sure it mattered. *He wants to be with me.* "You're not the man you were. I see the goodness in you. We can be anything we want to be."

That was what she wanted. Everything was different here. Rules and expectations that seemed important back home didn't exist on the frontier. It was on her lips to tell him the rest, tell him now when the disappointment in his eyes could only wound. But Josey spoke first, his need for confession apparently greater than hers.

"I would be the man you make me want to be."

Annabelle closed her eyes, hearing his words echo in her mind. *Can he really care for me the way I imagined love would be?* Josey looked at her, as if waiting for an answer. A moment of perfect happiness. *Why spoil it with premature confessions?* The sun shone on her back, she felt clean and warm and, what? *Loved.* That was the word. *This is how it's supposed to feel.* Annabelle leaned into him, her breath a whisper in his ear.

"How do I know all your pretty words won't flit away with the breeze once you've had what you want?"

"That's not how I am."

Josey could be so earnest, he didn't always recognize when she teased. There was something solid about him that Annabelle liked. Her tongue flicked lightly against his ear. "A man can be hungry until he's fed. Then he can forget he ever wanted food."

He leaned away, a crooked smile showing he was in on the jape. He rolled on top of her. "Until it's time for the next meal." Annabelle felt him stir, and her legs opened to him like the petals of a flower to the sun.

★ ★ ★ ★ ★

The next day the wagons turned north, leaving behind the North Platte. Josey ranged farther ahead than usual, his task growing more difficult with every mile. Bozeman's trail was no more than worn buffalo and Indian paths across alkaline flats, tracing along coulees that wound through forbidding cliff faces. The route followed a more direct route to Montana, but there were no signposts—and they were drawing near the disputed lands of the Powder River country.

The sun was setting as Josey rode toward camp. Instead of picketing his horse, he rode directly to where a circle of men had gathered. As he dismounted, Josey overheard talk about how the teamster called Caleb was missing.

Rutledge seemed worried about his hired driver. "He's gone off before on his own, but he's always come back before dark. I'm afraid something's happened to him."

"You think Indians?" Luke Swift asked.

"I would hate to think that." Rutledge turned to the Colonel. "Maybe we should look for him?"

The old man had been chewing on the stem of his pipe while the others spoke. He looked to Josey, and without a word between them Josey sensed his message was delivered.

"It's too dark to do anything tonight," the Colonel said. "We would risk losing more people in the dark or getting someone hurt."

"We can't just leave him," Rutledge said, wishing his words were true more than believing them. "What if he's hurt?"

Josey looked to the sky. The sun had fallen below a horizon of distant mountains, casting the land in shadow. "I'll range out as far as the woods once the moon rises," he offered. "Won't see much, but I might hear something."

The Colonel nodded, understanding the offer was more likely to give peace to the others than solve the dilemma. After a general agreement, the others returned to their fires. The Colonel lingered, a single eyebrow arched.

"Is it too much to hope the fool got himself lost?"

Josey shrugged. "Wasn't expecting Indian trouble 'til we got past Fort Reno."

"Worst Indian trouble is always the kind you don't see coming."

CHAPTER FORTY-EIGHT

The next blow came to the back of the head. Could have been the rifle butt. Or maybe the pearl handle of the captain's revolver. Caleb's eyes had swollen shut by then, so he couldn't tell. He hoped the handgun. Maybe his head would break those fancy pearl inlays.

Tasting dust, Caleb couldn't move if he wanted. He closed his mouth to keep from swallowing dirt. Heard the captain's voice from somewhere.

"Who else knows about the gold?"

No one. Caleb could no longer speak. He could only think the answer he had been repeating for—*what?*—hours? An entire day? His concept of time disappeared long before he became numb to the pain. The voices seemed as far away as Charleston.

"What did he say?"

"I don't think he *can* say anything. Maybe he told the truth."

"You're probably right."

"Are you going to kill him?"

"Don't be stupid. We need him to get the gold for us. Get him some water. And, get that bow Johnson took off the Indian. We're going to need that, too."

The emigrants had camped early that afternoon because of the heat. Alexander Brewster told everyone within earshot his thermometer peaked at over 100 degrees in the shade. The New Yorker seemed amazed, but even in the sun Caleb didn't sweat like he would sitting in the shade back home. They were near-ing high country. That meant it was hot, but only during the middle of the day when the sun baked them like potatoes in a stove.

They'd stopped a day shy of Fort Reno. After seeing to the oxen and wagons, Caleb slipped away with his pole, hoping to test the trout in a creek not far from the camp. At least the water would be cool, and time alone gave him an opportunity to think.

The others believed they'd beaten back the road agents, that Indians posed the only threat now. Caleb knew better. The captain wasn't going to let him get away with the gold. After the first attack, Caleb had expected another the following day. When it didn't happen that day, Caleb expected it the next day, all the way to Fort Laramie, when it dawned on Caleb the captain didn't want any part of Josey Angel again.

Instead of comforting him, the thought pricked at Caleb's mind. *What am I going to do when we reach Virginia City?* The captain would still be chasing the gold, and Caleb would no longer have the protection of the wagon train. He wouldn't be able to walk the street without looking over his shoulder, wondering when an attack would come. Because it would come. Of that he was sure.

Caleb had so convinced himself he would be jumped in Virginia City it never occurred to him he might be in danger in Wyoming. He didn't hear the horses over the sound of the run-ning creek, didn't hear anything until Harrison stood over him, both hands on his carbine like it was a club.

The first blow came to the face.

"You thought I was dead."

Caleb recognized the captain's voice before he could focus on his image. *I did.* Seated on a cot inside an old army tent, his hands bound behind his back, Caleb wasn't sure the captain heard him. They were alone. "Why didn't they kill you?"

"This lot?" The captain sniffed. The tent was large enough that he could stand so long as he stayed in the center. Somehow he looked as fresh as if he'd been sleeping in a hotel instead of camping in the wild. Even his clothes looked clean. "It wasn't hard to convince them I was chasing *after* you when they shot my horse out from under me. Had to kill Pickens, just to make the point of how angry I was."

Caleb looked around, wishing somebody was near enough to hear this, but it wasn't like the captain to be anyone's fool. Caleb needed to outthink the bastard if he were to survive the day.

"You were clever not to stay in Charleston. Where did you go?"

Caleb shrugged. He saw no harm in talking now. Might give him time to devise a plan. "Wandered around. Took some work where I found it. Tried to figure out what to do."

The captain found this amusing, his gabled mustache flattening into a smile. "All that gold and you were looking for work?" He slapped his thigh with his gloved hand. "So you weren't planning all along to double back to Charleston?"

Caleb shrugged again. He never saw the blow coming, and it spun him around, nearly knocked him off the cot. He tasted blood, saw bright pinpricks of light circling his head. The captain waited like nothing had happened. "It's important that I know." His voice calm, like a banker explaining terms of a loan.

Caleb spit blood. "Why?"

This time he saw the hand rise for the blow, and he shrank back, managing to roll with the force of it.

He spit again. "I didn't plan it. I didn't." The answer satisfied the captain, who relaxed, pulling at his sleeve where it bunched around his elbow. Caleb knew to avoid Charleston. It was only once he got the idea to go west, when he thought he would never be back again, that he decided to make one last visit.

"I went back to see Laurie."

"Laurie? Your dead wife?" The captain's confusion gave way to laughter. He paced the tent, Caleb turning to keep him in sight. The laughter seemed genuine, though Caleb found nothing funny in the situation.

"All this time I wondered how you outwitted me. I don't suppose you appreciate the irony of your response. A great strategist should always know to look to his blind spot—but, then, they wouldn't call it a blind spot if we saw it, would they?"

Accustomed to the captain's verbal meanderings, Caleb knew the bastard didn't need a reply. He merely needed an audience.

"We waited near Charleston for you. I don't have to tell you how dangerous that was for me. I didn't think you had the imagination to go anyplace else, and so when it had been months and you still didn't come, things got . . . difficult. It's best not to let thieves grow idle. They become distrustful. Some of the boys began to doubt my veracity."

Caleb saw a glimmer of hope in what the captain said.

"Taking the gold to Montana was a brilliant stroke. I suppose you intended to melt it down, pass it off as something you found in the hills?"

Caleb nodded.

"It wasn't your idea, though, was it? To go to Montana?" The captain didn't wait for a response. "Who was it? Was it Langdon?"

Caleb started to shrug, then flinched, wary of another blow. "That's what they say. I think Annabelle pushed him to it."

"Annabelle. That is another surprise. Another blind spot, I suppose." Caleb went along with the bastard's game. He had no choice. For some reason the captain wanted to know Caleb's motives. It was almost as if he resented Caleb's thinking of the idea first as much as he begrudged him the gold.

As they talked, Caleb tested the ropes binding his hands but gave it up. Even if he worked free and somehow overpowered the captain, he would be dead before he left camp. There might not be anyone standing near enough to overhear their conversation, but there were sure to be guards somewhere.

"You can have the gold. I never really wanted it. Just let me go."

The captain stopped pacing. His spoke slowly, as if instructing a child in how to tie his laces. "I will get the gold, Caleb. I was always going to get the gold. You don't have what it takes to be a rich man. You weren't born to it. It's why I picked you. Offering me the gold is not going to save you."

Caleb hadn't expected it to be that easy. It was time to make his play. "If you don't let me go, I'll tell the others it was your idea to steal the gold."

The captain smiled. "I've been wondering when it would occur to you to betray me, Caleb. You very nearly disappointed me."

He's bluffing. "I can get you the gold, if you let me go. Or I can tell Harrison and the others it was your idea to take it." His ace, for once, was the low regard everyone held him in. "Who's going to believe I thought of this by myself?"

Caleb braced for another blow, a cost he was willing to pay to frustrate the captain. Instead, the bastard acted almost gleeful. He strode past Caleb to the tent's opening and called for Harrison. A moment later, the slender gunman was with them, looking unhappy to have been excluded for so long. Caleb tried to look him in the eye, but his confidence ebbed in the glow of the captain's obvious delight.

"Tell him. Tell him what you just told me," the captain ordered.

There were too many angles, and Caleb had never seen them

as well as the captain. "It doesn't have to be this way—"

"Tell him!" The captain's scream struck almost like a physical blow, and Caleb flinched. "Tell him about the gold."

Speaking was a mistake. Caleb knew it. But he could see no alternative. "It was you," Caleb said, his voice barely audible, his eyes cast to the ground. "It was your idea to steal the gold."

Harrison swore. Caleb looked up in time to see him reach into his pocket for a gold piece. Swearing again, he handed it to the captain.

"Thank you, Harrison." He turned back to Caleb. "You see, we had a wager that you would blame me for your misdeeds."

Harrison was nearly out of the tent when he stopped and looked back to Caleb. "He didn't put you up to saying it, did he?"

"No, it was him! It was his idea all along."

Harrison held up a hand as the captain laughed. "Stop. I can't afford no more." He left the tent. The captain flipped his new coin in the air, watching it spin and fall into his hand.

"I told you, Caleb. I was always going to get the gold. Now with that out of the way, we're going to talk about what you can do to help me get the rest of it."

Caleb trudged to camp, footsore and shivering in air so cold he saw his breath. After the heat of the afternoon, Caleb couldn't get over the cold. He had experienced hotter days in South Carolina, and he had endured colder nights in the army. But those hot days and cold nights *had never been in the same damn day.*

Emerging from the tree line on the hill overlooking a basin of sage and cactus, he spotted the wagons. Their white canvas covers practically glowed in the light of a waxing moon. *Just keep walking.*

Caleb knew he was lucky to be alive. Once the captain was

confident no one else knew about the gold, he let Caleb go. For his plan to work, the captain said, there had to be an explanation for Caleb's absence from the wagons. Caleb would have liked an opportunity to suggest an alternative to the captain's plan, but both he and Harrison took too much pleasure in carrying out their part. Caleb could feel the bruises swelling his face. Hell, he could almost *see* them when he focused on the end of his nose. His left arm dangled uselessly by his side. If he turned his head, he just saw the arrow that protruded from the back of his shoulder.

"We have to provide a sense of verisimilitude," the captain said, practically singing the last word. *Bastard always had a sense of the theatric.*

A lone tree stood over a thicket of chaparral at the bottom of the hill, its scraggly branches reaching out in a manner that looked sinister in the darkness. It's always one tree in a field like this. One bull in the pasture. One cock in the yard. One stallion in the herd. Nature's way.

The one tree sank its roots deep into the ground, soaking up the water in the dry soil so that no other tree rivaled it. Its branches reached high above the brush to the sunlight, leaving all beneath to wither in shadow. Man was no different. Caleb's mistake had been viewing the war as a vast fire that burned away the big trees, creating openings for men like Caleb to grow from the ashes and rise high. The lone trees did not give up their position so easily.

The slow, painful walk through the bitter cold left Caleb time to think. The captain had his plan, but now Caleb began to perceive another path, one that might see him safely to Virginia City—with the gold. And the key to it all was the man whose presence on the wagon train Caleb had resented from the start.

There was a word for that kind of coincidence, but Caleb couldn't think of it. He started to doubt his mind. He thought he saw a horseman in the silvery light, a shape in silhouette that blocked Caleb's view of the wagons. He raised a hand in greeting, but everything hurt too much. His legs gave out as he recognized the rider.

Speak of the devil . . .

CHAPTER FORTY-NINE

The Colonel must have let slip to the private who met them outside Fort Reno that he was a friend of General Sherman because the commanding officer wore his dress coat when he greeted the Colonel and Josey.

"Gentlemen, it's so good to make your acquaintance." Captain Joshua Proctor was a tall, handsome man, almost pretty, with fair hair and delicate features he masked with a too-big mustache. He shook hands eagerly and Josey noticed a smear of mud as he drew back his hand. Proctor had dressed so quickly he'd left his shirt untucked in the back. Apparently, the captain didn't let West Point breeding keep him from aiding in Fort Reno's reconstruction efforts.

Fort Reno wasn't much of a fort, just a ramshackle collection of partially collapsed adobe and log buildings. The sod-covered quarters, guardhouse, sutler's store and magazine were on an open plain that stood on a shelf of land covered with thistle, saltbush and greasewood about fifty feet above the Powder River.

The official name was "Reno Station," but all the soldiers called it Fort Reno. Josey couldn't blame them. "Fort" sounded safer, and a sense of security was better than nothing. The emigrants were edgy after the attack on Caleb, and the soldiers seemed no more at ease. The single company of infantry left to fortify Reno busied themselves rebuilding the remaining structures and extending the fortified wall.

Josey listened as Proctor and the Colonel took each other's

measure, comparing where and with whom they'd served. "And you, Mr. Angel—" The captain's tongue seemed to get twisted in his mouth.

The Colonel laughed. "Everyone calls him Josey Angel."

Looking embarrassed, Proctor nodded curtly to Josey. "Of course, I'm familiar with your, uh . . . with you, sir. I was uncertain whether the sobriquet was to your liking."

"Just call me Josey."

Proctor relaxed once they settled to business. The Colonel told him about the attack on Caleb. "It's amazing he survived," Proctor said. "The Indians have killed nearly a dozen men—the ones I know about, at least."

"Open warfare?"

"No. Nothing so dramatic. Sneak attacks and ambushes, mostly. It started near Crazy Woman Creek last Tuesday. Four companies were camped on their way to resupply Fort Phil Kearny. A few Indians sneaked past the pickets, cut loose the horses and charged off on the bell mare. Stampeded all the loose horses and mules. In the fight that followed, two infantrymen were killed.

"It wasn't a full-out assault, by any means," Proctor added quickly. "But it was organized."

The Colonel looked to Josey. Neither liked the idea of leading the emigrants through the same area. "It might have been worse."

Proctor nodded. "It gets worse. Later, a patrol came upon several destroyed wagons. Covers were torn to shreds. Loot strewn all over. They found five dead civilians, another mortally wounded." He swallowed hard. A war veteran, Proctor had seen carnage. His pause suggested something new in the experience. "All of them were mutilated in the most horrible fashion."

"They told us in Omaha we would be safe, between the treaty and the forts."

Proctor shifted from one foot to the other, his eyes directed to his desk. "Yes, well, I wouldn't say they lied. . . ."

They were silent a moment before Proctor regained the initiative, telling them of his new commander, who had marched on to build two additional forts along the trail. "Colonel Carrington has ordered that all civilian trains be consolidated to protect against further attacks. The Indians haven't dared assault a well-armed wagon train."

He cleared his throat and straightened his coat. His focus returned again to his desk. "Your arrival is quite timely. News of this unrest has put me in a predicament. I have a company of infantry prepared to leave for Fort Phil Kearny, but we've been anticipating any day now reinforcements from Laramie, including a surgeon and the fort chaplain. Given the circumstances, I've been loathe to delay the company any longer than necessary, but the reinforcements will need a scout."

Realizing his shirt was untucked, Proctor stood straighter and fixed himself. He also seemed to remember he was the only officer in the room still commissioned by the U.S. Army.

"I've had only one scout I trusted to lead the infantry to Fort Phil Kearny and no one to guide the reinforcements once they arrive," he said, looking from the Colonel to Josey and back to the Colonel again. "Until now."

CHAPTER FIFTY

A full moon was rising when Annabelle stepped lightly from her family's wagon. She paused to listen that her father's steady snores did not alter before she stole away into the darkness.

It was a cloudless night, and cooler for it. Her mother had wrapped hot stones in blankets to leave at the foot of their mattress to warm the bed, but the rocks had lost their heat. Nights were peculiarly beautiful here, the rarity of the atmosphere magnifying the starlight so that it seemed there were twice as many stars in the sky as she remembered at home. Their light dimmed as the moon rose, shining like a beacon so bright Annabelle worried her efforts at stealth would be exposed for the whole camp to see.

No one stirred. They were enjoying a restful night in the relative safety of the fort. Few had slept the previous night after Josey brought Caleb Williams into camp, barely alive after a savage Indian attack. The burly handyman had lost consciousness and fell into a fevered fit from which he still hadn't recovered.

Annabelle made a wide berth around the watch fire of the men tending the stock. The previous night they had doubled the guard, and they hadn't set a fire because Josey said it would mark their position. Instead, they dug rifle pits, lying in wait for anyone intending to steal a cow or horse. Josey had been awake the entire night.

With less cause to worry tonight, Josey and Byron had kept the first watch by themselves. Annabelle counted the hours until she judged Josey's turn would be finished. After hearing the news that their wagons would be joining the infantry and moving on without him, she knew she wouldn't sleep. She had to see Josey again.

Since what she had come to think of as their "bath" in the river, heightened fears over Indians had made it impossible for them to steal away. Annabelle wanted to believe the circumstances were as aggravating to Josey, but he gave away so little of his thoughts. Niggling doubts nettled her mind like a loose thread she couldn't leave alone—even at the risk of unraveling her peace of mind.

Things happened so quickly that day by the river. With no time to think, the skeptical part of her mind couldn't stop what happened. Her doubts multiplied afterwards, and she'd been relieved they hadn't been alone since then. That changed at dinner when the Colonel shared the news he and Josey wouldn't lead them to the next fort. He might as well have said they were joining an Indian band for all the sense it made to her.

Her father had known. He never looked up as the Colonel spoke, even at the exclamations of surprise from her mother, her aunt Blanche and the others. Her father explained the logic of the decision after the Colonel moved on to the next cook fire. They would have a whole company of soldiers to escort them and would be guided by the legendary mountain man Jim Bridger. The Colonel and Josey would wait and lead the reinforcements coming up from Laramie.

Her father tried to mollify them. "Without our ox-pulled wagons to slow them down, they will probably make the next fort about the same time we do." As much as she struggled to quell her doubts, dread tormented Annabelle. Weeks of frontier travel had taught her this country was so big even a man as capable as Josey could get lost in it. *Especially if it were in his mind to do so.*

Annabelle found him beneath his blankets, using his coat and a roll of clothes as a pillow. He had been looking to the skies as if counting stars when she noticed him, his figure a shadow against the gray ground. His face glowed in the moonlight when he turned toward her.

"You don't look surprised to see me."

"I heard you coming."

She kneeled beside him, lowering her voice to a whisper. "What if I had been an Indian? Or a road agent?"

"If you had been an Indian, I wouldn't have heard you. You don't sound—or look—like a road agent."

"Aren't you glad for that?" She took off her shoes and slipped out of the quilt she'd wrapped herself in. Beneath it, she wore a white cotton chemise. The fabric was loose and light and left her calves and feet exposed. Josey had seen her so often in a boy's riding clothes, she wanted to come to him tonight dressed like a woman.

He lifted his blankets in invitation. "You must be freezing."

Eagerly, she moved beside him. He wore the clothes he had bought in Laramie. She nestled against the soft flannel shirt, shivering at the change in temperature. The cold slipped away, leaving her as comfortable as she'd ever been in a feather bed with downy covers. "I couldn't let you leave without seeing you."

"You'll see me again."

"Will I?"

"Don't you want to?"

"You know I do."

He looked at her, a hesitation giving her time to turn away, but she didn't, an unspoken request granted as her eyes held his. Their lips met tentatively, once, twice, again. He pulled her tight. Her thin nightdress left her aware of his body almost as much as she had been at the river when they wore nothing. Josey's next kiss left her breathless. He allowed her head to fall against his chest, and he stroked her hair, seeming to breathe her in.

She needed to unburden herself, to tell him what had happened to her. She couldn't live with the dread of wondering again when a man might leave her. With Richard, she had been sure one day he would decide his need for progeny outweighed any marital obligations. His death, ultimately, came as a guilty relief. Better to be a childless widow than cast aside as barren and useless.

With Josey, she felt a passion she had never known—and felt it returned in full. This was how love should be, how they wrote about it in books: unbridled emotion, feelings so unmanageable they frightened her, excited her, consumed her. She could no more stop feeling than she could cease drawing breath. The only thing that frightened her more than how he might respond to her infertility was the thought that she would never see him again, never have the chance to sort through the rest of her feelings.

That's what she should tell him, she decided.

Annabelle opened her mouth, still uncertain which word should come first—when she recognized the steady rhythm of his breaths as sleep. The poor man. Extra guard duty left him so tired he couldn't stay awake even with a woman pressed against his waist.

She nestled tighter against him. His legs twitched, but his breaths remained steady. She should sleep, too. Her body ached from the day's trek as it always did, but her mind whirled as active as at noontime. She recalled what it had been like to sleep with her husband, but thinking of that only brought back bad memories. Better to think of the man beside her now.

She allowed a hand to rest on his hip, her touch tentative at first, not wishing to wake him. It surprised her that he slept so well beside her. He'd told her he was a fitful sleeper. She smiled to think he rested more easily with her. *Why does he have to choose* this *moment to demonstrate that?*

She nudged him with her leg.

He moved but settled into the same position.

She pushed him again, using her arm along with her leg.

He stirred.

"Are you awake?"

He did not answer.

She repeated the question, louder this time.

He responded. Annabelle took a breath, thinking of how best to delicately broach the subject of her miscarriage and condition.

"I cannot give you children."

Annabelle rolled back and fell against the ground. After all that time strategizing the best way to share her secret, she had blurted it out, subtle as a church bell. It wasn't even what she'd intended to say.

He grunted in response without moving. Annabelle began to panic. *Had he not heard? Had he heard and feared speaking?* She repeated herself as she pushed against him so he faced her.

"I cannot give you children."

"So you say." He sounded groggy. "It matters not to me."

He attempted to roll away, but she stopped him.

"Didn't you hear me? Of course, it matters." Her mind whirled, searching for explanations for his reaction. She found none. "You might pretend it does not matter in the heat of our bed, but it will matter one day. Don't let me think it doesn't matter while you plot how to remove yourself from me."

He turned to her, blinking sleep from his eyes, his forehead creased.

"You are mine. You will give me children, or you won't give me children. If you wish to have children, we will take in orphans or Indian babies or bear cubs, for all I care. So long as you are contented. So long as you are mine."

He rolled away from her, the subject closed. Annabelle lay back, looking at the stars, their number diminished by the moon's brightness. She started to laugh, a release of tension. "I should have told you sooner."

"It wouldn't have mattered."

"I suppose not, not then." Passion has a way of clouding the mind, especially in a man. "It will matter more later."

He turned back to her. "I was dead to the world until I met you. You gave life to *me*. If the price God demands for restoring me to life is that I shall have no children, well, I have you. I have life. Nothing else matters."

Relief warmed her, but she didn't trust the feeling. "You may feel differently when you are older, thinking of the grave, with no child to carry on your name."

"No one can pronounce it anyway."

"Don't tease me, Josey."

"Would that I could be an old man, if you are with me. I never thought I would outlive the war. You believe you can't bear children. Ours is not to say." He smiled mischievously, his hand sliding around her waist to her thigh. "Besides, we've only just started. I intend to practice diligently."

She pushed his hand away. She wouldn't let him joke this away.

"It's not just a belief. I was pregnant once, but I was hurt and lost the baby. The doctor said I can't have children."

He rose on an elbow and looked at her. "Doctors can be wrong."

"I can't count on that." Her throat grew tight, choking the words. She blinked back the tears welling. She turned away, but he moved his hand to her face.

"It does not matter. Time will—"

"No." She put a hand to his lips. "Do not give me false hope. It will hurt more when I see your disappointment later."

"You won't see it." He took her hand, squeezed. "I am not he. He didn't love you as I do. You are mine. That is all I care about."

He kissed her, silencing any reply she might offer as his hands moved greedily over her body. *He is wrong. It will matter to him someday.* Then she stopped thinking.

CHAPTER FIFTY-ONE

Caleb drifted gently until a stiff breeze off the harbor set his boat rocking. His eyes closed, he breathed in salt air, ignoring the pain as his chest expanded, forgetting the soreness in his limbs. He inhaled again, but instead of salt or the rotten-fish smell of shore, he took in horse dung, pine tar, leather. Instead of the lapping of water against the boat or the shriek of a gull, he heard the creak of harness, the crack of bullwhips, the braying of mules, the rustle of wagon canvas flapping in the wind.

He opened his eyes. Waited for them to adjust to the darkness. He was in a wagon. He breathed again, his ribs pinching in protest against sodden clothes. An odd chemical smell cut through the others, and he knew it wasn't his wagon. Swallowing took effort. His lips were gummy. Lifting his head, he cringed, feeling as if someone were taking a hammer to it. More slowly, he lifted his head again. A small glow from the back of the wagon alerted him to another man's presence. Caleb's movements, slight as they were, drew his attention.

"Good morning. I'm pleased to see you're still with us." The man moved with practiced ease among the boxes and trunks whose forms emerged from the shadows as the man approached with his lamp. He took a seat on a box beside Caleb. "How do you feel?"

Impatient for an answer, the man put a hand to Caleb's forehead. Caleb started to speak, but his head grew heavy.

Thoughts formed slowly, like his mind trudged through waist-high water.

"Where . . . ?" His voice rasped. He needed water but couldn't remember how to ask for it.

"You're in an ambulance wagon. I'm Dr. Hines, the surgeon posted to Fort Phil Kearny, with the Eighteenth Infantry Regiment. We're in a train headed to the fort."

Nothing the man said made sense to Caleb. The darkness faded, or maybe his vision cleared. Dr. Hines was a fine-boned man, with a wispy mustache and a tousle of dark hair that seemed electrified.

"Water . . . ?"

"Yes, of course. I should have thought of that."

The little man moved almost noiselessly amid the tight confines of the wagon, reminding Caleb of a monkey he had seen in a street show. The doctor held a canteen to Caleb's lips, cradling his head with one hand. Caleb's throat was so parched the water burned. In his greed for more, he leaned forward and gagged, water spilling down his chin and onto his chest, cool against his skin. He coughed and collapsed, completely spent from the effort.

"Easy does it. We don't want you drowning now that the fever's broken."

Caleb struggled to breathe. "What . . . ?"

"You took a fever after the Indians left you for dead," the doctor said as he wiped Caleb's face and neck with a cool, moist cloth. "You might not feel it now, but you're a lucky man, at least compared with the others the Indians have taken. They did no permanent harm that I can see. I expect it was an infection that nearly did you in."

"Indians?" The doctor didn't seem to hear the question. Still feeling like his mind was under water, Caleb needed a moment to catch up. He remembered the captain and Harrison. Apparently, they had nearly taken their theatrical touches too far. Before he asked another question, the doctor lifted his head and brought the canteen to his lips.

"Slowly, this time. We've got a long day ahead of us."

Caleb obeyed. The water no longer burned. Caleb swallowed gratefully as the doctor laid his head back. His mind started to clear.

The gold.

Caleb might have leaped out of the wagon if he'd had the strength. Alarmed at his sudden thrashing, the doctor placed a firm hand on Caleb's shoulder. "Lie back, please. You're not strong enough to be moving around."

This was true. Too weak to resist even this tiny man, Caleb fell back. His mind, no longer wading, had taken flight. "My wagon," he managed. "Where are my things?"

The doctor misunderstood his concern. "You're perfectly safe. You're in a military train now." His voice controlled, soothing his patient. "It's Caleb, isn't it? May I call you Caleb?"

Caleb's panic invigorated him, and he grabbed the doctor's bony wrist with a strength that surprised the smaller man. "Where's my wagon?"

Wincing, the doctor attempted to pull away but gave up the idea. "Your friends went ahead to the fort."

I don't have any friends. "They left me behind?" In his anger, Caleb squeezed, eliciting a yelp from the doctor.

"They didn't leave you behind," he said through gritted teeth. "They left you in the care of a doctor." He explained, something about a military train and reinforcements. Between his muddled head and concern for the gold, Caleb couldn't keep up.

"What about my things? Do you have my trunks?" Caleb relaxed his grip, his strength already waning, and the doctor wrenched free. Hines leaned back, out of Caleb's reach, rubbing the wounded limb.

"I don't know anything about that. You had no need of anything when you were crazy with fever."

Caleb's mind whirled. *What if they found the strong boxes and opened them?* He stared at the canvas top. It was growing lighter. That explained the darkness earlier. They must have left before daybreak. He took a breath, calming himself. No one had reason to go through his things. He wasn't dead. The trunks were probably still buried under supplies in the back of the wagon, just where he left them. Even if he had been dead, they probably wouldn't find the gold until reaching Virginia City and unloading everything else.

"They shouldn't have left me."

"That's not what they did," the doctor said, careful to stay out of Caleb's reach. "They knew we would be following as soon as we arrived. They tell me our mules are faster than oxen. We might catch them before they reach Fort Kearny."

"When did they leave?"

"A day ago, I think. Captain Burroughs has a full company with him, bringing supplies to the fort. With the Indians stirred up now, they must have thought it best to move your wagons with a sizeable military escort." The doctor sounded cheerful. "You should rest. We'll rendezvous with your friends at the fort. I'm sure they will be pleased to see you so much better."

Caleb wasn't sure about that. Despite the doctor's confidence, it was hard to avoid a conclusion that the others had left him to his fate. Rutledge was probably already counting the wages he would save with Caleb's death. Well, the bastard could keep his money, so long as those trunks were safe. Caleb had plans. His life depended on it.

CHAPTER FIFTY-TWO

Riding alongside the wagons toward Fort Phil Kearny, Annabelle noticed how much the landscape had changed. One day they had been traveling over flat, brown prairie under a heat great enough to crack leather boots. The next day chilly mountain breezes compelled Annabelle to put on a shawl. The prickly pear and greasewood gave way to grasses so thick a horse couldn't be trotted through them. Groves of leafy willow and cedar grew along cold mountain streams so clear she counted the fish that hovered in place as if tethered to the banks. *No wonder the Indians value this land so greatly.*

The day should have seemed no different than any other. Josey rarely rode within view of the wagons, yet she felt his absence like a hunger pang. She was thankful Lord Byron was with them, driving a wagon in Caleb Williams's absence. It reassured her that as long as Byron was here, Josey would return.

Her last night with Josey should have been enough reassurance, she knew. Reflecting on it occupied her mind during the tedious hours of travel.

After they'd fallen asleep under the stars, Annabelle woke with a start, unsure of her whereabouts. Understanding rushed back as Josey kicked, murmuring, his arm twitching beneath her. It was still dark. His thrashing had pulled the blankets and exposed her back to bone-aching cold. His arm swung out, and only the blankets prevented him from striking her. She shook him.

"Josey, it's all right." His eyes snapped open, and she saw the confusion on his face in the dim light. "It's all right, Josey. You must have had a nightmare."

Josey nodded, still more in the dream than the moment. Annabelle leaned forward, her hand on his chest, feeling his heart hammering a rhythm like raindrops in a summer shower, his breathing nearly as fast. She shivered as he looked at her.

"You're cold." He tugged at the blankets and covered her. She laid her head against his chest, still hearing his heart. "I'm sorry I woke you. I didn't hurt you, did I?"

"No, of course not." She placed an arm over him. "Are you all right?"

"Like you said, it was a nightmare."

"It must have been terrible. Do you remember what it was about?"

"I think so. It was . . ." He hesitated. "The war." He shrugged, her head rising with the movement. "Go back to sleep. It's nothing."

She knew better. "When I was a little girl and had nightmares, my father would ask me about them. He said if you talked about your nightmares when you were awake, that would take away the fear when you went back to sleep."

He was silent a moment. "That may work for children, when the dreams are monsters. I don't know if it works when the dreams are memories."

"You can try."

"They're horrible things, Belle. Things I wish I hadn't seen, wish I hadn't done."

Annabelle thought back to the day the road agents attacked and how she felt watching Josey kill those men. They had threatened her family and friends. If Josey hadn't killed them, the bandits would have killed him or hurt more people in the wagon train. Josey didn't seem to enjoy fighting, but he didn't shy from it, either. She supposed it was no different when he had been at war. One side attacked and you either killed the man across from you—or allowed him to kill you. That didn't make him a bad man.

She pulled closer, wishing to cover him entirely, wrap him like a cocoon and make him feel safe the way he did for all of them. His body stiffened against hers, but in a moment he relaxed as she clung to him.

"You can tell me anything. I won't judge you."

His breathing became regular, his heartbeat back to a methodical rhythm. She kissed his neck without thought, the way she might comfort a child. When he spoke, the sound of his voice startled her.

"Belle, there are a lot of things I've done that I wish I hadn't." He shifted to face her, but his eyes cast down as he spoke, as if in search of the words he wanted. "Things that make me unworthy of you, I know."

"That's not true—"

With a gentle hand, he stayed her, his eyes finding hers. "I need to say this, so you understand. I don't mean to hide from you who I was. I think you know already."

She nodded. "I've seen. There's no need for secrets between us, Josey."

"No secrets, maybe, but memories, Belle. If I don't share more with you, it's because I want to forget and telling you will only make those memories a part of the new life I want to have." He looked at her, took her hand in his. "You have memories, too, Belle. Memories I wouldn't wish to share." She thought of Richard. In all the nights she lay with him, they had never talked like this.

Josey seemed to read her thoughts. "I would rather not know about your life with him. I can tell you weren't happy. I think knowing why would only give me an anger I can't vent."

"We both have secrets, I guess," she said, correcting herself. "Memories. We have memories that are best forgotten."

They lay back together. The moon was so bright, Annabelle couldn't see nearly as many stars as she had before it rose. Not seeing them didn't mean they weren't there. She wondered how long she would need to be with Josey before they created enough memories that the war faded from his mind like stars on a moonlit night. *I would like to find out.*

When she thought he had fallen asleep again, he proved he had other things in mind. She did not object. She was contented when he was inside her in a way she wasn't any other time. Even when the urgency of his need took over and his mind seemed removed from her, she was happy. *He thinks too much of death. This is life.* Their bodies were sweat-slicked despite the cool night air, and he slid against her smoothly. Abruptly, he stopped.

"Did you—?" She hadn't felt anything.

He shook his head, the movement rigid.

"Why—?"

He shook his head again. "I don't want it to end," he said, his voice tight, as if he were holding his breath.

"I'm afraid it doesn't work that way," she said. Her laughter shook her body.

"Don't move." He gripped her tighter.

She squeezed her legs against him, then allowed her hips to slide the tiniest of increments, down, then up. "Is it all right if I do this?"

"I wish you wouldn't." His eyes were closed and he breathed through his teeth.

"What about this?" She clenched something inside, a movement she hadn't known was possible before he was in her.

His voice sounded pinched. "You're killing me."

"I'm *loving* you. There's a difference."

"When it's done, I will slip from you. I'm not ready for that. I want to feel you like this as long as I can."

"And I want to feel this." She allowed her hips to slide again. He didn't protest. "You can't hold out forever." Her hips moved again, down and up. "And you will have to leave in the morning." Down and up. "So if we can't remain like this." Down and up. Down and up. "I will have to give you a reason—" *downandup downandup* "—to come to me again."

As much pleasure as the memory gave Annabelle, in the light of a new day, with her here and him someplace else, well . . . like a bug bite that wouldn't stop itching, the more she tried to put her doubts from her mind, the worse they plagued her.

At least she had no worries for herself and her family. A hundred soldiers surrounded their wagons. They even had a wagon hauling a small howitzer the soldiers said terrified the Indians, who called it "the gun that shoots twice."

In the Colonel's absence, a scout named Jim Bridger led their train. "Old Gabe" was a legend. *Give him enough time, and he will tell you himself.* Just as with the Colonel, Annabelle had struck up an odd rapport with the mountain man.

Bridger must have been over sixty, a little bowed by age yet enlivened with the charm only an old man can possess, capable of looking at a woman with a lascivious gleam while still passing himself off as harmless. He had come west as barely more than a boy, so long ago, he liked to say, "Chimney Rock was a hole in the ground when I first saw it." Despite a penchant for tall tales, Annabelle trusted Bridger. She sought him out while they were halted for a midday break.

"Hello, little darlin'," Bridger said with a wink and a crooked smile as he brushed the old gray mule he called Hercules.

Bridger swore by mules. Not only were they sure-footed, he told Annabelle, but their smaller legs made for a more comfortable gait than a horse. "Even at my age, I can ride all day and never get sore."

Done with the brushing, Bridger stood to his full six feet. "I suppose you've got more on your mind than the proper method of brushing a mule."

Annabelle nodded. "It's the other train. Everybody says I have nothing to worry about, that the Indians won't attack a military train, but I don't believe it's as large as ours. Do you believe they're safe?"

Bridger hesitated before answering. "The commander's right," he said. "All the Sioux attacks so far have been ambushes. A show of force will make them think twice." His eyes clouded over with a concern he seemed reluctant to voice. It was said the man had lived with Crow Indians, who hated the Sioux even more than white men did. The land they were passing through had been sacred to the Crow, but the Sioux had driven them out in a bloody war lasting decades.

Annabelle urged him on. "There's something you're not saying."

"It ain't my place to second-guess Colonel Carrington. He's the military man."

"You know the Indians."

Bridger smiled as if caught in another tall tale. He sighed as he pointed to the blue-clad soldiers lazing about on the grassy field after their meal. Safe in their large numbers, they gave no sign of being at war. "Lookit how young they are. Most of 'em have never fought, and those that have ain't fought Indians. They think with their rifles and cannon and military training no bunch of savages will ever beat 'em."

"The Indians have rifles, too, don't they?"

Bridger removed his hat and wiped the sweat from his face with a swipe of his sleeve. He nodded toward the dust-colored buttes that overlooked the valley. "The Sioux will skulk in them cliffs or wherever they can lie low under wolf skins, watching all the time. The moment you don't see any is just about the time they're thickest and you should look for their devilment."

Annabelle followed his gaze to the hills. It didn't seem like he wanted to frighten her, but she shivered, feeling more than the breeze off the distant Bighorn Mountains.

CHAPTER FIFTY-THREE

Caleb felt strong enough to insist on getting up when the soldiers stopped for water. Doc Hines warned him against it, and Caleb's legs quivered as he pulled himself up. Yet it wasn't his lingering weakness that would make him regret leaving the wagon.

They must have departed Fort Reno at an ungodly hour, for the sun hung low on the horizon. The doctor explained as they rode that the river near the fort was too alkaline to be much good, and they were limited in how much they drew from the fort's spring. They left in the middle of the night with plans to fill their water barrels at the next creek and push on to a campsite before the worst of the day's heat.

Caleb leaned against the wagon, hoping he looked stronger than he felt. The doctor told Caleb he might ride in front with the driver if he felt well enough after they stopped for water. Caleb wondered if the doctor hadn't been merely eager to be rid of his troublesome patient, but he wasn't about to complain. Unaccustomed to riding *inside* a wagon, he found the close quarters and constant rocking nearly as debilitating as the fever.

Their train consisted of five supply wagons, including one drawing a steam-powered sawmill, two ambulance wagons and a few horses belonging to officers. They were an odd assortment. Doc Hines had told him there were more than a dozen soldiers, nearly as many teamsters, a chaplain and two soldiers' wives, each with a baby. With the five officers new to the region, the Colonel and Josey Angel served as guides.

The wagons had stopped near a creek bed. A crowd of soldiers and teamsters gathered near the front wagon. Caleb hesitated when he heard the sharp voice of the officer in charge, a lieutenant named Wands.

"Keep the women back."

The warning drew Caleb forward, curiosity helping him forget his pain. Instead of the stream of clear water he expected, he saw a dry creek bed and the nearly naked body of a soldier— his identity made possible only by a square of blue uniform secured to his body by one of the arrows that pierced his back. The man had crawled into the sandy creek bed, so desperate for water he had been willing to dig with his hands to find it.

"Looks like they waited here," Josey Angel called to the Colonel from the tree line, a good twenty paces from the creek.

"Water always makes a good spot for an ambush," the Colonel replied.

More mindful now of the group's small numbers, Caleb saw no sign of Indians. He maneuvered among the soldiers for a better look and immediately regretted it.

During the war, Caleb had seen many dead bodies. Corpses mangled and twisted in every conceivable fashion and some Caleb would have deemed inconceivable before he witnessed them. None of that prepared Caleb for the sight of the dead soldier. The left side of the man's head had been crushed so that it resembled a melon dropped from a height. A patch of hair from just above his forehead had been ripped clear, and his ears were gone. More had been done to the lower half of his body, but Caleb looked away, glad for an empty stomach.

The man was just as dead as any he had seen in the war, but those bodies possessed an impersonal quality, men made corpses by the accident of a musket ball, their deaths motivated by larger objectives.

What had been done to the soldier in the creek bed was different. Methodical. Calculated. Caleb wasn't sure the soldier was dead when the Indians took his ears, nose and other things. *They enjoyed it.* Caleb shivered at the thought. The soldier's final release into death had probably been a disappointment to his tormenters, a premature end to their entertainment.

The reaction of the soldiers was mixed. Some calling to God, others angrily cursing the Indians, swearing a revenge Caleb hoped he wouldn't be around to see. One of the teamsters retreated to the trees and vomited his breakfast. His retching set off two others.

The young teamster who'd lost his breakfast swore under his breath. "Savages," he said, wiping his mouth with the back of his hand.

"Some things the Sioux did to the Crow would make this look like play," the Colonel said. "White men have done things just as wicked in the name of God."

The teamster looked uncertain. "God had nothing to do with this."

The Colonel shook his head. "When he dies, an Indian brave believes he will pass on to a place filled with wild ponies to tame, game to stalk and pretty young maidens to woo." The Colonel smiled at the thought as a few of the soldiers gathered close. "If his enemy has no fingers to pull back the bowstring, no tongue to taste the buffalo, no pecker to get a poke, well, that man's heaven becomes an eternal hell."

Lieutenant Wands interrupted and ordered the men to dig a grave near the trail. The soldiers seemed grateful to be occupied. Caleb sensed tension between Wands and the Colonel. The pair had stepped aside from the others and were speaking. Wands kept his voice low, and Caleb made out only part of the Colonel's much-louder reply: "—not this late in the season, after the snow melt. You just can't be sure." Wands reached out

246

to the older man, guiding him farther away from the soldiers. He looked no happier than the Colonel, who stalked off with him.

Weak and thirsty, Caleb found a spot in the shade, his condition and civilian status sparing him from the work detail. The wagon driver came over. Sam Peters was a squat, round man, with a jowly face that even a crescent of untamed whiskers couldn't hide. He looked like he had spent the war in the quartermaster's office, a little too near the food supplies, but the lack of deprivation gave him a generous nature. He offered a smoke. Caleb refused, afraid the tobacco would make him ill.

"Where are we, anyway?" he asked.

"Dry Creek."

Caleb thought the private was joking. "Did you come up with that yourself?" Peters shook his head, confused by the question.

"The name of this place is Dry Creek?"

Peters nodded, looking as if he might call the doctor for another examination of Caleb's head. *Oh, Lord.* Caleb would never understand how the Union won the war with this kind of planning and leadership. "Just like the army to hatch a plan that depends on finding water at a place called Dry Creek," he said, though it occurred to him the army might have the last laugh. Having failed to kill him during the war, maybe the army meant to rectify the oversight on the trail.

Wands, his face red with strain, yelled orders to prepare to head out.

"They say the campsite's by a river," Peters said as he stood, offering a hand to Caleb. "Guess the lieutenant wants to hurry and get there."

Caleb took Peters's hand, grateful for the aid. "I hope you're right. Doc says we're almost out of water."

As they walked to the wagon, Caleb looked back to where they had found the dead soldier. "So much for Dry Creek. Tell

247

me, where are we going to camp?" he asked Peters. "Indian Massacre River?"

He had meant it as a joke, but neither man laughed.

CHAPTER FIFTY-FOUR

After a midday break, Annabelle sneaked some sugar from the commissary wagon to spoil Paint. She intended to ride the horse that afternoon, putting from her mind the strange looks the marching soldiers gave her as she passed riding astride a horse and wearing boy's clothes.

They were still at least three days out from the new fort, the Bighorn Mountains to their west looking like they might stretch forever. As the wagons advanced, she noticed Jim Bridger hunched over a circle of white stones. Annabelle eased Paint toward him, realizing as she drew near that the objects were bones from an animal like a cow, only larger and bleached white in the sun.

"Buffalo," Bridger said as he looked toward her, his face pinched in a squint against the bright day.

Annabelle dismounted for a closer look. With its dark horns, the skull looked monstrous, the bones coming together in the beast's face like some kind of beaked predator. "I've never seen buffalo. I thought they would be everywhere."

"Used to be. Settlers have driven off them hunters haven't killed. I used to think there were more buffalo than stars, but now it's like the skies have growed dark."

Annabelle noticed odd scratchings on the thick side of the bleached skull. The marks appeared too regular to be natural, combining to form odd shapes and swirls. She asked about them.

"That's what I been ruminatin' over."

"They're not letters, not English anyway." Bridger wasn't literate, Annabelle knew, though she'd heard he enjoyed being read to. "Are they Indian letters?"

"Somethin' like that."

"I didn't know the Indians had a written language."

Bridger picked up the skull and ran a long, leathery finger across the marks, as if to read them by touch. "It's not so plain as English, but they have ways of transmittin' a message."

"Can you tell what it says?"

Bridger nodded and looked to her, as if judging how much to say. Annabelle feared what he might say, but she had to know if they or the others were in danger. "Tell me."

He stood, walking over to get his mule's reins and signaling with a nod that she should do the same with her horse. After he mounted the mule he looked back to her. "The message is a call to any Indian who passes to gather for a big battle."

Annabelle looked around the empty fields. "Where?"

"I'm not sure, but if I had to guess, I would say Crazy Woman Creek."

"The stream we crossed yesterday?"

Bridger nodded. "Kinda thought we was bein' watched. Any train headed north would have to cross there. It's the only good water."

"Josey and the second train—" Bridger grunted an agreement. "Shouldn't we tell the captain to go back?"

"Mm-hmm."

Annabelle stared at him, unsure what to make of his reserve. "Surely, the captain will want to come to the aid of the second train?"

"He has his orders."

"But that was before we knew the others were in danger."

Bridger's deeply lined face seemed to sag, and the scout

looked his age when he faced her. "Do you think your Josey would put *you* in danger, even if it meant he would be safer?"

Annabelle shuddered as if struck by an icy breeze. She looked the way they had come, past an ocean of grass to where she thought Josey might be, coming for her and unaware of what lay between them.

CHAPTER FIFTY-FIVE

From the crest of the hill, Caleb saw a line of cottonwoods and scrub oaks snake through the valley below. "That's Crazy Woman Creek," Peters said, his voice hoarse with thirst. The seat beneath them creaked as the round man adjusted his weight. "It's gotta be."

Caleb's hope surged but he saved his voice. They had been without water for hours, with the sun rising higher in the sky, temperatures soaring with it. The doctor provided updates every few miles. After he reported 100 degrees well before noon, they implored him to stop. It was better not knowing.

The path across alkaline flats had been clear, at least, and travel was easy, though they kept a deliberate pace to spare the mules. Doc warned him his fever might return, especially without water. Caleb felt weak but didn't complain. He would have to be carried before he would go back into the wagon, which was stifling even with part of the canvas peeled back.

The undulating line of trees appeared to trace the contours of a creek, but the papery leaves obscured the view. Caleb feared another dry creek might mean the death of them all. He squinted, wishing he had a field glass. The trees forked into two strands, creating parallel lines with what looked like a small, dry ridge in between. *There has to be water to have so many trees.* At the farther line of trees, between the leaves, flashes glinted like starlight. With a surge of relief, Caleb grabbed Peters's arm and pointed, still not trusting his voice. Sun wouldn't reflect like that off a sandy river bed. There had to be water.

Lieutenant Wands confirmed this with his field glass, sending word back through the wagons. It was hard not to race the mules to the water, but Caleb judged they were still a couple of miles off.

As the wagons proceeded down the slope, Caleb became convinced the first line of trees masked another dry bed, seeing no signs of moving water through the leaves. Nothing, it seemed, was going to be easy about this trip.

Their progress halted as the first wagons mired in the sand on entering the dry creek bed. Caleb feared they would have to double-up the teams to get through, but with enough soldiers lending a shoulder and the drivers whipping the mules bloody, they regained momentum.

"Doc, you might have to walk from here," Peters called back. He asked Caleb, "You think you can make it on foot?"

Caleb looked to Peters, allowing his gaze to follow the other man's full girth. "You sure that's the best idea?"

Peters chuckled. "I suppose you better drive. I'll push, if it comes to that. You're going to have to keep 'em moving once we get into that sand."

Caleb shrugged. He'd been driving a team of oxen halfway across the country. He doubted steering some mules through a sandy creek bed was any more challenging than walking through it himself. "Beats dying of thirst."

Peters and Doc Hines climbed from the wagon, and Caleb drove to a break in the trees where the path sloped into the creek bed. The wagons would have to slog a good hundred yards to the left to reach a point where they could climb out.

The ambulance wagons were in the middle of the train, behind a supply wagon and a Conestoga that carried the women and babies until they walked, too. Caleb waited until those wagons pulled far enough ahead that he wouldn't have to slow if they became mired. Getting Peters to walk proved a good decision, as he lent his wide shoulders and tree-stump legs to the wagon, keeping it moving so long as Caleb didn't let the mules quit.

Josey Angel had circled back from the front of the train. *Guess he doesn't feel like pushing.* His reins in one hand and his rifle in the other, Caleb admired his horsemanship to keep his balance in the sand. Josey Angel nodded toward Caleb. "Glad you're up again."

"Feel even better once we reach water."

Caleb expected some kind of reassurance from the scout, but instead Josey Angel studied the tree line that hid the creek beyond. "Me, too."

By the time they had all entered the creek bed, the first wagon pulled its way out. About a dozen men squeezed together to find purchase behind the wagon box to propel it from the sandy creek bed, the mules braying in protest.

Then the Indians attacked.

CHAPTER FIFTY-SIX

Lying in the shade of a rifle pit dug under one of the wagons, Josey pushed thirst from his mind, but the effort only exposed him to more damning thoughts. *I still should have seen it coming.* He didn't blame the officers for the ambush. The decision to spare the thirsty horses and go without scouts had been necessary. *I should have ridden ahead when we came to the creek.* It had been a perfect spot for an ambush.

It took remarkable effort for the teamsters to get the wagons out of the creek bed while Josey and the soldiers provided a covering fire. Most of the soldiers carried single-shot Springfield rifles, but the Colonel had them coordinate their fire so the Indians couldn't rush and overwhelm their position. Wands also had a sixteen-shot Henry, and the big lieutenant knew how to use it. He and Josey maintained a steady defense when the others reloaded.

With the Indians held at bay, the teamsters drove the wagons into a defensive circle on a ridge overlooking the dry creek bed. The drivers unhitched the mules and brought them inside the corral. One teamster stacked neck-yokes from the wagons to make a breastwork. Others emptied the wagons, stacking crates and sacks of supplies to build a makeshift keep. That's when the Colonel set a few of the men to digging rifle pits.

The Indians seemed content to bide their time.

"They know we can't last without water," the Colonel said.

While the others saw to the mules and wagons, Josey checked

255

his guns. Fighting always left him restless and jittery, like he'd been drinking coffee all day. Since his first battle, when he was so green he hardly remembered to fire his weapon, Josey had approached every fight the same. The methodical preparation of cleaning and loading guns shielded his mind from thoughts of what might happen. It was no hasty thing, loading a Henry rifle and four six-shot revolvers. A fight left no time to measure and pour powder, pack the ball, place the percussion caps. The routine helped keep his head clear, and Josey needed that now more than ever.

They hadn't been in the corral long before the Indians launched a sneak attack, loosing a few arrows into the corral before being driven back by return fire. Near as anyone knew, the attack came from a ravine on the opposite side of the ridge. Wands and the Colonel thought the ravine might lead to the creek. If the way did lead to water, the Indians would be waiting there.

Wands asked for a volunteer to join him in scouting out the ravine, driving away any Indians if necessary, and then leading a party loaded up with canteens and buckets to get water. Josey had felt every head turn in his direction, but his tongue, thick with thirst, held still. Finally, the chaplain riding with them stepped forward.

A well-built man of about forty with a thick head of white hair, Reverend White had the vigor of a man half his age. He must have had a reputation as a fighting man of the cloth for none of the others seemed surprised he volunteered.

With the two of them gone, Josey wrestled his guilt. *I should have led them into the ravine.* Wands commanded. He was responsible for seeing these men on to Fort Phil Kearny. He has a baby, a wife. Josey had looked away from her as she watched her husband leave the wagon corral. He hadn't been able to look at anyone. He felt their stares on his back, silent accusations of cowardice. *They are right.*

For most of the day's trek Josey had been lost in a daydream of a Montana ranch with a house overlooking a river. The clear head Josey usually kept in battle, a quality the Colonel once told him was more valuable than his marksmanship, had been lost in a muddle of conflicting emotions. Actions that usually came automatically required his constant focus as his mind drifted somewhere else.

Annabelle.

Though never heedless in battle, Josey knew he might die cowering in a hole just as easily as in a cavalry charge. When exploding mortars rain shrapnel everywhere, a man doesn't imagine himself immortal just because he wakes in a surgeon's tent. Such thinking is for the fresh fish who believe nothing evil can happen to them because it never has. Most die soon enough. Or, like Josey, they learn how fickle war is. Absorb that lesson, and a soldier knows he is doomed, a knowledge that can free his head from the distractions that might kill him before his time.

Today was different. Today, one thought filled his head.

I want to live.

It was a ridiculous thing to think in a fight. Of course, he wanted to live. *Every* soldier wants to live. Thinking it during a battle was no more useful than a cartridge box of daisies. Worse, it distracted him from the moment when a second's inattention might get him killed.

Annabelle.

Dwelling on her now only invited fate to cut his thread. Josey wasn't a superstitious man, but every soldier knew comrades who foretold their doom on the eve of battle. No one remembered the others who spoke with just as much conviction of their deaths, only to survive to repeat the prophesy before the next battle. Loving Annabelle didn't make Josey any more tempting a target to fate. *Thinking* about her when he needed to be focused, *that* could get him killed. *Loving Annabelle has turned me from Achilles to Hector.*

Hector always dies in the end.

Josey finished loading his rifle. The Colonel stood beside him. Josey avoided his gaze. *I need to forget Annabelle if I want to live to see her again.*

Josey had lost track of how long the men had been gone. Ten minutes? Twenty? No one spoke while they waited. The silence weighed on them as much as the heat. Josey found himself holding his breath to listen more intently.

A breeze rippled across the wagon covers, sounding like a sail on a river barge. From somewhere in the tall grass beyond the wagons, a quail cooed. Josey wanted to shush it, to preserve the silence even as it tortured them. So long as it remained quiet, he imagined the others were safe, that he wasn't responsible for their slaughter. They were probably nearly back, struggling under the weight of so much water, moving noiselessly in hopes the Indians would not discover them.

Unless they were dead.

Even now the Indians might be stripping their corpses. Josey shook the thought from his head. *We would have heard something if they'd come under attack.* Gunfire. War cries. Screams. Something.

No. Silence was good. Silence meant life.

Then the silence was broken.

CHAPTER FIFTY-SEVEN

Standing behind her father and Jim Bridger, Annabelle had to crane her neck to see Captain Burroughs. A doughy, splotchy-faced man, Burroughs had close-set eyes and a nervous habit of ceaselessly looking about. This was Burroughs's first posting in Indian country, and he seemed more determined to avoid a mistake than win glory. Pleas from Bridger and her father to turn back left him agitated.

"I can't run off willy-nilly," he said, his face reddening. "I have my orders: to see this train—with your family among them," he directed to her father, "—safely to the fort. I can't go off based on some primitive scratches on a *bone.*"

Bridger muttered under his breath, "Damn paper-collar soldiers." Annabelle knew she wasn't expected to address the captain but couldn't contain herself. "Mr. Bridger said it's a message."

Burroughs looked her way as if seeing her for the first time. "I wouldn't expect a woman to understand military matters." He looked past her without finishing his thought.

Tugging on the sleeve of his uniform, Annabelle wouldn't be ignored. "How will it look if a train of military wagons is wiped out by Indians? If the newspapers back East reported such a thing, why, the officer who stood by to allow a massacre would be *infamous.*"

Burroughs blinked twice, his eyes casting about as if looking for an escape that wouldn't endanger either body or reputation.

259

"Yes, how do you spell 'Burrows'?" her father asked. "Is it with a *W* or a *GH*? The newspapermen will want to know."

Burroughs blinked again. He looked at her father, then back to Annabelle, finally to Bridger. His face had grown as red as the stripes on the flag.

"I could lead the mounted infantry back," Bridger offered. "We would make better time, while you and the rest of the soldiers continue on with the wagons."

Burroughs turned away, looking to each wagon in the train, his head bobbing with his shifting gaze, reminding Annabelle of a woodpecker. He called to a lieutenant overseeing the wagons. "Gather the mounted infantry." He turned back to Annabelle. "For your sake," Burroughs said, the color draining from his cheeks, "I hope we have less need of those troops than the wagons behind us."

CHAPTER FIFTY-EIGHT

"Here they come!"

Josey saw first the hat, then the shoulders and torso of a young private, shuffling in a hopping gait with the weight of a bucket in each hand and at least a couple of canteens dangling from straps around his neck.

The first gunshot echoed out of the ravine before the last of the men emerged. At the sound, the young private redoubled his awkward shuffle. His face locked in a grimace, veins in his neck bulging. A burly sergeant behind him wasn't faring much better. Those in the camp shouted encouragement with what voices they had. More shots were heard by the time all six were moving across the grassy field to the wagons.

The reverend emerged next. His back toward them as he stepped from the ravine, he took aim with a revolver and fired. He turned and ran. Last came Wands, his hulking frame impossible to mistake. He brandished his rifle like a club, swinging down on an unseen target. *Damn you, man, where's your pistol?* Josey moved to a kneeling position and took careful aim past Wands's shoulder. He fired, cocked, fired again. The first Indian to emerge from the ravine dropped.

More followed.

Run faster. Josey tried to focus. *Just keep shooting.* The steady fire gave the Indians pause, but the soldiers' run for water had stirred them and there were too many to be held off. Josey reloaded. The soldiers returned, the buckets hastily set aside while every man grabbed a rifle and joined the defense, everyone shouting for the chaplain and lieutenant to hurry.

The Colonel directed the newcomers to positions around the corral. Josey finished loading and twisted the rifle barrel back in place. Wands drew closer, but the Indians were gaining. Josey couldn't see past the lieutenant for a clear shot—until Wands twisted and fell, his arms flung forward as if leaping for the shelter of the wagons, still at least ten paces away.

Josey fired once, twice, three times. The Indians were close enough to return fire, and Josey had to roll into a nearby rifle pit to avoid an arrow that caught in the bed of the wagon overhead. Some of the Indians had rifles, too, and the cloud of smoke from the exchanged fire hovered over the field between them, the smell of gunpowder burning his nostrils. Most of the Indians fell back or took cover. Everywhere he saw movement, Josey fired, his mind empty of any thought but the mechanical movements of aiming, firing, reloading. He rolled right at the sight of new movement.

"No!"

The Colonel and a fat driver emerged from cover of the wagons, scrambling in a crouched run toward Wands. An arrow protruded from his leg. They managed to lift the big lieutenant, each slinging an arm over his shoulder, and dragged him toward the wagons, Wands using his good leg to hop between them. *They just might make it.* Josey rose and stepped from between the wagons, not caring that he made himself a target. Advancing before the wagons, he fired off two shots at an Indian with a rifle.

"Hurry up."

The Colonel and the driver nearly had Wands back to the wagons. Josey moved toward the ravine, looking for any sharpshooters.

He heard the horses before he saw them, felt the pounding

hoof beats. He turned with a sense of dread. Three warriors on horseback charged toward Wands and the others. They had raced around the backside of the corral. The Colonel and the private increased their pace, too fast for Wands on his one good leg. He stumbled, dragging the others down before they recovered their balance. Josey raised his rifle and fired. One of the braves dropped his lance and veered off. The remaining horsemen were nearly upon the others as Josey fired again.

A second rider fell off his horse.

Josey cocked and fired again.

Empty.

He cursed, cast the rifle aside and drew two revolvers at his waist, firing wildly until his guns emptied, more in hopes of distracting the attacker than hitting anything.

It was too late.

With a deft swing of his arm, the third warrior clubbed the Colonel from behind, sending the old man tumbling into the deep grass even as the driver pulled Wands to cover. Josey screamed with all the voice he had, and the horseman turned toward him, his club held high as he whooped in triumph.

Time stopped. Josey saw the flare of the white-faced bay's nostrils. The muscles in its flanks pumping with effort. The Colonel lying motionless. The fat driver stepping out to pull the old man clear. All of it perfectly clear as if the scene hung before him in a frame.

Josey fell to his knees. His eyes turned skyward, closed against the blinding sun. *I feared death the first time I faced it, but death never stalked me. It was failure. I never thought to outlive the war because I never wished to live to see the day I failed him.*

The ground shook under Josey as the rider charged. The pistols dropped from his hands as he extended his arms wide. He heard the soldiers behind the wagons call to him, begging him to run. Josey felt as if he were floating above the scene.

Opening his eyes, he saw the wispy Indian brave, pale with wavy, dark hair plaited into two braids that framed a delicate, handsome face. A single hawk's feather twined in one of the braids, a pebble tied behind his ear.

The brave's war cries were cut off as his sad eyes met Josey's. Josey felt the horse's approach, its breath on his outstretched arm as it passed. *Why run when I can fly? Oh, sweet release.*

Chapter Fifty-Nine

Standing near the ridge the soldiers called Pilot Hill, Annabelle saw Fort Phil Kearny as if it were laid out before her on a map. Two crystal streams meandered through a valley between high rolling buttes that buckled and folded into the horizon. A thickly wooded island lay between the streams. The whine from a pair of sawmills and crash of falling timber carried across the valley.

The fort was mostly a collection of tents, though the men had marked its borders with a stockade of heavy pine trunks imbedded into the ground. Blockhouses, with portholes for howitzers, protected the corners. Mountains of board planks were piled inside, and the men had staked out locations for barracks, officers' quarters, warehouses and the other buildings that would make the fort more like a small village in the lonely valley.

From the amount of work that had been done, Annabelle would have thought the soldiers had been on the site for much longer than three weeks. *A threat of Indian attacks makes a wonderful motivator.*

Such threats are not conducive to hospitality, however. Colonel Carrington, the commanding officer, sent word that the emigrants could camp in the valley near the fort, but not so close that their stock would compete for the same grasslands as the fort's horses and cattle. After Annabelle proved a pest in seeking word of the second train, his officers compounded the insult by making it clear soldiers would come to them once news arrived.

The travelers occupied themselves with washing, baking and repairing the wagons. Even though they were safe, Annabelle did not relax as she worried over Josey and the second wagon train. An invitation from the fort commander's wife, Margaret Carrington, saved her from going mad.

Eager for new company, Margaret, as she insisted Annabelle call her, organized a picnic on a warm August afternoon for the officers' wives and the young women from the wagon train. They took their rest where a dashing stream near a thicket of chokecherry shrubs and cottonwood trees offered some relief from the August heat. A detachment of a half-dozen soldiers from the fort stood nearby as sentries.

"We found gooseberries growing wild on the other side of the valley, but I'm afraid we picked them clean," Margaret said. She maneuvered through the thicket, Annabelle close on her heels. "Gooseberries make a better pie, but at least we won't have to mind their thorns."

Annabelle gathered a small handful of the dark chokecherries. She tried one, surprised at how sweet it tasted. She wondered how to discreetly dispose of the seed until she saw Margaret spit hers to the ground. "You're not in Charleston any longer, my dear," she said, grinning like a child, lips stained by the berry.

Margaret was an attractive woman in her mid-thirties, though too thin in Annabelle's judgment. A chronic cough that she hoped the dry air of the west would cure inhibited her natural energy.

The soldiers spread blankets and erected a canvas cover with poles to shade the ladies from the sun, and they enjoyed a cold meal of chicken and bread. One of the soldiers used the grinder built into his carbine to start coffee, while another built a fire for the little pots called muckets.

Taking shelter in the shade, the women found no shortage of common elements in the stories of their journeys. Annabelle shivered to hear of the hardships the soldiers' wives endured during the past winter in Nebraska as they set out. Mrs. Bisbee, a lieutenant's wife, elaborated on the overland trek for more than a thousand men, a twenty-five piece military band, seven hundred head of cattle and some two hundred wagons, including the mowers, sawmills and sundry construction machinery needed to build the fort.

"My husband called it 'Carrington's Overland Circus,' " Mrs. Bisbee said with a birdlike twitter.

All the gay chatter kept Annabelle from dwelling on her worries, but they were never far from her mind. Her downcast demeanor, faraway gazes and inability to follow the conversation at times gave her away. Following lunch, as the women explored along the river, Margaret held back so they were alone.

Accustomed to being guarded in the company of women whose husbands were subordinate to hers, Margaret took to Annabelle like a long-lost sister. Annabelle laughed to hear stories of Margaret's two young sons, Jimmy and Harry, and their boyish squabbles over Calico, the small Indian pony their father had given them. She cried hearing Margaret tell of four children who died as babies.

"I did not wish to make you weep at my sorrows," Margaret said, offering a fresh handkerchief from a pocket in her dress.

Annabelle took it and dabbed at her eyes. "It's not that, not just that." Before she knew what had overtaken her, Annabelle found herself confiding about the loss of her baby, her determination never to marry again—and her sense that her resolve on that matter was eroding. Margaret proved an ideal confidante, mature beyond her years, but still largely a stranger. Nothing said between them could follow Annabelle as a secret to be divulged.

"This specialist who said you could have no more children, did you seek another opinion?" Margaret asked.

Annabelle admitted she hadn't. "I didn't feel up to seeing anybody. I didn't even tell my mother," she added, realizing how horrible that sounded.

"You should see another doctor. I would never trust the opinion of just one, especially about something like that. Men like to think they know more than they do, and that's a subject they are ill-equipped to master." Though too choked up to laugh, Annabelle appreciated Margaret's efforts to humor her. Then Margaret's voice turned solemn again. Though Annabelle never mentioned Josey by name, her new friend intuited the real problem.

"I suspect the ignorance of doctors is not your only concern. You are worried about your man."

Startled by her frankness, Annabelle flushed. "My husband is dead," she said automatically. As for Josey, Annabelle didn't know how to explain their relationship. "I am promised to no one."

Margaret chided her. "Perhaps not in any fashion that would be recognized in the drawing rooms we grew up in," she said, pausing to look at Annabelle. "We are not children any longer, and this—" with a sweep of her arm she took in the Bighorn Mountains and a horizon empty of any human presence "—is not a drawing room."

Annabelle smiled. She told some of what passed between her and Josey, though some things shouldn't be shared even between friends. "Until I know he's unharmed, I can hardly think of anything else," she said. She wiped her eyes again and breathed deeply to calm herself. "I am being silly. As a soldier's wife, you must endure this every day."

"You mustn't think yourself weak for your concerns. You've already lost a husband. Of course you fear the worst."

"My relationship with Richard was . . . different," Annabelle said.

"He is gone. That is my point. My Henry never served on a battlefield. His talents were better suited to raising troops and organizing them to fight. I think sometimes he wishes he had been bloodied. Some men won't trust an officer who wasn't. For my part, I was relieved I had no need to send him off, wondering if he would return to me."

She reached out and took Annabelle's hand in hers. "I admire your strength."

"You wouldn't call it strength if you knew my thoughts," Annabelle said.

"Admitting our fears does not make us weak," Margaret said, slipping her arm around Annabelle's waist. "It is only through them we discover the bounds of our strength."

Her new friend's words were still in Annabelle's head when the second wagon train arrived late that day. Annabelle insisted on going straightaway to the fort, but a rude and balding captain with alcohol on his breath barred her from entering.

One of the guards took pity on her, and she learned the Colonel had been wounded and taken to the hospital tent. Certain Josey must be with him, Annabelle returned to her wagon, confident he would come soon. When he hadn't come by the time the emigrants readied for bed, she decided to sleep outside. She didn't want her parents to hear when she stole away with him.

Beneath a blanket of stars, sounds that usually blended into a lovely lullaby stood out as discordant as church bells at night. Crickets chirped in the meadow. A light breeze rustled through the branches of the pine trees. Big Piney Creek murmured as it cascaded through a gorge. Wolves howled back and forth from the tops of ridges at either end of the valley. Annabelle heard everybody who woke to nature's call, their furtive footfalls echoing like hammer blows in her mind. She listened to everything but what she longed to hear.

Josey never came.

CHAPTER SIXTY

The second wagon train arrived at the fort late in the day. Doc Hines offered to allow Caleb to stay in a hospital tent, but Caleb wanted to get back to the wagons. He would find no peace until he knew about the gold.

The light from the cook fires led Caleb to the camp. The sound of wolves snapping and howling, drawn near the fort by the scent of the butchers' discarded offal, kept him moving. He had overestimated his strength, and the long walk over uneven ground in the gathering darkness exhausted him.

Someone must have brought word of the wagon train's return, and soon familiar faces surrounded Caleb. Langdon Rutledge embraced him like a prodigal son. Willis Daggett pounded him on the back with such enthusiasm the brotherly blows nearly felled him. Blanche Swift tenderly cradled his face in her hands and kissed him. No one but Laurie had ever appeared so delighted to see him.

He stood before them weeping, as much for joy as guilt, realizing even now he couldn't divulge his secret. As they guided him to a seat by a fire, filling his hands with food and drink, Caleb sensed their apprehension. As pleased as they were to see him, the absence of the Colonel and Josey Angel filled them with a dread that muted the joy of his reunion.

"Where's Annabelle?" he asked. Hers was the one face missing from the group.

"She went to the fort," her father said. "She wouldn't wait

once the soldiers brought word that your wagons had been seen."

Caleb was relieved he wouldn't have to explain to Annabelle what had happened. Before he said another word, the settlers peppered him with questions, and he told them about the Indian attack, his narrative disjointed, his ability to explain unable to keep pace with their curiosity. In their befuddlement, they pressed Caleb for more details. *How can I explain to you what I don't even understand myself?*

He wasn't sure he conveyed the desperation of the final fight. The only thing that had saved them from being slaughtered to the last man was the Indians' reluctance to make a concerted charge. While they waited for the men to return with the water, the Colonel had explained it just wasn't in the Indians' nature to sacrifice even a few of their braves to overwhelm and wipe out a foe.

Not all the soldiers believed that. They were a chastened lot by then. They had been full of themselves coming west: the army that had bested Bobby Lee now confronting nothing more than lice-ridden savages, fighting with bows and clubs against rifles and cannon. Their error proved a deadly lesson, and now they had an understanding of the ruthless opponent they faced.

Fearing the worst, a few of the men removed their shoelaces and tied them together, fashioning a loop at one end to go around their foot. They tied a smaller loop at the other end and attached it to the trigger of their rifles. The tortured soldier at Dry Creek was too fresh in their minds. If the corral were overrun, they would stand up with the muzzle of the rifle under their chin. The Indians wouldn't take them alive.

Caleb couldn't tell the settlers these things. Instead, he told them how the Indians melted away into the hills once Jim Bridger and the mounted soldiers from Burroughs's wagon train appeared from the north. His listeners made him go back to the beginning, so he told of the ambush, the desperate run for water. Gaps in his story tested their patience.

"What about Josey? And the Colonel?" Mary Rutledge's face pinched with worry. He told them how the Colonel had been struck down, how Josey Angel left the cover of the wagons, firing his weapons until exhausting his ammunition.

"Then what happened?"

He thought the woman might shake the answer from him. "He fell to his knees. We thought he was praying, at first."

The soldiers had watched helplessly as the pale Indian charged at full gallop toward the kneeling man, expecting to witness Josey's slaughter. Belatedly, a few thought to fire at the rider, but none could hit such a fast-moving target. To Caleb, it looked like Josey Angel was offering himself, whether to God or the Indian brave, it wasn't clear.

Just as his horse came upon Josey Angel, the Indian slid off to the side, reaching out to clasp Josey Angel's outstretched hand with his. The contact lasted for only a moment, but the momentum of the charging rider twisted Josey Angel in a half-circle, so that he was left facing the rider as he retreated toward the ravine, the hand that had touched his foe raised triumphantly as he whooped to mark his victory.

"He was counting coup?" Langdon Rutledge sounded no less amazed than Caleb had been at the time.

"That's what the soldiers figured." No one had been able to explain it, and Josey Angel never spoke about it.

When he returned to the corral, the men parted wordlessly before him, like he had been touched by something more than an Indian. He fell to his knees beside the Colonel, who was unconscious but still breathing. For a moment Josey Angel looked to the skies again, his eyes closed against the day's glare. Then he lowered his head so that it rested against the Colonel's forehead.

As much as Caleb enjoyed the attention, he couldn't tell another part of the story, about a conversation with Josey Angel before they knew help was on the way. It was a story he knew none of the emigrants would believe.

CHAPTER SIXTY-ONE

Josey found a deck of old Union cards in the hospital tent. Instead of spades, clubs, hearts and diamonds, they were adorned with eagles, shields, stars and flags. When the Colonel awoke, Josey sat beside him, idly shuffling. The Colonel's voice was barely more than a whisper. "You hate cards."

Josey continued shuffling. "You want water?"

The Colonel nodded. Josey set aside the cards and helped the old man lean forward and drink from a cup. The Colonel fell back heavily against the pine wood–frame cot, wincing as his head came against the tick suspended on the woven rope netting. Josey dealt, leaving six cards facedown on the Colonel's chest. He moved to show the Colonel the cards.

"I can do it." He tried to sound gruff but didn't have the breath for it as he shifted to a sitting position. Keeping four cards, he put the others facedown on the blanket that covered his legs and Josey did the same. "How are we going to keep score?"

Josey glanced around for paper and pencil but saw none. "I'll keep it in my head."

They both laughed at his joke. "You can't remember what game we're playing, most times."

"I can cheat this way," Josey said. He flipped over the starter card.

Before they finished the first play, the Colonel turned his gaze to the tent opening. It was mid-morning, and the camp throbbed with activity, a rhythm of sound from hammers and saws, shouted commands and responses. With the Indians so active, no one could rest until the fort stood strong.

"Do you want to sleep?"

"I want—" the Colonel smiled "—to not feel tired."

"The doctor says you should feel better soon. He thinks the swelling is gone, which is too bad. A bigger brain might make you smart enough to win this game."

"Smart enough not to kneel before a charging Indian?"

Josey winced. *Doc must have told him.* They had not spoken of the attack, probably never would. Josey still wasn't sure what to make of his encounter with the Indian warrior. He had expected to die. In the moment, thinking the Colonel already dead, the prospect relieved him. Now he wanted only to forget it. He had never failed the Colonel. His guilt squeezed like a chain bound so tight around his chest he struggled to breathe.

The old man reached for Josey's hand and squeezed, his grip surprisingly strong.

"I won't be ready to go with you."

"I'm not going without you."

"Don't be foolish. You have to lead these people to Virginia City. They can't wait for me."

"I can't leave you here. I owe it to you."

"What you owe me is to see this through." There was steel in the Colonel's voice and his eyes were clearer than they had been since his injury. "I gave these people my word. You must keep it for me."

Josey nodded, knowing he wouldn't win the argument. *You got what you wanted. Now you must keep your vow.*

Josey had gone to check on the Colonel the night he'd been wounded. He found Rutledge's teamster seated beside him. Caleb looked like he had lost a quarter of his weight, his thick features turned gaunt, but at least he was alert. Josey motioned to the Colonel.

"Has he woken yet?"

Caleb didn't bother to look at Josey. "He's the same."

The Southerner had never liked him. Josey found some comfort in that disdain now. He dropped beside Caleb. "You feel better?"

"Still drawing breath." Caleb wasn't exactly welcoming, but Josey felt too tired to rise and wanted to be near the Colonel. "The water helped," Caleb said after a spell.

Not that I was any help with that.

"What's that?"

Josey hadn't meant to speak aloud, wasn't sure he had. "I wasn't any help," he said. "With the water."

"You made sure those Indians didn't wind up in the corral. I'd call that a help." For the first time since Josey sat down, Caleb looked at him, glassy-eyed but focused.

"It should have been me who went for the water. Not Wands. The Colonel wouldn't be lying here if I'd gone for the water."

"You're right. It should have been you."

Josey nearly laughed, but it was a bitter sound. "You have a strange way of comforting a man."

"You want comfort, go to one of the women," Caleb said, his voice even. "You wouldn't have run out of bullets. Once your rifle was done, you would have pulled those pistols, I expect." Josey had thought the same thing. "Why didn't you go?"

The answer wasn't clear to Josey. He'd hesitated a moment, just long enough to consider the consequences. A delay no soldier could afford.

"I didn't want to die."

Caleb snorted. "Can't blame a man for that. Dying's not high on my list right now, either. Too much to live for."

Josey nodded. Since the war, he'd been drifting through his days, pausing only when the wind slackened and never for long.

Those were his good days, when the darkness of what he'd seen and done didn't make him wish for a quick end. The thought of taking root somewhere seemed as unlikely as surviving the war once had.

Things were different now. He fell so easily into the daydream of the Montana ranch. As Josey rode, his imagination covered the valley with cattle, a barn and a grand ranch house on a knoll overlooking the stream. He filled the house with comfortable furniture and kitchen things a woman would use. *What a fool I've been.*

He had dreamed of a future he knew he couldn't have. He had been wrong thinking he wouldn't outlive the war, but that didn't mean he could go back to being the man he once imagined he would be. The Greeks called that hubris, and the gods always punished a man for it. The Colonel paid for his hubris, just as Annabelle would pay for it if he didn't stay away from her.

"Do you believe in God?" he asked Caleb.

If the question surprised Caleb, he didn't show it. He shifted his weight from one side to the other. Stroked the whiskers across his jaw. "I don't," he said. "A god would punish the guilty, not the innocent."

"What if living is the punishment?"

"Then you should be thankful your colonel may find his peace. You don't look happy for him."

"Why should I? He doesn't deserve peace any more than I do." Both men laughed.

The Colonel did look at peace. His lips were chapped and ringed white, his face red from the day's sun. That much color was probably a good sign, but Josey wondered how much longer the old man could sleep before it harmed him.

He spoke a vow to himself. Some might have called it a prayer. Josey still believed in God, not with the blind faith of a child but with even greater certainty. That man was made in God's image he had learned to be true, for only God was so fearsome as man at war. There was nothing else in nature like it. A man doesn't ask mercy of such a god. Instead of asking anything, Josey offered himself for the task he knew God had given him.

God had made Josey an instrument of war, and the moment he turned his back on what he was, he put everyone around him in danger. *Didn't I learn that lesson in Kansas? Wasn't her death enough?* Josey wouldn't make that mistake again.

CHAPTER SIXTY-TWO

He left the woman's farmhouse in the morning. After a night with her, leaving was the last thing Josey wanted, but he couldn't betray the Colonel's trust by going AWOL. He promised he would return.

"You don't owe me anything." She wore the flower-patterned white dress from the night before, had somehow found time to freshen herself. In the bright light of morning, the lines around her eyes and mouth were more distinct, but when she smiled she glowed from within. He started to promise something that would make the moment easier, but she stopped him with a finger to his lips.

"Don't say anything you'll regret later."

He didn't understand, not at the time, but before he asked her meaning, she swatted his horse, and it lurched forward. By the time he looked back, she'd disappeared inside.

The hours couldn't pass swiftly enough that day. Josey avoided the Colonel and anybody else who might have asked where he'd been the previous night. He sneaked a sack of flour and a few other provisions from the cook wagons. It wasn't much, but it might help her after the soldiers moved on. He couldn't get away again until evening.

In the gathering dusk, he smelled the smoke before he saw it through the trees. He rode hard.

Flames licked at the roof, and smoke poured from the open door. Josey ran inside. Smoke overcame him within moments.

He couldn't see anything. He fell to his knees, coughing, fighting for air. He crawled to the back of the house, into the bedroom. A leg dangled over the edge of the bed. The white dress had been torn, fully exposing the lifeless body. Her vacant eyes stared toward the door as if at the last she had been looking for his return. He flung her over his shoulder and ran from the room, eyes and lungs burning.

He collapsed outside, his weight falling heavily on her body. For a minute, maybe two, he couldn't breathe. Air came in sips, like breathing through a knotted straw. The tattered dress clung to her back. Once he could breathe and see again, he arranged the material to cover her. He closed her eyes and took her hand in his, wishing to ask forgiveness but not allowing it for himself. The silver band was gone. Josey covered her body with a horse blanket he found in the barn. He mounted and rode to camp. Darkness had fallen by the time he arrived.

The bummers were infantry, their camp separate from the cavalry. Josey left his horse and rifle at his tent. Once among the infantry, he followed the lights of the cook fires. He nearly bumped into one of the bummers as he walked back from the latrine. He was even younger than Josey, a towhead with an overly large nose. Josey recognized him as the man who'd held the squawking chicken.

"Been busy?"

The man's eyes widened. Before he moved, Josey bull-rushed him, pinned him against a tree, his Bowie knife to the boy's neck.

"It wasn't me."

"Be quiet." Josey pushed the knife against his skin, drawing a trickle of blood. "Quietly, tell me what happened."

"It was the sergeant. He killed her."

"You didn't take a turn?"

The boy shook his head, so violently he almost slit his own

throat against Josey's knife.

"Was it the four of you again?"

The man nodded. "But it was the sergeant that did it."

"What did he do?"

"You know . . ." The boy feared speaking it aloud with a knife to his throat. He swallowed hard and winced. "She screamed so much, he started choking her. To make her quiet."

"And then what?"

The boy closed his eyes. When he opened them, he was calmer. "The sergeant told us to fire the place, so no one would know."

"She had a ring. The sergeant take that?"

The boy shrugged. "He must have. No one else was with her."

"Where's the sergeant?"

He looked to his left, in the direction of a fire.

"The others with him?"

He nodded.

"Anyone else with you."

"No. I'll show you," he said. "If you let me go, I won't say anything."

"Like you didn't say anything when he killed her?"

The boy closed his eyes again.

"I—"

Josey drew the knife across his throat with a violent jerk. He didn't care to hear the rest.

The other three were seated around the fire, just as the boy had said. One of the men crouched over the fire, pouring a cup of black. The sergeant already had his. He reclined against a tree, his boots off, legs stretched toward the fire so his toes glowed pink in the light through torn socks. Josey moved straight to him.

"Jesus, Shelton, you were gone long enough to shit a horse."

The sergeant had just enough time to realize his mistake before Josey fell on him and the knife was out and it was done. The other two sat dumbstruck. Josey whirled on them in a bloody frenzy of slashing. Only the last man had time to rouse himself. He reached for a revolver and Josey cut him. They struggled for the knife. The other man outweighed him by a few stone, but the life slowly drained from him. Josey held him down and waited, watching his eyes as fury gave way to fear, then to surrender, then to sorrow, a sinner's final penitence.

Josey rummaged through the sergeant's pockets and found the ring. He rode back to the farmhouse in the dark. The house had burned itself out. The stone fireplace remained, along with a few smoking timbers at the foundation.

After replacing the ring, Josey dug a grave under a tree behind the house. He found some leather strips and a pair of stakes in the barn to construct a cross. Then he kneeled beside her resting place. A day earlier he might have prayed. Instead, he cursed the men who killed her. He cursed himself for not returning sooner. He cursed a god so bloodthirsty the thousands sacrificed in battle couldn't satisfy him. Dawn cast a pink glow across the sky by the time Josey returned to camp. The Colonel waited on the path before the sentry pickets.

"We need to go."

Josey heard the sounds of camp, louder than usual for so early in the day. Amid the usual noise, he heard shouted commands as if the soldiers were readying for battle. "Where are we going?"

"Georgia."

Josey nodded. If the Colonel trusted him enough not to ask why they had to leave, Josey wouldn't ask why they were going to Georgia.

"I'm ready."

CHAPTER SIXTY-THREE

Colonel Henry Carrington looked more like the lawyer and man of letters he'd been before the war than an infantry officer commanding a frontier post. A stooped, thin man with a high forehead and soft dark eyes that looked sad even when he smiled, he found Josey at the Colonel's bedside in the hospital tent. They'd given up on cards.

"I understand from the doctor you are in no condition to travel," Carrington said to the Colonel after exchanging introductions. "While the circumstances are regretful, it would be foolish of me not to make use of what providence has delivered. We have need for scouts with your—" he looked to Josey as he considered his words "—martial skills. The Indians are not so pacified as Washington would believe."

"Yes, we had cause to see," the Colonel said. His hand moved to the back of his head.

Carrington's lack of field experience had been a frequent topic among the men headed to serve under him. The grousing stopped once the Indians attacked. Action was always the best tonic for camp gossip. So it was at Fort Phil Kearny, where Josey found the men were too busy to complain. Maybe Carrington wasn't much of a fighter, but he knew how to put his men to effective use with saw and shovel.

"Do you have plans to attack?" the Colonel asked.

"Not until we're ready. The fort must be completed first," Carrington said. He paced before the Colonel's cot, the movement apparently helping him focus his thoughts. Though not an old man, maybe forty, his deep-set eyes made him appear older. "We still must scout the territory more thoroughly. We have no firsthand knowledge of their numbers or position."

Carrington came to a stop, his gaze shifting between the two men. "That is why I need you." He resumed his pacing. "I know many of my men dismiss them as untrained heathens, but it is a mistake to underestimate the Sioux. Two-thirds of my mounted infantry didn't even know how to ride when we left Nebraska. I don't yet have enough officers to train them. My hope is we'll have time to drill once the fort is completed."

"You should start with target practice," Josey offered. "It's a different matter shooting from the back of a horse than it is standing in a line, especially with those long rifles."

Carrington dropped his head, mumbling something Josey didn't hear.

The Colonel looked to Josey, not sure he believed what he heard. "Did you say you don't have the ammunition?"

"It's true," Carrington said, speaking more softly. "We were promised one hundred thousand rounds at Laramie, but there was nothing for the arms we carried. We don't even have enough to shoot at the wolves that gather around the fort at night. Most of what we have are old Springfields." He looked at Josey. "If I could arm every soldier with a rifle like yours, I would take the fight to the Indians."

"Why don't they get you repeaters or at least breech-loaders?" the Colonel asked. "Carbines would be better for fighting from horseback."

"The war department claims the single-shot rifles cut down on wasted ammunition," Carrington said. His dark-ringed eyes looked even sadder.

The Colonel scoffed. "Sounds like somebody in the war department is getting paid extra by Mr. Springfield."

Carrington brightened. "You see how great my need is. Can I count on you?"

"I'm afraid I won't be much help to you, Colonel Carrington, and Josey will be needed to see these settlers through to Virginia City." He looked to Josey as he said the next part. "We gave them our word."

Carrington responded with a stiff bow of his head. "I respect your decision, but our priorities are not in opposition. Winter is the best time to seek out hostile Indians, when they are encamped for the season." He looked to Josey. "You could complete your mission and return by then. The fort should be done by Christmas. We'll begin our campaign with the new year."

I hope the Indians aren't ready before he is. Josey kept his doubts to himself.

An awkward silence fell over them until Carrington cleared his throat. "I see I have given you much to think about. I won't expect an immediate answer, at least not to this request." He placed his hand on Josey's shoulder. "I have one more thing to ask, and I'm afraid you will not be permitted to refuse."

Josey looked up, not sure what to say.

"My wife has insisted on your presence at dinner tonight." Carrington's beard parted in a smile at his verbal misdirection. "Mrs. Carrington is not a woman to be refused."

Josey stood. "I wouldn't think of it, except—" He looked down to the Colonel.

"Don't use me as an excuse for your antisocial behavior. I'll be asleep by then, and sleep better for not having you standing over me at all hours like some vulture."

"Excellent." Carrington beamed. "Mrs. Carrington will be delighted," he said to Josey before turning to leave. He had stooped to slip outside the tent when he looked back. He nodded and departed the tent without registering Josey's reaction to his farewell.

"I'm sure you will take comfort knowing you won't be dining alone with us. Mrs. Carrington has made sure to invite someone with whom I understand you are well acquainted: Mrs. Annabelle Holcombe."

CHAPTER SIXTY-FOUR

Margaret Carrington managed to fashion a formal dining setting within the fort headquarters, one of the first buildings constructed. A table Josey expected was used for meetings among the officers had been covered with a lacy, white cloth. Artfully arranged candles created a warm glow about the diners.

Even with a clean set of clothes and the loan of a jacket from Colonel Carrington, Josey felt underdressed. The fort commander wore his dress blue uniform, resplendent with brass buttons, gold braid and epaulets, while Mrs. Carrington had on a gown of blue that set off her eyes.

Annabelle was there when Josey arrived, wearing a gauzy, cream-colored dress he had never seen, her hair done up so elaborately he wondered how long she and Mrs. Carrington had been plotting this evening. Seeing Annabelle, Josey almost forgot his whereabouts. Her eyes found his from across the room even as Colonel Carrington formally introduced his wife. A flush came over Josey, his breath irregular. He couldn't look at Annabelle without remembering how it felt to hold her, without thinking that he would never have that pleasure again. The eye contact lasted only a moment. He couldn't hold her gaze, feeling like a coward as he looked away.

"I remember when you used to look at me that way, Henry."

"I hope I still do," Colonel Carrington answered his wife. He took her hand in his and bestowed a kiss.

Annabelle came to Josey, her eyes pinning him to the spot until she stood before him and waited to be kissed on the cheek. A coolness seeped from her, like a breeze off the mountains. Her dark eyes looked past him as she spoke. "I'm overjoyed to finally see that you are whole."

He had put off seeing her too long. He had known that, even as he continued to avoid her. A thousand times he thought of what he might say, but it never sounded right. He might tell Annabelle about the war. The hundred different ways he knew a man could look in the moment he dies. Bodies stiff and stacked like cordwood waiting for an unmarked burial. By torturing her with his memories, she might forgive his silences. *No. It's all a lie.* He wasn't afraid to tell her these things. What *he* feared were the questions that would follow.

How did you feel?

He could never tell her about the days he fired his rifle so many times he wore a glove to keep his hand from burning. He could never tell her about the boys and grandfathers at the Georgia farm who kept coming and coming. About how easy it was to lose himself in the routine of aiming, firing, reloading, so that it became a mechanical thing. About the pride he felt in being better at it than any man. *Ah, there's the thing.* The crispy black ash in his chest where his heart had been.

Josey remembered watching his father, so precise in how he displayed the goods in his store, following up behind Josey to sweep the floors a final time before leaving for the night because everything had to be just so.

"A man should take pride in his work," he had told Josey.

His father had been fortunate to find work that suited his skills. He hid his disappointment that Josey hadn't found his life's calling in the store. Josey found it on bloody fields in Kansas and Georgia. It wasn't that he enjoyed killing. Men who enjoyed it frightened him. No, Josey found pride in being good at something, at being better than anyone else. He enjoyed the way the Colonel depended on him. He had enjoyed the way other men looked at him and talked of him, at first anyway.

Was he wrong to find pride in being the best at his task? Was it any different than a base ball player who clubs the ball farther than anyone else? Was he a lesser man than a fiddler who makes his instrument sing a heavenly tune? *Of course, I am.* The shame and nightmares were proof enough, and no penance was great enough to forgive what he had become. He could never tell Annabelle any of this, and he saw now he could never be with her without telling her.

Mrs. Carrington displayed as much patience for a lull in the conversation as she would for a hair in the soup. Josey struggled to follow the small talk. He saw the women's lips move without hearing all the words. By closing his eyes, he followed a snippet before he felt obliged to look at his hostess, her words lost again in the dissonance.

He remembered every word of a favorite poem, every detail of long-ago battles, but he forgot Mrs. Carrington's first name or the names of her boys, even after she completed an amusing story about them. When Annabelle and Colonel Carrington laughed, Josey laughed, too, though he didn't know why.

Annabelle watched him, but she looked away when he noticed. She called him "Mr. Anglewicz," emphasizing her correct pronunciation. Another time, a look passed between Annabelle and Mrs. Carrington, but Josey wasn't sure of its meaning. He fought the urge to retreat from the room.

A gentle pressure on his arm brought him back. Mrs. Carrington looked to him expectantly. *How long have I been out?* Josey hardly knew how they came to be at the table, vaguely recalling two privates in clean uniforms serving a bubbly wine the ladies called Madame something. Over a soup made with canned lobster, Colonel Carrington spoke of Wyoming being a likely name for the new territory. Mrs. Carrington disagreed, but Josey hadn't followed why. He nodded dumbly.

"Exactly," she said. " 'Wyoming' might do very well for a county in—" she paused as she thought about it "—Pennsylvania. But it has no claim for application to the stolen land of the Crows."

"Surely, dear, the land is too big to be a part of Montana or Dakota."

She nodded between spoonfuls of soup. "It should be called 'Absaraka.' That means 'Home of the Crows' in their language," she added, seeing Josey's confusion. "The Crows deserve better treatment. They maintain the proud claim never to have killed a white man but in self-defense."

"They are also quite proud of their skills at horse-stealing," Colonel Carrington added, chuckling at his quip. The Carringtons continued like that, their verbal play a well-practiced dance that dizzied Josey.

The privates brought fresh elk steaks, salmon garnished with tomatoes, sweet corn and peas. More than once Josey sensed Annabelle watching him, but he no longer looked at her. He tried to follow the Carringtons as they went on about the Indian wars.

When the conversation turned to the events at Crazy Woman Creek, Josey grew warm. Carrington praised him, sharing with the women details of the battle drawn from his officers' reports and then hailing Josey's modesty after he declined to embellish the account. It wasn't modesty that held Josey silent so much as good manners in not wishing to contradict the fort commander with the truth of his cowardice.

Josey relaxed when an opportunity to change the subject came as one of the privates served a chokecherry pie. Soon, the women were joking about the army's lack of creativity in having two fort Kearnys on the western frontier, forcing Colonel

Carrington to explain that the Nebraska fort took its name from the Mexican War General Stephen Kearny, while their fort was named for his nephew, the one-armed hero of the Battle of Chantilly, "Fighting Phil" Kearny.

Looking at his plate, Josey saw the pie gone. He hadn't remembered eating it. Then everyone looked at him, an expression of curiosity on Mrs. Carrington's face, on Annabelle's one of rising anger.

"I'm sorry—"

Carrington rescued him. "Well, of course I told the boy he would have to see the wagons to Virginia City first."

Annabelle's mouth had fallen open, a question left to Mrs. Carrington to pose. "And then you intend to return?"

Josey watched Annabelle closely. "I haven't decided."

Carrington sensed his discomfort. "As I said, he must see to his responsibilities first." He cleared his throat. "How far is it from here to Virginia City?"

"We should be in Virginia City in another few weeks," Josey said, still watching Annabelle.

The privates cleared the plates, the dinner concluded, but Annabelle remained seated. She met Josey's gaze. "And you think then your responsibilities will be completed?"

CHAPTER SIXTY-FIVE

Early the following morning, Annabelle found her way to the hospital tent. The Colonel's eyes were closed. Annabelle pulled the empty cot next to his closer and sat on the edge. His weathered left hand rested on his chest, the skin speckled with brown spots and loose like an ill-fitting glove over the bones. She told herself the wounds made him look so wan, but she couldn't look at him in repose without being reminded of a corpse in a coffin.

"Are you an angel?"

A hint of mischief in the Colonel's eyes informed Annabelle he wasn't hallucinating. "I came to fetch you. We are leaving soon."

Too weak to move his head, the Colonel cast his eyes about his surroundings. "I fear it is my fate to remain here."

"That is not acceptable." She spoke in clipped tones to ward against the tremble in her voice. "You were paid to see my family to Virginia City."

"Josey will look after you."

"And who—" She used one of Margaret Carrington's handkerchiefs to cover her mouth, as if it were a cough that stopped her. "Who will look after Josey?"

"That task is yours now, child."

The Colonel hadn't moved, but his image blurred in Annabelle's eyes. She looked away, blinking hard to clear them. "He doesn't want me."

That had become clear enough the previous night. She had believed Josey when he said he didn't care that she was barren. She should have known better than to believe anything a man says in bed. Now he revealed his true feelings. Josey hardly looked at her.

After dinner, Josey had offered to escort her to the wagons. Margaret Carrington spared him that, having arranged for Annabelle to stay overnight in the fort. Margaret's words echoed in her head now.

"It's clear to any woman with eyes that boy still loves you," she said after Josey made his hasty retreat.

"Lustful looks aren't love."

"It wasn't lust I saw, not only lust, at least." Margaret smiled at her jest, but Annabelle was unmoved. Embracing Annabelle, she patted her head, a sister's comfort. "Battle does things to a man's mind. I've been lucky my Henry has never faced these demons, but I've seen it in other men. You must be patient with him."

Annabelle nodded, but she wasn't as confident as her friend. *I can't let him hurt me like this. I can't let* anyone *hurt me again like this.*

Now Annabelle felt the Colonel's hand over hers. Somehow he had found the strength to sit up, his hand clasping hers so tightly she winced.

"You must promise me you will look after him." Still not trusting her voice, she nodded, just to appease an ill man, and he fell back. They sat there, looking at each other, both trying to steady their breath. "I've never seen him more alive than when he is with you."

"Sometimes he can't even talk to me." The Colonel grew blurry in her eyes again. "He won't let me help him."

"You already do." The Colonel closed his eyes.

"Maybe I should go." Annabelle started to rise, but he

motioned for her to stay.

"A year ago I wasn't sure he would live this long," he said, his eyes still closed. "He drank then. Couldn't keep the bottle away from him. He would get into brawls. He's not a large man, but he fights like a demon when he's drunk or angry. We had to leave the states, head into the territories."

"I guess he prefers to be alone."

The Colonel's eyes snapped open. "Not at first, he didn't. At least in the bars, when he got stirred up, he had someone to hurt other than himself. Alone with me and Byron, he couldn't be rid of his dreams. Then I think he came up with a way."

The Colonel looked past her, his eyes moist in the growing light. "I took his guns from him. I don't know what scared me more, taking them or seeing that he would let me."

Annabelle remembered how Josey rode at the road agents. "Do you think he wants to be killed?"

"A man so filled with shame and guilt doesn't think he's worthy of living, much less being loved. You are Josey's angel." He reached toward Annabelle and she gave him her hand. His voice was hoarse. "You need to go. The wagons will be ready soon."

She kissed his sandpapery cheek, wondering if she would see him again. She wanted to thank him, thought to say farewell, but she feared choking on the words. As she rose and turned from the Colonel's cot, Annabelle recalled something else Margaret Carrington said, a notion with which she believed the Colonel would concur.

"You have a few weeks together until you reach Virginia City," Margaret had told her. "Let nature be your ally."

CHAPTER SIXTY-SIX

Little more than a week after leaving Fort Phil Kearny, the wagons came upon Fort C.E. Smith, the last of the three forts under Colonel Carrington's command. The soldiers had arrived only a few days earlier, so Fort Smith was little more than a camp of tents guarding the pass across the Bighorn River.

Annabelle didn't sense the same urgency in the construction of this fort that she'd seen at Phil Kearny. That didn't stop the men in the wagon train from carrying their guns in readiness. With the group on its own again, everyone felt the strain of vigilance. In their minds, sharp bluffs became watchtowers. Thick forests shielded Indian ambushes.

As they approached Montana Territory, they crossed cool, clear streams fed by snowmelt from the mountains. Caleb Williams and Willis Daggett caught enough trout to feed the entire camp one night. Signs of wild game became increasingly abundant, too. Every night they heard wolves howling, their number too great to count. Once Lord Byron pointed out grizzly bear tracks, Annabelle hoping she never saw up close the animal that left signs so big.

Then she saw her first buffalo. At a distance, they looked like great shaggy bulls. Some of the men wanted to ride after them, but Lord Byron convinced them they didn't have the horses to give chase. Josey shot one while scouting, but the carcass proved too big to bring to camp. He skinned it and cut away enough meat to feed the entire camp. The beef tasted lighter and sweeter than a cow. Josey gave the skin to Annabelle's mother, who intended to make a blanket for winter.

Even the stock seemed rejuvenated by the landscape, drinking their fill and growing fat on the abundant grass. Flocks of little brown birds Byron called buffalo birds alighted onto the backs of horses and oxen, picking off the flies and gnats that bothered them. The birds were so tame Annabelle's cousin Mark captured one with his hands, though her aunt Blanche convinced him to set free the terrified creature.

"This is God's country," Lord Byron told Annabelle one day as she rode beside his wagon. It was an unusual burst of loquaciousness for the big man, and she couldn't contradict him.

She'd felt awkward around Lord Byron at the journey's start, resisting the urge to tell him how well her family's slaves were treated. What little she knew from the Colonel and Josey of his past as a field hand in Georgia bore no resemblance to the experiences of household slaves in Charleston.

Now Annabelle drew comfort from his solid presence. Lord Byron had never looked at her with hostility, though she shuddered to see the scars around his wrists as he drove the oxen, grateful the long sleeves on his cotton shirt concealed more evidence of his tortured past. She wondered if she would ever overcome her shame to ask him about that life.

The wagons came together at a distance from Fort Smith to find good grass. The Bighorn River was nearly as wide as the Platte and too deep to cross safely without a ferry. Another wagon train camped ahead of theirs, waiting its turn, and it wasn't until the following day that Josey secured their passage. The ferry was just a roughly built, flat boat. The fort sutler charged five dollars for each wagon. As fast as the current moved, no one risked crossing on their own to save the money.

When her turn came, Annabelle stood beside the wagon with

Paint, keeping the horse calm while off-duty soldiers rowed them across. Most of the other wagons had already crossed, and another wagon train moved into position to be next.

Shielding her eyes from the morning glare, Annabelle watched a large number of riders arrive with the wagons. One of the riders dismounted and stood at the river's edge. He was a tall man and well dressed for a traveler. He strode off before she saw much more, but something in the way he moved sent a shiver along her spine, as if she'd been splashed with cold river water.

She eased to the boat's edge, seeking another glimpse of the man, but his face was lost to her amid all the other horsemen. Annabelle crossed her arms. The morning chill had melted away under the rising sun, but a coldness spread through her that she hadn't experienced for years.

CHAPTER SIXTY-SEVEN

After a restless night, Annabelle found Caleb Williams greasing wagon wheels. Twice the previous day she'd approached him, only to stop herself, convinced he would believe her mad once she gave voice to the suspicion that took root as they crossed the river.

When both a planting season and harvest passed without a letter from her husband, Annabelle began hearing whispers from those who feared for her well-being. She believed herself free of her husband only after Caleb returned to Charleston and confirmed that he'd been with Richard when a Union patrol shot and killed him.

All night she'd tried to think of a reason why Caleb would have deceived her. Finding none, she worked on convincing herself that she'd been mistaken in what she saw. The sun's glare off the water was in her eyes. . . . The distance was too great to be certain. . . . So much time had passed she couldn't know what her husband would look like now. All were true, yet all had the ring of a lie told to ease the mind.

Caleb seemed surprised but not displeased at her greeting. Removing his hat, his hair flat and sweaty against his head, he began an awkward reply that she interrupted.

"I saw Richard."

The doubts Annabelle harbored about her sanity disappeared in the shadow that crossed Caleb's face. He began to stammer but she interrupted again. "Don't lie to me. I'm not mad. I saw him at the Bighorn crossing. He was with some other riders."

Caleb's eyes grew wide. He looked about, as if worried someone might overhear, and guided her away. Annabelle nimbly stepped out of reach of his greasy paws.

"Keep your voice down," he urged in a harsh whisper. He led her among the trees growing close to the road where they wouldn't be seen. "How many riders did he have with him?"

"So you knew." Caleb looked away from her. "Don't lie to me. Not again."

His thick shoulders sagged and he fell to the ground, his back against the trunk of a pine tree, looking to the sky through the canopy of spindly branches. "I didn't lie. I told you what I thought was true."

"You told me you saw him die."

"I heard the shots. I believed him dead. The rest—" He looked at her, more sad than angry. "I told you what I thought you wanted to hear."

Annabelle didn't argue the point. She fell in beside him. "How long have you known?"

"The road agents. I recognized some of the dead. I knew Richard must be with them."

"Why would he attack us?"

Caleb allowed a sad smile to crease his face. "That's what he had us doing, during the war. We wore uniforms, at least at first, but before long we were nothing more than bushwhackers. We were supposed to be hunting Union patrols, runaway slaves, deserters. He just took what he wanted. We didn't need much convincing. We called him Captain Bastard behind his back, but there were no heroes among us."

It hurt to hear his words, but Annabelle didn't doubt them. She could imagine Richard as the leader of partisan raiders more easily than as a war hero. *Captain Bastard, indeed.* No wonder he chose not to write to her about his duty. Perhaps he had never intended to come home. "But why attack us?"

Caleb shrugged. "You're a beautiful woman. Maybe once he made his way home and found you gone, he decided to follow." Annabelle would have laughed at the suggestion if her stomach weren't roiling. Richard hadn't wanted her before the war. Following her now made no sense. "Maybe you hurt his pride by leaving," Caleb offered. "Maybe he wants to punish you."

That made more sense. Still, parts of this news Annabelle couldn't follow. She believed Caleb when he said Richard had been shot. Maybe Richard's wounds prevented him from coming home, or maybe the men he'd been running with wouldn't allow him. She recalled the men in Omaha who'd shown up again with the road agents. *Had Richard been following her that long?* "If he wanted me, why not come after me in Omaha?"

"If he caught us on the trail, he could take everything we had—and leave no witnesses."

The goods they carried held value but hardly enough to justify such risk. Annabelle wouldn't believe love had moved Richard to follow her, but other emotions motivated a man almost as powerfully. *Did he want to hurt me that badly?* She shuddered to think what would have become of them if the road agents had overrun their camp. Richard had been forced to modify his plans, perhaps bide his time for another opportunity.

"I suppose he didn't count on Josey."

After crossing into Montana, the wagons came to another stretch of barren, rough country, abounding in sagebrush, chaparral and prickly pears. The August heat punished the emigrants, and they saw fewer trees and little shade. Water grew scarcer and often tasted of alkali.

The train's pace slowed as they encountered rough hills and narrow ridges just wide enough for a wagon. Some sloped so steeply the drivers needed ropes to pull up and ease down the wagons. Near the east fork of a creek, Caleb saw rock outcrops that stretched for miles, as if a vast river of burning lava had once passed over the country.

The mosquitoes swarmed in thick, black masses. At night, the emigrants built smudges in hopes of driving them away, but the smoke provided little relief. After traveling in such close quarters for nearly three months, everyone's temper grew foul. Weary of the journey, they enjoyed no more nights of music or storytelling.

Since speaking with Annabelle about Richard, Caleb didn't mind the slow pace. Like a child who pushes a broken plate under a table in hopes it won't be discovered, he had put Richard from his mind. Caleb had promised to retrieve the gold and bring it to the bastard without the emigrants' knowledge, but Richard and Harrison had taken their desire for *verisimilitude*— the word still sounded like a song in Caleb's head—too far.

They had nearly killed Caleb. Riding under the protection of so many soldiers, Caleb had almost convinced himself the road agents had turned back once the threat of Indians became real. Annabelle's account made it sound like the riders had found safety by joining a sizeable wagon train. Caleb should have known. Richard Holcombe would never relent so long as he drew breath and Caleb had the gold.

Turning Annabelle's suspicions back on herself had been a clever move. Just like the vanity of a beautiful woman to believe a man would follow her more than two thousand miles, either for love or for hate.

Something she said brought to mind a plan Caleb had been turning over since his beating. Richard wouldn't stop so long as he lived, and Caleb had no intention of taking on the bastard himself. There was no need to so long as Caleb rode with a man as deadly as Josey Angel. If Caleb wanted to live *and* keep the gold, all he had to do was ensure one man's path crossed with the other. *It shouldn't be hard to arrange that.* He simply needed to exploit the one thing the two men had in common.

CHAPTER SIXTY-EIGHT

After leaving the badlands and making the turn west, the emigrants found the Rocky Mountains growing larger on the horizon. Seeing their destination—or at least some marker of it—brightened the mood among the company, though Annabelle worried the end of their journey couldn't come fast enough for Josey.

She hadn't exchanged more than a few words with him since leaving Fort Phil Kearny, and he looked worn down, staying so busy he borrowed her Paint to spell his own horse some days. No one spelled Josey. Annabelle's anger had turned into a hurt she knew would only become permanent once they arrived in Virginia City and he rode off to rejoin the Colonel.

After learning Richard still lived, she nearly went to Josey. If Richard meant them harm, Annabelle had to tell the others. But she hadn't seen Richard with the road agents. It was only Caleb's guess that Richard had been with them. And those men had made no move against the wagons after their failed attack on the prairie. In the absence of a certain threat, the idea of confronting Josey with news of her husband seemed like a desperate plea for attention—and the last sure way to drive him off forever.

As August drew to an end, the wagons crossed innumerable streams and climbed even more hills as they followed the Yellowstone River. It was hard work for everyone. Even the older women and children walked beside the wagons when the hills grew too steep. Parts of the trail were so stony the men needed pickaxes to clear the way for wagons.

With the threat of hostile Indians behind them, the miners chose to risk a brisker pace, and their train dwindled to almost half its number. Henry Miller, nearly recovered from his wounds, led the group in settling with Josey and Lord Byron for their remaining share of the scouts' services. For all his bluster and complaining, Miller seemed reluctant to part, needing Josey's assurances that it would create no bad feelings. Miller lingered a moment while the others started off, looking at Josey as if he had something more to say, then abruptly embracing the scout like a long-absent brother. Josey seemed as surprised at the gesture as Annabelle.

The train crossed the Yellowstone at a ferry operated by John Bozeman, one of the men who first blazed their trail. Bozeman lived in a small cabin on the side of the river. Annabelle imagined him as some larger-than-life figure, another Jedediah Smith or Kit Carson. She was to be disappointed.

Bozeman was a blond, apple-cheeked man who even while laboring wore a suit coat now that he was a businessman. Though Southern-born, he had forgotten the manners of his homeland and spoke with the oily glibness of a confidence man. He wanted ten dollars for every wagon and an additional fifty cents for each extra horse or cow that crossed on his ferry.

The impatient miners paid the fee and forged ahead. Josey rode along the river, determined to scout another crossing point. Only once he returned and started leading the wagons away did Bozeman bring his price down to five dollars. Josey agreed but had no kind words for the man he said was out to fleece the tenderfeet who followed a route so dangerous Bozeman had given up leading wagon trains himself.

It was late in the afternoon by the time they crossed. The ferry was a large boat with a rope strung over the river and connected to a series of pulleys. Annabelle made sure to be among the first to cross this time. Looking back, she feared she might see the same riders again, but no one came. On the opposite side of the river she found a tree where the bark had been peeled off. The names and dates of trains and individuals who had passed were written in pencil.

"Are you going to add your name?" Caleb Williams asked. She had come across with his wagon to be first on the other side.

"I don't think so."

"We're not being followed, if that's what concerns you. Not anymore."

In no mood for false comforts Annabelle asked, "How would you know that?"

Caleb seemed edgy. He looked about as if to make sure they wouldn't be overheard, his weight shifting from one foot to the other. "Not here." He stepped back from the river, bidding her to follow.

"No one is going to hear us. They're all on the other side."

The bank rose sharply at the crossing, and Annabelle struggled to follow him uphill even in her riding pants. Caleb didn't wait, moving off into the thick forest redolent of pine. He was out of sight by the time she crested the riverbank.

"Caleb? Where are you?" Seeing a deer track into the trees, she followed after him through the thick brush, growing annoyed with the man. About twenty paces into the trees, she prepared to turn back, when she saw a man.

It wasn't Caleb.

CHAPTER SIXTY-NINE

Annabelle was alone in an old army tent, large enough for two cots, though only one sat in the middle of the dirt floor. Annabelle pondered slitting the canvas on the backside of the tent and sneaking away into the night. First, she would need a knife. Next, she would need to cut the rope that bound her hands behind her back.

She no longer felt her fingers. Her shoulders throbbed from her arms being stretched behind her for so long. More angry than scared, she chided her foolishness at following Caleb, never suspecting he would betray her. Harrison had been waiting in the woods, wearing the same grin she'd seen when he challenged Josey in Omaha and negotiated with the Colonel before the road agents attacked.

"Mrs. Holcombe," he said in greeting, the name sounding like a slur from his mouth. The man couldn't smile without appearing to leer. Annabelle looked about for an escape or an ally.

"Don't make me draw my weapon," he said. "I know you can ride. I have a horse all ready for you. There's someone who would like to see you."

With a sweeping gesture, he directed her farther down the path to a glade where three horses waited. Caleb was already mounted on one. He wouldn't look at her. Harrison moved to help Annabelle mount, but she swatted his hand, stepping into the stirrup and hopping up easily. For a moment she considered making a dash, but the man held her horse's harness tight.

"He insists on your attendance."

Annabelle realized with a sinking feeling it was unnecessary for Harrison to identify her host.

As they rode, she tried to memorize every detail of the landscape so she could find her way back, but the more she concentrated, the more difficult it became to recall anything. All the pines looked alike. The hills they climbed and descended were nearly indistinguishable one from another. Questions swirling in her mind muddled her focus. *What did Richard want? Would he try to claim a stake of her family's new business? What was there to claim?* Annabelle didn't fear for her well-being. If Richard wanted her dead, this gunman would have killed her already.

She lost track of time, but they couldn't have ridden far because it was still light when they reached a campsite at the bottom of a ravine. Harrison prodded her toward the fire where a circle of about eight men sat. She recognized the big man in the Confederate coat who had been with Harrison in Omaha. A mulatto boy, maybe twelve, sat near the center, his eyes red in the reflected firelight. It was the tall man beside him who commanded her attention.

"Ah, Annie."

He came to her, looking cleaner and more handsome than any man had a right to on the trail, and planted a chaste kiss on her cheek. He stood back and smiled broadly, his thin mustache flattening to a dark smudge. "So glad you could join us."

Her reunion with Richard was blessedly short, though it left Annabelle as confused as ever. Without so much as a question or explanation, Richard ordered her tied up and hustled off. He seemed more interested in Caleb, and it had grown dark while she waited alone in the tent for someone to explain what was happening.

A sound alerted her to someone's approach. Harrison appeared at the tent's opening, pushing a trussed up man before him. He had been beaten so savagely, she almost didn't recognize Caleb. He collapsed beside the cot at the slightest nudge from Harrison, who left without a word to her.

"Caleb." Annabelle thought at first he might be dead, for he hadn't moved even after falling face-first into the dirt. "Can you hear me?"

With her hands bound, she managed to get into a kneeling position beside him. She leaned forward, putting her head against his back, reassured to feel the slight rise as he drew breath. He groaned and shifted beneath her, getting his mouth out of the dirt, his face swollen and red.

"Can you sit up? If you untie me, I might be able to get your binds undone."

He looked at her, but it seemed his eyes couldn't focus. "It won't do any good. We won't get away."

"We have to try." Annabelle pivoted her back to his. Her shoulders burned with the effort, but she scooted closer to Caleb, using her legs for leverage. When she judged herself near enough, she looked back to him.

"Now, see if you can get your hands on my ropes." He didn't move. "Caleb?" He breathed strangely. At great pain, she looked over her shoulder and saw him crying.

"I'm so sorry. I should have told you about the gold."

Gold? "None of that matters now." She shushed him, like cooing to a child, afraid his sobs would draw the attention of someone outside the tent. "All that matters is getting away."

She felt him moving behind her, breathing loudly through his nose, blowing out phlegm. He cleared his throat. His voice sounded stronger. "I'm going to get us out of this. It was my fault, but I'll fix this."

Annabelle wasn't confident, but his hands tugged against her ropes. If they got the ropes off, what then? *It's merely a tent.* Even without a knife, there had to be a way to get out from under the backside. Caleb worked at the ropes, but they weren't growing any looser. Her hands had so little feeling, she wasn't sure if she felt his touch or only his efforts moving her arms. She wondered how much longer they would be left alone.

"Hurry!"

"I'm trying." His efforts were accompanied with much grunting and uneven breathing. "I can't get my fingers loose enough to grab hold of the rope."

"Do your best," she said, not wanting to discourage him. "But hurry."

Josey will come for me. Despite everything between them, she knew that much, but she was just as sure Josey would be walking into an ambush. *Was that their purpose?* Harrison had seemed eager to challenge Josey in Omaha. *What did Richard have to do with that?* None of it made any sense to Annabelle. Caleb had talked about gold, just as the road agents had before the attack, but that didn't make sense, either. The gold was in Montana.

Annabelle choked back her curiosity, not wanting to distract Caleb. Escape was their best hope. Annabelle felt slackness in the ropes, a tingling sensation in her fingers, like pricks of ice or fire. "I think you're getting it, Caleb."

Then, another voice, only too familiar.

"Damn. I had hoped to interrupt as you were making your escape. Annie, you never cease to disappoint me."

CHAPTER SEVENTY

Annabelle and Caleb froze at the sound of Richard's voice. He hunched his shoulders and bowed his head to stand in the tent. The boy beside him didn't.

"Lucifer, check her binds." Putting his boot to Caleb's shoulder, Richard pushed so Caleb landed heavily on his back. He crouched before Annabelle while the boy pulled tight the knots. "I thought by now you would be much further along than this." There was a light in his eyes she rarely recalled seeing when they were together. "You're not very good at this game."

"I don't understand your game."

"You've never understood much, have you?" He popped up and moved past her to Caleb. The knots were even tighter when the boy finished and went to stand by his master, his dark face impassive to her pain.

"I don't think I want to understand."

This amused Richard. "That's probably for the best. What you don't know can't hurt you, right? Except you didn't know what a bad boy Caleb had been, and I'm afraid that's going to hurt you."

"Let her go, Captain. She had nothing to do—" The rest of whatever Caleb intended to say was cut off when Richard put his boot to his throat. The sound of the man's choking put a taste of bile in Annabelle's throat.

"It's too late to play hero, Caleb." With a final kick, Richard stepped back and allowed the man to breathe. "Caleb wasn't exactly a reluctant participant in this scheme, were you, Caleb?"

His breath coming in choking gasps, Caleb couldn't speak.

"I won't say it was Caleb's idea. Caleb has never been what you would call a man of ideas. But he was plenty ready to quit the army and ride off a rich man."

Watching Richard was like seeing another man dressed in her husband's clothes. He spoke with her husband's voice, resembled him in feature and manner, but it was a different man. *He can't be the man I married.* Annabelle wanted to believe that, but as she studied him, she recalled the times his mask slipped. A sharp edge of temper. A cruel glint in his eye. A cutting remark with no remorse. All of them dismissed as aberrations, waved away to the stress of life. In truth, they had been glimpses into a black soul she refused to concede belonged to the man she'd wed.

"I don't understand, Richard."

He turned from Caleb to look on Annabelle. "He really hasn't told you about the gold? I guess that's one time he wasn't lying." Richard kicked Caleb again for emphasis. "He was supposed to bring the gold, but Caleb tried to be clever." Another kick. Caleb had stopped reacting, and Annabelle wondered if he were unconscious or dead. "How do you forget to bring that much gold?"

The newspapers had been filled with stories of lost Confederate gold, as if some mishap of accounting had been responsible for Southern defeat. Annabelle had never believed any of the tales—until now. "You took gold from the army?"

His voice turned vicious. "The gold was for guns. The army was already beaten."

The extent of her husband's betrayal was horrible to contemplate, and Annabelle let her bitterness show. "You don't know that."

"I was there!" he screamed. She braced for a strike, but it never came. He leaned down, their faces only inches apart, a white-hot fury in his eyes. "The guns wouldn't have made a difference. We lost the war when England decided to remain neutral. Oh, but there were plenty of Englishmen who were willing to *sell* guns to us, if you sneaked enough gold into Mexico to buy them. What good would that have done? Another year of killing? We had seen enough of that."

Caleb roused himself. "I just did what you wanted."

"Yes, and after we had it, you were awfully quick to agree to steal it from the others, and even quicker to betray me."

"I thought you were dead."

"I would have been, if I hadn't convinced them I was trying to stop you." Richard looked to Annabelle. "I've always had a gift for convincing people of what I want them to believe, wouldn't you say, Annie?" Annabelle looked away.

"I can get you the gold," Caleb said. "Just let her go."

Richard kicked him again. "I was supposed to already have it."

Caleb's breath came in uneasy gasps. "I told you. They will trade the gold. For us."

Another kick. Annabelle winced at the sound. "You think anyone would hand over even a pinch of dust for you?" Richard kneeled beside Annabelle. With the back of his hand, he stroked her cheek as a lover might. She shuddered, but her reaction only seemed to excite him. "My dear Annie is now the key. I had planned on you being my insurance that no one would follow us. Your parents will give up the gold for your pretty little ass, I should think." He reached down and pinched her hard.

Annabelle hid her pain. "And then you'll let us go?"

Richard's smile was cold. "Yes, then I will let you go," he said in a voice one would use with a small child. He'd always been able to make her feel stupid in a way no one else could. She had given up trying to understand why. Yet even after seeing his savagery unmasked, a part of her hoped to appeal to him.

"Don't do this, Richard. You loved me once."

He laughed. "Don't be such a child, Annie." He grabbed her jaw roughly in his hands. "And don't look so hurt. Most men don't love their wives. Everything had to be so perfect in your world, didn't it? *You* had to be so perfect. Well, you aren't perfect, are you?"

He placed his hand heavily against her abdomen, and Annabelle struggled to keep tears from flowing. She wouldn't give him that satisfaction. She didn't know what to say. After the miscarriage, she had blamed herself for his inattention. Now it was clear to her: Her husband had probably put no more thought into their nuptials than he would in bargaining for a horse.

She had been too young to see it at the time. In her naiveté she thought he must love her if he married her. Later, a part of her had come to believe all the books and poetry and women's gossip about love were lies told to little girls so they would grow up obedient to their fathers and husbands, hoping vainly that they would be rewarded with the myth of love. Even with the lesson learned, she'd been quick to forget it with Josey. He could be so cold, no more capable of love than a wolf or other wild beast. And yet, when she was alone with Josey, there were moments of sweetness and gentleness that she had never seen with Richard.

Richard watched her. "I suppose you believe the soldier boy loves you."

"I don't know."

"Oh, come now." He prodded her with a finger, nearly pushing her onto her back. "I saw you riding together. A husband can tell when another man has eyes for his wife. Has he had you yet?" His hand fell to her leg, his forefinger tracing the curve of her thigh. The fabric of Annabelle's riding pants suddenly felt too thin. "Do you believe his love will last once his passion has been satisfied?"

Annabelle grew dizzy. Richard smiled at her, and she was more frightened than before. "I suppose there's only one way to find out. But now that you know I am alive, I wonder: Would you be a bigamist? Would you bring God's scorn upon the man you love?"

Still fighting off tears, Annabelle stoked her anger, hoping it would ward off despair. "Why do you care?"

"It amuses me to think of it. And amusements are so hard to come by here." He smiled at the boy, still standing impassively at the tent flap. The boy didn't look anything like Richard, even accounting for the difference in skin color, yet Annabelle wondered if he was the son she'd been unable to give Richard.

"I suppose the point will soon be moot. Harrison's had his eye on you since Omaha. The man's besotted. I suppose he's weary of squaws and whores, though I tried to explain that one hole's as good as another. He'll understand once he's had you, I suppose."

Annabelle cringed at the thought.

"Now, now, dear. I'm not going to just *give* you to him. He's going to have to *earn* that sweet meat." He squeezed her thigh. "I told him he could have you only after he killed soldier boy. He's been aching to do that almost as much as—" Richard's hand moved roughly over her body, forcing her legs apart even as she squirmed from him "—well, you can imagine. If he's smart, soldier boy will never see him coming. So you see, my sweet, you've got no cause to worry about bigamy, unless you decide to marry Harrison."

He looked away, as if in deep thought. "Something tells me that after Harrison's through with you, that won't be an option."

Richard rose and turned. Caleb was on his feet, too, having somehow managed to work free from his ropes while Richard talked. With hands clenched together like a club, he struck Richard across the back of the neck, sending him sprawling to the ground.

Caleb stepped forward, his boot drawn back to kick Richard when the boy sprang out from his post by the tent flaps. Annabelle saw a flash of silver in the lamplight. Caleb, off-balance, tumbled back against the tent post with the boy on him. He landed hard with a grunt as a whoosh of air escaped his lungs. The boy stood, and Richard rose to join him, petting him on the head. Annabelle had to crane her neck to see Caleb, the wide handle of a Bowie knife lodged in his gut.

Richard leaned over Caleb, his voice almost tender as he reached for the knife. "You won't be needing this," he said. With a sharp twist of his wrist he pulled the knife free.

CHAPTER SEVENTY-ONE

Annabelle knew she would soon be alone. She sat with Caleb's head in her lap, stroking his hair, more for her own comfort than his at this point. She had not moved as she counted down the hours until morning, and her backside and legs had grown numb from the weight of his head and shoulders. Having Caleb there had provided some warmth as the ground grew cold beneath her, but the warmth had drained away from him along with everything else.

She had been so furious at Caleb's betrayal, the idea she wished now for his survival seemed absurd. Yet she prayed, realizing her fear of being alone outweighed her anger at Caleb.

Any woman would have pitied him. Left alone together, she did what she could for him. Tearing away strips from the bottom of her shirt to use as bandages, she had tried to stop the bleeding. Wild-eyed, Caleb had thrashed so much at first he bled even worse.

"Stay calm, Caleb. We'll get you a doctor soon." She spoke in smooth, measured tones, as one might talk to a nervous horse.

Caleb saw through her empty promise. "It won't matter. I've been gutted."

A note of plaintive surprise in his voice broke Annabelle's heart. She had him hold the bandages to the wound to staunch the blood and guided his head onto a small pillow she'd found. She sat down and slid her body under him, smoothed his hair with her fingers, like stroking a cat. The motion calmed him.

"I saw a man gut shot once. It took him hours to die. He begged us to kill him, but nobody would. Oh, God, I'm so sorry."

He went on like that for what seemed hours. Annabelle tried to quiet him. Told him to save his strength, but speaking seemed to keep him from thinking of what happened. He told her about the gold, told her how he believed Richard was dead but couldn't tell her what had happened. He even confessed how he plotted against her, hoping to pit Josey against Richard.

Even as Caleb confessed, it was Annabelle who was overcome with guilt—first, for wishing him dead because of what he had done. Later, for praying he would live, knowing his suffering would continue, just so she wouldn't be alone. When he begged her forgiveness, she gave it without hesitation. When he asked her to kill him, she demurred.

"You can't ask that of me. I've never killed anyone, and I surely wouldn't know how."

"You don't have a knife?"

She told him no.

"What about a rock? Is there a rock here?" She hoped his delirium portended a quick end. Instead, he lapsed into an uneasy sleep. He had been that way for hours.

Annabelle resisted the urge to move, even as she started to lose feeling in her legs, afraid she might wake him and renew the conversation over his murder. As she stroked his hair, she noticed the small pillow beneath his head. Her hand stopped.

The pillow, so threadbare and dirty it had nearly turned gray, lay flat against her legs, with barely enough down to make a difference in his comfort. *It might serve another purpose.* She pushed the thought from her mind, resumed stroking his hair, thinking they might both be blessed if his sleep turned eternal . . .

Annabelle might have dozed herself. She woke to the warbling, flute-like call of a meadowlark. No light leaked into the tent. She sensed more than saw the gray cast of pre-dawn through the canvas. She no longer felt anything below her waist. She shifted beneath Caleb's weight but stopped when he stirred. He woke with a smile. "I was dreaming of Laurie."

"That's good." His smile confused her. She wanted to think it signaled a recovery but feared it was more like the gray light of a false dawn. He turned his head, exposing more of the pillow beneath him. "You should go back to her. I'll wake you when Josey comes."

"Do we have any water?"

A canteen lay by the front flap of the tent. "I'll get you some." Grateful for an excuse to move, she lifted his head just enough to slide out from under him. The pillow stuck to her legs, leaving his head to rest on the ground. She moved to replace it but changed her mind.

Annabelle nearly collapsed as she rose, her legs giving way beneath her. She crawled to the canteen. Sharp pricks attacked her thighs, like the bites of an army of ants. She shook the canteen, relieved at the sloshing sound inside.

She brought it to Caleb, raising his head so he could take a mouthful. Most of the water spilled over his chin, but he smiled and thanked her.

He was still in a mood for confessions.

"I wanted you. You had to know that. I thought you were the prettiest girl I had ever seen, and I thought I deserved you, now that I was going to be a rich man." Annabelle took his hand and shushed him, afraid of what he might ask of her. "I never loved you, though, not the way I loved Laurie."

Annabelle hadn't known Laurie well but believed she would have liked her from the way Caleb spoke. Ridiculously, Annabelle felt a pang of jealousy, not for Caleb, but for the devotion he still held for his wife. She'd never known that kind of love.

"Laurie must have been very special."

Caleb nodded. "Laurie made me want to be more than I was, and I don't mean rich. That never mattered to her. I lost my way without her."

He closed his eyes. His face had lost most of its color. His thick features had softened into serene repose. "Laurie made me a better man, and I loved her for it."

Touched by his words, Annabelle stroked his hand, hoping he might imagine it was Laurie who stroked him, that he might rejoin his wife in sleep. His eyes opened. "That's how Josey loves you."

Annabelle stopped, wondering if she'd imagined him saying that. Tears that had clouded her vision as Caleb spoke of his wife rolled down her cheeks. She wiped them away, recalling how cold Josey could be. "He doesn't love me, not really."

"He's afraid to love you, is all."

She dismissed Caleb's words, wanting to shield herself from the hole growing inside her, like the wound slowly eating Caleb from within. Men liked to talk about the effects of a woman's love while they pursued it. With Laurie only a memory, Caleb talked about his love more eloquently than she'd ever heard him speak of anything. In having a woman's love, men treated the daily obligations and inconveniences that came with it like forgotten chores around the house.

"I suppose he's afraid to be a better man," she said.

She expected Caleb to contradict her, to take Josey's side as a final act of contrition to the man he'd hated and betrayed. Instead, Caleb nodded slowly and closed his eyes. His hands fell away from where he'd been holding the cloth to his wound. He whispered something. Annabelle leaned in to hear him repeat it.

"A better man won't survive what's to come."

CHAPTER SEVENTY-TWO

Long before anyone else awoke, Josey forced himself to eat a cold biscuit. His stomach roiled and burned with uncontained anger. *Caleb will be dead before this sun sets.*

Josey hadn't slept much in days and not at all the previous night. No one had realized Annabelle and Caleb were gone until all the wagons crossed the river. He had been preoccupied. The chance that at any moment one might topple off the ferry left him frazzled and so short-tempered he had gotten into a shouting match with John Bozeman over how long it took. Dusk had settled in by the time Mr. Rutledge alerted him to the pair's disappearance, too late to initiate an effective search.

Josey found it hard to believe Caleb would take Annabelle, but he thought of no other explanation for their disappearance. They had left Annabelle's horse, and they hadn't taken much in the way of supplies, so they couldn't be far. Josey's best hope was to pick up their trail in the light of day. He'd spent the night tending a burning rage, the kind he thought he'd learned to keep tamped down. Even Lord Byron knew to keep his distance with Josey in such a mood.

Once the pale dawn grew bright enough to see, Josey kicked out the fire. He'd forced himself to be patient but couldn't wait any longer. He rolled up the blankets that had gone largely unused and kneeled down to tie them into a roll. His rifle and pistols were on the ground beside his leather bandolier when he heard a stirring behind him.

"You're up awful early. Any special plans for your last day?"

Recognizing the voice, Josey bit back a response. He turned only his head, slowly. Harrison stood watching him. The dandy gunman wore a fresh shirt for the occasion. His choice of words wasn't lost on Josey.

"Just about to clean and load my guns. Want to help?"

Harrison was quick. He had his revolver drawn and pointed by the time Josey had his hand on the rifle. Josey gripped the rifle by the barrel and raised his other hand, palm open.

"Why so edgy, Harrison?" Slowly Josey moved his free hand to twist open the rifle's magazine sleeve. "It's not even loaded."

"Let's see it stays that way," Harrison said, pointing his gun to Josey's head. He moved close enough to kick away the bandolier with Josey's spare cartridges.

Josey turned the magazine sleeve back in place. "Have it your way."

"Yes, that's what we're going to do." Harrison took another step and backhanded Josey with the barrel of his pistol.

The blow knocked Josey to his side and drew blood. He stayed down until his vision cleared, using the pain to focus his mind. *At least this helps explain Annabelle's disappearance.* Josey wiped away the blood with the back of his hand.

"I guess I was wrong to blame Caleb. Where's Annabelle?"

"She's where she belongs—with her husband."

Harrison was enjoying himself so much, Josey didn't want to give him the satisfaction of a reaction. The man's grin showed him he had failed.

"Your captain," Josey said, knowing the answer came too late.

"You're not as ignorant as I thought. Since she's still married, I guess that makes her your whore."

The words were intended to provoke, but Josey's anger burned more like a furnace than a spark of powder. He shrugged off the news. "You came all this way to reclaim a man's wife?

That's a love story for poets."

"I don't know if you can call it that." Harrison licked his lips as he watched Josey. "Captain intends to give her to me." Another grin. "Her and my share of that gold you've been hauling all this way."

The gold again. Josey rose, making a show of holding the rifle by the barrel as he settled against a boulder that had served as a windbreak for his fire. "I guess I'm not as smart as you suppose."

"Spoils of war," Harrison said, his eyes lighting up at the thought. "We figure that sod-buster's got it hid in his wagon."

So Caleb was one of theirs. "And you want me to bring this gold to you?"

Harrison shook his head, trying to look downcast but enjoying himself too much. "The captain's seen enough of you." He waited for Josey to get his meaning. A cat playing with its prey. Josey's grip on the rifle tightened. Harrison directed him with the gun. "Go ahead and drop that if you don't want a bullet in your head."

Josey studied the rifle. "I suppose you'll be taking this for yourself. Ever fire a Henry?"

Harrison shook his head, licked his lips. They were chapped from the habit. "We used to call those 'the damned Yankee rifle you could load on Sunday and fire all week.' "

Josey nodded and smiled. "I never found that I made it last that long."

"I bet you didn't." Harrison grinned again. "It's a fine weapon. I'll take good care of it."

Josey ignored the comment. "The thing about a Henry is you have to be careful. It's got no safety, if you've got the hammer cocked." He moved his hand along the barrel as if to demonstrate to Harrison.

"Just keep your hands on the barrel."

"You don't trust me?"

"No."

Now it was Josey's turn to grin. Still holding the rifle by its barrel, he extended his arms toward Harrison, as if making an offer of it. "You're not as ignorant as *I* thought."

With a sudden movement, Josey drew the rifle down hard so the hammer struck against the boulder. With the hammer resting on the rim of the chambered cartridge, the gun fired without Josey even touching the trigger. The impact struck Harrison in the chest and sent him staggering back a step. He kept his feet, looking at Josey with an expression of disbelief that shifted into something else as he put his hand to his chest and drew it back bloody.

"I lied about needing to load the gun." Josey stood and levered in another cartridge as he approached Harrison. His second and third shots put Harrison on the ground. Josey stood over him as he levered in a final shot. "Any man who tends to himself before his guns isn't worth much in my view."

CHAPTER SEVENTY-THREE

The pain returned, twice in strength of what it had been. The hurt nearly blinded Caleb. He wondered again at the cruelty of life, that even as a man's body loses the last of its strength, what still works should be the part that feels pain.

Caleb looked to Annabelle a final time and nodded. He wondered if she would be strong enough to do what he asked. *Could Laurie have done it?* Gentle Laurie had loved him. Annabelle never held any affection for him. Caleb wasn't sure if that would make the task easier or harder. *I suppose I'm about to find out.* It amused some part of his brain that he'd turned philosopher at the last.

She spoke, but he didn't make out the words. Didn't matter. Her pleasant tone reminded him of Laurie.

The cold ground felt hard beneath him, but he was thankful to no longer be in her lap. Her attentions made him feel worse for what he had done. She moved beside him. He wanted to see what she was doing but didn't have the strength. *God, it hurts.* He closed his eyes, imagined himself somewhere else, but the pain held him here. His belly burned. His legs were heavy. He tried to shake free from the numbness. No response. He went to lift his arms. Again, nothing.

A woman's voice, hollow and far away as if he were hearing her in a dream. *Maybe this is a dream. If I pinch myself, will I wake with Laurie? It's been so long. Where has she been?* He started to rise to see his wife, but he managed only to turn his head, shift his gaze down.

Blood had gathered in a pool near his waist. It glistened darkly in the gray morning light. Its stench filled his nostrils, left a taste in his mouth that he wanted to spit out but couldn't.

He asked Laurie for water. Felt her hands on his brow, blotting the sweat with a handkerchief. She said something. His heartbeat, quick but weak, fluttered like little bird wings in his chest. They flapped in time with a humming in his head.

It seemed odd that he thought so clearly in a dream. He was grateful to be asleep. He no longer felt cold with Laurie. The pain was gone. She stirred beside him, then hovered over him, her white dress filling his vision. He closed his eyes. Tomorrow would be a new day. He might fish. Or go hunting. When he woke, if he didn't oversleep, Laurie would be there.

Once Josey knew to look for the gold, it didn't take long to find the sturdy trunks buried at the bottom of Caleb's wagon. He needed Lord Byron's help to lift them out.

Once they had the trunks unpacked, Luke Swift swung a heavy pick against the locks. Mr. Rutledge opened the first trunk. Josey couldn't see inside, only Rutledge's reaction. It was enough. For a long moment, Rutledge didn't breathe. Then he released his breath in a gasp as he uttered a word Josey had never heard Annabelle's father speak.

"How much . . . ?"

"It's a fortune." Rutledge had the look of a man lost. He opened the second trunk, his eyes growing even wider. "It's beyond calculating. A few ounces of dust would buy a man's meal. A few nuggets might buy him a horse. This—" He shook his head. "Kings have fought wars for less."

Rutledge closed the lid, leaning over it as if his weight might prevent anything from escaping. "We can't tell the others about this."

Josey wondered how much trouble Rutledge might have been if it weren't his daughter at risk. He was relieved not to find out.

"It's too late, Langdon." Annabelle's mother came upon them, most of the rest of the camp trailing behind her. "I've already told everyone."

"We're here to help," Bill Smith said, turning to Josey. "If there's anything we can do."

If Rutledge were surprised, he was diplomatic enough to hide it. Alexander Brewster put an arm on his shoulder. "No one will stand in the way of seeing your family made whole again," the camp's Yankee preacher told him. "We came west to make our fortunes, but not at the cost of our souls."

Others, both northern farmers and southern businessmen, took up the sentiment, and Rutledge thanked them. He said to Josey, "I'm the one who hired Caleb. I put us in danger. I should be the one to go."

Josey shook his head. "That's what they wanted. They even sent a gunman to make sure it wasn't me. The surprise might give me an advantage." *I'll need every edge I can get.* He already pictured how it would go, though he chose not to share that.

While the others moved the gold from the trunks to saddlebags, Josey saw to the horses. He would divide the load between his horse and Annabelle's Paint. The women parted before Josey to create a path to the horses. Josey kept his head down, avoiding their gaze. Mrs. Smith said, "Be careful, Josey." Caroline ran toward him but stopped when he looked at her. Tears filled her eyes and she choked back whatever she'd intended to say. Josey kept walking.

Once the saddlebags were loaded, Josey was eager to leave. Mary Rutledge waited, seated on a stone by the edge of the trail. Josey resisted the urge to pass her without a word.

"I know you'll get her back, but make sure you come back,

too." When Josey merely nodded, she added, "I mean it."

"I know."

"I don't think you do."

She's probably right. Turning it in his head, he saw a way to get the gold to Annabelle's husband without getting killed. And he saw how he might get Annabelle away. But he couldn't see how to do both. Not that it bothered him much.

By already thinking himself dead, he wouldn't be distracted from what he had to do. It was simpler that way. It was simpler than picturing a life with Annabelle. Josey wasn't sure he could walk away from her, even though he believed she would never be safe with him. He would never know any peace for worrying about her. A man could love something too much for his own good.

He didn't figure Mary Rutledge would understand, so he kept it to himself, watching her like a schoolchild waiting for a teacher's dismissal. She knew him well enough not to press.

"I don't know what's happened between you and Annabelle, but none of it matters now." She spoke in a low, urgent voice that held his attention more effectively than a scream. "A woman will forgive almost anything of a man who loves her wholly. All he has to do is ask."

He nodded and looked away. The silence didn't seem to bother Mary. She came to him and kissed his cheek. "I want my daughter back, and I don't want her to be alone anymore. She deserves better."

On that we agree. Josey thanked her and led the horses onto the trail, feeling the truth of what Mary Rutledge said tugging at him. When he turned back, she watched him still. "What you ask," he called to her, "it's not a simple thing."

Later, he would have time to reflect on her final words, wondering if she spoke of his seeking Annabelle's forgiveness or his walking into a likely ambush. *Maybe it was both.*

"If it were simple," Mary Rutledge called after him, "we wouldn't need you to do it."

CHAPTER SEVENTY-FOUR

Josey found the road agents' camp near a creek at the bottom of a ravine, not far from the trail. Trees near the water shrouded their numbers. Josey liked that he could approach from above, even though his descent would make a quick retreat impossible. Retreat wasn't in Josey's plans. His best hope was that a man like Richard wouldn't anticipate that.

Still out of view from the camp, Josey tied off his horse to a pine. He transferred all the saddlebags to Annabelle's Paint, then slipped the rifle scabbard between the fender on Paint's saddle. He didn't need to check the Henry to know it was loaded. Same for the four pistols he carried.

The pine-scented breeze that had blown along the trail above the ravine stilled in the noontime heat. Birds in the trees fell silent. Despite the sleepless night, Josey felt alive and alert. For the last year and a half, life had rolled past Josey like the Missouri, its waters dark and murky so a man never knew what he might find on wading in. A rock might turn underfoot and send him tumbling into unseen currents. Before he knows what's happened, he's in a wagon train to Montana. He's with a woman. He's imagining life on a ranch. No chance to consider *how* it happened or whether it was *right*. A man tumbles in, nearly drowns, and when his head comes up for air, well, he finds himself here.

Josey slowly led the horse into the ravine. The creek at the bottom was one of those clear, cold mountain streams. Josey liked that. Water gurgled musically over smooth stones, and a man could see every one of them. Some men would rather take their chances in the slow, murky water, but Josey liked to see where he stepped, even when it meant wading into fast waters. Soon he would have a look at what faced him in the ravine.

And they would see him.

Annabelle saw Josey first. She'd been scanning the hillside since two of Richard's men brought her out of the tent that morning, knowing Josey would come, that it would have to be him, despite whatever Richard planned. The more time that passed without Harrison's return, the more certain she became, the more agitated Richard grew. He knew it, too.

Josey carefully led her horse on a zigzag pattern across the scree that covered the top third of the slope. The horse kicked free a few loose stones and they bounded down the ravine, alerting the others.

"Don't come alone, Josey, he'll kill you," she shouted.

Richard came to her in a flash, backhanding her with such force that it spun her around, left her face in the dirt. The blow dizzied her, and she tasted blood but managed to call out, "There's eight of them."

Richard rewarded her with a kick that caught her around the waist and collapsed her. He held his fist before her eyes. "Say anything more and I'll kill you. He'll be dead before he can get to you."

Richard looked disappointed when she gave him no reason to strike again. He turned to watch Josey's approach. "Josey Angel," he called. "I should have known. I told Harrison to shoot you in the back. I guess he was too proud."

Josey gave no indication of hearing Richard as he led the horse across the stones. He waited until reaching surer footing before speaking. His voice carried into the ravine so that even without shouting they heard him.

"I cured him of that."

Richard made a show of laughing at Josey's joke. To the others behind him, he whispered, "Kill him as soon as you've got a clear shot."

"He's too far off, and the horse is in the way," the big man in the Confederate coat said. He had taken a position behind a cottonwood tree, its trunk too narrow to fully conceal his body.

Richard called out, "You have the gold?" Josey pointed to the saddlebags. Richard seemed to be waiting for Josey to say something. *He doesn't know Josey.* Finally, Richard said, "Well, bring it here."

"Let Annabelle go."

"Get him to come closer," one of the men with rifles whispered to Richard. His words drowned out whatever else Josey had said. Richard told the men to be quiet.

"Where's Caleb?" Josey repeated, so quiet Annabelle sensed Richard held his breath to hear better.

"He didn't make it. The deal is for Annabelle." Josey's silence tested Richard's patience. "You still want her, don't you?"

"Let her go, and I'll bring you the gold."

Richard laughed, standing upright over Annabelle. He was the only man not taking cover. "Bring the gold, and I'll let her go."

"Just go, Josey," Annabelle shouted. "Protect the others."

Richard turned on her, striking her savagely with his closed fist. Annabelle collapsed, her world turning black for a moment. Then she saw pinpricks of light even after she closed her eyes.

"I can beat her all day, and you can stand there watching," Richard called, "or you can bring me the gold."

Annabelle grew nauseous, her mouth so dry she couldn't swallow. She held her breath to still her heart and hold down the bile. She no longer saw Josey and barely heard his response.

"Send up two of your men. Unarmed."

"I'm glad I never had to face you in a poker game, Josey Angel," Richard shouted. "Even when the deck is stacked against you, you act like you're holding all aces. What do you have up your sleeve this time? I hope it's not another rock."

Annabelle's head throbbed as she watched Josey draw his rifle from the scabbard, lifting it high.

"That's your answer, one rifle?" *He's trying to draw Josey closer.* Richard watched her too carefully for Annabelle to risk a warning. Loud enough so Josey heard, Richard said to the men behind him, "Show him he's not the only one with a fancy rifle."

A chorus of shots exploded from the trees behind Annabelle, so loud she couldn't hear her own scream of alarm. A few shots struck the ground beside and in front of Josey and her horse. Josey pulled hard on the startled horse's harness to keep Paint between himself and the men below, and Richard laughed to see Josey crouched low behind the spotted horse. After the fusillade ended he said to the others, "See the coward, boys? All he can do is bluff now that he's lost his advantage."

Josey steadied the horse. His voice carried as clear as if he stood beside them. "The rifle's not my advantage."

Richard stood over Annabelle but looked to Josey, his curiosity getting the better of him. "So what is?"

"My advantage is you expect to live out this day." Josey paused. He stared at Richard, as if the other men, the ones with drawn guns, didn't exist. "I don't."

CHAPTER SEVENTY-FIVE

Josey nearly drew the Henry on seeing Richard strike Annabelle, but he couldn't get off a shot—not a good one—without a risk of hitting her. Richard stood over Annabelle, taunting him. Josey hadn't considered how her presence would cloud his thinking. He needed to narrow the odds.

Two men stepped out from cover. He didn't hear Richard's command, but the newcomers dropped their gun belts and walked toward Josey. One was older and didn't look good for much beyond cooking and keeping camp. A thick white beard ringed his face, and he moved with a limp that made him wince with every step. The other man was young, clean-shaven but for a wispy mustache no thicker than his fair eyebrows. His features were soft but not his eyes. He looked eager to prove himself.

Their strides were short and unsteady on the uphill climb. Josey pulled his pistols as they neared, one pointed at each man. He motioned to the younger man when they got within ten paces.

"You, stay." To the old man he said, "You, come look in the bags."

Richard called from the bottom of the hill. "What did you say?"

The young one answered. "He said for Peco to look in the bags." He looked uncomfortable being made to stand in place, feeling exposed without his guns. Josey knew the feeling, wondered if the man kept a knife in his belt or had a pocket pistol on his back. *Don't get nervous, boy.*

"Well, go on and look," Richard shouted.

The old man made a wide berth around Josey and approached the horse from the side. Josey held the gaze of the younger man, feeling the horse move as the old man tugged at one of the saddlebags.

"It's gold," he shouted, a mixture of surprise and relief. "All four bags," he said a few moments later.

"Leave it," Josey commanded. "Now step away."

The old man hopped away to rejoin his partner. He grinned widely, seeming to move with less pain after seeing the gold.

"Satisfied?" Josey called to Richard.

"Not until I have it—and you're gone. Give the gold to my men."

Josey nodded. The young man smiled as he stepped forward, like he was in on a secret. The bullet passed neatly into his brain at a point between those fair eyebrows.

Without moving, Josey looked to the old man. He had just enough time to start raising his hands, his mouth open to form whatever words he thought would save him.

The bullet caught him in the throat. He dropped to his knees, his hands clutching at his neck, blood spurting between his fingers. It would have been an act of mercy to finish him, but Josey wouldn't waste the bullet. Both shots had been fired so quickly, no one by the creek had time to react. Josey took a step back, careful to keep the horse between him and the others.

"What are you doing?" Richard screamed, crouching behind Annabelle. "Do you want me to kill her?"

Josey shouted his response, loud enough to be certain every man heard. "Now you have two less to claim a split." Less loudly, he added, "Let Annabelle go and I'll ride down." Josey counted on Richard's greed winning out over his fury.

The old man had collapsed to the ground, his death gasps

growing fainter. Richard, still using Annabelle as a shield, called out. "You come closer."

He needs to be sure I can't get away with the gold. "I'll come closer once she starts walking up."

For a moment, it was a standoff. Richard must have decided the hill was steep enough Josey couldn't get away because he helped Annabelle to her feet. Josey used the time to reload the pistols. Then he holstered them and drew the Henry as Annabelle took her first steps up the hill. Richard moved forward with her, halting her with a hand to her neck. "I'm not letting go until I have the gold."

"Just go, Josey," Annabelle said, her call followed with a cry of pain as Richard jerked on her loose hair.

Josey led the horse forward a few steps. He'd moved past the scree, into the grass on the slope of the ridge. He wanted more solid footing when things started. He was still too far off to be sure of a shot, but he brought up his rifle, using the horse's saddle to steady his aim. "Let her go now."

"Shoot and she'll be dead," Richard said. "And you'll be next."

"Maybe. For sure, you won't live to spend the gold. You let her come, and it will just be us. And the gold."

Richard looked to either side, as if reassuring himself the other guns were still there. He drew his pistol and pointed it at Annabelle's back. "She'll be dead before you can get back up that hill, if that's your plan."

"I'm planning on coming for you," Josey said.

Richard grinned. "Then the price will be paid in full."

Annabelle started. Her steps were unsteady, and she used her hands to scuttle forward when the slope grew too steep. Josey moved toward her, measuring his pace so that they would pass at a point still far enough away to make the gunmen hesitate.

As she drew nearer, he stole a glance. Her face was red and

looked to be swelling where Richard had struck her. Her hands were covered in blood, though there were no signs of any other wounds on her. She was out of breath, and her eyes looked glassy and distant. Twice she nearly stumbled, each time Josey forcing himself not to rush to her. He waited until she drew close enough that only she could hear.

"My horse is at the top of the hill. Call to me when you're in the saddle and then ride. Ride east and don't look back. The wagons are camped in the next valley. Byron and your father will be watching for you."

Annabelle stopped two paces from him. Her eyes found their focus. "He'll kill you, Josey. He won't let you leave."

"He'll try."

She came to him, extending her arms to him. "I love you, Josey. You don't have to die for me. Drop the gold and we'll ride off together."

Annabelle moved to embrace the man she loved, but Josey wouldn't even look at her, stepping back and repositioning his aim on the man watching them from below.

"We'll both be dead before we can clear the hill," he said.

The hardness had returned to his voice, as if there had never been anything between them. *He feels betrayed.* "I'm so sorry, Josey. You have to believe I didn't know Richard was still alive. I thought I saw him, on the ferry, but I didn't believe it—"

"You don't have to apologize." He looked to her, just a moment, and she saw the deadness in his eyes. "I need you to go, Belle. I can't do what I need to do if I'm worried about you."

He handed a pistol to her. "Take this. Just in case." She hardly believed what was happening. He wanted her gone. *He means to die here.*

"The rocks won't make it an easy climb," he said, still not looking at her. "I'll give you time, but I need to know when

337

you're safe."

Annabelle recalled the first time she'd seen Josey at the campsite outside Omaha. Even in the glow of firelight, there had been a pallor to his face, as if all emotion had bled away. She had known men wounded in the war, men with missing limbs and scars, marks that would never go away. *Josey is no different.* Annabelle couldn't see or understand his wounds, but they were there, as surely as if a cannonball had taken his leg. *I thought I could make him whole, but I might as well have hoped to reanimate a severed limb.*

She moved close enough to kiss him on the cheek, her body brushing against his as she found her balance, but she sensed no warmth from him. Fighting back tears, she stepped past him, hoping she had the strength to finish the climb.

Richard called. "She's safe now, Josey. Toss the gold from your horse and you can join her."

"I want to be sure you can't follow her."

Annabelle fought the urge to look back. It required all of her concentration to keep her balance on the tiny rounded rocks that spread across the rim of the slope. Her legs quivered. *What would they do if I collapsed?* Their standoff would be complete, and she might as well die of humiliation. She no longer cared. She *wanted* to die. Only the certainty that they wouldn't allow it kept her moving. Her failure to finish the climb would only delay their deadly game. They wouldn't permit her to frustrate it entirely.

It's better to crawl off someplace where no one will ever find me. Josey had made her feel like she could know joy again. He made her happier than she'd ever been with Richard, but the feeling had proven no more genuine. Josey's deception felt like a worse betrayal because she should have known better.

Cresting the hill, she saw Josey's horse tied to the tree, just as he'd said. As much as he'd hurt her, her life had meant more to him than his own. She owed him for that.

"I've reached the top," she called. The scene below hadn't changed, as if it were a tableau of toy soldiers arranged for a child's amusement. Josey held the rifle, standing behind the horse. *My horse.* Richard had taken cover behind a tree, but she didn't doubt that Josey's first shot would find some part exposed. She had started the day with two men who held a claim on her. *Will there be none by day's end?*

Josey lowered his gun. He took the reins in one hand and began to lead the horse down the slope. Richard stepped from behind the tree.

It's begun.

Annabelle was supposed to ride away, but she couldn't leave. *How long will he wait before shooting Josey?* So long as Josey held the rifle with just one hand, Richard could be patient.

Then it happened. The first shot echoed through the ravine like a snapping tree limb, jolting Annabelle even though she'd been anticipating it. The shot hadn't come from Josey, Richard or any of the men by the creek.

CHAPTER SEVENTY-SIX

Josey flinched at the crack of gunfire, expecting to feel the impact. Nothing. He didn't wait for another, jerking on the reins and pulling the horse to the ground, dropping behind its haunches so that he was covered when the whole fusillade exploded.

Gunfire echoed through the ravine so that it seemed all the guns at Gettysburg were ablaze. Seeing Richard crawl to the trees as if he'd been hit, Josey couldn't make sense of it. *What's happening?*

Paint whinnied in pain and started to rise unsteadily. The sudden movement left Josey partly exposed. His lower leg burned, as if he had been struck with a poker just pulled from the fire. The wounded horse struggled against him, leaving Josey no choice. He pulled a revolver and finished the horse, then buried his head in the nape of its neck and pulled his legs tight against the horse's lifeless body as more shots tore through the air around him.

All hell broke loose, the reverberations playing tricks so that it sounded like gunfire came from all around him. Josey knew he'd be dead if any of Richard's men managed to flank him to the higher ground.

Focus on what you can control. That's what the Colonel had taught him. The high ground that had prevented his quick escape now saved his life, giving the men below a poor vantage so long as Josey held some cover.

Josey risked a look toward the creek, drawing a shot that thumped into the dead horse's side. *Don't panic.* He needed to be sure Richard's men weren't moving to get a better shot from behind him. Josey could safely look down the slope from a spot beneath the horse's neck. By watching for powder smoke, he saw where the shooters were. He counted six. They were hunkered down, just as he was. Six shooters near the creek weren't enough to account for all the gunfire he heard.

Josey looked back. On the slope above him and in the tree line that led into the ravine he saw telltale puffs of black powder explosions. *Who are they?* Lord Byron might have gone back for the cavalry at Fort Smith, but that was too far away. *A patrol?* Carrington didn't have the manpower to send men this far north.

Movement from behind the trees near the creek drew his attention. *They're on the move.* He no longer saw Richard, but someone maneuvered for a clear shot, firing and running for new cover.

They probably wonder if I'm dead. The trees were poor cover, especially while Josey held the high ground. The runner had just made it to a new spot. He was a heavyset man in a red shirt, and the tree obscured no more than two-thirds of his body. Using the dead horse's haunches to steady his aim, Josey inhaled and held his breath before pulling the trigger.

The first shot took the man in the hip, knocking him back a step and down to one knee, his rifle held out like a crutch as he sought to regain his balance. Josey had to roll on his side to cock the lever and ready a new shot, but the man stood fully exposed when Josey fired a second time. *One less to worry about.*

The others by the creek had forgotten about him, more concerned with the fire they were taking from above. Josey might just lay back and wait for the new arrivals—whoever they were—to finish off Richard and the rest of the bandits. Josey kept low while gunfire rained down on the ravine. All he had to do was make sure no one flanked him.

Yet something was wrong. The more Josey watched, the uneasier he became. Soldiers would have concentrated their fire. They would have followed up a fusillade with movement to gain a better position. The men atop the ravine weren't taking advantage of their position. Having recovered from their initial surprise, Richard's men were changing tactics.

This is a screening fire. They were pulling back, and the guns from above were doing nothing to press their advantage. Soon, Richard and his men would melt away into the trees. Richard may have been hit, but that didn't mean he was dead or even badly hurt. *If he escapes, he will come back.* Annabelle would never be safe.

There wasn't time to construct a plan. Josey took three deep breaths and sprang from behind the dead horse. He ran, gritting his teeth through the pain of every footfall on his bad leg. By the time he reached the creek, he no longer felt it. His body and mind focused on the charge.

From the smoke of their return fire, Josey saw the men were moving along the creek to his left. He would be approaching from behind. Time slowed. Josey heard every heartbeat, like a war drum landing with each step in the moist ground. He practically tasted the earthy smell of rotting leaves as he bounded through the creek with small, quick steps over uneven ground, the water cold against his legs as he splashed through.

Another twenty paces and he saw the first one, a tall, wiry man, his back to Josey as he aimed to the woods above the creek. Josey was faster. He fired before the man got off his shot. Josey levered in another shot. The man had crumpled beside the tree he'd been using for cover. Still running, Josey was on him before he recovered and put the second shot into his head as he passed. He would leave no one living at his back.

The mottled sunlight through the trees created odd shadows amid the brush, roots and leaves. Careful of his footing, Josey leaped over a fallen tree trunk, ducked beneath low-lying branches, leaves whipping across his face.

He passed the point where Richard had been. *He's still out there.* The fleeing road agents must have heard Josey's rifle shots. The next man waited behind a tree, stepping out with his pistol for a clear shot. Josey leaped for cover. The bullet passed so close he heard it, like a mosquito at his ear.

Josey fired wildly from the ground. Once, twice, again, not caring where he aimed, just forcing the man to cover. Josey levered in a new cartridge as he rolled, hearing another shot pass him. He kept rolling behind a larger tree, fired again, rose and ran for the next tree. The other man must have had the same idea, and they nearly collided. Josey swung the stock of his rifle at the man's head, feeling it soften beneath the blow. The impact tore the rifle from his hands. He drew the knife from his belt as he spun away from the man's desperate grasp. As the man fell to his knees, Josey completed his arc, catching him under the chin and drawing a blinding red spray. Josey wiped his face with his sleeve. He picked up a tomahawk the dead man had been holding and moved on.

The sounds of gunfire slowed. Between shots, Josey heard nothing but the pounding of his feet and heart. He smelled blood. Hoped it wasn't his. Found the next one in the act of reloading. He was just a boy, his dusky face round like a cherub's.

Seeing Josey, he dropped his rifle and turned to run. Josey caught him in the back of the head with the club end of the tomahawk. The boy fell forward so heavily Josey thought he must be dead. He paused long enough to be sure, pulling back the boy's head to expose his throat to the knife. *Leave no one.* Josey ran.

Slipping the knife in his belt as he ran from tree to tree, Josey drew a pistol. The big man in the Confederate coat stood behind a copse of young cedars. Josey shot as he moved, automatically raising the gun so the spent percussion caps would drop free, ducking low after firing the last round from the pistol.

He couldn't see the gray coat, only the barrel of his rifle extended beyond a tree as he fired blindly from his cavalry carbine, probably a seven-shooter. Josey waited for him to reload before moving again, coming at him from the side.

Crouching low as he ran, Josey burst to his right, hearing the first shot pass wide. The repeating rifle spit again, but Josey kept moving so the tree trunk interfered with the gray-coat's aim. As he charged, Josey emptied another pistol, pinning his foe behind the tree until he fell on him.

Throwing his full weight and all his momentum into the larger man, they both crashed to the ground. The gray coat got the worst of the impact, but he was bigger than Josey remembered, and he knocked Josey off with a swipe of an arm as meaty as a bear's. Josey rolled to his feet, but the big man was nearly as quick. Gasping, he brought up his rifle like a club. Josey ducked under the swing, rolling away from his reach and pivoting up. He stepped forward for another try.

Josey brought the club end of the tomahawk onto the gray-coat's knee. He screamed as his leg buckled. Rising with the momentum of his swing, Josey brought out the knife, slicing into the other's back. Another shout of pain. The gray coat reached for him. Lost his balance. Josey knocked him back and fell onto him again. Raised the knife. Brought it down. Again and again. The other stopped moving. Again and again. Seeing red, stopping only when he sensed someone else. *Richard?* Josey spun wildly, reached for his last pistol.

Breathing heavily, Josey blinked, not sure he saw clearly. Lord Byron stood over him, a rifle in his hands. At his shoulder stood

Rutledge. Luke Swift, Bill Smith, even the preacher Alexander Brewster. All were armed with rifles. Byron stood silent, a look of concern mixed with something else. Josey imagined how he looked to them, eyes wild, chest heaving, covered in blood, and he knew what he saw in Byron's face.

Horror.

Josey didn't care.

"Where's Richard?"

CHAPTER SEVENTY-SEVEN

Annabelle had been unable to look away once the gunfire started. She forgot all her anger toward Josey once she saw him in danger.

It took a minute for her to realize the gunfire came from the top of the ridge where the tree line descended partway into the ravine. Relief overcame her on recognizing her father, Lord Byron and some of the other emigrants. They had put Richard and his men on the defensive, but they couldn't save Josey, who remained exposed on the slope leading to the ravine.

I can't ride to him. Even if Annabelle safely descended the incline, they would be shot before they escaped. She had to find another way. Recalling that Richard's men had been using a deer trail through the woods that led up from the creek bed, Annabelle led Josey's horse there.

As gunshots echoed through the ravine, she moved carefully despite her urgency. She couldn't help Josey if she broke his horse's leg in a hasty descent. The sound of gunshots grew fainter as she followed the trail into the woods, then a switchback brought her nearer to the sound again. At the bottom of the ravine, a path led off from the creek. If she worked her way around the campsite from behind, she might get close enough to Josey so that he could run downhill to her before being seen by Richard or the others. They could ride to safety together.

Annabelle slowed her pace. She couldn't determine where

the shots were coming from, but the gunmen were near. The pace of gunshots had slowed, but she didn't know whether that was good or bad for Josey. She prayed he was still alive.

The path wound between trees and over broken ground of stumps and brush. She no longer heard the gunfire through the thick forest. She feared she had turned herself around in the woods and gotten lost. *What if I can't reach Josey in time?* Maybe the fighting was over. *Was Richard dead?* The possibility seemed too much to hope for. It was more likely the arrival of the others had frightened off Richard and his men.

If Richard fled, where would he go?

Too late, she realized the answer. She heard something moving in the brush, too loud to be a squirrel or bird. In a panic, Annabelle looked back, but the narrow path afforded no room to turn a horse, at least not quickly or quietly. Before she could think of something else to do, he stood before her, looking as surprised as she.

He recovered more quickly. "Annie. I didn't know you still cared."

Limping, his pants stained with blood, Richard failed to project his typically dapper mien. His smile looked forced, his thin mustache arched over gritted teeth. "How thoughtful to have brought a horse."

He was nearly to her when Annabelle remembered the pistol Josey had given her. She drew it quickly from the belt around her waist, pointed it the way Josey had taught her.

"Stay back." She held the gun with one hand, drawing back the hammer with the other.

"Don't be ridiculous. If you intended to shoot me, we wouldn't be talking," Richard said. The look in his eyes didn't match the confidence in his voice.

Annabelle needed both hands to hold the heavy gun, trying to remember what Josey said to do to fire a second shot. She wasn't sure she could hit anything at a distance, but she liked her chances with Richard standing directly in front of her.

His voice softened. "You don't want to shoot me, Annie. Just let me get by, girl. You can keep the horse. You'll never see me again." He extended his hand.

Tears blurred Annabelle's vision. "All I ever wanted was to be loved," she said, managing not to choke on the words. "Was it because I lost the baby?"

He looked over his shoulder. Annabelle heard more gunshots, but not like before. There were long pauses between shots, but they were growing closer. That meant only one thing: Josey was coming.

Richard knew it, too. In his impatience, the charm dropped away like a discarded robe. She saw the man beneath.

"Our parents wanted a child, not me. Once my father died, you think I was going to allow you to trap me?" The gunshots grew louder. "You pushed me to, let's say, *extreme* action."

Annabelle recalled Richard's talk of selling the land after his father's death and traveling abroad. She had thought it was his reaction to the grief of losing the child. "What are you saying?" Holding the gun fully extended made Annabelle's arms shake. A tear ran down her face. She resisted the impulse to wipe it away.

Richard saw his moment. "You were always stupid. You didn't lose the baby from the fall. I brought in a doctor, a *specialist,* to make sure you did."

His words had their intended effect, falling on Annabelle like a physical blow. She reeled, stumbling back a step, squeezing the gun more tightly lest she drop it even as Richard lunged for it. The explosion in her hands shook her entire body and set her ears ringing. The recoil knocked her back another step. The smoke burned her nostrils and eyes.

Richard stood before her, surprise in his eyes. His mouth

dropped half open in a question he dared not ask. His eyes lost their focus. He looked beyond her toward something far away.

Blinking away tears, Annabelle watched a crimson stain appear on his shirt, sticky with sweat and clinging to his body. With his every breath, the stain grew wider.

Richard moved a step toward her on unsteady legs. Annabelle stepped back, careful to keep beyond his reach. She recalled Josey's warnings about the snake he had shot in camp. Even then it posed a threat.

She kept the gun pointed at him, hoped he didn't see the tremble in her arms. Richard took another step, then stumbled to his knees. He looked up to her, but Annabelle didn't think he saw her. His voice was hoarse as he reached for her.

"I am your husband."

Annabelle pulled back the hammer on the pistol with her thumb. With both hands on the gun, she tightened her grip to still her trembling arms and closed her eyes as she squeezed.

"You are *not* my husband."

CHAPTER SEVENTY-EIGHT

Riding to the top of a grassy ridge, Josey took in the undulating hills on either side, some smooth and green, some blanketed with evergreens. He smelled the pine on the crisp air, and he breathed it deeply, his lungs aching, like drinking too-cold water on a hot day. Summer faded fast here. The mountain held more snow today than yesterday. The river that meandered through the valley still flowed strong and fast, but he saw from its banks where it had retreated from a high-water mark of summer snow-melt.

Josey had been riding all day, the first time he felt normal in almost a week since Mary Rutledge stitched his leg. The leg wound had been made worse from his running around, and he had spent the last days of their journey on his back in the Smiths' wagon, Constance Smith so attentive that he feigned sleep when he wanted to be left alone. After receiving assurances that Annabelle was well, his questions about her had been ignored. Just see to himself, they told him.

Josey knew about Richard. They told him that much, though he didn't know the details. He'd lost more blood than he realized at the time and wasn't clear on how they got him to the wagons or how they found Annabelle. He knew better than anyone what she was going through, and yet they hadn't let him see her. Or maybe she hadn't wanted to see him. *It might have been better for everyone if that Confederate with the carbine had a better aim.*

Mr. Rutledge came to see Josey in the Smiths' wagon. He said all the right things, inquired politely about Josey's recovery, asked if he needed anything. His discomfort was palpable.

Josey squirmed to watch him until he broached the subject of the gold. Rutledge thought it best they divide the money among everyone equally, and the rest of the emigrants agreed. The gold had been stolen from a country that no longer existed, and everybody who had unwittingly risked their lives carrying it halfway across the continent deserved a share. That troubled no one's conscience, but Rutledge seemed to think he needed Josey's approval.

"Lord Byron, too?"

Rutledge nodded. He'd been prepared for the question. "Of course. It was his idea, you know, for us to follow you."

Josey had figured it out just before he charged after Richard. Somebody hit Richard with the first, carefully aimed shot. Once everyone had taken cover and started shooting back, it didn't surprise Josey that the settlers hadn't hit anything else. It hadn't mattered. They'd drawn the fire away from Josey long enough for him to end it. He and Annabelle, that is.

"Annabelle?"

"She will be fine," her father said. "Her mother says there's nothing some rest and food won't heal. Her body, at least." He looked at Josey as he said the last part. No one knew the lie of that better than he. "What about you?"

Josey shrugged. He knew Rutledge wasn't asking about the leg. "I wish you hadn't seen what happened."

Rutledge watched him closely. "We needed you—" he struggled for the right words "—to be like that."

"That's when you were more afraid of them than of me." Josey didn't ask how the others felt now, but Rutledge seemed to anticipate the question.

"These people risked their lives for you," he said.

"They came for Annabelle."

Rutledge looked away. "She was already safe when we opened fire. You alone were in danger then."

He was more comfortable talking about the money. They were still counting it, so he wasn't sure how much each share would be. "It will be enough to make us all quite comfortable in our new homes."

The statement hung between them. *Home.* It had been so long, Josey hardly knew what the word meant. It brought to mind faraway paradises of mythology. Avalon. Elysium. Eden. Home. Josey had dreamed of a home here, a dream only half-remembered, then lost on awakening.

Rutledge studied the threads on Mrs. Smith's comforter. *He can't even look at me.* It was one thing for them to believe he had killed many men in the war. They felt safer as they traveled a strange and hostile land. It was something else to have witnessed it, to have it in mind every time they came together in town, every time they extended an invitation for a visit.

With all the death in the war, Josey had never killed a boy, not up close at least. He had killed that dark-faced boy without hesitating. *What kind of man does that?* He wondered if Rutledge and the others would ever look at him the same way, could feel an easy companionship around him like at the campfires, look to him as one of their own instead of one apart. *The dog in the yard. That's what I am.* Josey wondered, too, if he could look at them without remembering what had happened. He had traveled more than a thousand miles to forget the war only to create new memories that would haunt him here. *How far will I have to ride to forget that boy's face when I cut his throat?*

The first morning he felt strong enough, Josey rose so early no one could object to his standing on the leg. It started to throb after a few steps, so he took to his horse, leaving before anyone knew.

Riding off would be best for everyone. Go fetch the Colonel. Give the old man his share of the gold and leave him and Lord Byron to build something with it. They could get some horses and drive cattle here. The Colonel would die a wealthy gentleman rancher.

Within a few miles, Josey forgot the pain in his leg. He rode all day, passing some potato and wheat farms near Bozeman, a town of only a half-dozen buildings and a smithy. Virginia City was a real town, lots of buildings, some of them made of stone, filled with people, saloons, even a hurdy-gurdy where for a dollar a fellow might dance with a girl and have a shot of whiskey.

Josey had no interest in going there. He retraced his steps, calculating how far his valley lay between the two towns. The dream still was buried in his brain somewhere, drawing him to this place of grassy hills and gurgling water.

The wagons caught up late in the day. Lord Byron drove the front wagon, waving his hat in greeting. Josey looked for riders but didn't see Annabelle. He'd heard she had taken to riding off on her own during the days. He understood the solace of solitude.

"I thought you'd done got yourself lost," Byron said when Josey rode up.

"Not like I didn't try."

Byron smiled. "I thought we'd camp here for the night. Leave the hills for tomorrow." He always seemed to know Josey's mind.

Josey looked past him to the row of wagons. "No trouble today?"

Again, Byron anticipated the true source of his curiosity. "She rode off ahead. I thought you might have come across her on that hill."

"I didn't." Josey wasn't used to Annabelle riding off alone.

"Which horse did she take?"

"She took *mine*," Byron said. His gap-toothed grin showed he didn't mind. "She said you killed hers."

"Hers? I tried once to give her that horse. She didn't want it."

He intended the remark as a joke, but nothing sounded funny to him. He watched the drivers maneuver their wagons into a corral without guidance. Many of them waved his way or called out a hello, but they stayed at their work.

While they unhitched the teams, Josey retraced his path to the hilltop, where the green land spread before him like folds in a bed comforter. Josey imagined he could see all the way to Omaha. *How far had it been?* Measuring the journey in terms of distance or days seemed insufficient. His whole life stretched out behind him in miles and months too many to count.

The laughter of the women and children gathering wood for cook fires drifted to him as Josey turned away. Nestled in the next valley was his favorite spot, a wide grassy field split by a stream with water so cold a man would never need ice, far enough from Bozeman and Virginia City that few would come here by accident. A horse grazing beneath a wide-canopied tree that shaded a bend in the stream surprised him. *Who else knows of this place?* He found his binoculars and looked again.

The late-afternoon sun reflected off the water and cast a white glare that dazzled his eyes. Shielding the light from his glasses he made out a form, a shadow against the glare, seated near the water beneath the tree.

The shadow rose. Even in silhouette, he knew her. Her back was to him as she watched the water play across the round stones in the riverbed. His eyes burned after looking so long in the light, and tears blurred his vision. The sunlight reflecting off the water created a glow around the outline of her body, the way artists drew angels in church paintings. *Dark and bright.*

She had both in her, too.

He could go to her. He could tell her that's how he saw her. He could tell her a thousand other things that filled his head all the long days he lay in the wagon hoping she would come to him. But she hadn't come. *Wasn't that enough of a message?* If he let her go now, he wouldn't have to see the cloud in her eyes as she wondered if the dark in him might one day turn against her. He wouldn't have to see the regret or, worse, the fear, cutting through him more skillfully than any bullet ever had.

He watched her until the sun dropped behind the mountain. A final ray, like a pinprick of starlight, winked and disappeared. In the shadow that remained, a snow-cooled breeze descended upon the valley and surrounding hills. Josey shivered and imagined he saw her do the same. She moved to the horse. She would be leaving this place soon. Josey had to decide.

Riding off in search of another opportunity would always be easier than setting about the hard work of building something. Moving among strangers would always be easier than living with the hurt he caused those closest to him. Imagining all the things he could tell her would always be easier than saying them. Courage is easy at a distance. She was here before him, she and everything he wanted. All he had to do was get close.

ABOUT THE AUTHOR

Derek Catron was born in Alexandria, Virginia, and divided his childhood between Detroit, Cincinnati, and Orlando. He's backpacked throughout the West and spent part of one summer camping along the emigrant trail to Montana. An award-winning investigative reporter and feature writer, Derek lives in Florida with his wife and daughter. *Trail Angel* is his first novel. Read more about the author and *Trail Angel* at derekcatron.com.